Best wishes
from Adam Corres.

RAFFLES AND THE MATCH-FIXING SYNDICATE

Adam Corres

*Re-inventing, for another age, the infamous
characters created by E.W. Hornung*

**Grosvenor House
Publishing Limited**

First Edition, Published in Great Britain by Grosvenor House Publishing, 2008

●

With acknowledgement to West Island Cricket Club, who meet with triumph and disaster up to three times a week and bring their own teas.

A note on continuity:

I have drawn the opening line of this story from the beginning of E.W. Hornung's first Raffles novel, The Amateur Cracksman, published in 1899. It's fun doing something new with the characters, but also important to honour the past.

ISBN 978-1-906210-62-5

For Eva, my darling girl,

Ne'er was one to be praised so far,
nor in such dark a cloud so bright a star.

Troilus & Criseyde

Contents

Chapter 1

The Scene of My Disaster

The scene of my disaster was much as I had left it. The computer's lights blinked uncaringly, feebly beckoning me to have another go. A cup of cold coffee, abandoned in a tense passage of play, seemed to bore into my mind with its own obscure accusations.

Why had I deserved this terrible month, this host of my downfall, this death-knell? Should I blame technology for making it easy? No, I cannot displace that responsibility. This was my own fault and smashing the computer would be obtuse when the bailiffs might be happy for it. What economies could I make to recover these losses? I thought to cancel my subscription to the internet, telephone and satellite television, but what would be the point, when their direct debits would soon bounce limply at my bank.

How many years could I go without, I narrowed the list, without anything? What job would pay enough to satisfy my creditors? I firmly pushed away the thought of borrowing more for the chance to win it all back. Time to grow up now, time to see the addiction for what it is. Never more come tapping upon my window pane. Never more.

Kneeling, empty as straw, I ejected that evening's recording. Cricket was a game of the light, but today they'd played it under artificial brilliance, when all around the match there gathered a clamouring swarm of shadows.

By now I was used to the time difference. The summer sport of old England was played in one hundred and twenty two countries in their own summers, in their own daytimes, in their evenings and under their own bitter floodlights. Cricket, a gentleman's game, a field of honour. I could recall my childhood and the smell of newly mown grass. I could feel the warmth of the sun on my whitened back and the anticipation of those electric half-second chances which could turn a match. Described by one as 'duty, service, battle and sport', I had felt it change in my lifetime. Professional, commercial, unending, out of our hands and surely out of the control of gentlemen.

Alright, so I was probably going to have to shoot myself. I was glad to think my parents were gone and would not know of it. Had anyone crashed so fast and so far? I supposed they had, but I recoiled to think how I had wasted my advantages. Born into a respected family, a public school education, pump-priming funds to my name and a good start in a solid military career. Until this. A month, just a month and all I had left was insubstantial. They had made it so easy.

'No, I'm not going to accept it. I'm not going to shrink away like a boy in church who's abjectly soiled himself. If it's the last thing I do, I want a ruddy explanation.' I paused awhile in thought. Who could answer to such a demand? Where could I source my Jabberwock? Well, I knew one cricketer…

Ten minutes later I clattered up the granite steps of the Albany and imperiously demanded to see Mr Raffles. I had nothing to be afraid of now; my course was set and the sharp-witted doorman of my last remaining club could jump at my command or measure his length on the flagstones.

It was not the club I remembered any more. All things scanned in black and white. No longer amusing were the old wooden wheelbarrows, which porters used in antiquity for the transportation of drunken members back to their lodgings. No longer terrifying were the library regulations, or the list of 'dues' – members who had forgotten to pay their subs and had not written in with their resignation, often having died (some of these accumulated membership fees dating back over two hundred years). 'They're gentlemen. If they haven't formally resigned, they might pop in.' Rubbish. I had no time for it. I had no time for the plimsoll-black tulips in the window boxes to mark the anniversary of the execution of the King of France, with French things dropped for the day and brie left like a dangling hook on the menu at lunchtime. 'Brie, Risley?' 'Would Sir require the Welsh brie or the Somerset brie?' This passes for a joke in clubland.

Raffles was different. Unlike the run of members, the businessmen who lunched until they were fat and complained at the already completed crossword, their only concession to fitness being a short potter to St. James's park to scatter bread-crumbs at ducks in hope of walking-off their indigestion. Raffles was no country member either. The lost aristocracy who come up to London once a year and rush away from the place as soon as they possibly can. Almost certainly maintaining a club because they can find accommodation there at one hundred pounds less than the Savoy and a hot dinner at fifty pounds less than the Grill Room. There are probably other places, but when you're out of touch, you can't trust those. Food poisoning, rats, decorative food, food with *height*, waiters who don't understand. Raffles was different.

Come to think of it, Raffles is the only one I know who's been thrown out of The Ritz twice. Once for playing the piano in the Palm Court and once for being in the company of a lady dressed in inappropriate clothing. Of course, I missed both occasions. I've never been thrown out of anywhere.

A.J. Raffles, who played cricket for Middlesex and the England eleven, an all round success, occasional toast of the tabloids, a charmer of the social scene and invited simply everywhere. His people had owned this building, this rock of St. James' Square, but had given it over to the club, all but an ample flat in the roof-space which was to be forever theirs. Raffles lived there alone, like a hunter atop an elephant, in appointed luxury. His visitors forever vetted and filtered through the Albany Club's hall by a doorman retained on their payroll. That took care of journalists, unwanted associates and all the friends he'd shrugged off. All but the most determined and that, tonight, was me.

'Bunny! You splendidly ridiculous marauder, what is all this noise?'

He disarmed me with my school nickname. Perplexed, I twisted around to find him. Only afterwards it occurred to me that I didn't hear Raffles arrive. His ability to be quite the supreme centre of attention at a vast gathering or sidle into a room with rubber-soled anonymity is a contrast I've never entirely grown accustomed to.

'Most unusual' he observed. 'Are your carpet slippers an oversight, a sudden whim or a current fashion?'

'Raffles', I interjected, 'Will you let me get a word in edgewise?'

'No', he replied after marginal consideration. 'You're a military man. Do you know how the mediaeval Japanese debriefed their assassins?'

'What? No, I don't think that came up in basic training.'

'Ah', said Raffles, 'You probably had toothache that day.'

'I did?'

'Thought so. The scheme was that the assassin, the Ninja, what you will, returned from his mission and was not permitted to speak. They took his pads off, decanted him into a cool, dark, cave and told him to get on with his dinner. After a couple of hours, when he'd had a chance to calm down and sort the story out in his head, he'd be called for a balanced report. So, Bunny, I'd like you to sit down, sink a glass of something definitively Hebridean and get this in proportion before you blast me with it.'

Raffles hadn't changed much since I'd first encountered him, except in terms of complexity. He was in his thirties now, but still spoke to me in much the same way as the days when I was tasked to run around after him at school. Despite years of scant acquaintance, he still looked at me as if I were an interesting tangle of hair clogging up his doormat and still spoke to me as if he, one of life's prefects, were addressing some otherwise fascinating variety of inconveniently awkward pleb. Yes, I was one of the 'plebs', a kind of junior with the duties of a servant, to his year at boarding school. When I reached the age and status to earn a pleb of my own, the school suddenly abolished the privilege, which at the time, and with a dim understanding of the ethics of forced servitude, I thought to be grossly unfair.

Through the club now, I ascended his private stairway in a daze. My rage distracted, dissipated, I began to wonder what I was doing there. What would I say to excuse this intrusion? I certainly didn't want his charity or his whisky. Raffles was the only professional cricketer I knew. The only man I thought might understand, although how could I ask one man for justification? Steady on. This was madness. I should go.

Raffles indicated a battered and upholstered chair as the apartment door was closed behind me. I thought I heard a key turn in the lock, but my mind dismissed the possibility. I'd give my account and then Raffles would act as if all decently apologetic and kick me out. So he should. It was another racing certainty and all at once it pulled at me, cold and distant and inevitable as one of our lot in the ski-jumping.

I gazed absently at his eclectic bookshelves. Becker's Practical Engineering, an A to Z of London, Gentlemen & Players, The Prince, Cotswold's Outdoor Equipment catalogue. On his desk were invitations from the MCC, mail-shots from charities, a bank statement from Coutts & Co., letters, business proposals, appeals, invitations, invitations simply *everywhere*, letters and cards from admirers, even one with interesting stamps and a broad green prison postmark smudged across it. Raffles was everything I was not; charming, capable and irritatingly effortless. I'm sure he did it deliberately.

Re-surfacing from the direction of the kitchen, my tormentor appeared once more carrying his old wooden serving tray and a lukewarm club dinner.

'Here, eat something, you look like a Xerces butterfly with a pin through it. I know. My cousin has cases of them and they share your vapid expression to an uncanny extent.'

I didn't want to, but on Raffles' insistence I demolished his dinner and realised I'd not eaten properly for days.

'Thank you', I said at last. Then, as if I'd forgotten, he fixed me with a clear blue eye and I knew I could no longer avoid recounting my story.

'If only I could wind back the clock a month to when this debacle started!'

Raffles rolled his pragmatic eyes. 'The facts might be more helpful, Bunny.'

I explained about my original clever idea, which I'd drunkenly scrawled on a nightclub napkin. I was so confident. Oh yes, it had sounded a good bit of harmless fun. There was a gambling website, you see, called 'Betfine'. It operated in a new way, which threw all the rules into the air like so many fortune sticks. A challenge, I'd told them, which demanded fresh thinking. It was a relict to engage the traditional bookmaker service, offering their set odds for the customer to accept. Betfine matched amateur members of the public, willing to accept bets as a bookmaker would, against equally amateur members of the public who could wave money and say whatever it was would happen.

Spotting that every horse at the races had a market both for and against, I reasoned a strategy. It was no longer necessary to pick a winner. It was not necessary to offer odds on every horse, as a traditional bookmaker would. Nowadays, all you had to do to gather up the money was identify a single horse in a field of perhaps twenty which absolutely couldn't possibly win. That done, I'd accept all those idiots' bets on it. Bring me the sick and lame of the racing world, bring me the three-legged donkeys and the outclassed selling-platers. Show me anything without hope and I'd give you odds against it!

Unfortunately, a number of them had won. Raffles rolled his eyes again. I thought they must be quite seasick by now. I watched as they broke their curve on the furthest chandelier and he leant back on an anxious cushion.

'I had a supernatural knack of picking fifty to one winners! Only I'd accepted bets on them!'

Raffles indulgently suffered a few more of my exclamation marks before gesturing me to continue.

'In the army, we were taught that all military plans can quickly become losing plans if they are not adaptable, so I altered the strategy. I reasoned that website members must be offering artificially generous odds on these outsiders. If something were available at 50-1, it would probably win one race in twenty five. Still unlikely to win, but in every hundred bets, there should be four 50-1 winners and a profit of £104, including the four winning stakes back. Less, of course, Betfine's five percent commission on the winnings.'

'Well', I explained confessionally to Raffles' clear blue eye, 'I never again picked a winner. Isn't that downright odd?'

Raffles stared at me as though I were a puddle of the first water, but seemed loathed to interrupt, willing me on in my confession.

'Horses were clearly not for me' I continued, 'so I decided to chase my losses with something I understood. Something comfortable and unthreatening. Something like cricket.'

There's the rub. As you know, in test matches, there are four possible options: win, lose, draw or a tie, being precisely the same score. A tie voids all bets and, as in abandonment, the stake is returned. Therefore, for my purposes, there were three options to consider. I just had to select, on about day three of a five day test, which option was no longer possible and accept lots of bets on it! Easy.'

'Remarkably easy.'

I wasn't sure I liked this patronising tone.

'Since, in this modern age, I'm sure you've noticed that run-scoring has become much less restrained, the thought of a drawn test match in five days of good weather, because they ran out of time, is an increasing rarity. So, I just had to check the weather and take bets on a draw or simply find the team which couldn't win!'

'Bravo.'

'I did alright, with more wins than the statistical average. Test matches, however, don't happen often enough for me. As my confidence grew, I gravitated away from the drip of small winnings made consistently, gradually, in the manner poker players have called 'the grind'. I wanted more money and I wanted to win it faster. One day cricket seemed the game for me.'

Yes, well, name your poison. At last, Raffles the Test match purist chimed in.

'One-Day cricket is really little more than a slap-around before the pubs open. It's anything but consistent. The result can very quickly turn either way. Good batsmen are no longer predictable because they swipe across the line rather than playing proper cricket shots. It's no test of quality bowling either, when they lash out at every ball and good players get themselves out off rubbish.'

It was true. One-Day cricket was more about keeping your nerve and riding your luck than cultivating the impenetrable technique of the five day test match. I told him of matches that went well. Matches that made me bet even more. I told him of matches that went badly wrong; the sequence of uncommon and unlikely events where certainties turned against me.

'I was already thousands down when the World Cup started.' My audience nodded diplomatically. 'It was the warm-up matches that did it.'

Raffles lifted my now empty whisky glass out of my hand and took it out to the adjoining kitchen.

'Tea/coffee?'

'Yes, fine. South Africa had scored just 91 runs for eight wickets down when I chose to bet against them.'

'Logical. You would have taken poor odds though.'

'I did. Within an hour and a half they'd added over a hundred runs for the last two wickets! Too late to reverse the bet of course, the odds had changed against me.'

'I saw it. 192 all out.'

'In my hesitation I had thought, 'surely this score is reachable?' so I let the bet stand.'

Raffles stepped out of the kitchen and placed a cup in front of me. It was a mixture, half tea and half coffee, but I was too preoccupied at the time to notice.

'Within a few hours they'd bowled out the opposition for only one hundred and fifty-seven and I had a major loss. Then there was India, with freak results against Bangladesh and Sri Lanka. You'd

7

think test playing nations like the West Indies, Zimbabwe and Pakistan could beat Ireland, wouldn't you?'

'You seem to be saying that all these matches involved the most unlikely sequences of fortune, almost always in favour of the weaker side?'

'Seem to be saying? Yes I am saying!'

'Has it occurred to you that good old, down to earth, complacency might have a hand in it?'

'Are all big teams complacent against small ones? Aren't they strong enough to recover from a bad start?'

'South Africa did. You said so yourself.'

'What about the others? The final match, tonight's, was the shocker that broke me. Oh, that was awful!'

'I cradled him with fearful eye, for I knew that he was sure to die. Poor Bunny'

'If you're going to be sarcastic, why are you still listening?'

Raffles grinned warmly. 'Well, there's precious little entertainment in this town...'

I cut him short. 'Oh, for heaven's sake! I'm in agony here!'

'Don't worry Bunny. The pain only lasts about ten minutes and then your balls drop.'

The unexpected vulgarity was like a strike in the face. I swear that moment put ten years on my head and I should have thanked him for it. It was my turn at last to sit back in silence.

'You brought a recording', Raffles said quietly.

'Yes, it's in my coat'

'No, it's here' said Raffles, transferring it smoothly from his pocket to the player. I wouldn't be surprised by anything any more. Not now. Clearly there's more in the world than known to my philosophy.

The half-filled spool took Raffles' attention and he considered the chore of rewinding. 'It's been stopped at the starting place' I chipped-in coherently.

We watched the match from first ball to last. Mostly in silence, with Raffles re-playing some passages of play, ones where I could see very little that might be of interest to him. He scribbled some sums and then gave up and went for a calculator. Some miss-fields, some shots straight to fielders. Raffles was particularly interested near the end. Pressure had clearly got to the batsmen and they froze, unable to score. With five players in hand and needing just four runs to win from the last ten balls, six balls went through without a single run coming off the bat! Then, in sheer panic, four wickets fell in a row for nothing. Four balls, four wickets that ruined my life.

'The short game has more to it than...' He tailed off. 'Bunny, you've stirred my interest.'

I wanted my answer. 'Raffles, how can it be? How can I be so sure of the result and then the impossible happens?'

He paused and reached for a packet of cigarettes. He picked them up, turned the box over and put them back in their place again.

'I've given up of course. It's no thing for an athlete. If they're in the house, I'll not smoke one, but if there were none, I'd feel obliged to go and buy them. It's strange, but there it is.'

'Raffles, tell me why? Why am I losing?'

'Should I give you a morality tale?'

'If you must, but if there's any more bilge about medieval Japanese pyjama people, I'm leaving now.'

He blinked. The delay was just long enough to remind me I was getting his time for nothing.

'A long time ago, in 17th Century France I believe it was, a group of wealthy aristocratic patrons rounded up, entertained and employed, a number of the finest and most respected mathematical minds from universities across the continent. They were tasked to calculate for their employers the odds of winning in all permutations of gambling at tables. For two years they corresponded and totalled their spotted dice and clubs and diamonds, their wheels and shoes and house commissions. At last they announced the findings complete. Hooray, or indeed 'Zut Alors!' the sponsors cried. We will soon know how to win at gambling!'

'Excellent! What did they say?'

'This is absolutely true, mind you. The group of patrons asked 'Is it possible to consistently make money at gambling?' The mathematicians replied 'Yes, yes it is.' 'We're not talking about minimising our losses here. We do mean making a real profit.' 'Yes, it can be done' said the wise owls. 'Tell us!' they demanded.'

'Yes! Tell me!'

'Buy a casino.'

'Oh.'

This was a bit of a let down.

'Really. That was the only recommendation. It isn't strictly true, of course. It is possible to make a consistent profit if you have access to better information than both the Public and the bookmaking industry. It is possible if you are an exceptional specialist in a single sport and are strong minded enough not to lose your profits straight back to the industry on another sport. Otherwise...'

'Yes?'

'You must cheat.'

'Oh. I hadn't thought of that.'

'Evidently. One more thing.'

'Yes?'

'Betting is an addiction. Risking money and winning money generates dopamine, a chemical which irresistibly stimulates the pleasure centres of the brain. In essence, gambling has the same effect as sex and heroin without the associated liquids.'

'So you've studied addiction too, have you?'

'Yes. I have one myself, although you'd never guess it. No, don't ask. Just lay off the betting for now.'

'I will.'

I would have agreed to anything at that point. Raffles made a long arm, ejected the recording and handed it across.

'I can see how they did it Bunny. It was a rather clever conceit.'

'What was? I don't understand.'

'That's because you've never been a bowler. You've watched cricket being played, but all you've seen is a series of events on the surface, a facade. Imagine watching a play from the stalls and then watching the same play from behind the scenes. It's a completely different way of understanding it. You see the skill to play shots, the hand-eye co-ordination, the speed of reaction. Well, young man, when you get up to first class cricket, that's not enough. You need to know what's going on in the player's minds. You need to know the statistics, the percentages, of how they play their shots and where they fail. How to frustrate them, put them in two minds, work on their confidence or their pride, draw them obligingly into error.'

'Cricket's two old war-horses are analysis and psychology' he continued. 'You can groom them all your life, but one day they'll turn round and bite you. When a first class cricketer steps up to Test level, it's even worse. You don't bowl men out like you do in the shires, you really have to *think* them out. Perhaps not the tail, but the top seven

10

batsmen certainly. I'm talking about the underpinnings of the game, Bunny. The mind-set of the players, what's processing in their thoughts, the neatly thought-out traps that are silently set for them. That's the toughest nut to crack, perhaps, but in this case you've been outdone by something else. Something always ticking along behind the scenes. That game was lost not by the tail, as you almost certainly think, but in the middle overs. Someone sabotaged the mathematics.'

I still didn't catch his drift, despite the dunes piling up around me.

'I'm still confused.'

'When bowling in one of these short matches, players are constantly running the numbers in their heads. Total to get, less total so far, divided by the remaining overs. Four an over to get, perhaps, at the start. Is the required rate climbing or falling? Are we winning this or is it slipping away? Are we 'on the right side of the equation?' Bowling a few balls the batsmen can't hit increases the mathematical pressure and can induce an error. The required rate goes up; the batsman plays a rash shot, then a wicket will certainly increase the pressure and then the fielding side senses a win. Why is one side winning? Because for an over or so *nothing happened*. The run rate went from five required up to six. Would you look for that, Bunny? Would you run the numbers, if you hadn't played the game?'

The lecture drew more. 'Sixty to win from ten overs, for example, is a requirement of a run a ball. Less than a run a ball is usually within the capability of a batting side, but more than that and the game should be won by the bowlers. If a batsman scores fifty runs in one hundred and twenty deliveries and then gets out, he'll put dreadful pressure on the tail-enders who might be left to score at two a ball, something usually beyond their capability. That player with a solid fifty on the board can throw a match, above suspicion, when it looks for all the world as though the last men in were the ones that lost it by shelling their wickets cheaply in a desperate hunt for runs.'

'You're saying it was fixed?'

'It was somewhat affected, yes.'

'The whole team?'

'No Bunny. I think just one player. Khalife, their number three. The suggestion of a calf injury was most likely feigned. He looked brave as he stayed at the crease, supporting his partner, scoring twenty one runs from eighty three deliveries. The batsman at the other end was playing shots, so it didn't look conspicuous. He tried to increase the tempo as he watched the required run-rate climbing, unluckily hitting his best shots straight to fielders. He got himself out trying to smash that huge six over long-on.' Raffles replaced a marbled volume in the bookcase. 'Caught by one of only three fielders in the deep.'

'It looked good, Bunny. Rugged stuff. A few big shots, runs on the board, it looked like he was *trying*, but the sixty two deliveries he didn't score from made the difference. The rate when he came in: 3.8 an over. The rate required when he handed over to the next man: 6.2. I'm sorry to say the theatrical community have missed a great talent.'

'Oh, hell. I can't believe I've been so stupid.' I murmured pointlessly.

'It's only money, Bunny. You can rebuild. How much are you in for?'

'Oh, a ten thousand loan, twenty thousand drawn on credit cards, another thousand on overdraft...'

'Even so. It's nothing to an average mortgage.'

'No. It's worse than that. I was chasing my losses, so I needed some more money to bet with. I went to the Officer's Mess yesterday, Raffles. I thought I could use Regimental funds, just as a temporary thing you see. They won't stock-take until the end of the week, so I thought it wouldn't be noticed.'

My leg began shaking involuntarily. A strange, half-felt sensation.

'It wasn't really stealing. I was going to put all of it back in the morning. So that's it then. I've lost my money, my commission, my fiancée, my honour and soon it will be my liberty as well.'

'Your fiancée too?' Raffles questioned.

'Yes. Charity Blake. Strickland-Hocket's step-daughter. You know, the politician with a foot in the media.'

'The 'cash for questions' man? Private Eye called him Mr Sticky-Pocket?'

'That's him. Charity and I have been engaged since New Year. I've had to write her a letter breaking it off. I couldn't think of anything else to do.'

'Oh, my silly friend. Although, all is not lost.'

'You'll help?'

'I have to. Normally I wouldn't waste my time on your petty addictions, but the mechanism you've outlined is a matter of professional concern.'

'How so?'

'Your favourite gambling website has changed the game. In the past, the financial incentive was always to pick a winner. Now you can win money if you know who's going to lose. If you're often sure of who can't win, you can earn a favourable second income. If you can *ensure* failure, you can make a fortune. That fact turns professional sportsmen like me into targets.'

'I'm so sorry.'

'Don't be. It's just another layer of complication. Anyway, sometimes the targets strike back. That's only sporting, wouldn't you say?'

'Thanks A.J. Thanks for understanding.'

'Correct. Understanding and caring are quite different.'

Raffles returned to the bookcase once more, turning his back and running his fingernail across the spines. He spoke softly, strangely unsure.

'There is another reason. You helped me once, although you might not remember it. Noblesse oblige.'

'Raffles? However would you find a match-fixer to strike back against?'

'The easiest way would be through the website which records their predictions. I'm sure the greatest clairvoyants in the world would stick out admirably. However, the database encryption would be, I think, a task beyond my talents. Chin up. We'll find another way.'

'If we can show it was fixed, I mean, there must be a way to...'

'No Bunny. They'll consider a case from the Albany Club, but they won't from Albany Prison. You're not in a position to look for justice. First of all, you need to avoid it. We must reimburse your regiment.'

'You mean, I can get the money back?'

'Yes', said the bowler of England's most perplexing deliveries, 'Although not from me.'

'Ah. I hadn't meant to...' I began.

'I'm not saying it can't be got. We just need a little working capital. You'll help me with that, won't you Bunny?'

'Of course!'

'Do you know how wide the English Channel is?'

The question threw me. 'Yes, I think I do. It's about twenty six miles, isn't it?'

'Which illustrates a point. You know a lot Bunny, but at a pinch, can you make money at it?'

He was actually going to help me. I stared in awe. 'I'm in your hands. Just tell me what to do.'

Chapter 2

In the Regimental Museum

My Grandmother used to weave knitted pictures on squares the size of a spread palm, to be ultimately stitched together into bed blankets. You won't immediately appreciate why I mention that, but bear with me. She knitted image after fantastic image. Stonehenge, city streets, strange mythical animals, a bonfire, pyramids of the Giza Plateau, a page of sheet music by Dvorak, a tiger, even the New Forest complete with deer and mushrooms. Beautiful, colourful and delight-ful images reflecting all there was to see in the wonderful world of Mankind, flower and beast.

Then, one winter's day, her husband died. After a few weeks of empty and hopeless shock, she returned to her knitting. Only, this time, she knitted those squares in a muddy green wool. Square after square the same, featureless, in hopeless progression. The boot-scrap-ings of abandonment. Mud green, endless, headless and lost.

There is a point to this story. The reason, if you're wondering why I threw in my lot so completely with Raffles, wasn't just down to perfect loyalty for getting me out of an almighty scrape. Before the evening I dropped in on Raffles at the Albany... Well, let's just say, I felt my life was just like that blanket, with its pictures and colours and wonders and then routine muddy dreary void, only... only the other way around.

Before I forget, there is a post-script to this story. When I was five, I gave my Grandmother a collage of pressed flowers, hoping to cheer her up. I included a pressed fly, because I happened to have one.

I'm not one for mentioning these things, but I suppose I should, given the context. In my schooldays, a year or two after A.J. Raffles was dazzling everyone as Captain of Cricket, I became the Captain of Shooting. Since ours was foremost a cricketing school, my tenure passed without notice. It was something I was good at though, something I could actually do. Shooting at great range always fascinated me. I speak of targets at a mile or more, for clarification. Banchory Field Target Club. Braemar. Bisley. Aboyne. Real shooting; curling distant dots through the sky and into something hard. Shooting as art.

It's not just the requirement to remain unexcited, since adrenaline affects the aim like a wavy sea. It's not just the need to slow the heartbeat with thought alone or to control and almost stop breathing. Naturally low blood pressure really helps. It's the ability to concentrate down, placing yourself in a trance-like hibernation, until the world fades out, hearing dulls away and all you know is the tunnel vision of the concentrated mind, reaching out and sensing, feeling for the target. Self-hypnosis perhaps. Breathing as it breathes. Close enough to touch it through the scope, to feel the way it's going to move before it does so.

Then, down fifteen lenses of parallax-vision light-intensifier sights, to visualise the trajectoral curve of the shot, to superimpose the non-existent curve of invisible gravity onto the field-depth of that tunnel and, without reference to the universe or time or pressing need, drift into sleep inside that telescope. When the rifle fires, it comes as a shock, an alarm clock to spoil the daydream. In this semi-trance, I swear you don't remember even pulling the trigger. It's an action of the subconscious mind.

The thing you do remember, the thing that's plainly, physically impossible, but all the great gillies will tell you they've seen it, is the black dot. The impression left on your retina which can only be the back of the bullet. I've seen it. I've seen... I've experienced something A.J. hasn't, which probably makes me a specialist. Raffles has been known to court specialists as a safe-cracker might gather his lock-picks. All those odd little twisted shapes; you never knew when the unusual ones might come in handy. I couldn't imagine how I could be any use to him, particularly as he had always made fun of my interests. Violent sports and situations, in particular, he was not so much disturbed by as openly amused.

That's a confusing statement. What I mean by it is this: He believed, as a central touchstone of his philosophy, that intelligent people had no need to waste their time on aggression. They should be able to foresee locations or situations that might lead to it and 'design them out of their lives'. Unless, of course, they didn't want to, but I'll come to that; that later version of Raffles, as yet unawoken.

Raffles has been known to sit in shock as someone explained how they'd spent two hours a day for six years of their lives learning Aikido: "You've spent 4,382 hours learning how to kick people?" or listened in surprise to praise of the various versions of karate or boxing, "Is it easier to walk up to someone and punch them to death or ask Bunny here to pot them from a mile away?"

A firearm was a tool to him, a superior tool to a fist. As with all tools, screwdrivers and hammers and bicycle pumps, he could not understand an association with enjoyment or sport in the use of them. A tool moved whatever it moved and then you put it down. If a better tool came along, you threw away the old one.

It is for blood-sports though that A.J. reserves his greatest disrespect. Raffles, I'm afraid, doesn't understand. He doesn't appreciate the art, the self-control or philosophy of hunting. I once said to him "Raffles, if you want to bring down a magpie, you have to think like a magpie." He spent much of the next year inflicting upon me such witticisms as "Bunny, I'll be out this afternoon collecting mushrooms in the woods. Remember Bunny, if you want to hunt mushrooms... you have to *think like a mushroom.*"

I know he tried shooting once. On Founder's Day, I think it was. He sat cross-legged in a row of boys at the field-target range and sang to himself to pace his breathing. "Su-su-sudio, all my life [bang] just say the word, Su-su-sudio [bang]" and such golden oldies as "I see [bang] of green, red roses too, I see [bang] for me and you and I think to myself, what a wonderful [bang], yes I think to myself, what a wonderful world..." and just when you thought he'd finished and could concentrate on your own shot "[bang]". He managed to come tenth or so out of about forty, almost certainly not by skill, but by the inherent ability, his divine gift, for putting everyone else off.

This next idea will probably take some thinking about, so I'll leave the analysis up to you. I might have hit upon a hypothesis: There are two kinds of winning sportsmen. The first kind win their games by delivering a better performance than their opponents. The second kind, despite being able to compete as equals, can also win by affecting opponents thinking to the point where they under-perform. Type A would obviously outnumber Type B, but I have to say that Type B might prove the more fascinating.

Where was I? Oh yes, *think like a mushroom.* I do remember that Raffles had a special hat for hunting mushrooms and, when he left the school, it was forgotten, hanging on a peg behind his study door. I took that hat and placed it upon the head of a Guy Fawkes for the autumn term's bonfire night. As a strange co-incidence, being some decades later, I came across a copy of the old bomber's handwritten confession, as published on the British Museum website. The looped 'f' letters snagged my skimming attention and I do remember looking at the page again, closely this time. What shook me, the thing I have never entirely got over, was that Guy Fawkes had, exactly, my handwriting.

Fate – pah! Throughout a struggled and insecure life, the less tangible of my sensations have hinted and jested that fate might have something special in store for poor old Bunny. Something I felt instinctively I should give a wide berth on sight or generally keep ahead of as long as possible. Raffles, for example, would have 'designed it out of his life' early, but for lesser mortals like myself, that isn't an option. Getting chopped from the regiment was just such a precipitous slope and I had trusted in Raffles, not my own native wits, to hoick me out of it. Does that sound helpless? My defence has to be, of course, that my own native wits had hoicked me into this godawful mess in the first place. There are times and places for native wits, comedy clubs in the colonies for example, but this was one of those times when I had to be sure. A time to turn to reputation. I just hoped and prayed that he wouldn't let me down. What he had in mind, I didn't know.

That day, I reported in and took over my duties as O.I.C., that's Officer in Charge of, our Regimental HQ and Museum, Birdcage Walk, London. It was quite an honour, but the endless repetition of the job could easily put the bearer on auto-pilot. Repetition, let's be frank, is the dullest thing in the world and just what the Army's best at. With the duties of my particular role the institution had excelled itself. Repetition, let's be frank, is the dullest thing in the world and... see what I mean?

You can probably tell by now that I'm not entirely cut out for the Army. How did I get here? Well, I'd say it was the awesome power of not knowing what to do with my life, not being entirely cut out for anything, and ultimately doing what other people had expected of me. I don't really bother with jealousy, but I do envy people who've always known what they wanted to do and haven't dispersed their time on little bits of everything else. Focus, that's the point. Sorry, I've been rambling again.

Think about this objectively. Here I was making sure that a stone building in the most secure part of London would be kept safe from passing vagabonds. A building housing a tempting haul of thirty desks, cloth flags, some twisted old metalwork from WWI and incidentally the spiritual home to two battalions of top notch soldiers who could put 15,000 bullets per minute through the button holes of any foreign uniform the Queen might suddenly take offence at. Yes, it was pretty safe. I was a military cipher.

Between eight and ten, I did my tour of the building. I confirmed that the non-opening windows were not open, observed two specks of dust and signed three documents. The most important of which was a release form to grant access to a window cleaner. It was always exactly the same window cleaner every time. I had thought to give him a photocopy, but changed my mind as I wouldn't want to land him in any trouble.

I finished my tea and hid the mug behind a magazine about regimental climbing expeditions. Some of ours went to Everest last year and came back pencil thin from burning calories at altitude, but with fingers so fat from frost-bite that they couldn't fit them through their trigger guards. One of them hasn't fully recovered, so has taken light duties here, mucking out the mascot. That isn't easy. Our mascot's a great heaving lummox of a wolfhound and, in deference to rank, appears to be allowed to dump whatever it likes wherever it likes, whenever it feels the mood. That plays merry hell with the carpets. If I'm ever battalion commander, I'm going to have the bugger shot and replaced with a mole.

Ten o'clock each day and the doors are flung open. Well, not exactly open. This is a theoretical concept. Our regimental museum is supposed to be open to interested members of the public. They simply have to get past the two fully armed bayonet-flashers at the gate, whistle for the Sergeant, who then decides if he likes the look of them, rings a bell inside and I come down to see what all the fuss is about. If someone wants to come in and view the museum, which is hardly topical I might add, I'll do the tour. It isn't often.

It isn't often, but it was that day. Three groups in all, museum for the touring of. 10.15: An old soldier explaining a few old glories to his grandson. I retired discreetly into the background and picked up the few titbits of history I didn't already know. 10.44: A postman from Amersham nervously tracing his ancestor from an old army cap found amongst ancient chocolate wrappers he'd pulled from under a floorboard. I remember he spent ages looking at the mangled bugles from Passchendale, with which one of our illustrious corpses had once sounded the advance. On the next occasion he'd not been around to do so. When the postman turned, I could see the tears. That taught me 'past' doesn't mean the same as 'gone'.

11.26: A confident type from – hang on, this was Raffles. Raffles in a shady hat, but definitely Raffles.

'Morning Bunny.'

'Well observed. Yes, it is the morning, I know all you cricketers wake up at two and I'd appreciate it if you'd call me by my rank if anyone's listening.'

'Certainly Bunny, but there's no one listening. They've put you in charge of the Marie Celeste.'

'Yes, well. The first battalion's in Cyprus. The second are off on manoeuvres. They're chasing the Queen's Sutherland Highlanders up a random Cairngorm.'

'No wars then?'

'There's nothing to do, Raffles. As we speak, there are Ghurkhas in bushes protecting osprey nests from egg collectors.'

'Pleasant enough weather for it. Isn't that a job for the Guards?'

'What do you want? I thought you were going to help me out of my little situation? I didn't expect you to turn up here making social calls.'

'I'd like to see where the money should be returned to.'

'Returning it isn't the problem. I can do all the returning I'll ever need. I just need *something* to return.'

'If you say so. Perhaps you'd give me a tour of the Museum then, as I've come all this way?'

'If you don't take the mickey. This stuff's very important to some people you know.'

'I know. Why has your dog got a box around its neck?'

'It's not my dog. It's the mascot. It's also a colonel.'

'You're joking?'

'No. It's tradition.'

'Oh, that.'

'Don't make fun of it.'

We walked the stairs and the length of a heavily beflagged corridor in increasingly chilled silence.

'The box?'

'The box contains the key to the strong box, effectively a safe, that's kept behind the painting of the Colonel in Chief in the Staff Office here' I indicated.

'The horse?'

'No, the individual sitting on the horse.'

'So, not all your fellow officers are...'

'No, they're not. Just the dog, okay?'

'Yes.'

'This is also my office, when I'm on duty.'

'Someone else's when you're not.' It was a statement, not a question. 'Someone else's tomorrow?'

'Yes. Major Gish-Browning from Second Battalion.'

'Related to the inventor of...?'

'The Gish, yes, it's a kind of motorised field gun. There's a risk he'll discover the funds are gone when he's on checks in the morning. If he's thorough, which he might be. Strange bloke; Irons his underpants. I volunteered for the next three days in a row, to cover you see, but they've stuck to the rota.'

'Where are we now?'

'This is the museum. The exhibits are, I am sure, to your taste.'

I showed him the bugles, including the one of that poor soldier who stood up and led the regiment over the top at Passchendale, the Victoria Cross he'd earned and appended commendation. Raffles noted the flag which flew over Port Stanley after the re-take of the Falkland Islands and asked what part the Regiment had played. I explained, as tour guides do, and he nodded in thought. I wondered if he'd leave here with a little respect for us? It was surely too good to last.

'Does your Sergeant like cricket?'

'Hates it.'

'Good. I thought he didn't recognise me.'

'If you played darts, it might be a different matter.'

'If I played darts, I'd hardly be fit enough to get up those stairs. Bunny, I am going to ask you to do something and I would like you to follow my instructions without question. If you don't, you will be lost. Do you understand?'

I nodded. What was he up to?

'This bottle contains an ether chemical which does the same sort of job as chloroform. It just vanishes a little faster. Take it.' I took it.

'I'm going to have a wander around the museum, during which you can chat to the Sergeant and we'll have ourselves an impression of separation.'

'Okay.'

'You'll need some form of swab. I suggest using one of these knackered old flags.'

I was right. It was too good to last.

'I will return at 4pm exactly. I would like you to knock the Colonel out...'

'Knock the what?'

'Dog. Chloroform. Apply one to the other, it doesn't matter in which order, but do try to swab the right end. I'm not sure you'll last long in this job if you're seen wiping the dog's bum with a Union Jack. I had hoped you'd pay attention, Bunny. Knock out the blasted dog and send the Sergeant to call a vet. Got it?'

'Um, yes.'

'You must tell him to call Greenaways Vets, okay? When he's gone, you can take the key from the dog, open the safe and adopt a concerned expression. I'll arrive, pre-vet as it were, hand you the money...'

'There's money? What money?'

'There will be money, but I have to collect it. In the meantime, don't try to understand. Just run along downstairs and have a cup of tea, as I soak up the human misery of your museum and help to establish your innocence.'

'Innocence? I thought we were returning the money? Where are you borrowing the money?'

'Excellent, Bunny. That's the most innocent face ever composed. Freeze it there and go! Go on!'

I'd been talking to the Sergeant for a full ten minutes before it dawned on me that I'd been told to "run along." Who did Raffles think he was? Apart from my guardian angel, obviously, the cheeky slug.

12.10 A panama hat slid between Raffles and the sun, glided down the short gravel path and doffed itself at the guardsmen. Off it went toward Buckingham Palace Road where it signalled an aimless taxi.

Pacing about seemed my best and only option. The guest list had dried up and so I worried unhelpfully until ten to four, when I could stand it no longer. The caffeine I'd ingested from five cups of tea didn't help much either.

I'll pass on this hint for free, in case you ever need it: Catching large dogs isn't easy. In fact, Sir Arthur Conan Doyle gave us a whole book on the subject. Just to compound the problem, our large dog wasn't especially compliant. Not interested in food, not interested in playing, the mascot weighed as much as a man and spent most afternoons sleeping on its face. I probably could have got the key without drugging it, but I stuck with the plan - Raffles had warned me about the dangers of thinking.

I levered up the Colonel's head as gently as I could for a bonce that stuck to the floor like the stoney brow of a forty ton sphinx peering for a missing scarab that's rolled under an inconvenient wardrobe. With a flag ready, appropriately a Regimental Standard for the Regimental Mascot, I soaked a few banners of immortal victories and pressed them up the dog's nose. It didn't like that at all, but soon lost the power to stand up. The smell of cleaning fluid was everywhere. Oh no, how was I going to explain that? I had a brainwave and quite impressed myself.

'Sergeant! Sergeant! The dog's swallowed half a bottle of cleaning fluid! Quick, call for a vet!'

'Straight away Sir!'

What was the name of the vet? Oh hell.

'Sergeant! The vet is called Greenlanes or Green something. Make sure you get the right one.'

'Yes Sir.'

He ran off and was soon to be heard shouting into the phone, shouting back to me, followed by a little more shouting at the guardsmen. If in doubt, shout. That's the NCOs way.

I got the feeling I was meant to be doing something. Ah, yes, that was it. I loosened the box fixed to the dog's collar and unhinged it without trouble. The hound, resolutely immobile, snored comfortably. The key popped out and it wasn't long before I'd crossed the room and turned it in the lock. There was one dodgy moment when the royal picture almost fell off the wall, but I fielded it like a county colt. The strong box fell open before me. So far so good. I waited for Raffles.

I waited fourteen minutes. In case this eventuality ever befalls my readers, I'd say this is a horrible length of time to baby-sit a drugged wolfhound. For those of you with the sternest constitutions,

I'd recommend five minutes at most and even then only if you've had a sniff of the whisky.

The vet arrived, escorted up the short gravel path by a pair of quick-time guardsmen. It was quite surreal to see him attempting to two-step too, something he patently couldn't do, but he must have felt it was expected of him. A white coat whooshed past the Sergeant and into the building. Did vets wear white coats? I supposed they must do.

The gate was unguarded for the first time in years. I pressed my nose to the window pane and willed Raffles to come through it. He didn't. They'd called the wrong vet, hadn't they? This was going wrong. I thought I'd better face the door when the vet came in, which he did and Lo! Behold! And all the usual exclamations, I saw that it was Raffles.

'Guards! Back to the gate! Sergeant! Cup of tea for the visitor please.'

'Sir!'

He went, much to my relief. I knew there wasn't any tea because I'd finished it. That's tactics, that is. I was even more, in fact very, relieved when Raffles handed me a pile of bank notes. In wordless rapture I shook his hand and returned the missing funds to the strong box. The key went back to the attachment on the collar and we both sat down on the floor alongside the elongated form of the monstrous hound.

The dog hadn't woken and frankly looked as though it could snore its way through the winter. I'd say the only difference between this scene of workplace bliss and the thought of accompanying a hibernating bear was the smell. Few hibernating bears, if any, get to see a couple of privates on fatigues sent in to shampoo them. Actually, they might do something unusual in the Gloucester Fusiliers, but to be fair, that's just a rumour. If any of you out there ever find yourself alongside a sleeping bear, or a wolfhound, I would like to take this opportunity to remind you that there are much more wholesome things you could be doing. If you must do it, just don't put any videos on the internet, alright?

'Hell! Raffles! What happens when the real vet shows up?'

'They won't. I rang them up and told their receptionist to ignore the 4pm call as it would be part of a security exercise. They were most helpful.'

'Where did you get the coat? It has the right logo and everything!'

'They were *most* helpful.'

'Oh.'

The clearing-up operation was a matter hardly worthy of your attention. The dog recovered, had some water and returned to sleep. Raffles went home and I updated the duty roster until it was time to hand over the keys. As with hotels, we always have a full half an hour handing-over time, which can be frustrating on the occasions when you'd like to go and there's no reason to stay, but you can't. At the end of a difficult day, I did my duty and got away.

After a quick call to thank Raffles again, I relaxed a little and slid into a soapy bath. What a relief.

The telephone rang. I ignored it. Ten minutes later it rang again. Oh for heaven's sake. I let it ring. Ten minutes after that some heavy boots clobbered up the stairs and some men I found a little harder to ignore banged repeatedly on the door panels.

'Okay, okay. I'm coming.'

More guardsmen. What now?

That night went very badly. I'd been recalled to HQ to explain how, as officer for the day, I'd gone home without noticing the fact that the only VC in the museum, together with its commendation and bugle, had been stolen.

I couldn't explain. I could only suggest the postman who'd coincidentally failed to leave a legible signature in the visitors' book. After all, he'd hung around that display case a very long time. Not enough to go on and I was indeed for the high jump.

'Unless you'd like to pop out and win us another one' added a sour-faced Major-General.

I learned my fate in the morning. Suspended from duty pending a court-martial for dereliction of command. Super. I'd probably lost my career, but could still be forced to serve a term in Colchester prison before being kicked out. Super. I'd dissect that postman and put slices through every letterbox in Amersham if I ever got hold of him. Was there anyone, anywhere, more put-upon than me? I called Raffles to explain what had happened. He didn't seem that surprised, but he always was a cool one.

'Is there anyone worse off than me?' I asked him.

'Well, yes. Divide the US debts to the rest of the world by their population and they each owe us thirty thousand, so that's two hundred and thirty million people in your position across a single country. In fact, if you could persuade them to pay up, you might be square.'

'That's economics. No one takes it seriously. What I meant was, I just can't think of any individuals who are in more of a fix than I am.'

'Bemoaning one's lot is unbecoming, don't you think? Do you believe yours was the only life the result of that match ruined? Twenty eight million pounds changed hands on Betfine alone, you know.'

'I suppose not then, but…'

'I have a little more breaking news for you, from the sun-blessed sands of Jamaica. The Coach of your losing team was found dead in his hotel room this morning.'

The news caught me entirely off-guard. I couldn't speak for a few moments.

'If he was as upset as me at the team's performance, he probably had a heart attack. I had no idea cricket could be so stressful.'

'Quite, it has the highest suicide rate of any sport in the world, but the Coroner disagrees. He's reported death by manual strangulation, compounded by salivation, vomiting, diarrhoea and muscular incoordination, consistent with cypermethrin poisoning.'

'Seriously? Hell! Have they made an arrest?'

'No. The media are circulating a rumour that he had a blazing row with three players after the defeat. There was even a suggestion of bribes. No solid allegation of course. Just faff and speculation.'

I found this news barely credible, but then I'd found the initial result beyond belief. So, one man at least had a worse day than I. Perhaps, I thought, our destinies might be connected.

Chapter 3

Catching the Post

I've always tried to be chivalrous. I suppose that's because everyone has always automatically presumed I would grow up to be a gentleman. The difficulty I've found with that is, I get a terribly strong feeling that I'm designed for a former period of history. What I mean is, in nutshell terms, I feel I'd be perfectly well adjusted to life at any point in history between the late Middle Ages and perhaps Edwardian Britain. I feel like a horse-drawn cart on the motorway now. Out of place and reluctant as a goat with candles on its horns at a Haitian party. Am I making sense? Probably not. I'll have a pot at it metaphorically:

I had a cousin with knobbly knees. These were knees so knobbly, so gnarled and nutty, that no other knobble on any other kneelet in the kingdom could have given the judges pause for so much as a moment's conferral in any knobbly knee competition you can possibly imagine in this world or the next. I'm sure you can picture lots. Come on, no need to be bashful. This is the twenty first century and we can talk about such perversions now.

Anyway, Albert, we can call him Albert for it wasn't his name, failed to capitalise on his birthright. Could he find a knobbling competition to enter? Anywhere? What happened? Did they all end with the 1970s? Perhaps there's a secret world of plastic surgery that nobody ever mentions. So what then of Albert, born twenty years after his time? 'Is there any point' he thought 'in wearing these short trousers any more when no-one even bothers to whistle?' Where then, was his glory? Do we see processions rolling 'neath triumphal arches, as the crowds kneel before him? We do not. Do we see international recognition from princes and potentates? We've checked the post and there's nothing so far. Do the great British public hold his name like a precious nectar bead betwixt their grateful lips? No they don't. Why? Because it's stupid, that's why. Being chivalrous is the same. It gets you funny looks.

Raffles had asked me a question. My wandering mind refocused back to the drawing room.

'Charity Blake? I've known her, off and on I suppose, since I was about fourteen. I remember the very first time I visited their house, I sat on the chinchilla. I think I still have the bite mark.'

'No, no, please keep it to yourself.'

'The family are quite interesting. On her mother's side, she was related to the great Victorian explorers of Polynesia, Willoughby and Finge.'

'Both of them?'

'Yes. I forget which was which, but one of them was her Great Grandfather and the other, during a second expedition through the region some twenty years later, became her Grandfather. Partners to the end.'

'Oh, well, that sounds... reasonable.'

I remember this all took place on a Tuesday; the day of the great god 'Tue'. Honestly, that's who it's named after. If you don't believe me, go look it up. I have no idea what it was that Tue did exactly, but I'd say he or she was pretty lucky as it's hardly worth commemorating. Tue was probably massive in the years 120 BC to 225 AD, with festivals and all that dancing about with nothing on, but nowadays the day of the great god Tue merely means the day they come to collect the dustbins. Poor old Tue, consigned to the dumping ground of history.

'Charity lives at The Turretts, Horrington Park. You know, overlooking the Serpentine. That's where I sent the letter.'

'Is she Strickland-Hocket's daughter or niece?'

'She's the niece. He doesn't have any children and must have accepted responsibility for Charity after her parents died.'

'She's well named.'

'Yes, but she says she'd like to change it to something that doesn't remind her of the fact quite so often.'

'Let's review: You posted the letter, declaring bankruptcy and breaking your engagement, in the red pillar box outside your building at 9.45pm the night before last. The letter would have been collected when the box was cleared at 9am yesterday. There is therefore no chance the letter would have been delivered yesterday morning and the second post of the day has been abolished due to progress.'

'Yes.'

'So your letter will be delivered after 9am this morning.'

'That's right. Although nowadays they deliver the morning post in the afternoon.'

'Charity Blake will be circling Hyde Park on her unnecessarily expensive pony for most of the morning, after which she will return to the house?'

'Yes. She begins at home. The pony's quite obvious - it has white socks.'

'You mean it has white legs, a pattern commonly phrased as 'white socks'?'

'No, I mean she really puts it into white socks. She has a theory about traffic fumes pooling on the floor.'

He didn't dignify that with a comment, probably calculating whether Charity could possibly be worth the effort. I thought so. t least I used to. There was a time, when I was aged about sixteen and my hormones were simmering, when I dreamt of bringing her the largest bunch of flowers ever grown. Very often my dreams nded badly. Not with rejection, necessarily. In this particular dream, the bunch of flowers was sometimes so large that it destabilised the rotation of the planet. We kissed and then the Earth crashed into the sun. I blame Douglas Adams. Raffles snapped me back to reality.

'Strickland-Hocket leaves home at 8.15 am, regular as clockwork, and there are no servants, yes?'

'None. He's too tight with money. Charity has to do the cleaning herself and he generally eats out.'

'With her?'

'I don't think so, no. I get the impression she doesn't particularly like him.'

'That's settled then. We'll break in.'

'We can't just break in.'

'Alright, then I will. When they deliver the letter, I'll pick it off the mat and be out in a minute.'

Sometimes, Raffles amazed me. In the Army they teach us all to be resourceful, but I hadn't truly appreciated what that meant until I'd trailed around for a while after A.J. Raffles, the cricketer.

'Isn't that chargeable housebreaking or something?'

'It's hardly burglary, Bunny. Try to think of it as a supplementary away-fixture.'

●

It was 7.30am and sleep hung heavy like the felted walls of a Mongol Yurt, but not here. Sleep had so far eluded my adrenaly-flushed mind and slunk off to hang heavy over those lucky Mongolians instead. Yes, I'd been thrown into the street again, by Raffles, in such a kind-hearted way as a fellow would hardly notice it. He'd parted with instructions to meet him at 8.30am on the railway station. "If I'm to be thrown into Wormwood Scrubs Prison this afternoon, I intend to do it with my teeth clean" he'd pronounced, with reasonable consistency.

I haven't actually *been* in a Mongol Yurt, but it stands to reason that's what happens.

The minutes passed slowly until 8.30am, the appointed time to find Raffles at the railway station. I know this sounds strange, but I felt extremely relieved to see him holding the actual tickets. I should explain. When we were about fifteen years old, A.J. and I were permitted by the School to attend a national 'Triple-As' sports meeting in Nottingham. I think that first of all I should explain the explanation.

Raffles was representing the region in a singularly English event known as 'throwing the cricket ball'. I was representing the old School at hurling the discus. Don't laugh. The circumstances were odd, to say the least. I used to sling discusses all afternoon, athletics being a compulsory element of enforced education, and regularly notched up divots in the lower-scoring circles. My scores read something along the lines of: 2,3,3,2,2,2,3,3,3,2,3,2,2,3 etc. You begin to see the form? Then, out of the blue, I threw a twelve. The dratted iron plate scooped into the sky like a salmon leaping to escape the immediate catering arrangements of a neatly positioned Grizzly Bear and whoosh, there it was! I stared at my own hand. My hand stared back at me. Neither of us could believe it.

"I believe I heard a whoosh" exclaimed a wandering unit of academic staff. "Were you responsible for that whoosh?" "Yes Sir, it was I." "You threw a thirteen?" "A twelve, Sir." "It's cutting the line. We'll call it thirteen." "Yes Sir." "Clear your plans for Saturday, you're off to the Triple-As, you snotty little chimp." So there I was. The beginner's luck golfer plonked onto the first tee at the Open with a crowd of three thousand and Arnold Palmer watching intently to see if he can pick up any tips. No, it was worse than that. I not only had to do it again, but I had to do it *in short trousers*.

Shall I start again? Thanks. Glad you're still listening. To re-cap: I was extremely relieved to see Raffles holding the actual tickets. On that day long ago, we were told to report to the Bursar's office for our rail passes, schedule and tickets. We did, but there was no Bursar to be seen. Would the Bursars of Harrow and Eton have crippled their school's chances in the Triple-As with such an inappropriate absence? Would the Bursars of Gordonstoun and Roedean have nipped off to a Bursarial conference at such a pass? Would the cash offices of Stowe or Bembridge have let the side down in quite this manner? Would bursars as far as Millfield or Wellington College have, frankly, naffed off for an early lunch? No, they wouldn't. They were too polite. What about the myriad bursars in the sphere of state education? Come to think of it, the situation wouldn't arise as they'd sold off their school playing fields for housing development and wouldn't be going anyway. Ah-hem.

In conclusion then, we also wouldn't be going anyway as we didn't have enough money for the trip. Between us, we had about two pounds in cash, which was an achievement in itself, since the school was officially a cashless economy. Raffles, stubbornly determined to go, instructed me to fetch two glass beakers from the Chemistry Lab and to meet him in the village. I met him in the village. He'd spent our two pounds on a live chicken. Jolly good, we now had two beakers, one chicken, a complete absence of two pound notes and we still weren't going. Marvellous. I wondered how many fellow competitors from Shrewsbury or Rugby would be wandering about their villages like the ghost of Banquo in one of those new experimental interpretations of the play featuring two beakers and a live chicken. Not many. I wasn't happy and the chicken was borderline livid.

With seconds to spare, we arrived at the doors of the train. A.J., sod him, had told me it would be alright, but still I hesitated. "This is First Class." I'd pointed out. "That's right. In you go" he'd replied pushing me firmly inside with a leather sole and a couple of well-aimed blakeys. I sat down and pulled out a book. Perhaps, I thought, if I'm not seen talking to the chicken man, people won't think I'm with him. Raffles disappeared to the lavatory and returned after a while with a tightly tied plastic bag. "I shouldn't go to the lavatory if I were you. There's a stinkingly evil scene in there. Goethe might have promoted his book with a woodcut of it." "Oh, okay, thanks for the advice." "My pleasure. It's an even worse mess in there now I've killed that chicken." "You've done what?" At least I think I said "You've done what?". I may have jumped out of my seat and gabbled something unintelligible, which is what I usually do on these occasions.

Raffles opened the plastic bag, took one beaker out, re-tied the crinkly structure and handed it back to me. The bag was disgustingly warm, which wasn't overly reassuring. I instinctively held it upright. A.J. winked like a stage magician, the kind who entertain at children's parties and not the kind who chop up their rabbits in railway lavatories. He off-loaded, spun about and left me with five minute's worth of uncomfortable pause. Raffles reappeared from the direction of the Guard's compartment. "Don't worry Bunny. It's all arranged now. You can read your book." I read my book, but I must admit, I kept glancing over the top of it to see if he was still sitting there and not extending his reign of terror to any of the other passengers. It was okay, he'd found an abandoned newspaper to persecute instead.

When we eventually arrived at Nottingham Central Station, I was as surprised as anyone to see an unnecessary amount of policemen entering the carriages and re-directing people leaving the train. 'It's okay lads, off you go. Get clear as quick as you can. That's it. Move along.' We muttered thanks and moved through the cordon of officers. Strange days, strange days.

Should I tell you about the Championship? Is it relevant? Well, I've clean forgotten what Raffles did in his event, but in mine I threw a five, so came back to the paddock with not only my second best ever score, but also as a barely creditable last. I'm sure it was mostly the result of the latent tension buzzing around my system than any gasp of athletic ability, but the pleasant surprise had me walking on clouds through the rest of the afternoon and, feeling deservedly First Class this time, all the way home. The funny thing was, when we arrived back at our home railway station, there they were again. Dozens of provincial police scurrying about, directing us through emergency exits and generally managing the situation.

When we got back to school and handed in our wreaths of laurel before the apoplectic masses, I asked A.J. a question that had been bugging me all day. 'Raffles, how did we manage to travel half way across the country in a first class carriage when we hadn't got any money?' 'Oh, that's easy. We didn't have any tickets.' 'What?' I almost went through the floor. They made floorboards of oak when they built the refectory, so I didn't manage the legendary feat on that occasion. 'What?' I repeated, for emphasis. 'When the guard finds his attention drawn to a locked travelling trunk in the luggage compartment that apparently has a pool of blood seeping out of it, he'd have to be made of pretty solid stuff to think checking tickets was still a priority.'

I couldn't help thinking, if Raffles had been born in 15th Century Florence, Machiavelli would be out of a job, dead in a ditch and taking whole wooden spoonloads of the blame.

Where was I? Oh yes, lost in history. Clutching our tickets, we found ourselves diverted onto the rail-replacement bus service outside the exit to platform three. That would be the noble chariot to ferry fate, in the form of us, to the very home of Charity. Did I say I loved her? No, I didn't, did I. In hindsight, I'd say that at the time I was rather unclear on the matter, but you know how it is. Love is blind. Infatuation is very often 'blind man's buff'. Let's face it, she had her moments, but could also be a pleasantly borderline idiot. So could I. The only difference is, I've changed.

To pass the journey, I asked Raffles what he thought about the burglary and how I might state the facts at the upcoming court martial. I had been given quite a long time to prepare my defence, or more traditionally plenty of time for an honourable defendant to dispose of myself and avoid the humiliation, but could hardly engage a leading defence barrister without felling the dog and raiding the strong box again. I discounted this. There were certainly better options, but unfortunately at least three of them involved the Thames.

'The medals and so forth would have been stolen to order.'

'By the postman from Amersham! He specifically asked me where to find them.'

'Sure, why not? It's hardly relevant who removed them. The issue of consequence is to whom they were sold.'

'Military history has a market value? I hadn't really thought of it in that way.'

'Absolutely. At battlefields like Rourke's Drift they have to shoo the metal detectorists away.'

'Where would someone sell a Victoria Cross?'

'To a Victoria Cross collector? Bunny, you really have to learn to think these things through.'

'There are Victoria Cross collectors?'

'Yes there are. The families of long-dead cross winners enjoy their everlasting glory, but are not necessarily equipped with an everlasting supply of money, so they sell them at auction. It happens every few years or so. There are known to be three major collectors.'

'How do you know?'

'Christies, in King Street St James, just around the corner from the Albany. I made a desk enquiry.'

'So that's where you were! I could have done that.'

'No you couldn't. Think it through. You would have looked suspicious. To be blunt, I had to shake you off before I could go near the place. If the Police asked the auction houses about recent activity, they might have connected you to the scene and then... openly canvassing for the sale of a fantastically rare and recently stolen commodity?'

He had a point. I frequently found I couldn't argue with his logic, but what really irritated me was his patronising habit of not telling me what was going on. I presume he thought that providing explanations where they have not been asked for would be an unconscionable waste of his time.

'So who are the VC collectors?'

'Hawkins, CEO of Farnworth Circuitry and Software. In the City, he has a sterling reputation for honesty. Tungsten Marriot, a Canadian who made his name in silver bullion. Rumour has it that he isn't credit worthy any more, so I doubt he'd still be able to afford a VC.'

'Are they worth a lot then?'

'At a legitimate public sale, the last one sold for £280,000.'

'How much?!'

I don't think I had ever been flabbergasted before. Surprised, yes. Shocked, occasionally, but never this.

'The third candidate is much more interesting. Dishonesty is his middle name. I would bet my reputation against left-handed batsmen that your missing contraband can now be found at the London residence of Lord Bunting.'

'Lord who?'

'Bunting. He's fascinating.

'Is he a cricketing lord then?'

'No, no, he's one of the 'modern' variety. Classless society and all that. As I understand it, he's a 'mover and shaker' in the film industry. Apparently, he moves and shakes like nobody's business although I can't say I've witnessed the antic personally.'

'He's there on the 'services to industry and culture' ticket then?'

'I suppose he must be. I can't think of any other reason for it. I understand he invented a horror movie character called *Soda Man*, who inflates American teenaged backpackers until their clothes part at the seams. They generally burst after that and soggy bits drip down the walls.'

'It's art then.'

'Culture, arguably. The critics say his films are in such commercial demand that they go straight to video without even waiting for a cinema release.'

'Ah, I understand.'

'Bunting was elevated to the peerage in the New Year Honours list, on the Prime Minister's personal recommendation. You know, of course, that he wants people from all walks of life in the upper house?'

'Oh, yes, I had heard that.'

'Then there was all that nasty business about secret donations to fund the Prime Minister's political party. They had him down for £750,000 you know? It emerged as a 'loan' on token interest, to be written-off after five years. Of course, that's a dreadfully embarrassing coincidence for the Prime Minister. People might think the two things are connected.'

'Indeed.'

'He's also this country's foremost collector of militaria. Medals other people have earned. Banners other men have died for. If anyone's in the market for your museum's VC, it's going to be him.'

'Are you sure there's no one else?'

'No. There are others who could afford the price, but are they interested enough? There's Eugene Drobek of *Personal Hoovers*, the dandruff and fluff-collection specialists, but he mostly buys the George Cross. They say he has five and wears them at dinner, before which he sucks dust off his guests and measures it.'

'Lovely. Alright, presuming it's Bunting, what can we do?'

'Nothing. Without evidence, you haven't a chance. The Police won't touch him.'

'Alright' I swallowed stoically 'I'll accept my fate.'

'Sometimes you have to. Did I tell you the story of Canterbury, 1992?'

'No, but we're nearly there, so if you're going to, you'd best make it quick.'

'I was a teenager in my first season for the Middlesex Second Eleven. We were playing a seasonal warm-up match against a touring team of middle-aged former professional players from the Indian state sides. For them, it must have been a final fling of the pill before accepting the limitations of age.'

'Sounds fun.'

'It was. I had a great time trying to tear them out with my spin and watching every tenth ball go sailing over my head to the boundary. Honours were even. I'd never been played so well, so they actively forced me to bowl better than I had ever done before. Our seam bowlers bent their knees in submission, but I wasn't about to give up. I tried to bowl the old boys a few genuine corkscrews.'

'Excellent. Never say die.'

'Chasing down their score with the bat, our side suffered a collapse. I found myself playing for an honourable draw against exquisitely aimed leg spin. Now, the thing I'd been taught about leg spin is that if the arm passes wide of the bowler's ear, it's an attempted leg spinner. If the bowler's arm clips their ear, i.e. passes vertically, it can not possibly be a leg spinner. It must either be a googly, turning the other way, or a ball which continues straight on.'

'I knew that.'

'The old boy bowled. The bowling arm clipped his ear. I swept my bat inside the line and played to drive the straight one, leaving the pad to block the googly. It broke firmly to leg and removed off stump. An impossible ball. Against nature, physics and the laws of reality... just impossible.'

'Bad luck.'

'No, you aren't following this at all. Being out didn't matter to me. Losing didn't matter. What mattered was that I'd done everything right, I'd covered every possibility, yet I had to accept my defeat anyway.'

'How very philosophical.'

'It also taught me that only a fool takes teams like India for granted, at any level.'

'You do realise, I'll be strangely comforted by all this when the court strings me up?'

'Up you get. We're there.'

We were there. My attention must have been wandering, since Raffles recognised the house before I did and I was the one who'd been there before! As a child, of course, I'd visited often and the sooty grime on the white stones of the gateway looked as though it hadn't been wiped off since. Strickland-Hocket was a real cheapskate, wasn't he? It was a wonder the object of my adoration had anything to eat.

Having slipped through the gate, we angled left and peered out from a screen of whispering green bamboo.

'Stay here' instructed Raffles 'and throw a pebble at the door if anyone but the postman comes back.'

As I'd watched him sneaking out of school, I saw him now. Climbing on window fames, bracing on gutters, finely balancing on a ledge, forcing a catch. I couldn't see a burglar alarm. Was Strickland-H really too miserly to pay for one to be fitted? Despite being the older man. I assured myself that he was better adapted to the task, as a professional sportsman. I liked my sport too, but it has to be acknowledged that I wasn't in anything like the same league as Raffles. To put this in perspective, my greatest afternoon of sporting achievement involved a pretty hard-fought game of 'wang the welly'. I annihilated six or seven opponents, although three of them later turned out to be girls. At least I had assumed they were girls. You can't be so sure nowadays, although the throw's a dead giveaway. Ah! Most professional. A.J. was in.

I waited. Nothing happened. I waited and waited. The postman duly arrived and delivered some letters. As he walked away, the door opened a fraction. That was the end of it; Raffles didn't come out. I wondered what he could be doing. Just before my watch reached the mark where I'd waited and waited and waited, I decided it would best to go in after him. I passed through the open door without opposition. A Japanese lacquered desk in the entranceway caught my attention. Not the desk itself, you understand, but the flurry of post laid along it. Most of the letters had been read and then left as a sort of open litter in lieu of an appointment diary.

I ploughed through its crop of papers, desperately looking for my letter. An account from a dressmaker, something about a new website and tickets for *Ultrasound*, although why she'd push off to a Midge Ure concert without me, supposedly her boyfriend at the time, I couldn't imagine.

I turned and spotted today's letters still in the shadow behind the open door. So, they hadn't been picked up after all. Where the hell was Raffles?

'It's you!'

It was her.

'Charity! I thought you were...'

'Riding? I've had to give that up for a while. I'm spending much more time these days catching burglars.'

'I'm not a burglar!'

'Perhaps not, but you're friend is. Don't look at me like that! You only got close to me again after all these years so you could tell your friend how to rob Daddy.'

'No I didn't! I was trying to surprise you and he said he'd help me get in.'

'Is that the best you can do? It's pathetic. If you've run out of money, you could have asked. I would have understood. We were engaged to be married, you know.'

'Were?'

'Were. I won't marry you now, even though that's going to make the future very difficult.'

'I can explain.'

Actually, I couldn't.

'Don't bother to even try.'

Phew!

'Your accomplice broke in, I locked him in Daddy's study and you came in to see where he'd got to.'

'If you have it all worked out, what are you going to do?'

'I'm not sure' she said decisively.

A police car howled up the drive, scattering gravel. They are awfully loud, aren't they?

'I called the Police' she explained, helpfully. 'They're looking for two of you. One in the study and one behind the bamboo in the garden.'

'So you're going to turn me in?'

'No. I'm going to let you go. It will be the last thing I do for you.'

A pair of burly policemen marched in, their radios squawking excitedly.

'Madam, where are they?'

'One's locked in the study – the door off the landing – and the other's shot across the lawn that way.'

Rather efficiently I thought, he repeated this into the radio. More police would attend to the runner.

'This man is?'

'My fiancée.'

'Thank you. Please stand aside, we'll take the one in the study first.'

He motioned the second officer into readiness to break down the door.

'Would you like to use the key, Officer?' asked Charity without a hint of sarcasm.

'Thanks.'

Crash, bang, wallop – what a picture. The window within had either imploded or exploded, but either way, it showered glass.

'Damn' said the second policeman. Between them, they operated the lock and barged their way through into the now vacant study. It was radio-time again.

'Echo Zulu, this is 7583, over...' squawk.

'Receiving you 7583, over...' squawk.

'Two suspects have exited the Turretts, proceeding over the wall on Horrington Park and Central, over...'

At that point, Raffles ran down the road, past the gates of the house, shouting 'I've got the other one!' and the Police rushed out to help him.

I remember how we all recorded statements, like a pack of excited spaniels. The police remained irritated by the evasiveness of their quarry, but at the same time thrilled to be assisted by a famous cricketer who happened to be passing. One young policeman shyly asked him for an autograph. Statements completed and witnessed, nothing further to do, we wished the police luck and said, if that was it, we were going to our homes. All except Charity Blake, of course. She had to live here. She had to live with the consequences. I kissed her cheek farewell, for the last time, and looked down and away from those eyes filled with the chill hatred of the betrayed. I walked away into a plethora of alternative futures.

The journey was a quiet one. Raffles had shaken hands and hailed a cab. I'd earned the frosty stare, I can still see it when I close my eyes, and taken a slower path: the rail-replacement bus service back to town.

It was a pity about Charity. I couldn't be sure she'd been serious about our relationship anyway. When I settled down in the old apartment, with its scuffed floors and velvet curtains, it was as if a great lens had changed, flicked, and for the first time in years I properly focussed. I didn't love her.

This, the place I'd called home and rattled around in for the past few years, at least when not on duty at barracks, was now nothing but a hollow shell. I poured an undiluted glass and slumped. Surely I could do better? I could walk away from my den without looking back. I felt I had at last grown and hatched from here and now was the time to fly. Do parasitic worms hatch into butterflies? Ouch. I was being hard on myself. I had always had a healthy sense of self-loathing. I'd pay the old boy back somehow, even though there was nothing he wanted, except a little loyalty.

I don't think I've always had an inferiority complex. I think it comes and goes whenever my life veers and jolts and pinballs between confidence and crisis. I do remember how my parents behaved. Always so self-assured and confident. Sometimes they would stare at me as if I wasn't entirely theirs.

Every December, my parents held two parties. An A Party, followed by a B Party. The A Party was for all their real friends. The people who were close enough and distinctly civilised enough to get along with each other and be trusted not to spoil it. At the A Party, they served Islay Malts, Spey Royal, three kinds of gin, Chateau Ott and Burgundy. To the B Party, a week or so later, were invited all the people who would be dreadfully upset if they weren't invited at all, but were not close enough, nor trusted enough... perhaps not quite 'us' enough to make the A Party.

I know that someone at the B Party once arrived with his own collection box for the RAF benevolent fund and rattled it under our guests' noses. Unacceptable, but strangely anticipated. He was the type. Guests at the A Party thought they were at the only party, since they saw the same faces every year. Equally, the Bs thought they were at the only party, because they saw the same people drinking the same sort of table wine each and every year. I was in on the secret though. I could see what my parents were up to.

As a child, I was at a boarding school. Sorry about that. Honestly, I just went where I was told. 'Get on the train, enjoy the complete lack of heating and we'll see you again, a little tougher and taller, in about three months.' I know someday there'll be a revolution and I'll be persecuted for this. It's just my sort of luck. I also remember, although it didn't strike me as unusual at the time, that *always*, by the late-December date I arrived back from boarding school, my Parent's A Party had already happened.

I thought I'd seen A.J. for the last time, back in '88, in the audience of a smoking concert organised by the Cambridge University Light Entertainment Society. Upstairs at The School of Pythagoras, I think it was. He must have been an undergrad at the time, but I never thought to ask what he was reading. I'd seen Raffles playing raucous piano for C.U.L.E.S., or more often read his name on fly-posters about the town, so I suppose he would have got in that night on free tickets. He'd brought along some ephemeral shock of blonde he'd been dating at the time. She was most likely something in amateur dramatics and, it could be said, quite something else in a slippery cocktail frock. I didn't intrude with clumsy hellos.

What brought it home to me, the thing which really told me he'd got his life sorted out and I hadn't, was the manner in which we went home that evening. Raffles, shaking hands, reflecting regards, decanting his girl into a throbbing racing-green car and tooting away. Me, padding away un-noticed. Wandering down the public footpath, wandering and wondering if the white patches under my feet were rare lichens or just chewing gum, through the arcade, dobbing my head round the door of the pool hall and then down to kebab-row with Beanbag and Tigger, Cider Joe and Fatbacked Mary. They asked where I'd been. 'Oh, nowhere.' That was my last time at C.U.L.E.S. I didn't even get all the jokes. I bet Raffles got all the jokes. I bet he laughed and put everyone at their ease, even when they weren't being funny. Oh dear. This was the stress, or the relief, or perhaps the drink talking. Churlish of me. Sorry.

I'm not one for jealousy, but I can't help feeling irritated by nature's successes. At last, I could think of Raffles as a housebreaker and a common thief. That was a comforting thought, or at least it drew me from the deepwaters of my ongoing aggravation with him to the mere irritant shallows. Until, that was, I considered that he'd fallen from grace only and purely to save me. In which case, it was absolutely no consolation at all. He'd probably only helped to make me feel worse. I realised I wasn't making much sense. Time, I think, for two night's worth of sleep.

'Thanks Raffles' I conceded under my breath, although it made no difference in the end. I threw Charity's letter on the fire. It curled and ignited. Now then, Fatbacked Mary, I wonder what happened to her?

Chapter 4

From All Our Suffering,
a Parthian Shot

Recovering from adventures isn't fun. They never mention the bit about calming down afterwards, these Rider Haggards and Sax Rohmers and W.E. Johnses, do they? I'm sure their poor characters had to do something to cool their heels when the criminal gangs and Fu Manchus popped off for their annual skiing holidays. Norland-Smith, for example, almost certainly went fly fishing. He was just the type. Although why anyone might want to catch a fly, I couldn't imagine.

I'm sure Bulldog Drummond would have played Rugby. I could just imagine him picking up the ball and playing against the whole town of Rugby, all at the same time. Alan Quartermaine, back in the metropolis with a pocket full of emeralds following some spectacularly lucrative adventure, would almost certainly slope around to his patent leather bootmaker, his patent leather whipmaker and then he'd be off to Madam Wong's Slap Emporium for the rest of the afternoon to give them a bit of a test. That's the bit we are never told. That's why none of them could ever keep a girlfriend.

They say the unusual is relative. In that case, most of my relatives are extraordinary.* As a matter of commonality, they mostly infest the

---

*Raffles only has one living relative, as far as I know. He seems to be some species of cousin, married with a child, living down in Suffolk. They've fallen out with Raffles, so can't be considered as on speaking terms. I know they visited A.J. once and when the cousin's wife didn't want more wine, she put her hand over the top of the glass. Raffles, brought up to know you mustn't do this, (it questions the host's ability to pay for a single wasted glass of wine) just kept pouring it over her hand and across the table cloth. After a year or five they forgave him for that incident and invited him for a weekend at their house instead. It seems they then asked him if he wouldn't mind babysitting for a bit and took the opportunity to disappear out for dinner. Then there was a bit of a rift. Raffles' rifts are legendary. By the time they returned, A.J. had taught their baby how to undo its own nappy.

42

same village. I'm not sure if that's because they're genetically indisposed to travelling or whether they just happen to approve of the soil conditions. Pigeons are the same because they have magnets in their brains. Personally, I can't stand the place for more than a couple of days, so only shovel down the river to visit the tribe when I have something expressly formal to say.

I'd spent a weekend down in the country since my last encounter with the unsettling world of A.J. Raffles. Have you ever been to The Uphams? As the locals will tell you, there are three villages: Lower Upham, Middle Upham and They Don't Like It, collectively known as 'The Uphams'. My padding feet reluctantly closed the ground on Middle Hall at Upper Upham, which is only technically excluded from The Uphams per se to make room for the preceding joke.

I considered it my reluctant duty to break the news to the Manders ilk that wheels were turning that might well lead to my discharge from the Army. They didn't take it well, although there was a general consensus that Her Majesty might be fractionally safer now that I wasn't allowed to stamp about under her windows doing my best party impression of guard duty. That was my Uncle. A nasty man who once described the chore of shaking hands with ordinary village people as 'a firm grip of the basics'.

In fact, I suspect they'd rather been counting on my getting myself killed and earning the family a constipated photo for the mantelpiece with a dusty medal draped over it. The continued existence of a real, living, three dimensional me – still capable of letting them all down – appeared to be scant compensation in the eyes of the family. Do you know, I didn't care? I wouldn't be judged by them any more. There were enough other annoyances to contend with.

For example, having bought a 1st class railway ticket down, I found myself directed onto the rail-replacement bus service to Brighton station, just in time to catch the rail replacement bus service to Southampton which connected seamlessly with the rail replacement bus service to Plymouth, after which there was a train. It didn't have a first class carriage and, being shortened by half for profitability reasons, was so full that I had to stand up for the rest of the way, but at least it fulfilled the remit of a train. Good old Cornish Regional Railway Co., they at least had a train and ran a railway service on a Sunday, unlike the rest of the network.

I sometimes wonder if they couldn't publish a timetable with the very worst travel times of the year given as guides between destinations? From my own experience, I could submit one entry to the editor: Flight from Athens to Gatwick Airport on a Sunday, one and a half hours. Rail and ferry travel from Gatwick to the Isle of Wight, another nine and a half hours. That's the bit the brochures exclude. On a bad day, you can fly to Australia in less time than you can cross two English counties by rail. Caveat touristei.

Of course, the Public are conditioned from birth not to complain about such things. Just get on with it. I'll never forget the occasion when I arrived one winter at a rural station in Hampshire and found that the connecting train had already gone. I had to spend all the night on a station bench as the temperature dropped to an outstanding minus sixteen. One of the departing railway staff, who'd just locked the waiting room, laughed out loud at my predicament. No, worse still, he pointed and then laughed out loud. "You're going to have to sleep out all night mate! Ha ha ha ha!" To paraphrase Gump, 'Life is just a box of bastards; you never know which one you're going to run into next.' When I hear that these people are taking their regular bouts of industrial action for improved pay and conditions, there's a part of me that remembers that night and says aloud 'Just fire them. Fire them all, kick them hard and say 'Grrrrr!' into their ears on the way out.'

Is this getting un-necessarily angst-ridden? Sorry, but my mind was on little else as I took the usual series of rail replacement bus services back to London. Other forms of public transport shouldn't escape the flames of wrath either. I once took a bus to Bournemouth, which changed its destination markings after I got on it and I ended up in Aberystwyth. Since there were no trains from Wales to Bournemouth that day, I took a taxi back to London at a price of a few hundred pounds and avoided all busses everywhere from then onward. It's hardly possible to avoid rail replacement busses though, especially since the southern line has been dug up for semi-permanent weekend engineering works since the sunny second Tuesday in April, 1894. They're quite happy to sell you a ticket for a train though, knowing full well there are no trains running. Honestly, they're complete and utter shents.

By the way, this is called displacement anger. That's right, I've just invented it. Some things have gone wrong, some things have gone right (if awkwardly) and now I'm just in one of those moods that you have to put up with for a few days before it falls away. My apologies to everyone, backdated to the beginning of my life. How very English and self-deprecating. I'm apologising again!

Did you know that the famous computer printer companies can sell their laserjets, inkjets and dot printers at under production cost? You see, their core business *is really* to sell the ink. Why couldn't the Southernshire Coastal Railway Company be honest about what they do and just sell their customers bus tickets? If I had a pound for everyone this rail operator has upset... insert a depiction of fields full of commuters gnashing their teeth, one specialist gnashing-conductor, circled by ant-like volunteers going around and between them all with clinking buckets to collect all the gnawed pound coins for re-minting.

I arrived in town and took an underground connection to Green Park, with a view to drop in on Raffles at the Albany.

That reminds me, since I'm on the subject, - no, don't hold me back - of the London Underground strike where the ombudsman said season ticket holders were entitled to £40 compensation to make up for all the days of travel they had paid for in advance and subsequently lost from closures. I wrote in with my evidence and claim, asking for the forty pound reimbursement I'd been officially awarded. A few weeks later, they posted me a letter containing a cheque for £20 together with a note explaining that they'd deducted a further £20 'administration fee'. As you can see, I don't have much luck with public transport. It's usually Aberystwyth all over again.

I launched a tirade at Raffles. Yes, I know, inflicting this sort of thing on your friends is supremely bad form. I vented my frustration over the transport system and right across his bows within the first minute of him opening the door. He probably wished he hadn't. After all, what could he possibly do about it?

'Raffles, I am determined to write another letter of complaint. I will be harsh and shall pull no punches.'

'Yes Bunny, but there are only so many complaints you can make before they post you a turd.'

I hadn't thought of that. He was right. They probably had a special department for ignoring complaints. They'd probably invested in a binary optical recognition sorting machine to ignore the stacks of complaints with ever improved efficiency. They probably thought customer complaints were an annoyance against them! That was, after all, the modern way. That was the thing that moved thousands of commuters a year off the trains and into the gleeful hands of the car salesmen, and Lo! The gaping hole in the ozone layer shuffled and yawned and cracked its insubstantial jaws even wider.

Too cynical? When the Greeks developed the Cynical School of philosophy, they named it after the word for 'yapping dog'. If I had become too cynical, it was only because they'd finally driven me barking.

'I'm sorry to bother you with this, A.J. I know there's nothing to do. I just feel like revenge, that's all.'

'Fair enough. It's no use damaging the company itself. The staff would simply carry on as usual somewhere else and do exactly the same thing to someone else. The only solution would be to hit them personally. Let's remove their pension fund.'

'You're joking.'

Some of Raffles's jokes weren't in the least bit funny. It was five, perhaps ten, minutes before I came to the conclusion that he really wasn't joking after all. It's only now, when I come to explain to someone else – oh, I don't know. What I mean, I suppose, is that it's extremely difficult to convey the consummate ease with which Raffles can lull a person into accepting that what he's talking about is perfectly normal. It's like listening to a lullaby.

The truly insidious thing is that if I'd questioned his proposals, he would have reminded me that he was merely helping me do what I had wanted. It was my plan then, apparently, although I'm pretty sure I hadn't intended to be drawn into common robbery. My opinion was soon corrected. As the plan unfolded, I could see that it was to be a very uncommon robbery.

'It won't be a proper robbery. It should be seen as a temporary re-distribution of assets. The aim will be to put it on the public agenda. We find work at the pensions company, at the necessary level of financial access, then transfer as much as we can to the central railway ombudsman's fund which compensates passengers for failures of service.'

'How do we ever get that?'

'I have it here. I've just been inadequately compensated myself by electronic transfer. Playing the surprised customer, I've asked for details. My bank have given me the name and number of the company account that the payment came from.'

He threw me a newspaper, in the margin of which was written 'BR (compensation), Cortis Bank' and a line of numbers.

'Hang on a minute! This is very prepared. You asked for the account number before I even mentioned it?'

Raffles leant over and tapped the date at the top of the newspaper. He'd been thinking about it for weeks.

'Did you think you were alone in your frustration? I, also, have grown tired of the bus.'

'Understandable. So, you propose we clean them out and show them up. Then what?'

'Initially the pension fund will collapse. They'll still have their shares and bonds in certificate form, but they'll lose their liquid assets. No cash to invest with, you see. One hundred thousand fund members, who've made their contributions as usual, will have to be told and the media will find out automatically. The next stage will be an FSA investigation, which will quickly discover where the money went. The funds will then be returned, by court order if necessary, and the Press will rake over the whole issue of terrible service in public transport until someone in power does something about it.'

'So we just highlight the problem?'

'We will also cause them as much grief as they've dumped on us. Then we're even.'

I wobbled. Certainly they deserved it, but I could be well out of my depth. I know I should have pulled out of the scheme right then. Unfortunately, my inquisitive nature and the bond of trust I by now owed A.J. wouldn't let me. The leading factor though, the one which persuaded me to agree to it all regardless, was that the spectator in me dearly wanted to see how Raffles could possibly pull it off.

No, to be honest, I think I'm easily led. Raffles, who'd read the literature he could get on hypnotic suggestion, must have used some cunning ploy to relax my usually lawful nature because, otherwise, I can't quite work out how I went along with it. Unless it was angst. I only have to see a train to feel angst. 'Grrrrr!' in their ears, 'Grrrrr!'

Ah-hem.

In the early evening, we'd rattled down some seedy steps in Golden Square, off London's Soho district. At the time, you couldn't ask me why. In a basement establishment, through a much sprayed-upon doorway, we entered a club less respected than the Albany and, thankfully unobserved. Shadows, tables in recesses, some form of stage with a tropical island scene painted behind it, a line of cabins?

'Hey, look Raffles. They've got private hidden tables, just like the Savoy Grill!'

'Bunny, this is as far from the Savoy Grill as you can get.'

My eyes adjusted to the light. I could see a bar and there were people at it, at the bar that is, although there seemed something strangely wrong about them. Okay, bite the bullet, I slogged over to get in a couple of pints and left Raffles to secure the table. I just hoped I could identify him again in the gloom when I came back. That was the point when I had the fright of my life. The people at the bar were, I mean they were dressed as... well, I mean to say, I can't say, if you see what I mean? Is that appropriate Madam... or Sir? Oh dear. Thanks A.J., for exposing me to this niche in the folded tapestry of life. Actually, as niches go, this was more of a perspirational crevice.

I've always found embarrassment to be the worst thing you can do to a Briton, but I took it on the chin. The barman looked at me, disappointed I hadn't made more of an effort, then served up my two pints of best Yorkshire Bitter. Another patron made a joke about the head which I decided not to understand and I found myself free to run for cover. Alright. Not so bad. I found the right table and leaned back, relaxing into the shadows.

'There's someone I want you to meet' said Raffles.

'Is she pretty?' I asked hopefully.

'Look around you. Do the maths.'

From that, I supposed we were meeting a male person, but probably one with *complexities of dress*. I made inroads into my pint. At about the three quarter mark, I slowed my drinking somewhat, trying to put off the inevitable moment when I'd have an empty glass and be compelled to go to the bar again. I'd have to have had a lot of drinks before I'd make it to that particular bar again without feeling extremely self-conscious. Come to think of it, that's a bit of a catch-22. Ah good, a waitress! Raffles signalled before I could raise my arm. Talk about 'two great minds' and all that.

It wasn't... It was... I mean to say I'm not sure what it was, but 'it' begins to cover it. Not that I'd wish to offend anyone who'd made *that much effort*. It was also covered by feathers, ruffles, lace, neon garters and something that looked suspiciously like a balloon in the hair. Okay, so it was a man, but you can appreciate the point without having it rubbed in your face. Altogether the effect was designed to challenge, provoke and fiercely shock the prudes of England. Old-fashioned prudish people like me. Oyoyoyoyoy. Take me back to the country. I ducked behind a defensive beer.

'What are we doing here Raffles?'

'I want you to meet someone.'

He stood up and shook hands with... um. I could only suppose this elaborate costume comprised some form of cabaret entertainment. How had Raffles met... I mean to say? Surely they hadn't? Eeeuuw, I didn't want to think about that.

Raffles spoke to our painted visitor first.

'Long time no see! What would we do without the magnificence of your company? Jason, I'd like to introduce Bunny here, who's going to front-up our little job.'

We engaged in uncommitted how-do-you-dos.

'Bunny, meet Jason Pinder, the finest club singer on the transvestite circuit and also, *shhhhh*, the most dramatically dressed forger in London.'

Ah, okay. Light dawned. It hadn't occurred to me that transvestites had a circuit, but I supposed I could get through life without overly exploring this information.

'Hiya! Hiya!' said one of the other customers, interrupting Mr Pinder. This one was wearing metallic gold shorts. I wondered how anyone would ever find a metallic gold short shop – in the Yellow Pages?

I took this opportunity for a swift aside to Raffles. 'A.J., he's a, you know...'

'A hominid?'

'Um, yes?'

'An absolutely *raving* hominid. Most of these types aren't, you know, but he's the exception to prove the... Ah, Jason, anything the matter?'

'No trouble. That's the lovely Syorg. He works at the hospital.'

'Oh' I ventured, 'what does he do?'

'What doesn't he do?'

I probably shouldn't have asked that. It was time to show an acute interest in the bottom of my beer glass.

By the way, no, I did not say 'cute', actually. I said 'acute', although I did say bottom. I'm only making that point because I know what you historical revisionists are like, with your naff little theories about Sherlock Holmes having a suspiciously close relationship with Doctor Watson. Raffles and I are not. Okay? Just not. I'm glad we've got that clear, so I don't want to hear any of you piping up in a hundred year's time when nobody's around to nail you for slander and making grubby little accusations to support your own private agendas. Jeeves was engaged. Wooster was serially engaged. Sherlock Holmes was in love with the Countess of Bohemia. Alright? Enough said.

I'm sorry, but I'm not very well adapted to this whole politically correct modernism thing that everyone else seems to soar through without experiencing the least discomfort. In fact, I'm not sure how to cope at all in these sorts of circumstances. I mean, I wouldn't want to be judgemental, but everyone's trying to read between the lines here and it's so easy to say the wrong thing. Frankly, some of these people look as though they're *inserting things* between the lines. Okay, so I don't know how to react. Slap me.

I can't believe I just said that. It's all the fault of the décor. Soft furnishings have an awful lot to answer for. Have they put something in my beer? I'd just like to point out that I was drinking straight, honest, Yorkshire bitter, not one of those fashionable Japanese lagers flavoured with citron yeast or something equally daft like that. Although, despite the low light, I could see they'd put a small turquoise parasol in it. Perhaps it was heliotrope, but that's just a matter of detail.

Oh dear. There I go again. Objectively, I hadn't been confronted with anything particular awkward yet, but it was just the suggestion that... Oh, I don't know. Look, I learned my cricket in Harrogate, where running leg byes is still considered tantamount to homosexual activity and I can just imagine the wave of panic that would roll through North Yorkshire if I were to be seen here today.

What I mean to say is that I go red, for heaven's sake. Where does one apply for a training course to deal with these situations? In brief, I'd rather not be involved, if it's all the same to you. Not that I've any objection – free country and all that – but I've never been comfortable with embarrassing face to face confrontations.

Admittedly we're great at confrontation in the military, no problems, but in those circumstances you can sort it all out with honest-to-goodness gunfire. It's all so much harder when you have to tip-toe around these issues and their associated reactive, emotive, personalities like a dizzy ballerina in a glassworks. Admittedly, I'd barged into their back yard and as such didn't have a nodule of moral high-ground to stand on, but even so. I blamed Raffles for this. Why did we need a forger anyway? Tickets for the cricket?

'Jason, if I had your phone number, this would be so much easier.'

He gave Raffles his phone number and the piece of paper found its way to me. I didn't want his phone number, particularly. Strange man. Oh my god, it had a heart on it! I felt like passing out, but I didn't much like the thought of being revived. Time to look around for the hidden camera.

'What's the job?' a question directed at Raffles, luckily. He still hadn't told me what he was up to.

'We need to be sure of getting Bunny here placed at the Challener Harris Corporate Pension Company. They're advertising a managerial post in the investments section of their Finance Department and we simply must have it.'

'I understand. A shining CV, a good degree, accountancy qualifications, professional memberships, the backdated work history and fully checkable references?'

'That's it exactly' said Raffles. Good, I thought, this was going to be quick. 'When can we collect it?'

'If you're prepared to pay my fee, I'll cancel my gig down in Putney and you can pick it up on Saturday.'

'Six days? You're a fast worker!'

'Not really I'll just adapt a CV I've done for a friend. He wanted to be an Oxbridge Blue, of all things! Just like that one I did for that novelist back in Maggie's government. I don't blame him though. Those committees to select political candidates can be so cruel, especially given the old-fashioned views of those constituency chairman.'

Good heavens, this man could make or break entire careers if he wanted to. Raffles' too, I should imagine. What a thought. What a risk.

'If you don't mind my asking, why the C-H pensions company?'

'Unusual, I know' said Raffles. 'Bunny here is going to infiltrate them to expose corruption and malpractice, on behalf of his readers and millions of other maltreated rail passengers.'

'A journalist? Alright, I'm up for that. I certainly approve a poke in the eye for the railways. The things they do to my hat boxes. You won't be mentioning my name, will you, my brave little moral crusader?'

'No, of course not!' I assured him. 'I'm just trying to make a stand. This is a bit like the story of the finger and the dyke.'

'I don't think I've heard that one darling.' Another freezingly embarrassing moment drifted by. Have you ever seen an iceberg? Well, imagine a pink one.

Raffles came to my rescue. 'Look, over there. Isn't that the ex-Member for Beckenham? I wonder how he'll claim this on expenses, 'urban social research'? Another of your guests, Jason?'

'No, not mine. He's just here being happy with the boys. No story there but the usual. Between you and me, he's a bit old for it. Liver spots are so unattractive.'

'I think they're trying to attract your attention. Are you due on stage?'

'Not for fifteen minutes, poppet. Leave it with me and I'll see you next week. Oh, by the way, real name or fake name?'

'Fake, please' said Raffles.

'With a real National Insurance number?'

'If you can.'

'Lovely meeting you' he said as he bounced away.

'Isn't that A.J. Raffles, the cricketer?' said a voice that cut through the bustle. 'I never knew he was a *player*.'

Whoever it was had stressed the word 'player' and faces were turning in our direction.

'Yes, I believe you're right! It's amazing who's on the scene nowadays!'

'Another glimpse of Bertram' murmured Raffles.

'What did you say? There's so much noise in here.' Someone was singing.

'I said, I think it's time we left'.

I agreed. Half an hour ago would have been the perfect time for me.

●

Days passed, as did the uncomfortable sensations of embarrassment. By my usual scale, Raffles had exposed me to a ten year's worth of the fear of embarrassment in a single sitting. This was the main thing in life I really couldn't cope with. I still couldn't believe people went to that sort of place for fun.

It was a Sunday when Raffles summoned me. We had lunch at the Albany, a wonderful cheesy fish pie, talked of this and that, then relaxed into broad club chairs with the papers.

'Your new CV' said A.J., handing me some pages. 'Would you mind adding your unutterable scrawl to the bottom line?'

I signed the name indicated in the place indicated on the application letter.

'Well done. I made a couple of copies in case you signed your real name out of habit.'

I read through my new CV and shuffled the various certificates of qualification. AAT Accountancy, BSc, Manual Handling; he had been thorough.

'A professional bit of work, I thought.'

'Yes, very professional.'

'His evening job's blatantly conspicuous, wouldn't you say, so who'd suspect him of having an equally impressive day job as well?'

'Who indeed?' I replied enigmatically.

Great. This page said I could swim. I've always wanted to swim.

'What is that?'

'I found it in this Sunday newspaper supplement.'

'And?'

'It's an advertisement for a little plastic press which turns direct marketing into fire-lighting blocks.'

'You've considered purchasing some rubbish advertised in junk mail which solves your problem of what to do with junk-mailed advertising rubbish?'

'Um, so you don't think I should encourage them?'

'Correct. See if it burns, would you?'

'Oh, all right.' I consigned it to the flames of the Albany Club's copious log fire. Where do they get their logs in London?

'Bunny?'

'Yes.'

'What's the other one?'

'It's for a company in Reading that's selling half priced water-diviners. I know, I know. On the fire.'

What a pity. I'd always wanted to try that too.

●

Days passed, as did the uncomfortable sensations of cheesy fish pie. I don't think I have an allergy and I must say I'm not entirely convinced it was the fish, blame-wise that is, but there it stands, for the chronicles, if you see what I mean, without spelling it out. Next time I'll have the duck. I'm okay with duck. Where was I?

Raffles had applied in my name for the advertised position at the *Challener Harris Pensions Company*, a limited investment company involved solely in the administration of *The Southernshire Coastal Railway Company's* pension scheme.

The return address on my application letter, care of my apparent previous employer, was that of a large office building at Carrington House in Regent Street. As Raffles explained to me, the occupiers of these offices come and go. If any post arrived for an addressee no longer in residence, it was their custom to place the unclaimed letter on the radiator in the entrance hall downstairs and so give the owner a chance to retrieve it. We retrieved it, after six days of dodging in and checking. I had been invited to interview!

There is little I can say about that interview, other than it went well. There were three other candidates, to pit their working expertise against mine, and we did a sort of clerical test. It fairly wore down my typing finger. I'm fairly sure the clerical test didn't swing it for me. It's likely that my assumed accountancy chatter and misplaced confidence had little to do with my appointment either. I think what really impressed them into giving me the job was the fact that the other three candidates weighed the pay against the demoralised demeanour of existing staff, proposed working conditions etc and then swiftly dropped out.

'When can you start?'

'Now.'

I had my first ever office job! I couldn't stay long though, as someone might find out I couldn't actually do it. There's always a snag. I went home, changed, slept for eight hours, changed, came back again and started work. My induction came from the very Finance Manager I would be replacing.

I've always thought that working in a British office is rather like the Muppet movie *Labyrinth*. You struggle through the endless horrible nonsense, arcane incompetence, the tricks, traps and pitfalls to the point where you finally get to meet David Bowie at the end.*

Although, without the bit about meeting David Bowie.

On my first day came the first demoralising whiff of damaged people:

'You actually applied to be here? Good grief. I suppose I'd better give you the whistle-stop tour then, since everyone else is working remotely or, as you might notice, not remotely working.'

'What's your name, Mr...?'

'You don't need to know my name. I'm going.'

Welcome to sunshine alley.

'That's the office of the ex-Managing Director. He used to do a lot of pheasant shooting, but then suddenly told us he'd given up. Then it turned out that one of his other companies, a cut price stockbroker, had receivers stalking the premises. He said that, under the circumstances, he'd pass over his Directorship to someone else, until he'd resolved the situation. Then someone put two and two together – you can't hold a shotgun certificate when you've got a criminal record, or a company directorship for that matter. If the fraud case doesn't go well, I don't think he'll be in the office for the next few years. That means there's a place on the Board going.'

Inspiring.

'Which neatly brings us here, to the office of the General Manager, Jenny Lamplighter. She's our resident card shark. She turns up to work at about ten thirty and plays solitaire on her computer for the first hour. She'll then take a look through her in-tray, panic, not be able to face it and look for something else to do instead. She goes to about seven hundred meetings a year, which is about six hundred and fifty more than necessary. Other departments ring us up sometimes and ask why she's attending their meetings. Then there'll be a long lunch 'negotiation' and she'll do an hour's work before playing solitaire again from half two until four, then she'll burst out of the room saying to anyone important that she's been far, far too busy to have a break yet and she'll have to go to lunch from now until five, then home.'

'Incredible.'

'Yes. We all think so. It's displacement activity. She can't face work, so she finds reasons to be away from her desk, which means more work piles up. It's either that or she retreats into the make-believe world of computer solitaire. If you have to knock at her door, just politely turn away for a second so she can flick it off the screen and pretend she's been composing a difficult email. You can talk about it – *everyone knows*. She plays computer games in work-time for two hours a day for 225 days a year, which means we've already paid her around ten thousand pounds this year to play cards!'

'Can't anyone do anything?'

'No one wants to stick their neck out and be the first to say. She'll snap their nose off, frankly.'

'She'll defend herself by attacking them?'

'Yeah. She also networks with all the directors, so they'll have her ear. I saved her from public humiliation at the Christmas Entertainment last year, not that she's even aware of it. The junior staff had a sort of comedy slideshow on the big screen in the conference suite. They were going to make all sorts of references to Jenny working hard and, each time, have the solitaire cards spring up and click over in the background. I said they should pull it out of the show because it undermined her position. That was before she attacked me. Thoroughly stabbed me in the back. It's all very sad and pathetic. At least, you'll think it is until you find she's been taking the credit for your work and blaming you for her mistakes behind your back.'

I began to see why he was leaving.

'She wants to build up 'performance management' cases to use against her own staff. The idea is to replace ten support staff without compensation and make 'a salary efficiency' by 'centralising services'. After saving the money, she can then bargain for the loose directorship. She just has to build up a fake track record of poor performance for each of those ten staff before she can push them out. She can't do it yet though, which is why you've been appointed, at less than my salary I might add. You've got eighteen months mate. If she invents a list of insane accusations against you and says 'sign at the bottom of the page to agree we've had this conversation', don't sign, okay?'

'I won't.'

'Last week she rang up sounding slurred and told us to put 'no smoking' signs in the poolcar. Look around! Do you think that's the priority? She also sends emails from home, copied to as many people as possible and timed at weekends and evenings, to make it look as if she's slaving away at her desk. They usually end by questioning how people who actually work here, the ones who actually turn up and sit at their desks all day, are filling their time!'

He continued. It was like being hit by wave after wave of negative energy.

'Like most office blocks in Britain, this place is completely dysfunctional. The rail company realises their contract won't be renewed, because of all the complaints, lack of investment in replacement track and the usual profiteering, so they aren't bothering to run the service properly. If you get a five year contract and after three years you realise it won't be renewed, what's the point of investing in long-term safety? We're all stuffed if the rail operator is closing anyway, so the managers here don't care.'

'The railway will still be there though. It will still have staff and they'll continue to pay for pensions.'

'The new rail company will immediately transfer the employee pension fund to their own pension provider. This place goes down with the ship. Sorry about that. Although I'm not sorry.'

More big bad waves rolled in.

'That office belongs to Maureen Twigg. She's nuts. Don't think I'm saying that because she's vegetarian. When she makes baked potatoes, she won't put whole ones in the oven. They have to be cut in half first.'

'Really? Why?'

'When the steam escapes, it squeals. She thinks the potato's alive and screaming. Bless her little cotton mind.'

We walked past a drinks machine. Ah yes, coffee, the opiate of the offices. Two secretaries were ahead of us and I couldn't help overhearing their conversation:

"So there I was, walking down the High Street and I looked across and saw her on the other side of the road and she was walking along and she hadn't seen me and she had these very high heels on. So I was looking across the road and I was in flats and I was walking along watching at her and thinking how come she doesn't fall over wearing those really high heels and I walked straight into a lamp post."

'Good morning ladies' said my guide. 'Did you know Mr Larsen's been trying to reach you? He's desperately trying to get into his email and he thinks he's been locked out. Have you changed the password?'

'Yes. We have to change them every twelve months. I *have* emailed him the new one.'

'Of course you have.'

I turned back with a question for my induction manager, but he'd already cracked-on with his commentary.

'At least Maureen's doing a hell of a lot more to save the business than Fanny Adams in the office down the corridor. She telephoned in earlier saying she's at home with the plague. Undiagnosed, as usual. She told me to email the staff, so I did. I explained she was spending the day at home because 'she's got plaque.' If she says anything, I'll say it was a mis-key.'

'Ah, okay.'

'Seventy-one days leave so far this year, according to her calendar. She does a six hour week, if you knock off all the mornings at the gym and the hours chatting to her friends. She's completely protected by the General Manager though. She goes in there, sits cross-legged on Lamplighter's office floor and kicks her shoes off to chat. It's all really weird. No one knows for sure, but most people think they're either related or there's some kind of blackmail going on. She delegates almost all of her work and no one's supposed to notice – they're both getting away with murder.'

'And you?'

'I've been here so long, it's depressing. When I cleared my desk and turned my keyboard upside down this morning, enough skin and hair fell out to make a new person.'

I wasn't warming to him.

'Meet the fire doors.'

I wasn't sure how to react to that. Should I say 'hello fire doors?'

'An object lesson in the daily problems of operating an office building under modern regulations which exist to prevent anyone doing anything. For example: The double doors set into the corridors throughout the building must, under the disabled access legislation, be kept open at all times. Not doing so would be against the law. The double doors set into the corridors throughout the building must also, under the health and safety and fire prevention legislation, be kept closed at all times. Not doing so would be against the law. The organisation has therefore opted to try and comply with both sets of legislation by propping one half of the double doors open and leaving the other half in the closed position. Although this still obstructs wheelchair access and allows fires straight through, the company lawyer had advised that it should provide a partial defence if the business were to be prosecuted under either Act.'

Glorious, I thought. As in 'defeat'. This was turning into an insightful morning for me. Until today, I'd thought it was just the passengers who got upset. If this disgruntled worker was anything to go by, everyone associated with the transport system in any capacity might be affected by this universal malaise. Perhaps it wasn't a transport-industry-specific condition. We were in the pensions business, after all.

I thought of my pension. A spotty youth in red braces, representing the Regal Sunshine Partnership had mis-sold me a pension scheme in the late 1980s. He said I could pick components and put fractions of the investment in equities, property, bonds, commodities etc. I chose 100% property and they lost more than half my pension in the first two years! That was in the 1990s, when London property prices quadrupled. I've since decided I could do better for myself than the average British pensions company in a fruit machine arcade. Perhaps not, in hindsight.

How on earth, I asked, could you lose most of my money on property? They explained that they'd mostly invested in the rental of City of London office blocks, which they'd valued too high, to inflate their assets and attract more investors, then entirely failed to sub-let to companies. The auditors said 'if the property has this value, the rent should be that much', which was more than anyone would pay. The blocks stood empty, the fund evaporated and the investment managers paid themselves their 'golden farewell packages' as they hawked their glowing CVs around the City and the Bourse.

'In this place, you'll soon see that everything's delegated. They might ask you to buy and sell some stocks. They can't even manage that for themselves. They can't even monitor what the offices have done without asking them to produce a report. They'll then take that report, re-type it and put their own names on the bottom. That's why they ask for reports to be emailed. It saves them time. The middle managers have been avoiding responsibility for so long, I think none of them remembers how to work the controls.'

'Which means, practically that is?'

'They can't do the actual investing because they've spent so long at lunch, they can't remember the process. We have to do it for them, or rather you. You can't trade stocks without their level of log-in, so we have to log-in as them and do the actual work. I'm going, now, so that mean's you'll have to do this. It's going to take about three days to get you security checked and set up on the system, so under your mouse-mat there's the ex-Managing Director's log-in name, password and systems PIN number which gives you access to trade. Here's my key to the office. Good luck.'

'Thanks. If the ex-MD comes back, how should I recognise him?'

'Well, there's one sure way. When I sat behind the senior managers in the last finance presentation, I could see the boss has one ear larger than the other. I thought at the time, was I really the only person who'd seen that?'

'Ears, check.'

'That's the Gents, that's the cleaning cupboard, the server room, staff kitchen…' It went on and on.

'Where's my office?'

'Right at the start mate, so we'll walk all the way back, shall we? It's not your fault. I need to pick up my coat anyway. At five o'clock I'm gone and then I'm on a plane to New Zealand. I'm sick of covering for them and, guess what, I'm leaving.'

As we passed the General Manager's office, we could see through the glass pane in the door that she was indeed playing solitaire, as he'd predicted.

'She's asked Maintenance to rearrange her office furniture so the computer screen faces away from the door. She's also asked them to obscure the glass panel. That way she can play cards all day every day and still claim overtime.'

'Any more advice?'

'Yeah. Don't invest a penny in the company pension scheme. So many managers have taken early retirement on full pensions because of stress, aged about fifty, that there won't be much left of the pension fund when you retire. Oh yeah, and I've put a bit of meat in the General Manager's pencil pot, but don't worry, she won't find that for a week or two. Hey – heads up!'

I looked down the corridor at a pair of approaching suits. Four-button coat sleeves; hand made suits, which probably meant power.

'That's the Regional Director with the Auditor. They're sure to see what Lamplighter's up to!'

It was true. As they walked past her office, the Regional Director did a double-take at the card playing on the screen. The Auditor, barely a step behind, stopped too and peered through the glass strip of the door.

'No, that's not right' said the Regional Director.

'Oh, you noticed it too?'

'Of course. That's just wrong on so many levels. She should have put *the Jack* on the Queen.'

I spent the rest of the day doing something clever. Oh, alright, I admit it might have been Raffles who suggested it. I found five separate people and asked them to each run through with me one fifth of my responsibilities. I left each of them with the impression that I knew the other four fifths and that was why I didn't need to ask.

At last, I found the borrowed password and logged-into the financial system. It looked straightforward and my access level appeared high. Excellent. I could see the cash trading accounts, how much was in them and how to transfer the money. I could see the stocks and bonds. If I instructed the broker to sell those, it would be three days before the money arrived. Too long. The clock turned to five and I thought I'd better log-out of the system.

He'd done a good job. I was thoroughly antagonistic toward the organisation and it was still only my first day. I supposed it was fair - he'd earned some sort of legacy after the way he'd been treated. At least it would make it easier for me to do what I was about to. I left.

Yes, I left, but I didn't completely leave the building. The cleaner's cupboard was a bit small and anyway there were cleaners prowling. To cut to the chase, I hid in the bog. I'd recommend a maximum of three hours if you're going to hide in a lavatory. The automatic flushing of the pedestals every ten minutes and the background hiss of the strip-lights will drive you out of there in the end. That's why squatters never squat in lavatories, despite the free hot and cold running water. In this case, the convenience was a convenient hutch until shortly after eight o'clock, but I don't think I'd want to do it again. I got so bored, I even cleaned the lavatory for them, which I can't imagine anyone will ever thank me for.

I removed myself from the water closet. Why had I waited so long? Most of the staff had left at four. It was the work of a moment, call it five minutes, to open the office, warm up the computer, log-in and start transferring cash to the BR (compensation) account that Raffles had given me. What the hell? Cry Havoc! I instructed in the sale and transfer of the stocks and bonds too. If the transactions were stopped, it wouldn't matter. If, as the Finance Officer said, none of the managers knew what was happening, or could even monitor the situation without him, then the deals might just go through. What fun this was!

When I'd done as much as I could, I telephoned Raffles, waiting as arranged at the call box downstairs, and said I'd be dropping out through lavatory window at 8.30pm, or thereabouts. Before I went though, I thought it best to take the application papers back with me, if I could find them. Of course! They were in the General Manager's office.

I couldn't get in. I wandered around and tried to gain access via a blocked-up door adjoining the photocopying room. No, that wouldn't open at all, despite my brutish forcing. This wasn't going at all well. I called Raffles again, but it wasn't answered.

'Oh, for heaven's sake Bunny' and up, through the lavatory window he came.

'Quiet! You'll wake the Vogons.'

Raffles pulled out a plastic cash card and sprung the lock in seconds and, if I didn't know the man, I'd swear he'd practised. Come to think of it, I was perpetually amazed at his varied expertise. I mean, that was too confident a trick for simple luck, so where would he have learned to do that? Getting locked out of a dressing room at the MCC?

Concentrate now.

No, not you. Me.

In the third filing cabinet, we found the Personnel papers. Mine were filed under 'A', presumably for 'accepted' or perhaps 'another one'. Who knows? Gathering them up and slamming the cabinet shut, which Raffles always did with the edge of his hand to avoid leaving finger prints, I almost shattered a pair of vodka bottles which had been left in there accidentally. She'd probably confiscated them from someone. Time to go. Time, I thought, to never come back to this asylum.

A noise in the corridor stopped my heart. Not permanently you understand, obviously, don't be thick, but quite long enough for me to inwardly panic. My learned accomplice had frozen too and then moved only his lips to whisper.

'A security guard, I think. Who can say? Perhaps a regular patrol?'

'Raffles? What happens if the Police catch us?'

'Then we treat every ball on its merits.'

A torch-light passed. We froze. A torch-light hesitated, thought about it for a moment and shone back in our direction. A cone of fuzzy brilliance lit up Raffles' black leather shoe. The security guard dropped his torch and ran.

'They're not paid to confront. It isn't in their job description' said Raffles with a roll of the eyes.

'What are you doing?'

'The torch.'

'We don't need it!'

'You wouldn't deny me a souvenir?'

A few moments later, I descended into darkness from the lavatory window. It was quite a long way, but when you've been around Raffles for a while, descending into darkness becomes a lot easier. As Raffles exited the window, I checked all the documents were there by the sodium glare of a municipal street light.

'Hey, Raffles. This reference letter is on St James's Palace letter paper. This is a reference from The Queen!'

'I know.'

'You know?'

He paused, then spoke with painful care.

'Well, it is a reference from *a Queen*.'

That night, I had a dream. In it, the General Manager played her game of solitaire for fully four hours. My dream was very tranquil, as you can imagine. Then, as she pretended to be working, one of her juniors burst in and broke the news that the funds were missing. She initially shooed them away and claimed she was concentrating on the figures. In that case, said the junior, she would already know. She didn't know. Pitter patter, pitter patter. The solitaire cards, like little dry scales, were falling. They fell out and scattered, a few at a time, from the fantasy of her computer screen and out across the desk in front of her. What an untidy mess they made of the real world, those little cards.

A week later, I read the news in a paper. It was a strange feeling for me. The whole thing had passed so smoothly, so quickly, that I still didn't feel I was any part of it. I rang the only person I could ring, under the circumstances.

'Raffles, Raffles! Have you seen today's paper? The Southernshire Coastal Railway Company has announced it's lost its entire employee pension funds! That means the stocks as well. We've done it! We've actually broken the bank!'

I had a flashback to the Dambusters control room. "Barnes, you said it could be done and I doubted you, but after this you could sell me a bally pink elephant!"

'I know, it made yesterday's evening paper, although I'm very much surprised you spotted it. I thought you read papers from the back page inward and stopped when you ran out of sports?'

'Yes, well. I was looking for this, wasn't I? For the first time in my life, I've got a good reason to read the front of the paper. It says here, they've even launched an appeal for public donations!'

'I know that too. This morning I sent them a letter saying I'd enclosed a cheque for twenty pounds.'

'You're kidding!'

'Less a £20 administration fee.'

I laughed heartily until Raffles stopped me.

'I've been picked for England.'

Chapter 5

An Occurrence in South Africa

' South African Airways, Flight SA252, proceed to Departure Gate 17' flashed a mute screen at Heathrow Airport.

That was quite a relief, really. Not because I don't like waiting in airports, no – perish the thought. British airports were made for waiting in. Some people enjoy it so much, they spend whole weekends there. Alright, we've still got three minutes, so I'll explain.

I wandered around the airport shops and, unable to find any overpriced bargains to buy just for the sake of it, sat down at a vacant internet terminal. Having pushed in the last of my coins, I slotted my hand luggage between my knees and clicked my way out of reality.

Start – Open Browser Link – Google – "South Africa"+"tours"-click.

The first website I visited wasn't much use to me, apart from the map, since their tours cost three or four thousand pounds and last twelve days. At least they guaranteed you would see 'The Big Five', which presumably meant elephants and tigers and things. Perhaps that was India? Of course it was. In Africa it would be lions and tigers and things. It would be useless to mention the big five to Raffles. He'd think they meant the Test Matches.

I clicked on.

The next site wasn't a good advertisement for the country. In fact, I found it morally objectionable. Marketed mainly to America, the *High Calibre Tour Company* encouraged wealthy customers to pay $18,000 for the chance to send their sons to a South African 'Lion Farm', at which they could fire a long-range rifle at point blank range into a hand-reared, caged, lion. The site featured a page displaying photographs of beaming children, holding rifles, standing with one foot on top of a lion carcass. I could almost picture them showing the photos to their friends at school. 'Turn your son into a man', read the sales patter.

Apart from its very existence, there were further oddities to catch my eye about the site. The first was that someone had bothered at all to fit the rifles with telescopic sights. Display, presumably. It would be like fitting spoilers to a car which never left the garage. The second was that, on the far budget end of the range, they'd offered the chance to shoot a flamingo for $50. Maybe this was for visitors who wanted to shoot the Big Hundred & Fifty-Six? 'Turn your son into a?' Give your son a guilt complex, probably.

'South African Airways, Flight SA252, proceed to Departure Gate 17'. Good. I wanted to get away.

We'd decided to travel early, in light of the recent unpleasantness. A.J. said England wouldn't care – he'd just send a receipt to the ECB and get his ticket reimbursed later. There seemed to be a problem with Middlesex and an important fixture in the County Championship, but Raffles said they could all go hang because of some perceived slight against him – I think they'd passed him over for a benefit year or something like that, but I don't know the details. My flight, un-claimable from the ECB of course, found itself magically settled from Raffles' pocket.

After all the grief and heart-rending I'd been through in the last two weeks, I looked forward to my unexpected sunshine holiday. It would be just the thing to take my mind off Charity and, more to the point, what she must have thought of me. Yes, this was just the ticket, said a firm grip.

The flight passed uneventfully. Alright, it didn't, but I was just trying to save the trouble of explaining Raffles' inhuman behaviour when he's bored. This particular long-haul flight turned into one I'll not easily expunge from my memory. Come to think of it, I'll never travel with him again. There! A decision.

I suppose you want to know? Oh, alright then, if you must. Raffles, perfectionist that he was, chose his targets with precision. If anyone recognised him, they'd be no good. On the whole, he selected people he didn't think he'd normally get along with. A cast to act the victims in his cruel and insidious plays.

Firstly, insisting upon economy class, he took a window seat in a row of three. As the other passengers placed themselves, he'd stoppeth one of three and introduce himself, usually as someone going to a conference. On this occasion he was a global authority on the fasci-nating Stone Age artefacts known as 'Clovis Points'. He listened patiently as they opened up their own life stories, dreams and misgivings, to such a learned and worthy audience. In short, he charmed them. When the breakfasts were delivered, all colours and textures and cellophane wrappers on neatly plasticized trays, Raffles would stand up, smile and say he needed to go to the lavatory. Patiently, laboriously, the two passengers blocking his path would pack up their meals and stand for him.

Poor things, they looked. Standing in the aisle with trays aloft as Raffles shuffled past them. Poor things indeed as Raffles paused and placed his own meal in the middle seat, so his set of tray-bearers could not sit back down again until he had finished. When Raffles returned, as he did after an un-necessary time, seats were retaken grimly, like hills in wars in low countries, and no one complained because *he was such a pleasant man.* Complaints would be churlish, as the cold food dripped from their forks and the red wine, with a suspicion of witch hazel, failed to save it. 'Would you like to hear about the reduced efficiency of taste-buds and nasal referencing in studies taken at altitude?' He charmed them again with his ridiculous talk of Clovis Points and taste-buds, things to be observed in the hair of famous scientists and a mnemonic to help remember the distinguishing characteristics of isthmuses, peninsulas and archipelagos. They were charmed again, forgiving and entertained, until lunch arrived and Raffles did exactly the same thing.

When they finally regained their seats, he charmed them again. I don't know how, it was cringe-making and I couldn't look. I suppose they thought him absent minded, with very bad timing, but otherwise a good man. A few hours later, the two fellow passengers were becoming restless. Wondering perhaps if it was conceivable they'd get a warm dinner. By this stage, someone must have asked the stewardess if the passenger in the window seat was indeed the person they thought him to be. The Stewardess called, just as the trolley made its pass to serve dinner. She hopped to one side to let it through.

'Excuse me, are you Mr Raffles?'

'Yes, that is my name.'

'The Captain has asked me to see if you would like to be upgraded, as a special guest of the airline.'

The other two passengers looked pleased at the news.

'Thank you, but no. I'm having such a delightful conversation with my new friends that I'd really hate to upset them.'

Oh, okay then, they must have thought. It's a pity, but... *what a charming man.*

Trays in seat-backs slumped down, bottoms shuffled and dinner landed. They began to eat. Oh good, he's not going to do it, oh he has. No, I'm sorry, I couldn't watch this.

By the time we'd landed, unbuckled our buckles and unslung our bags, Raffles had them all promising to visit some imaginary Clovis Point museum somewhere in the hills of Montana and ask for Jed. As we disembarked, they apologised to him, which until that day I had assumed you had to be English to do.

So this is South Africa, I said to myself as I passed through the airport arrivals zone which might have been any airport arrivals zone in the world. The luggage always takes a while to come through, doesn't it? I nipped into the wash-room to wake myself up with cold water. A conversation between the stalls and the wash basins took my notice.

'So who was that nutter?'

'A.J. Raffles. He's a famous cricketer, down for the Tests. Completely eccentric, but he averages 29 with the bat, nearer 40 in the domestic season, and keeps the Test players down to 21.5 with the ball. He's in and out of the national team because he's notoriously unpredictable. In first class cricket he's taken nine wickets in an innings five times and had over one hundred five wicket hauls. They have a saying: "Spin bowling doesn't work at Lords before July, unless you're A.J. Raffles." He also helped Middlesex secure the Championship two years back, on a flat batting wicket too. Lancashire lost four or five of their middle order for single figures. Star names mostly and Raffles skittled them.'

'You're kidding.'

'I didn't want to say I recognised him' the traveller said, washing his hands and pulling an *Atherton's Barmy Army* shirt out of his kit bag, 'He probably hates sycophants.'

'What was all that about 'Clovis Points'?'

'Beats me. Fancy a beer?'

I decided not to tell Raffles. He'd earned his laugh. Not *yet* anyway.

A.J. breezed through Customs. They stopped me, as they always do. I used to mull over the idea of demanding to view the HM Customs staff teaching facilities, as my right under the Freedom of Information Act, and then tear down all the posters with my image on that they are without a sniff of a doubt using for training purposes. Were HM Customs lecturing their counterparts in other countries nowadays? I only ask because they're up to it too. An obvious drug mule walked past me and through the green lane unmolested, followed a minute later by a dozen more. They probably all had fake passports, but the moron from Customs seemed more concerned with the threat posed by my toothpaste.

'Did you pack this suitcase yourself?' 'Are you visiting for business or pleasure?'

Hardly the most imaginative of the world's brigade of thugs, customs officers never offer options like 'Business, Pleasure, Money-Laundering or Criminally-Motivated Escapology, Sir?', so I can no longer be bothered to volunteer honest information. Trolleys, tannoy announcements, hire company chauffeurs lamely holding name boards, you don't want a description of all the usual airport ejection procedure, do you? Thought not. Get away as fast as possible, that's what I always say.

Forty minutes. It took forty minutes to get shot of that airport and find a taxi. An hour or two faster than I'd expect at most British airports, so comparatively not bad at all.

We arrived at the team hotel, a spacious palace encircled by discreetly bushed chain-link fences. At first I thought they'd brought us to the wrong place. 'Um, excuse me. I'm not the Governor, actually', then I found out that all hotels on the coast look like that. 'Perfect Stay – Hotels & Resorts of South Africa' read the sign. Although naturally cynical of advertising, I began to believe they could be right.

Raffles and I flopped into comfortable armchairs and knocked away the dust of travel. The peacocks were underfoot, but that's just the way it is with peacocks. Maharajas had to put up with it and so did we. In just a moment or two a dutiful receptionist checked our passports and reservation codes. It was all very civilised. We ordered tea. In barely five minutes, steaming cups swirled softly on our table.

'Nothing like a nice cup of tea' I mumbled.

'That's true. This is nothing like a nice cup of tea' observed Raffles.

We stewed thoughtfully and watched the late-afternoon sun sink atmospherically behind the flight of vultures and down toward the shark-infested sea. It was all very peaceful and liberating.

'I've always approved of Pete and Dud, but I have no wish to become one of them. In *No Exit*, Sartre said that hell was being locked forever in a room with your friends. Don't let your friends, or the things you like best, turn the key behind you, Bunny.'

'What?' I hadn't followed that at all, so guessed he was still talking about tea.

'I suggest we just drink it. Anyway, it could be worse. There might be fruit floating in it.'

'I've opposed re-introducing cricket to the Americas for precisely that reason.'

'Very wise. You can't have cricket without proper tea. It's simply not done.'

'Were you aware that cricket is the only game with meals scheduled into it? A Test match has ten meals and stops ten more times for drinks. One day cricket is something of a poor cousin in that respect.'

'What do you think of one day cricket, Raffles?'

'Vertical baseball, little more.'

'I knew you were a snob. You were a snob at school.'

'In a test match, you may have to set a plan and bowl something quite brilliant to get someone out. In one day cricket, they're often just swinging at everything, so it takes the great bowlers out of the game. The most successful one day bowlers just dabble everything along from wicket to wicket, no energy on the ball, waiting for the batsman to take a risk. Can they be proud of their wickets? Did they get the batsman out, or did the batsman get himself out?'

'Is this because you, the great Raffles, go for lots of runs in short matches? They don't give you any respect, do they? That's quite funny really.'

'No. It just means the wickets are worth less. It isn't history, it's... fun.'

'So, you're a purist. Proper bowling. Historic batting. White clothes and picnics.'

'The Test's the thing.'

'Would you play in the England one day side if they asked you?'

'They did ask me. Can you see me in coloured pyjamas with a name and number on my back? Can you imagine how unspeakably embarrassing it would be to ask for viscose pyjamas at my tailors?'

'You are a snob, Raffles.'

'Damn right.'

He thought about it for a while, gazing distantly across the coast.
'I am what I am.'

'Who said that? Jean Paul Sartre again?'

'Popeye.'

As a waiter flitted past, Raffles effortlessly lassoed him at all of
twenty yards and requested a telephone be brought to the table. I have
no idea how he does this. They always ignore me. Hailing a cab from
the other side of the street, that's the other thing he can do and I can't.
Remarkable, I call it. They wouldn't notice me if I used a flare gun.

'Hello, Clive? Yes, It's Raffles. Of course I'm in the country
already! I wouldn't miss this series for anything. Oh, don't worry, I'll
get turn at the Wanderers. Didn't Tayfield take 9 for 113 there in '56?
– and I'm feeling devilish lucky this time. You just watch my offie! Ha
ha! Oh, really? I'll wander over and prove it on your snooker table if
you want me to! Two snooker tables? You old plutocrat, you. Yes,
absolutely, but I know what you 'Boks' are like – all the furniture
outside and all your plants indoors! The sun's going to bleach that
cloth, you know. How's the family?'

The conversation rattled on for a while in this fashion, so I slunk
to the bar in hope of any drink more palatable than hotel tea. Ten
minutes later, I came back with something mostly green, yellow and
red with a par-boiled baby banana floating in it.

It wasn't my fault. No, it really wasn't this time. I expect you've
had the same experience where you've drawn up at the bar, perhaps
you had to rope your sweaty horse to a post before entering though –
some places are classy - and had to wait behind another customer
before asking for the perfectly normal drink you were absolutely,
unswervingly, intending to ask for. There's the rub, as the Bard and a
thousand sports physiotherapists have noted before me.

What happens when you have to wait three minutes in a queue to
be served? Your mind wanders, that's what happens. You find yourself
reading the cocktail list, or at least I did. 'The Coelacanth' looked rivet-
ing. 'Long as a Giraffe' caught my eye for a moment. Then, I saw it. The
only one without a picture. 'Garden of Proteas', the house cocktail.

'What would you like, Sir?'

I hate direct questions when I'm not concentrating. They're so
intrusive, I usually answer any old thing, just to push the questioner
away.

'Garden of Proteas?'

Okay, you've probably guessed it anyway. I'd just forgotten whatever it was I'd planned to ask for.

'That'll please the staff, Sir. We haven't sold any this week. It's based on all the colours of our national flag.'

'Oh-ah.' I added, with mediocre interest.

It arrived. It landed. Small insects and sugar lumps scattered to shade and cover. Bar cloths curled at the margins of my vision. I expect the inventor thought 'patriotic, nutritious and fruity', but my overriding impression was 'psychedelic lavatory bowl'. What really got me though was the banana. How, exactly, is one supposed to despatch a banana floating in a drink? I wasn't convinced bananas were indigenous to South Africa anyway. Weren't they from South America or somewhere? Confused as usual, I wasn't sure. It occurred to me that the Dutch weren't particularly indigenous to Africa either, so maybe the banana represented them.

'Thank you' I speculated, as an afterthought, and backed away. To save the scene, I hurriedly placed the glass on a vacant table and went back to the bar for a beer. Thankfully, it was a different barman.

When I finally got back to our table, Raffles had completed the call. 'Beer, Bunny? At ten o'clock?' To my enduring horror, a helpful waiter buzzed up to our table and set the bananaesque monstrosity in front of me. Raffles took one look and reached for the beer.

'Do you know what this is, Bunny?' asked Raffles, holding aloft a piece of paper.

'The Munich concession?'

'It's Arjan Khalife's telephone number.'

'You're kidding? No, hang on, I'm getting confused. No, don't tell me. Was that the one...? Weren't you chasing his sister?'

'You're being flippant. Think about the name 'Khalife'. Where have you heard it before?'

'The slow-scoring batsman from the World Cup!'

'Well done. The problem is that Clive just thinks he played badly – nerves, pressure and a bit of bad shot selection. I trust Clive's opinion more than most, so that really gives me pause. He tells me they're saying that Coach wasn't murdered after all. In fact, they're saying the match wasn't fixed.'

'What about the poison? The 'super-dooper' whatever it was found in his blood-stream?'

'Cypermethrin? A military defoliant noted for its unstable molecular structure, which breaks down quickly in the presence of oxygen. It biodegrades into gasses after a few hours, which stops it getting from the soil into run-off water and then away into the food-chain. Unsurprisingly, in the second toxicologist's report, it was not found to be present.'

'No evidence then?'

'Nothing. Natural causes exacerbated by a heart condition, according to dear old Scotland Yard. Bunny, you were right first time.'

'Was I?'

'Although... I know what I saw. Clive was watching one of the ex-South African players closely as well, as it turns out, along much the same lines.'

'You didn't notice him?'

'A face in the crowd? Hardly. Have you heard of Bryce Hedges?'

'Nope. I've heard of Foxy Fowler.'

'Forget about Foxy Fowler for a moment, would you?'

'Okay. He doesn't play any more then, this Bryce Hedges?'

'Let's just say he's travelling an awful lot for a retired person.'

'My auntie does that. Cruises mostly.'

I got the stare. Only a grade IV this time, but it was definitely *the stare*.

'Clive's seen him in a lot of places, making a lot of deals with a lot of current players. Clive doesn't think he's asking them to guide any tour groups. He's emailed the ICC with details, but he says they haven't even bothered to reply.'

'You haven't written off Khalife though, have you?'

'Not yet. He's still the first point of enquiry. Off the record, Pakistan lost their Chairman of Selectors because of him. He was a tad bitter about it: "We select a man capable of hitting and yet he does not hit." Fairly damning, without being an accusation. He can't prove it of course. World Cup nerves and all that. It hurt them though. It hurt you.'

'Quite. I don't suppose I can punch him on the nose over the phone then?'

'No. Unfortunately Alexander Graham Bell failed to design that possibility into the system.'

'Okay then, so what's the plan? We threaten him, he breaks down and then admits everything?'

'Simple, but effective.'

'Really?'

'No. I think sneakiness is the way forward and now is the time to grasp the nettle.'

'What are you banging on about, Raffles? Next you'll be making me suffer more of your ancient oriental botanical bilge and them I'm afraid I'll have to…'

Raffles rolled his eyes, lifted the receiver and firmly set my drink back in front of me. I looked deeply into the substance and wondered why it might be developing a deepening froth.

'Khalife? Excellent. Raffles. Yes, A.J., England.'

They exchanged amicable pleasantries for a while as I poured my drink into a compliant shrub. Khalife was naturally familiar and yet still firmly on guard. A.J. was soon making heavy weather of it.

'Arjan, I had word during the World Cup that there might be some business to be had… yes, business opportunities. No, not sponsorship as such. No, no, I already have a bat maker. I'm talking about *business opportunities*, Arjan. No one ever asks the England players, so it's up to me to do the asking, you see? Your sister? Charming girl. How is she? No, really. I'm fully aware that I'm single, but my home is a London club, Arjan. They won't allow women in. What? No, I don't want to speak to your parents. Please don't make this more difficult than it has to be.'

Raffles removed the receiver and bonked it against his forehead a couple of times.

'Look, I know you're *connected*. No I don't care about that, it's your business. Arjan, Arjan, *I know*, okay? No, that's not a threat. We're old friends aren't we? Remember Lahore three years ago? The most exciting night-life on Earth? Ha, ha! So you do remember! Excellent. No, all I'm asking you to do is a little favour for me. Just take down this phone number and email address, then pass it along to your connections. 'Expression of interest', that sort of thing. You'll do that for me, won't you Arjan? Good lad. Then I shall owe you a favour, to be called in at your convenience. Yes, it's a deal. Witnesses? Who needs witnesses? Ha, ha. Pen and paper? Splendid. Jolly good. Here goes: a.j.raffles@mddxcc.co.uk, mobile 077-294… Arjan, Arjan, no, of course I don't think there's anything wrong with her. What? Oh, wonderful, hello Mrs Khalife. How are you today?'

The ball was in-play.

We made our way back to the hotel lobby, just in time to see our luggage arrive. I previously thought it was only in Asia that cricket fever took hold so readily with the public. Here too, I could see the phenomena in evidence. Un-noticed before, one side of my patent leather suitcase had whitewashed stumps daubed on it. I wondered how much of the contents had survived the luggage-handlers' tea break.

I collected my key and, declining the assistance of a porter, carried the decorated bag to my room. A junior manager towed me around, identifying the bathroom, the fridge, mini-bar, spare towels, describing how to use the remote control and, smiling like a gracious monarch of old, presented me with a drink, which clobbered into existence on a silver tray behind him.

'A Garden of Proteas, Sir, with our compliments. The bar staff told us what you like.'

'It's based on our national flag' added his demonically helpful waiter.

'Thank you, thank you. So kind. Everything is just wonderful'. Reeling, I closed the door.

It wouldn't flush, of course.

Stubborn and floating, the green baby banana gurned at me from its sunken pool. It bobbed up and down merrily. In the end, I had to break the little bastard up with a coat hanger.

Chapter 6

Of Pistachios and Polymaths

Sometimes, in one's idle moments, one has to speculate why one one one one one one. Doesn't that sound superior? No, please don't write in. I'll have another bash at it. Sometimes you simply have to speculate why you're different to other people. So there. What I mean to say, if you don't mind plumbing the fathoms of deep dark psychology for the very nub of this, is why do some people seem to do so much better in life, given similar resources? I really can only spare a single paragraph for each of these people:

C.B. Fry, for example. He'd earned a degree from Oxford, Captained Sussex at cricket, Captained England at cricket and, never losing a Test Match, took 30,886 first class runs at an average of 50, scored 94 centuries including six in consecutive innings, 166 wickets, 239 catches, held the world long jump record (23ft 6.5 inches), won both the long jump and 100 yard sprint at the world's first international athletics meeting, played football for England, played in the final of the F.A. Cup, played rugby for the Barbarians, taught at Charterhouse, became a Captain in the Royal Navy, wrote speeches for India at the United Nations, spoke a dozen languages, served as the British Ambassador to somewhere I've forgotten, on the tip of my tongue, and rescued survivors of some sort of disaster by personally swimming across a freezing river and carrying them to safety on his back. You think I've finished? I was just drawing breath. C.B. Fry was able, from a stationery position on the floor, to spring backwards onto the mantelpiece. Winston Churchill served this man as his servant at school for heaven's sake! He topped it all off by being offered the throne of Albania and turning it down because he was much too humble. Useless.

Fry's career is dazzlingly useless to us without contrast. Let's take a breathless moment to search for a little perspective. What happened to the boy who sat behind him in prep? What, exactly, did he do?

Shakespeare then. What happened to the uncomplicated corn-fed village girl to whom he first read Ovid? Did she get confused, run back home and spent the afternoon milking ducks? We shall never know.

Douglas Noel Adams. A polymath to the core. He wrote scripts, articles and played Julius Caesar whilst still at school. He collected a degree from Cambridge, wrote a number one radio series in which he blew up the world and then began the story, wrote the best ever episodes of the scientifically imaginative television series *Doctor Who* when he wasn't even supposed to be the writer (he was meant to be the Editor), acted in the *Monty Python* team, wrote one of the best comedy sketches of all time, wrote the most original science fiction genre novel of all time (one of the greatest bestselling novels of all time), inspired the invention of the internet, foresaw and suggested the modern world of portable wireless computing, visual mobile communications, inter-active live databases and web browsers, encouraged humanity to see the ivory towers of established wisdom from a different perspective, with subtlety and humour, until people questioned the absurdities that have persisted in our world *because they are too normal to ever be questioned*, taught us the value of imagination rooted in the laws of reality, educated millions to understand hugely complicated philo-sophical questions as if they were common fodder, lectured the world's great universities in technologies of the future, the value of biorefugiums in the conservation of endangered species, evolution theory and much more, tried desperately to save at least a dozen species from imminent extinction (all apart from one are still with us) and asked mankind to please scientifically evaluate all those deeply held beliefs from the Bronze Age about the existence of pesky deities.

Okay, so tell me, what happened to the bloke who played the Vogon guard? Contrast man, contrast!

For yet another example, take the case of Heinrich Schliemann, a voracious self-educator who left school aged fourteen after one year of proper classical education (after which his father was caught embezzling the church and could no longer pay for it). He became a sailor at fourteen, made a fortune in Baltic commodities by his twen-ties, spoke thirteen languages and wrote his diary in the tongue of whichever country he happened to be in, opened a bank in California and made a fortune within two years re-selling gold dust, went to Russia and completely monopolised the trade in indigo and then the supply of gunpowder to the Russian Government for the Crimean

War, became bored with business and retired aged thirty six, learned Arabic and disguised himself as a nomadic Arab to tour Mecca, read the Iliad in the original Greek, published a book on archaeology, submitted a thesis on Troy written in ancient Greek to the University of Rostock, then nipped out to by a bucket and spade, discovered the lost city of Troy and the golden hoard of 'Priam's Treasure', excavated Mycenae and Tiryns, squinted upon the golden face of Agamemnon, dominated Mycenaean archaeology and came to be regarded as the founder of modern archaeology.

What happened to the other junior clerk in the Baltic trading office? Give me contextual reference, *please.*

A.J. Raffles. A cricketer for Middlesex and England. Think of one of the great batsmen of the last two decades. No, don't tell me. Look up his Test batting average in your Wisden. Got it? Now look up his Test batting average *against A.J. Raffles.* Halved, yes? What do you mean you haven't found it? Oh for heaven's sake, page 246. This would be the same A.J. Raffles who spoke four or five major languages but, when abroad, exclusively stuck to English anyway, only using his knowledge to listen to what other people were saying. A.J., who was thrown out of woodwork classes aged nine for building a chess board with three extra squares to give himself a tactical advantage over opponents, who won *The Times* cryptic crossword aged ten, *La Parisian's* cryptic crossword aged twelve and took his Latin and Greek A Levels a year later. Banned from woodwork, Raffles took up metalwork with technical drawing, then designed and built the first 'honeycomb' aqualung re-breather system* - which came to nothing when his parents wouldn't fund the patent or the safety testing. In a fit of existential angst, he gave up metalwork and studied philosophy, attempted to form his own religious sect as an experiment and gathered over seventy devoted followers across the world, who eventually insisted upon meeting him. Their devotion vaporised like the dew when they found he was spotty and barely sixteen. Forced to play a musical instrument at school, he took to the piano with ease and played regularly until the age of seventeen. He then refused to play ever again after presenting *Rachmaninov V*, which he was rather disgusted to find his piano master failed to recognise. Cambridge University followed, with an oar and a cricket Blue for his kit-bag. Did I mention the actress? You know, the one from the Richard Curtis film? An excellent self-taught chef (he had to be - our school and his parents hadn't a clue how to cook), winemaker, photographer, literary classicist, amateur engineer, sculptor, athlete, artist and tactician, he can now be found at chess tournaments, cricket matches and any number of reasonably fashionable nightclubs with highly tarnished reputations. There are some days when I can do nothing more than sit back and hate him.

No, that's too strong. I'm not annoyed, as such, with Raffles orchestrating further and greater crescendos whilst I spend quiet days plodding along with my comfortable little ditties. It's just that he seems to have so many more keys to his disposal than I have. It's almost as if I'm learning to play from a manual and other people are not only self-instructed, but have the regular use of at least two other *secret notes*, for which you have to be a great composer before you're even told about. Of course, they'd make an exception for Raffles. He was so bloody charming after all.

It was as if he had these people in mind when the great orator Cook told of the *Holy Bee of Ephesus*, which circled our Lord on the cross thrice, thus signifying something completely beyond the reach of human understanding.

It's not that though. It's this:

Such people are rare and different. With an hour and a log fire, I've tried to analyse the phenomena as best I can. My main lab-rat to study had to be Raffles, since the others I've mentioned had all

---

[A]*During that school term, Raffles took to wearing a red woollen hat in the manner of Jacques Cousteau. It was around this time that I first heard his expression "you pay for your trip on the way out" – a diver's reference to hanging around in long decompression stops on the way up to see off the feared nitrogen narcosis. As the traditional red hat of a deep sea diver, Cousteau wore it to remind everyone that although he was the ship's captain, he was first and foremost a working undersea explorer. Raffles wore the red woollen hat after his first series of self-taught dives in the English Channel. As a point of historical record, whenever it snowed, the school sent us swimming in the sea as a toughening-up exercise. I'll never forgive them for that. When A.J. dragged himself out of the water and picked his way up the rocky beach, his frozen body would reflect in shades of white and blue and then the red hat would slip on, suggesting to me the abused frame of some great and patriotic martyr. Then, I remember, one wet Wednesday evening in the Common Room, we watched an episode of Cousteau's Undersea World in which the crew had formed a human chain to pass Northern Sea Otters or something from one place to another. It was no longer just Cousteau in the red hat. The whole crew of the Calypso had bought one! Raffles' face was a picture when he saw that line of swaying red hats and we all knew how diluted his currency had suddenly become. We never saw him wear it again, have a hero or follow a herd. From that day on, he was his own man. Actually, he'd be pretty damn embarrassed if he knew I'd told you about any of this.*

succumbed to the randomised flows of temporal positioning, geography and fate that conspired to keep us apart. In other words, they managed to avoid being locked up in the same freezing boarding house as me for six years.

What did I observe? Well, I'd like to sum it up in a moment for you, if that's possible. We were playing a game, you see. We always did, on Wednesday evenings in the summer. The problem is that, in schools, you have to divide up into two teams and the teams are not always fair. People pick their friends. People gang up against the weak until they're unstoppable. A clever boy called Ben Crowder, probably emigrated by now, suggested a solution: "Choose names for two sides." Crusaders & Paynim, Hyenas & Vultures, Spartans & Athenians, it didn't matter what. "When someone new turns up, simply call out to determine their affiliation." We tried it with a game of British Bulldog, thus.

'Who goes there? Saxon or Celt?'

'Saxon.'

'Who goes there? Saxon or Celt?'

'Celt.'

This was working.

'Who goes there? Saxon or Celt?'

'Norman.'

It was Raffles. Never a team player, that summer evening he played on his own as a side against everyone. He lost of course, but at another level he outplayed us all, as individuals.

Do these people have common characteristics, I asked myself, in greater frequency than ordinary people? Some stood out. They were all risk-takers. They decided what to think about the world and their place within it based upon the factual evidence they could actually see, not other people's established wisdom. They jumped at their chances as contemporaries dithered. They had an insatiable interest in everything, specifically how things work. A child-like fascination? Perhaps. An inability to comprehend spite? Frequently. Many had a complete lack of shame or any other psychological encumbrance. The law and the other rules, burned into our behaviour patterns, were often guidelines to them. Some were manically depressive or mentally ill, but that seemed to be another side of the same coin. 'Larger than life' was a common notation. It's not just natural aptitude then, nor exceptional intelligence. It's being born into the world and throwing yourself headlong and early into spellbound exploration. I wonder how many got themselves killed before being noticed? How would they have affected more ordinary lives?

They find it all so easy. They don't even have to s t r e t c h. If you asked the likes of me to juggle six jam donuts, we couldn't do it. If you asked them, they could. It's as though their jam donuts have naturally stuck together in the great bakery of providence and they'll always find it pretty easy to juggle their six in two clumps of three. It's when they find it *oh so predictable* and extend themselves to seven jam donuts, two éclairs, one Viennese whirl and a star-shaped spotted macaroon that I find myself getting a bit tetchy.

What about Schliemann then? I *certainly* could have done that. Not the languages and fortune in business, obviously. I was thinking more of the sunny holidays and knocking hundreds of little holes in the Peloponnese. You know - snorkelling about until you find something. Perhaps I should have been an archaeologist. I've always had an underlying urge to dig up the Greek island of Aegina. Possibly Poros too, who can say? I don't know why, but maybe it's all to do with a subconscious desire to inflict latent revenge for my pistachio nut allergy. Not that I'm allergic to pistachio nuts, per-se. At least I can't be sure. What I can say is that when I stare fixedly at a pistachio nut ice-cream, it looks exactly the kind of thing I would be allergic to. Aegina is brim full of pistachio nuts. Green ones. They litter the ground.

On the subject of subconscious urges, I sometimes feel a strong desire to blush, but my regiment disapproves of such things.

Retracting this observation to the point where I wanted to make a point, the point is this:

When I see people like Raffles gliding effortlessly through life, achieving all that they aim for, I do sometimes wonder whether their minds work differently to ours.

Chapter 7

The Diamond Party

The sun blinked. The sun blinked again, or maybe it was me. Raffles had already gone through the ostentatious courtyard and entered the sponsors' much-publicised *Diamond Party*. This was just the sort of event I never got invited to. However, I had been invited today, courtesy of the Press Pass that Raffles had managed to cadge for me. Another crumb from his table. It meant wearing a name badge, but despite being a second class citizen, I am sure I would have really enjoyed the party, but for the inevitable sight of A.J. charming the living pants off everyone. He'd started with the Press.

'What are you going to call your autobiography, Raffles?'

'Oh, hello Fred. Couldn't your editor have you ask me in London? It would have saved the air fare.'

'Ah, Mr Raffles, you know my paper can't afford those London nightclubs. It's much cheaper if we come out here.'

'Ha, fair enough. You'll be my guest next time, won't you Fred? Autobiography you say? Isn't that supposed to be at the end of your life? I think I'll settle for *The Man Who Had Problems With Strawberries.*'

'Can I quote you?'

'Sure. Just make sure they use one of my good photos. You know – *the ones from about five years ago.*'

The journalist laughed, Raffles smiled back and took his chance to get away.

'What was that about?' I wondered.

'They'll ask questions about strawberries for the rest of the series and make all sorts of dire fruit jokes. Even when there are several players who's performances they could write about, they'll write about mine because the tabloids love bad puns. It should keep my name ticking along in the back pages for months. At least they won't think to ask *anything else*. That's the media for you. Throw them a fish and watch them clap their hands.'

We were accidentally absorbed by a tribe of business men and women who played a pathetic game of one-upmanship against each other. Boasting about cars, their properties, recent deals, dinners with first name politicians that I'd never heard of, in short, their pumpkinesque wealth and influence. The women dripped with diamonds. The men, inwardly upset that the conventions of gender denied them necklaces and tiaras of their own, wore diamond cuff links and collar studs. One man in particular wore a fat gold and diamond tie pin, presumably designed as a safety precaution to be large enough to jam any office shredder that he might be ridiculous enough to feed his tie into. They talked, but didn't listen. They boasted, but were not impressed. They made sure everyone remembered their names, so I deliberately forgot them.

Blah blah from Blah Corporate Energy; Fwah fwah from the Embassy of Fwah; Yak yak, Chairman of Yak Accountancy; Plink clink, a magnate of Klonk Shipping – "If ever you need an oil tanker, just ask." Idiots.

Raffles introduced himself with a handshake.

'Raffles, non-entity.'

They believed him. We moved on.

I observed the journalist who'd been interviewing A.J. I made mental notes of the mannerisms, appearance and cheek he used, sharking the room for another victim. So, if I had to pass for a journalist, this was what I should be. At that moment, the glorious Captain of the South African XI made his entrance and the press man broke formation and stooped his conquering stoop.

'Hi Hansie! Can you spare me a few minutes of your time for the Syndicate?'

'What, here?'

'Well, yes. Selected journalists have been invited.' He waved a Press Pass.

'Yes, of course. Fire away.'

'As Captain of South Africa, you're on the selection panel. Is that right?'

'Yes, yes I am.'

'My readers would like to know why you've selected a jobbing seamer in the squad instead of the more proven bowlers everyone had expected to see.'

'You can't keep talent out, can you? India made that mistake. In South African cricket, we pride ourselves on picking the best players available for the squad on the day. Why stick with the same old names, even if they're the names you're used to?'

'Are the players selected on their current form in State cricket?'

'It's taken into account, yes. The real thing you have to develop here is an eye for talent. I'm not going to give you names, but the player you're referring to will show how reliable he is in the Tests. He's good at containment and he's a fine cricketing brain. I'm proud to give him a chance.'

'So he'll play in the First Test?'

'Why not?'

'Well, perhaps it's just that his current form in domestic cricket doesn't justify inclusion. The readers might be aware that this particular medium-paced seam bowler is a Cape-coloured player and it could appear that the squad is being selected according to some racial quota system imposed by the politicians.'

'Oh, don't be so stupid. The squad is entirely selected on merit from the talent available at the time of the series. I would be pleased, honoured, to entrust the nation's chances to any one of them.'

'What if the statistics suggest someone else should be there on merit?'

'Look, there's a difference between past achievements and the promise of coming achievements. I have full confidence in the strength of natural talent emerging throughout our Rainbow nation. I'd like all South Africans to hear this message: If you're good enough, YOU can make the cricket team! Get yourself down to your local club and play the game! I'm only South Africa's Captain because someone better hasn't pitched up yet and taken my spot. Tell them: If you're good enough, you're welcome to try!'

'A challenge to the readers?'

'Yes. South Africa deserves the very best team it can raise. I'd never guarantee an established player's place or even my place ahead of that rule. Sure, one day that policy will apply to me. Sir, I am a Christian. I believe in many races, but one nation under Jesus. That's my credo. I don't think in terms of races and politics because we are all God's children. So what if one of our boys has been in the oven a little longer than I have? Who cares? I just want to know if the team can rely on him, if he'll raise his game when it gets tough. I just need to know if, in the late-cut, he keeps his head down and rolls the wrists!'

'Well said. So, to recap, the players are selected on the basis of future merit, on results they haven't produced yet.'

'What paper are you with?'

'The Bugle Group. Although, as I said, we're syndicated around the globe.'

'I'm sorry. We'll have to leave it there. I don't talk to your paper and I won't discuss anything with syndicates. Good evening. Please enjoy the buffet.'

'That's a great pity because...' He found himself talking to the air.

All this while, during my eavesdropping, Raffles had been talking to a girl called Yula, or possibly Una. She had a friend called Jo-Jo, or was she a sister? Whatever she was, I think she'd already wandered away. As my attention drifted back, I wondered whether I was supposed to be following their conversation too. Perhaps not then, as they were talking about me.

'Why's your silly friend called Bunny?' asked Yula, or possibly... never mind.

'Ah! That's an old school nickname. He turned up one term looking harmless, then shot the school rabbit.' – Raffles, obviously.

'So he's cool after all! Jo-Jo thought he was your pet doggie!'

'Admittedly he has a tendency to snap at moving objects. I think it's only because he's still a bit traumatised from leaving the Army. He was an officer you know.'

Delighted, Yula swung off into the fray with her news of the pooch, knocked a many elbowed path through to, presumably, Jo-Jo and clattered away in girlish excitement about shell-shocked war heroes being much more exciting than dowdy old cricketers. So flirtatious, so easily distracted, they completely forgot to come back and talk to me.

'Hello' said a passing Sports Psychologist 'I specialise in functional patterns.'

'Do you? That's interesting.'

Oh dear.

After ten minutes of talking about the importance of a player's unthinking trust in his own knee caps, ten minutes of my life I'll never, ever, get back, Raffles rolled up to the rescue. The Sports Psychologist gave Raffles a peculiar look, as if a researcher studying the migration of sharks from orbit had returned home to find quite a long one in his kitchen, conversation dried and he edged away. Most unusual.

'Bunny, isn't this a charity ball?'

'I believe so. It was billed as something of the sort.'

'Yet I don't see anyone giving. I wonder if they've really thought this concept through. Wouldn't you say that some of the wealthy businessmen and political noises, who probably spend most of the days behind electrified fences counting their groats in palatial luxury, might make a little contribution to the AIDS relief and mosquito-eradication charities they've mentioned above the door?'

'Yes, but you can't make them.'

'Look at the couple at that table, for instance. Oh, and the daughter. They've got half a million in ice hanging off their necks!'

I must confess, I'd also seen the three-string diamond necklace with the triple set of larger roseate diamonds clustered in the centre. It sparkled like a harbour on the Riviera.

'What are you thinking of, Raffles? You're surely not going to give them a speech?'

'I've a better idea than that. Will you help me with a little practical joke?'

'If you must. Don't embarrass me though. You know I hate that.'

'In the... what's it called? In the portico, that's the word. Whoosh. Over there,' he indicated with a flap of the hand 'you'll see a white box on a white background. That's the fuse box for the lighting system.'

'How do you know?'

'It has 'Fuse box for the Lighting System' stencilled on it. It's either the truth or starkly original graffiti. Don't worry about the details Bunny. Leave all the reading and writing to me.'

I wondered if it was too late to withdraw my assistance, but Raffles was on the march.

'Just turn the power off, there's a good lad, count to twenty seven and turn it on again. Think of it as a bit of a rag.'

I remember his 'rags'. On Founder's Weekend he stuck foam rubber to the bottom of his shoes, stood in magnolia paint and walked a footprint trail from the plinth of the Founder's statue right across the drive to the gents lavatory and back. At Cambridge, he dismantled another student's Volkswagen and reassembled it outside their study, which happened to be on the second floor landing. 'Rags' were dangerous. In my experience, 'rags' got you caned.

Even so, I had a little remaining loyalty to him and none whatsoever to them. In for a penny... I tripped the fuses.

Eighteen, nineteen, murmurs, twenty one, twenty two, susurrations, twenty three, twenty four, twenty five, a scream, not good at all that, fuses down, oh, they were already down, fuses up then and the lights went on.

'Well done that man' called a voice. I bowed instinctively and then saw they'd meant Raffles not me.

'Lucky I was close by' he said. 'When the light went off, I felt sure someone went for the charity box, so I jumped across and sat on it!'

'Hooray!' yelled Una or Yula or – oh, why do people insist on giving their children stupid names? I shall call her, no I won't, better still I'll stop mentioning her altogether.

'Raffles, you're not used to Africa, are you?' called out one reveller 'It was nothing more than a power cut. We get them here all the time.'

'Oh good. What a relief I won't have to sit on this box all evening!' He did a handstand on it instead.

More laughter and a cheer or two. I think he'd broken the ice. Good old Raffles. I went to the bar.

I watched as the reporter did his rounds. I watched as the organisers tried to put people at their ease again. I watched a lady crying. I felt I'd seen her before. Clearly distressed, an insistent partner held her arm firmly against the table and refused to allow her to rise. He seemed to be explaining something in words of one syllable. Something important? They seemed to reach some sort of agreement and he relaxed his grip. She stood up, spilling her drink across the tablecloth, and struck off in the direction of Raffles. At least now I'd find out what happened, if only by the roundabout method.

Then it occurred to me. This was the lady in the three string diamond necklace, only I hadn't recognised her because... there was no necklace! I know she'd been there all along, but – and I'm sure this goes for everyone – we were now looking at her face. I'm sure that some women get this all the time, even without necklaces, but for this particular lady the diamonds were sadly her only natural advantage.

I zoomed in. By the time I got there, a floor full of rapidly revolving revellers having upset the smoothness of my zoom, Raffles had already signalled me over and set about introducing me to the upset lady.

'This is a friend of mine, assigned to the tour. Brigade of Guards, off duty. Between the three of us, we can get to the root of it.' He reversed the introductions.

'The lady would like to withhold her name for the time being. Her husband is a well known industrialist and prospective political candidate. It would be wise to avoid a scandal.'

'Scandal?'

'A crime.'

'You need the police, not us!' I told her.

Raffles placed his hand on my shoulder. 'It is a matter of some delicacy.'

'Oh, one of those.' Surely he hadn't got her pregnant? The lights were only off for twenty seven seconds.

A.J. steered us both to an alcove away from the ballroom traffic.

'Madam, if you wouldn't mind fully explaining the circumstances?'

'Theft! It's a theft Mr Raffles! What should I do?'

'You should explain. Your husband obviously doesn't want to take any action. Why is that?'

'They took my necklace! In the dark, Mr Raffles! I felt the fingers on my neck! I'll never forget the feeling of the dreadful fingers!'

'Dreadful fingers, okay. Why don't you want us to call the police?'

'My husband won't permit it. You see, it was a… it was a bargain, Mr Raffles. There aren't any authentification papers.'

'You mean it was paste?'

'No, nothing like that. It was just that my husband…, oh, Mr Raffles!'

'Your husband did what? It really would be so much easier if you'd explain.'

'My husband bought it from and I.D.B.'

'What's that?' I asked.

'An illicit diamond buyer' volunteered Raffles. Trust him to have heard of it.

'My husband said that if the papers started calling them 'blood-stained diamonds', it would do more damage than they are worth. He wants to be in government, Mr Raffles. He told me to let them go!'

'I'm not sure. I still think this is a police matter' I suggested. They won't care where they're from, will they?'

'It's not just that.'

Raffles intervened. 'She's also worried her husband will do something terrible to the thief if he catches them.'

'Mr Raffles! I know by what methods he became as powerful as he is today and it wasn't by forgiving the poor fools who tried to exploit him.'

'Would he buy you another one?'

'Perhaps. I don't know. Please Mr Raffles, do something!'

'I quite understand and I will do what I can to find them. Look after her Bunny. I'll return shortly.'

He returned with the Police.

The remains of the evening went badly. We were questioned and we were searched. We stood where we said we were standing when the lights went out and people were asked to confirm their neighbours' locations. Luckily, I was confirmed as having been seen on the other side of the room and thus cleared of suspicion early. When nothing material was found in the room or on the person of any living soul, the fun dissipated. The thieves had got away. Poor old rich Mrs not-allowed-to-know-her-name. Poor old Mr lynch-the-culprits. Not that poor. I suppose they could afford another.

As an afterthought of the various policemen who no longer had tasks to occupy them, it was decided to break open the charity box and confirm that nothing had been taken from there. This task accomplished, the closest of them, the one with his head in the great box and his feet suspended in the air, let out a strange yelping noise not dissimilar that found on the soundtrack of the popular documentary *Meerkat Manor*.

Triumphant, South Africa's finest son held aloft a sparkling jewel of the night. Most people failed to notice it because, distractingly, it was attached to about seventy others. Yes, this was the missing three string necklace and what a beauty it was too.

'Evidence' said a senior copper 'Wrap it up'. He turned to the relieved couple and advised them to bring their identification certificate for the stones to a police station in the city before making a formal recovery of the evidence, to follow the usual cataloguing for potential criminal proceedings against the thieves.

The husband, I'm sorry but I never discovered his name, experienced a sudden attack of charity.

'There's no need for that, Inspector. I prefer not to ruin the occasion by demanding arrests.'

'May I remind you, Sir, that a crime has been committed this evening.'

'I disagree. Someone put wealth into the hands of a charity. That's the best place for it. If I'm elected to serve this country, this damn fine country, they'll be plenty more of that! No crime has been committed here today. Just a humble donation. Why don't we auction the necklace and the charities who've made us so welcome tonight can keep the proceeds!'

That earned the greatest round of applause I've ever witnessed. The auction raised an enormous number of South African rands and, although I can't for the life of me recall the conversion rate, everyone seemed pretty impressed as the various plutocrats vied to outbid each other. The lady who'd arrived with it turned her head and couldn't bring herself to look. What a prize though! Three strings of little stars with a triple cluster of... oh, the centre-piece didn't seem to be there now. Perhaps I'd confused the necklace with another. Yes, probably the daughter's, now that I think of it.

After the auction, the guests remained excited and talkative. Raffles seemed to be leaving via the atrium, but then broke his stride for a chat to the snubbed detective, recently in charge of the scene. I followed and, waiting for A.J. to disengage himself, heard a little of their conversation.

'It doesn't matter if it was a publicity stunt in a good cause. We're talking about thieves here, Mr Raffles. The person responsible is a thief, nothing more, and I mean to put him in a court room. In England, your legal system does everything it can to protect the rights of the criminal. Our system guarantees a different kind of justice.'

'Guarantees?'

'We try to give justice to the victim.'

'Well Inspector, that's all very fascinating, but far beyond the understanding of a simple sportsman. I must say though, I would love to come along and see the court proceedings one day, if time permits.

Especially if you fine fellows apprehend that daring jewel thief before our tour is over.'

'That, Mr Raffles, is an excellent suggestion. You would be an honoured guest of the Police Department. A great gesture, not to mention the beneficial publicity it might bring to those charities represented here tonight and of course in support of respect for the law. Yes, Mr Raffles, you would be welcome. We'll catch him and then we'll invite you in for a tour of the Station.'

'Most kind. Good night and good hunting, Inspector!'

'Good evening to you, Mr Raffles.'

Raffles smiled and began walking out.

'Sir, just one formality, before you leave.'

He was going to search him. The Inspector was actually going to search him!

'Surely, Inspector' said Raffles as the policeman investigated his pockets 'the jewellery is no longer missing? Is there any point to this?'

'It won't do any harm to be sure. We haven't done a full inventory yet and, between you and me Sir, most of these worthy citizens can't remember how many diamonds they arrived with.'

'Ah, well, that explains it. It's reassuring to know we're in safe hands. Good night Inspector!'

Raffles caught me by the elbow and headed for the exit. I spoke first.

'Do you feel affronted? I thought that was pretty intrusive. Lots of people were watching and he frisked you like a common thief. I'm surprised you took it so well. Honestly, if it were me...

'Honestly?'

Without breaking stride, we walked beneath a sparkling chandelier and Raffles, with one deft pass of a high bowling-action, swept a bunch of glass tear-drops from their place in the fringe of light.

'Another souvenir, I suppose?'

It took half a minute before I made the connection. Those weren't cut glass baubles, were they? Those were the three centrepiece stones from the diamond necklace. He'd stolen them!

'People never look up, Bunny. They're conditioned not to. If you want to hide your secrets, paint them on the ceiling.'

I couldn't find any words for this action. He'd actually stolen something, in front of everybody. He'd actually stolen their diamonds without being noticed! It might never be noticed. It felt as if nothing had happened. What a strange, underhand, rather criminal thing to do. No one has ever accused my family of cheating, stealing, lying or being deceitful and when they have, they've at least had the decency to accept our explanation for it. This incident however was absolutely, utterly, inexcusably shameless. It certainly wasn't expected of a member of the First XI.

Could I turn him in? No, because he'd turn me in. Perhaps he wouldn't, which would make it even worse. Sometimes, hanging around with Raffles is like picnicking in the Bolivian rainforest. One minute it's all relaxation, tea and scones then, just when you're getting settled, something poisonous and unspeakable shimmies up your trouser leg.

'Would you mind explaining your actions today? I couldn't help noticing, you know, the whole *stealing things* theme to this evening. I mean to say, are you going to put them back? What, exactly, has just happened?'

'We needed a little working capital. The fundraisers needed funds. An opportunity presented itself.'

'Doesn't that make you, I mean to say, aren't you therefore a somewhat thieving person?'

'Bunny, the meek shall inherit what's left.'

'What's happening to you Raffles?'

'Do you know how the most successful fraudsters operate when they find a wallet?'

'Find? You mean steal.'

'They take out a single credit card and return the rest of the cards and the wallet. That way, the owner won't report the card as stolen because they will believe they have temporarily mislaid it.'

'Yes, jolly good. You would like to say you've been very clever tonight, but let me remind you that society frowns upon crime and the law doesn't bother downgrading sentences for the clever ones.'

'You didn't say that last time.'

'What last time?'

'When I took and sold that medal to repay your debts. Haven't you worked out by now that the visit to Strickland-Hocket's mansion was merely a ruse to collect it back from the buyer?'

'What? You don't seriously mean to tell me...'

'Bunny, you really are spectacularly naïve. At least you've stopped frowning.'

'You said it had probably been sold to Lord Bunting, the militaria collector!'

'Absolutely correct. Strickland-Hocket was elevated to the Peerage in the New Year's Honours list. He has adopted the title of 'Lord Bunting'. If you ever read any further than the sporting section of your newspaper, Bunny, you'd know that.'

'So you stole it back? When you were waiting in the house for the letter, you broke into his study?'

'Well done! You almost always work it out for yourself in the end, Bunny. Yes, I took it back. He knew it was stolen property when he bought it from me. We negotiated over the internet, as it suited neither of us to meet in person. He said he knew the provenance and then used that knowledge to haggle down my asking price. I very much doubt he will complain to the Police or the Army, do you?'

'Raffles' I spoke clearly, with hushed deliberation, 'where is the medal now?'

'I posted the whole lot back to your regiment on the morning we left, the medal, bugles and commendation. I've included a sad little note which explains how remorseful the sender is about their impulse, simply wanting to feel close to their long-lost ancestor. There's also a final thought of pity for anyone who might be reprimanded.'

Raffles might have told me, but I couldn't complain. At least he'd worked hard to finish the job.

'One of the first acts of a Lord, a Peer of the Realm, was to buy stolen goods?'

'Yes. Tell me, do you feel *respectful*? Society, as you call it, has collapsed. The Establishment taught us to disrespect it, to doubt our own conditioning. Rather a shot in the foot by our rulers, I thought. Our strata of what was previously called 'Society' will be the very last to realise the truth. In that respect, Lord Bunting and I are leading the pack.'

'What are you talking about?'

'Bunny, you believe in constructs. It's part of your psyche. Constructs are ideas built up in your mind which have no practical existence other than as persuasions by which humanity can be herded, motivated and controlled. To most people, under pressure, they are disposable concepts. To you, they are so far above criticism that it wouldn't occur to you to evaluate them.'

'Do you mean loyalty to flags and things? That's normal military cohesiveness.'

'No it isn't. Not under life or death pressure, when the reality dominates. Most soldiers on the front line carry on fighting not for Queen and Country, but out of loyalty to their small group of mates, their platoon. You are the exception; you're not like that. Even if it were you alone standing between your flag and all the horsemen of the Hunnic Empire, you'd fight until you died out of sheer unshakeable belief in your constructs: Queen, country, flag and always putting tea in before the milk.'

'They're very important.'

'They're all in the mind. Apart from the milk thing, obviously. If everyone around you believes in them, you find yourself believing in them. It's very hard to reach your own conclusions under such pressure. Wouldn't you agree, you've met only a microscopic fraction of the people in your country? It's just an artificial line of convenience around a population on a map. The concept of country equates to a sort of club. You serve it, believe in it and you pay into it your taxes and then, if you get into difficulties, the club comes back and rescues you. I put it to you that the club no longer works. The criminal, the lazy and feckless have already adapted to exploit this. You can pay in your taxes all your life, but there will not be a pension for you when you retire because the money will have been spent or given away.'

'That's cynical, Raffles.'

'No. That's what the government has actually admitted. It's everyone for themselves now. Successive authorities have taught the people to have no respect; to be selfish. If a man is loyal to his country, politicians ridicule that person as 'A Little Englander' – they laugh openly at loyalty. They say it is embarrassing and racist to be loyal. They are laughing at you, Bunny. The answer? Don't be loyal. Don't be loyal to their version of England. The England which you were conditioned from a child to be loyal to has gone – sunk beneath the sea. If the country simply isn't your country any more, if it's been dismantled, cancelled and some other outfit is using the name, why pay the membership taxes?'

'Democracy. Peace. Right of abode.'

'You could have that in New Zealand, Canada or the Virgin Islands. Why not re-pitch your flag? Apathy? If you're going to stay put and be a victim out of your lingering sentimental attachment, at least ask yourself: why should I continue to obey the rules?'

'I like the law. I mean, I like the fact it's there. I'm comfortable with British democracy.'

'You really don't follow the news, do you? Britain is not a democracy. Britain's highest form of political power is a completely unelected foreign government called the European Commission. The Public have no right to vote for anyone at all in the government which rules them. My sincerest congratulations!'

Ah, now, I wasn't falling for that. If you don't like the European Union, you should stop obeying the law? Illegal and widely detested as it might be, I could see the two things weren't connected. Surely Raffles didn't care at all about this stuff? It sounded to me like an excuse - or the manifesto of a Unabomber.

'You say 'your country' and 'you are ruled'. Does that mean you are not?'

'I am loyal to my country, I still wear its colours, but I have already told you that it's ceased to exist. It was cancelled, abolished, demolished in the interests of progress. I would like to be ruled by a democratically elected government. Every mainstream political party believes Britain should be ruled by an unelected foreign power. What's the point of voting? To make the coup d'état look legitimate? Why weren't we asked if we wanted this? It was because we would have said 'No', which the politicians insist is the wrong answer, *so they didn't ask the question.* They just did it. They ended democracy and cut me, and thousands of others from all possible backgrounds and classes, adrift. I don't believe in the illusion they've replaced it with. Their new flag is just a meaningless cloth attracting more hatred than love.'

'So you're a patriotic nihilist hedonist?'

'Bunny, you miss the point. I am happy and free. I accept the destruction of everything I was brought up to believe in as a wonderful gift. I am stateless, free from the infections of birthright! I can choose my own allegiances, I can risk-assess the law, I am transnational and, above all, I can think for myself.'

I'd had enough of this. I liked my constructs. I openly admit I'd support the reigning monarch even if it was a gooseberry lollipop, but beliefs like that mean you don't have to worry about things and *I really like* not having to worry about chaotic things that go on *else-*

where. In fact, not having to worry is one of my favourite sensations, right at the top of the list with being asleep and getting stuck in New Year traffic with a tipsy Charity Blake, although I could wave good-bye to that one. She'd be rubbing red wine stains off someone else's trousers next year. Was Raffles seriously suggesting I should edit my allegiances?

'Raffles, is there any reason for staying in my company? I mean, if I'm so predictable and harmless.'

'On the contrary. You are a very capable asset.'

'What the hell does that mean?'

'Calm down old friend.'

That shut me up. I'd never once heard him use the word 'friend' before. Was he dying or something?

'Bunny, how well do you know the history of military psychology?'

I couldn't help thinking that only a civilian would lecture an army officer about such a thing. I let him ramble along in the same patient spirit a doctor might use when patients come in, sit down and diagnose themselves with all the training of Hippocrates's hamster.

'If one massed group of soldiers are invited to fire upon another group of soldiers, or civilians, researchers believe that the majority choose to miss. Despite their training, they find it very difficult to put bullets into real people standing unprotected in front of them. There have been instances, in the first war, of entire twelve-man firing squads failing to hit a person tied a mere thirty yards from them.'

Actually, I'd heard of this. Apparently no one could face shooting Mata Hari in the first salvo.

'At the site of the battle of Gettysburg, for example, an archaeologist recovered a muzzle-loading musket which had a barrel charged with a column of no fewer than twenty six shots. The Union soldier had loaded, aimed at his Confederate countrymen, pretended to fire and repeated the exercise until he could load no more. That same researcher claimed that in any group of thirty soldiers, only two do the actual killing. These, he said, were the psychopaths.'

'I don't think that's accurate. What about fiercely committed volunteers or people protecting their homes?'

'Yes, but they would use minimum force and cease when they'd achieved their aims. You, Bunny, would not. You would fire and keep firing and bring down as many as possible and feel guilty about it and fire again and keep firing and killing people, real people, until an outside factor forced you to stop. For you, it wouldn't be a matter of choice. It wouldn't even cross your mind that there could be another option. Your constructs are so deeply embedded that you can't think outside your given parameters.'

'That's balls, frankly. Why would you think that?'

'1982, The Falklands Crisis. When you were a snip of a child, you told me you could have fought that one better. You had a good plan. The enemy forces in occupation of the islands claimed it as their land. Fine, you said, ask them if we can remove all British subjects from the Falklands and repatriate them.'

'So what? I wanted to get civilians out of the way?'

'That done, you thought it best to position aircraft carriers to the south of the islands, seven hundred miles from the mainland being out of range of the enemy, and patrol the waters between the islands and the mainland with submarines. You'd impose a complete air and sea blockade. With no losses on your side and no supplies reaching theirs, their forty thousand soldiers would starve or freeze to death in an Antarctic winter within two or three months.'

'Oh, for God's sake.'

'If they asked to surrender, you said, you'd reject it replying you wouldn't want to end it yet, since you had all sorts of new weapons to test and there'd never be a better opportunity than to try them out on them.'

'Enough. Please?'

'The few that survived, you said, could be collected and taken off for a very long imprisonment. Our side would have almost no dead and, when the families of every single enemy soldier found them to be either dead or gone for decades, with no exceptions, who would ever want their sons to fight against us again? It would stop all future conflicts, you said.'

'I was a child, aged about twelve. It was a plan for toy soldiers.'

'No. It was a good plan. Syracuse enacted something similar on the Athenians. It's inhumanly efficient.'

'I've grown up, okay? I've had training. I can lecture you on military ethics! I am not that child, alright?'

'One thing remains. If I asked that child to give me the best tactical solution, he'd give it without any filtering. You still have a blind-spot for lateral, cynical, questioning thought. How should we bomb a wooden city? With fire, of course.'

'That's just stupid. It's not me. I think of alternatives. I am perfectly civilised, alright?'

'Civilisation quickly turns to messy hell if you stop asking questions. 'Civilised' is an end product of social conditioning. It is your programming which you can't snap out of. It's commonly believed that messy minds aren't dangerous. You have a pure and predictable messy mind, operating within the constant approval of ingrained constructs. You are potentially very dangerous. You have a little subservient policeman inside your disorganised mind who stops you being free.'

'Oh, bog off. I'm surprised you don't want to be truly free. Go on - live in a shack in the woods, Raffles. If it's helpful, they say putting a tinfoil lining in your hat stops the secret police reading your thoughts.'

I know that was lippy and (even worse) unoriginal, but laws and civilisation and things aren't open to question, are they? I really felt as if I'd wandered into an infamous 1950s Cambridge study meeting where either Philby, Burgess, Blunt or Maclean have just thrown their latest super-whizzo suggestion into the ring "I know chaps! Why don't we support the other side for a change?"

It wasn't exactly that though. Raffles wasn't supporting the other side of the coin, was he? Raffles' proposal was to abandon loyalty for nothing at all. "Everyone aboard? Remove the rudder!" Absolute animism. I remembered the words of Joyce Grenfell, who said "Anarchism is all very well, but my question is: Who will be responsible for the drains?"

Ultimately, this wasn't a vision of the future I could subscribe to. I could see that by choosing to live in this way, you helped destabilise established order. You helped to make this future happen faster. In my experience, no rules and survival of the fittest works in your favour really, really well, right up to the point when you've bust your ankle. Then they find you. Raffles may have thought it attractive to predate on the failing carcass of civilisation, but I do wonder if he'd miss the old beast if it wasn't there and risk-takers like him had to operate without a safety net. No, I would not yield to this new thinking. I might document it though. Yes, I should record it in case anyone ever asked how the hell he got like that.

'The other problem is, you always believe what you're told.'

'Do I? I wasn't aware of that.'

'Quite. Bunny, you can't fence the future out. Do you acknowledge your everyday unthinking loyalties? Yes, I too have allegiance to the Queen, but not a blind one. I have evaluated the facts and decided for her. She can't be corrupted. I can't be sure of anyone else, so I award that the highest value. It's important to anchor yourself to someone or something or you can forget who you are. Politicians can be bought and sold or use temporary power for their own purposes, they can be helped to power and then owe their job to a handler, but a monarch *is the country*. It's in their interest to do it properly. As far as I'm concerned, she's the only solid reference point we have left.'

'You're not entirely lost then.'

I couldn't be sure in my mind of what he really meant. If the Queen goes, the collapse of society will be an open secret? I'm not sure. I couldn't think the Public would watch crime become a legitimate activity without cobbling together some form of order. I have a lot more faith in my fellow man than has A.J. In a blinding flash of intelligence, I have those, no honestly I do, I wondered if this could be a cry of help. I was supposed to be incorruptible too, wasn't I? I thought so anyway, but Raffles was making inroads. Was he worried that if I went, he wouldn't be grounded in right and wrong? In reality? Perhaps that was it (I told you I was bright), he needed me or it wouldn't be long before he'd seriously embarrass himself. He'd never admit that though, not Mr One Man Island.

'You really can be unbelievably negative sometimes. You just have to come to accept that that's how the system works.'

'The System works? Gosh!'

He paused in startled contemplation.

'There is a System?'

'I don't think this conversation is going anywhere, Raffles. Your existential rage really isn't my concern.'

'Bunny, I'm losing you, aren't I? I haven't outlined the crisis in relevance to a subject which panics and stabs at the very root of your being.'

He paused, seemed to look through me for a few seconds and carried on.

'Bunny, we grew up in a world in which the industry standard for salt and vinegar crisps was blue. Twenty years ago, the nature of society slipped over a boundary, representing a disintegration process, after which we can no longer reasonably expect to have control over anything. Instead of replacing the colour/flavour associations of the bags, the colours mean nothing any more. It's chaos and regression.'

Actually, he was right, that did upset me. Being pedantic though, I think that *Bones*, by Smiths Crisps, were in a black bag as early as 1974. They got away with it though because *Bones* were in a different shape. They were shaped, in fact, like bones. I'm not sure why. Perhaps we should write in?

I looked up and Raffles seemed to be waiting for an answer. What was he talking about again? Oh, yes, self-destructive waffle, wasn't it?

'A.J., I think this can mostly be put down to the London effect. When you see twenty thousand people pass by every day, you begin to think human life is directionless and irritating. The countryside isn't like that. You can value people's lives and opinions because you have spare time to listen to them. You should come and see my village. That hasn't changed much.'

'Look around! No more Miss Marples! Their entire generation has gone extinct! Except, I concede, a few hanging on in their last remaining fringe habitats on the Isle of Wight.'

'I know some.'

'Are any of them under seventy? Society has mutated. The country you adore is now infested with verminous chavs, all hooped gold earrings and pink jump-suits. Can you imagine what they are going to become? Chav grandmothers? Do you think they'll replace the principled generation you were brought up by? Will they go to tea with the Vicar? You think London has a pigeon problem? Ha! You just wait until that lot fill the place up with twenty million useless progeny. Bunny, it's inevitable. These people breed so much faster than us. They are replacing our world and it will discontinue.'

'Raffles, this is a rant. If you start talking about superior classes, I really am going to go off you.'

'It isn't about genetics, it's about attitude.'

'Think about it carefully, would you? These same people turn up and buy tickets to watch you play cricket. They subscribe to satellite television channels which *fund your career*. Face it Raffles, they pay your wages.'

'No, they turn up and buy tickets to watch the football. They much prefer a quick fix of unthinking tribalism with the chance of a fight afterwards. The civilised minority follow cricket.'

'That's a gross generalisation.'

'Yes, but often a disturbingly accurate one. Just think, Bunny! Think of a country run by people like that. Countries only function if the population believe in them. What of the Public now? Just look at your pension scheme, for example. People won't pay into a pension because they don't believe they'll get anything back. They are sure the government will steal it, so the State has to make payment compulsory at source. Society favours the selfish, the rule-breakers and the ones who ignore the spirit of the thing. I'm not talking about thieves. It's much wider than that. I'm talking about everyone and their neighbours. They see the country as a pot to take from.'

'Not all of them.'

'Whether good or bad, 'Society', or 'Class' systems, meant structure. There is no structure now. It's all chaos. There's nothing left to respect, nothing to be proud of. If our rulers have dismantled society, taught us to be embarrassed by it, then we are free…'

'Free to commit crimes?'

'Why not? Being a professional thief nowadays is just like any other occupation. There are occupational hazards, yes, but the excitement and the rewards outweigh those. Life is about gathering experiences! Risk is just another path to explore.'

'What happens when the Public think it's equally acceptable to burgle you? Who will you complain to?'

'Not the Police. No, that wouldn't be sporting, would it? I expect I should do the same as we did to that railway pension company. Hurt them in kind.'

'If someone steals your bike, you can hardly transfer their money to a compensation fund!'

'Oh Bunny, Bunny. When will you wake up? There was no 'compensation fund'. The funds were transferred to 'BR (compensation)', an account in the name of Mr Bertram Raffles, my convenient twin.'

'You kept the money? You haven't got a twin! You haven't even got a brother!'

'No, but I once had a cousin by the name of Bertram, who died at the age of two from a hole in the heart. Bertram now acts as my marionette. Since finding his birth certificate, the opening of anonymous accounts and even the directorship of a limited company, have been matters without the least thrill of complication.'

'I'm sorry, but that's disrespectful and actually quite sick.'

'Yes, but effective. I had the idea from yesteryear's actors of television and stage.'

'Oscar Wilde, you mean.'

'For one. Have you heard of the concept of an 'evil twin'?'

'What?'

Overloaded with information, it took me a while to mentally process the deluge. Interpreting our recent activities in their new perspective then, it meant... It surely meant that I was now a genuine criminal! How did that happen? A defence lawyer wouldn't bother mentioning my original motive now. Their advice would be getting it over with and pleading guilty. The strange thing is, I found myself even further taken aback to hear the word 'yesteryear' employed in ordinary conversation.

'What?' was the best response I could muster.

'Simple. The main 'good boy' actor slips out of view, sticks on a thin black moustache, then returns and causes havoc. This, of course, damages the spotless reputation of the main character until it is revealed at the end that character B was in fact his evil twin. Bertram Raffles is my evil twin. The BR (compensation) account, together with BR Enterprises and Bertram's Online College for the Uncommonly Gifted, a registered charity I might add, are all "moustache accounts".'

'When you tire of it all, will you find something even more dangerous? Tiger-baiting perhaps? Ski-boxing?'

'Why not indeed? Why not try everything you can?'

'Raffles, are you seriously telling me that you, who have all the respect in the world, would like to live at the same level of morality as some brain-dead hoodie stealing from a corner shop?'

'No, but they will inherit the Earth. The corner shops will close under the weight of it.'

'What's wrong with you Raffles? Where does all this weirdness come from?'

'It has crossed my mind, that's all.'

'What has?'

'A leaf from the forger's book. That someone with a famous and very public career might enjoy a second profession of which the public would never, ever, suspect them.'

'As a burglar? A safe-cracker?'

'Perhaps. Just think of it Bunny. Oh, to fill the sports pages with one career and the crime reports of the very same newspaper with the other!'

'Raffles, listen to me. Do you know what happens when a passenger train goes off the rails? It experiences, for the first time, the freedom to ignore someone else's rules of direction and then a few seconds later everyone ends up dead in a ditch, wrapped in scrap metal.'

'No. It doesn't have to be like that. Don't you see? We're different! Mankind is not a component of the system. Society formed around humanity. If it fails to serve, life should still be free to disregard it.'

'Civilisation should regress? You are going mad.'

'No. I'm becoming uncommonly sane.'

'Oh. Is that better? I'm not sure. I don't have any other lunatic friends to compare you with.'

He brooded. I don't think he'd ever discussed this thinking before. I felt honoured by his confidence and yet still extremely worried for him.

'Bunny, I'd never intended to keep the money for my personal use. The BR account is now quite empty, as are all my savings funds. Every penny is currently sitting in our gambling account on the Betfine website.'

'Well, that's alright then. Perfectly explicable.'

'We will need as much money as we can get if we're going to break that match-fixing syndicate.'

'Raffles, tell me, what's wrong with an honest career?'

'Well, I admit there are lots of honest jobs out there, but they usually make you wear a paper hat.'

'It's thrill seeking, isn't it? Do you really think crime is worth the effort to bring you some adrenaline rush that an honest job won't?'

'I suggest the third option is to progress in both. One for respect, one for income, both for the adventure.'

'Should I buy you a cape?'

He laughed and banged me on the back.

'Come, let's away to prison. We two alone will sing.'

I didn't think that was particularly amusing. How did I get drawn into this? I didn't want to be his accomplice, even more so on inevitable day when the authorities muscled in. I certainly didn't like the sound of African justice either. He might get a shock when "They took it altogether too seriously. Thirty years."

'Let's get a drink.'

Good, something I could relate to at last.

On the way to the bar, I remembered an old joke about the Lone Ranger and Tonto, his Native American side-kick. It went something like this:

'Tonto! There are Apaches to the North of us and Sioux to the South. The Blackfoot are closing from the East and the Cheyenne have cut off the plains to the West! We're completely surrounded. It's just a question of who's going to catch and scalp us first. What are we going to do?'

'Who's "we", Paleface?'

Chapter 8

The Day we Played the President's XI

For such an intensely secretive mind, our discussion after the diamond party was the first of A.J.'s aberrations, his leaks from the script. I wondered if it would be the last, since he hadn't persuaded me to agree with him. What would I have said about him a week ago? Let us see.

Raffles was a mine of information. In other words, he was deep, dark and it took a great deal of effort and heavy industrial machinery to get anything out of him. On the rare occasions when he did explain or, heaven forbid, tell you what he was thinking, you could see it coming a mile away. Why? That was because he firstly passed through an obvious mental ritual.

He'd listen to the question, turn his gaze directly to the questioner and freeze. With a steady head, as if preparing to face a ball, he'd look straight ahead without blinking. He then seemed to run the answer through in his head, beginning a process, assessing his own response, to calculate whether it might be used as ammunition against him on some future occasion. Would the papers misquote him or make a story out of nothing? Would giving away secrets compromise his cricketing skills and affect his ability to compete? Sometimes he might revise and edit his answer, sometimes he'd smile and then not answer at all. On occasion, he'd do his best to be open and honest, but listeners felt the presence of a boundary there. If they interrupted or used a follow-up question, it was an unspoken risk that the conversation rights might be withdrawn.

I wandered about my hotel room the next morning trying to think of a subject that might draw him again. When I had one, I came down the stairs and sought him out.

'A.J., why have you always refused the county captaincy?'

I got the stare.

Tick tock, tick tock. Would he answer?

'Bunny, do you know what captaincy really is?'

Gotcha.

'Yes, I think so. The captain attends to the toss of the coin, decides the batting order, changes the bowlers when they get tired and chooses when to declare or whether to impose the follow-on.'

'Yes, that's what a reliable, steadfast, losing captain does day in and day out.'

'Losing? I thought they all did that.'

'Human beings add a level of complication.'

'Such as?'

'Cricket is a complex reality. There are specialists, but no experts. How should I describe it? Perhaps like this: Without further intervention, the players will give their average performance and put up an average fight. If a player is having an off-day, they will not be brought out of it. If a bowler is having a once in a lifetime performance, he'll be rested on cue at eight overs and the momentum will stop. If an opposition batsman looks too good to get out, the bowlers will concede the fact, submit, and in so doing they'll make it true by their actions, not his.'

'Are you talking about motivation?'

'No. I'm talking about psychological babysitting. Cricket isn't a game of chess. Each piece on a cricket ground has a mind of its own. In chess, a rook's ability to perform doesn't differ from day to day. As a captain, you aim to control the opposition and your own team. A nip here, an encouragement there - sheepdog thinking. The hope is to manipulate eleven opposing minds into disarray and eleven of your own team's minds into stability and focus. Most players can't see where they are in that equation until it's pointed out to them. Especially the one's who've lost their tempers. Captains have to jump on that.'

Raffles signalled a passing waiter for something, but I wasn't paying attention to that. He noticed my expectation and resumed.

'If you want some players to try harder, you might have to reassure them of their own abilities and tell them how well they are doing. Other players, doing the same job, react best when told 'You're rubbish this morning. My granny could have put that last ball away. Are you sure you wish to be described in the programme as a fast bowler?' Some players are self-motivating. Those are the ones you can forget about. The vice-captain is one. The other is our most unassuming bowler, Hinden. He's like Bill Bowes or Glen McGrath in that respect. He just comes in, does exactly the job he was selected to do and maintains his accuracy in all conditions. You can tell exactly when the opposition batsmen are winning the psychological game; The Captain brings Hinden back on to bowl. The others aren't disciplined enough to regain control.'

'Since you understand this stuff. Wouldn't you make a good captain?'

'It would be an inconvenience for me to become a county captain. The enormous weight of personalities I'd have to carry through a long, long season, you understand? Learning their thinking, motivations and weaknesses, inside out, just in case it could make the difference in a tight finish. Understanding cultural differences and not offending expensive international hirelings. It's a real day's work to get a world class performance from a world class prima donna who will always think they know better than you, who's convinced they're doing your county a favour by taking their money, who thinks they can send *you* back to the pavilion for *their* sweater.'

I agreed I wouldn't need that, as if I'd ever be in the position. Then I applied it to Raffles. Yes, he'd be far too polite to send someone for his sweater. He'd struggle on without it though, right up to the point when they noticed, felt they might be letting him down and fetched it without him needing to ask. Then he'd be self-depreciating. He'd feel good, they'd feel good – on with the game.

'Most players find their batting averages slump as soon as they take the captaincy. Other players' problems take up so much of their thinking that they can't apply themselves properly to their own game. Yes, it's an honour, but also a poison chalice. Imagine learning the opposition's weaknesses too. Altogether that's seventeen counties worth of memorising and guessing where the little mental cracks can be found. Did you know, county players get on the phone to each other after a match and exchange observations? There's a whole network to be understood. If you dismiss it, the web of minds will be used against you.'

'Test captaincy then.'

'Even worse. An opposing national captain will then try to break you down as an individual. He'll use dedicated analysts who'll watch all the videotape they can get of you. If he can make his opponent question his own abilities or answer to the team for a string of noughts, that's half the battle won. This would reduce my enjoyment of the game, not to mention the freedom to do what I do without scrutiny.'

'What exactly is it that you do, if you don't mean bowling?'

He blanked me.

'However, I have never been put in the position to accept captaincy before because my county has never asked me. I've been considered, I think. They've certainly sounded me out, but never directly asked. You see, they don't think I'm a team player. You'll never be offered the Test captaincy if you haven't skippered a county side. Spinners aren't the first choice for that because they're not always guaranteed a place in the team.'

'Why? That seems very unfair.'

'No, it's absolutely practical.'

I was surprised at the craftsman's lack of defence for his own art.

'You'd drop yourself from a team?'

'Yes, on some surfaces. Fast bowlers and seam bowlers can take wickets in any conditions. Spin bowlers on flat, unfavourable surfaces can be easy meat, unless they're top quality thinkers. If a spinner plays well at Adelaide and then gets dropped for Perth, he might thank his captain. Two of the greatest batsmen who ever lived said "spinners should not be bowling" and yet, the top wicket-takers of all time are the finest spinners. It's an enigma. There are the one or two brilliant spin bowlers in each generation who are automatically selected at the national level and they are never, ever, dropped. Young man, I'm simply not one of them.'

'I thought you were pretty good. Everyone says so.'

Again, the obvious path was ignored. Pride, most people's Achilles heel, had no hold on A.J. Raffles'.

'There's another reason for not asking me, that of history. The England team almost always invites a batsman to be captain. They still believe the ability to construct an innings and create a score is a more positive motivation to his followers than the bowler's ability to generate failure, chaos and anxiety.'

I could just about follow that. The team was formed in two parts, attack and defence. Defence was the home and you built them around you – House Carls of the game. Attack was something you sent out to raid – Charioteers, loose and unpredictable individuals. It would be harder to build anything around them. They were too fluid. They made individual on-the-spot decisions without reference to authority.

'Why have you done so well at Test level when you believe you're not one of the best?'

I got the look. Would he? Yes, he was actually going to answer!

'I took a good man's place to get into this side. He was a lion in a placid little pride and I forced him to stand aside before he was ready. His farewell speech was... spiteful, which most people put down to jealousy. He said this:

"A.J. Raffles is not much more than a jobbing county cricketer. I don't think he's good enough to hold a place in a regional side for more than a couple of seasons, let alone play Test cricket. I don't understand why he's even got a career. Just watch a tape of his bowling, one delivery at a time. He doesn't do enough to get a decent batsmen out. Okay, so he gets a lot of turn, but you can see it coming. I have no idea why he's got so many wickets this season, but it can't last."

'That', said Raffles, 'was just over eight years ago. I've been in and out of the Test team ever since.'

'So, you proved him wrong. Forget about it.'

'You don't understand. He was close to the truth.'

'What can you possibly mean? You're the trickiest bowler ever to play for England!'

'Another exaggeration, Bunny? If you analyse my bowling ball by ball, mechanically, it's true that it shouldn't trouble Test batsmen. So, ask yourself, why am I still able to get them out? Although you won't see it in the score book, how am I able to generate conditions which help my fellow bowlers to get batsmen out? It's called thinking. I think them out.'

'I've heard of that, but I don't understand it.'

'The best bowling is a blend of mechanics, observation and thinking. My predecessor, my first Test victim, was right – I am not one of the finest natural bowlers and, in those days, he could bowl better deliveries than me. Throughout my career, I have relied on psychological skills to set my victims up. Captaincy is not for me because my game does not sow or nurture or support. I find a way into their minds, I undermine and then I burn.'

'Is this what you call 'gamesmanship'.'

'Not exactly. Gamesmanship is a category of thinking, similar to lateral-thinking. Potter described it as "The art of winning at games without actually cheating."'

'Potter?'

I should have mentioned that Raffles had a habit of presuming everyone knew who he was talking about.

'Originally recorded for fun, Stephen Potter identified many practical techniques which survive repetition. I have merely devoted my professional career to the further development of his original field of study.'

Intrigued, I pushed for further information.

'What are these techniques?'

'The first and by far the most important will be to "break the flow". Potter's expression, not mine. If a player is absolutely in his stride and starting to dominate the game, you must do something or say something or otherwise interrupt his timing to make him start again at square one.'

'I still wouldn't know what to do. I mean, can you clarify that?'

'Batsmen don't just stand there and bat. There are a lot of invisible things going on. As a batsman, you must monitor several simultaneous situations in your head: The fielding positions – estimating distances and gaps to see if there's a run here or there, the different types of delivery that the two bowlers operating at the moment can produce, the number of balls left to bowl in the over, footwork, the line you need to protect if you want to avoid an LBW, whether your fellow batsman might run you out, where you are standing in relation to your stumps, whether the wicket keeper is moving up to stump you, how many overs to survive until the next break, when the captain might declare, where is the field fast or slow or sloping, which fielders have a weak throwing arm, is the close fielder right or left handed and which is his bad side, is the bowler making marks in the pitch with his follow through, will the next ball be the slow one or the out swinger, watching the bowler's wrist and remembering the hand action for different deliveries. How many runs to avoid the follow on? How many runs to his fifty? Where is the pitch deteriorating, whether the new ball is due, the tactical situation of the game...'

'Okay, I get the point.'

'Now then, Bunny, could you hold all that information in your head if I asked you... 'Where did you get that shirt?"

'I'd forget everything I'd been concentrating on and...'

'Have to start again. Exactly. This technique is called a memory-dump. My expression, not Potter's. Memory works as if a single object has been lit up in a dark room. If you're retaining multiple 'illuminated' situations when a new memory is searched for, that room resets to black and lights up the single object searched for and then, by connection, the other memories and sensations associated with it. If the question is unexpected enough, the mind drops everything it's doing to concentrate on the new problem. It's quite instinctive.'

'I had no idea.'

It works best of all with anger. If someone is very, very, angry and you ask them an unexpected question, they'll find it almost impossible to get that state of anger back. You've pacified them with a single question. Good, yes?'

'Brilliant!'

'Can you find anything to complain about in the context of a match?'

'No. It's great. I had no idea.'

'A lot of county cricketers could be Test cricketers if they could play the mental game. I suspect I'm not good enough to remain a Test player without my box of tricks. Remember Bunny, gamesmanship is an art to get the very best players out. It can't be wasted. It's best saved for the old and experienced hands, who know it all and steady the ship. Those are the wickets I want. The wickets that actually mean something.'

'This is dynamite! Is it ever used against you?'

'Of course. A question to imply bad sportsmanship works best to unsettle English players: 'You're not going to run me out backing up, are you?' The English worry about 'what you think of them' for the rest of their lives. More often, we encounter crude insults - the Australian technique known as 'sledging'. It's not gamesmanship, it's not even intelligent and won't often work on English players. We know what they're doing and so we dismiss it as pathetic, but it still upsets many Asian cricketers. Sledging is a rough club to gamesmanship's surgical steel.'

'Sledging's still used then?' I asked, since I'd often heard of it.

'Less so, since its effectiveness has diminished. Some batsmen even take it as a compliment; thinking the bowler isn't good enough to get them out conventionally and is showing how pathetically desperate they are - a 'try anything' solution. If they're rude to you of course, it's alright to be rude back, but if you're witty, the other fielders will laugh at their own player's expense and – guess what - you've turned the tables.'

'I see. Not pleasant though. They still get away with it?'

'Yes. Some are fined for ungentlemanly conduct, but most get away with it if no one complains. It occurs less often in Tests where the stump microphones in place, but yes, it does happen.'

'What other techniques are there?'

'There are hundreds. Some of them haven't even been tested. In the origins of gamesmanship, Potter suggested encouraging one's opponents to take the game less seriously and then feel guilty for not doing so. He would encourage opponents to over-analyse. Many's the time I've drawn a batsman out of his crease to cover perhaps the only four potential threats to their wicket. Then I've deliberately bowled a wide ball to the wicket keeper and had him stumped. No one practices defending a wide.'

'In a Test match?'

'In a Test match. Okay, here's a question. If you asked a batsman what's the most efficient way to score off a fast bowler, they'd say to use the bowler's speed against them. In other words, if the ball reaches them at eighty miles per hour, all they need to do is correctly angle the bat and it will deflect away to the boundary with the momentum *the bowler* has given it. So, how do you get a confident batsman out?'

'Use his confidence against him?'

'Well done. If a batsman plays a shot which in my estimation would have got him out once in three swings, but on this occasion it goes for four and the crowd cheer, what should I do?'

I looked blank.

'Encourage the shot. I'll walk up to him at the end of the over and say "Incredible. That last one was straight out of the MCC coaching manual, wasn't it? I'm not sure everyone saw it, actually, as your bat-speed was supremely fast. Good for you! I don't mind conceding a boundary to brilliance. It's good for the game." So, he's confident, yes?'

'Well, yes.'

'I've also planted the idea that not everyone saw it the first time around, so… I bowl the same ball again.'

'So he plays the same shot again and, one time in three, he's out! He's out and he likes you for it!'

'Have you heard of 'pint pot python'?'

I hadn't heard of any such python and said so.

'At Test matches, pints of beer are sold to the spectators in plastic cups - a health and safety precaution to save the lives of anyone who might inhale them. In the late afternoon, the crowd often assemble long strings of these cups, which are passed from head to head along the rows of seating. This phenomena is called 'pint pot python' and usually gets a cheer if not much else is happening. Why is not much else happening? That's because the batsmen do not feel under threat from the bowling and the crowd do not sense a wicket is about to fall. They're amusing themselves.'

I knew this feeling. I'd seen it on television too.

'This is surely the ideal time to point out the pint pot python to the settled batsman and say "They're not putting you off are they?", then perhaps round on one of your own players with "Was he distracting you?", "I say, the batsman here won't stand for this sort of irritating behaviour." "Silence!" Defend the batsman's rights against something he wasn't even aware of and then speak as if he'd complained to you about it. He should then join in himself to explain that he really didn't try to complain about anything. Where's his focus? So, Mr Batsman, do you feel as comfortable now?'

'I should write this down.'

'You should. I won't repeat it. Distraction is also of immense value. There is no advantage in cricket from feigning an injury as no one can be fouled or sent off. However, it is a useful ploy to draw attention away from a minor change in the field or the setting of a trap. When I limp bravely back to my mark in the middle of an over, who'd think to look around and see if I have the same field settings? It's like moving a chess piece when your opponent turns their back, only – it's allowed. They play the same shot as before and yet now... there's someone there.'

'Brilliant!'

'Cheating?'

'Um, no. It isn't against the laws of the game.'

'Most of it's just a matter of perspective. One man's disadvantage is another's clever trap. Potter suggested making intentional 'mistakes' to gain advantage over an opponent. For instance, what happens if you leave a helmet or an article of clothing on the pitch and the ball accidentally hits it?'

'The batting team are awarded five runs. That's why they always leave the helmet behind the wicket keeper, isn't it?'

'Yes. Bunny, do I have your word of honour that you won't give my little game away?'

'Yes, absolutely.'

'I have a new ploy which I'm saving for the Test matches. The South Africans have a player who's unusually circumspect in playing my bowling. He won't step out of the crease and he won't hit the ball against the direction of spin. His weakness is that he is otherwise very, very greedy for runs. When I come on to bowl, he scores more from the bowler at the other end to restore the run rate. I can no longer allow this to happen, so I've developed a ploy to tempt him and I'll have his wicket yet.'

'Which is?'

'The helmet will not be placed behind the wicket keeper, as expected. The helmet will, carelessly if you will, be left on the floor at short mid-wicket.'

'Yes, but he'll try to hit it. That's five runs every time!'

'Then he'll be hitting against the spin. My close-catchers will know and they will be waiting.'

'Clever. Not against the laws then?'

'No, but after I've used it, they'll legislate and within a year it certainly will be.'

'You've got ploys for batting and bowling, but what about fielding?'

'Have you heard of Colin Bland?'

'No, I don't think so.'

'A famous South African fielder. He had such a good aim that he fully believed he could hit the stumps from anywhere on the pitch. So do I, in fact. The difference being that he was generally right. In one Test the England batsmen could see that he was so far back, they could easily run two, so they trickled the ball towards him and did so. As the bowler ran in next time, Bland moved two steps closer and they did the same. As the bowler ran in the third time, Bland moved four steps closer, the batsmen turned for two as they'd done comfortably before as Bland returned the ball like a thunderbolt and effected the run out.'

'Are there any more?'

'Of course. Here's one predominantly for use in village cricket. Ask the opposition's advice for a fictitious match you have coming up next against a stronger opponent. It will make them feel that the match you're currently in is such a formality it's hardly worth playing out.'

'Do you analyse everyone?'

'Yes. A tool from the field of play has become a habit outside the game. It amuses me to do so.'

'What insights do you have about me?'

'You contrast well with the new Tour Manager because he's a visual thinker. He would enjoy a film if you chopped out most of the dialogue and blew the budget on special effects. If you want to get through to him, you'll have to speak in pictures. Teletubby stuff. You are a words thinker. You'd like a film with three actors locked inside a box, provided the script sparkled. You'd leave the cinema quoting it.'

'How do you know?'

'By listening. You naturally use descriptive word play in your speech patterns and throw in those classical quotations all the time. None of them are things you've read recently, indicating you have become either too busy or too lazy to read.'

'What makes you say that?'

'You misquote more often than not, especially when under pressure. As long as the quotes come out the right way, I know I can push you even further.'

'You can push me? You're wrong, Raffles.'

He carried on as if he hadn't heard.

'You went to a mediocre public school and then failed to live up to family expectations.'

'It was a good public school.'

'There are only four good public schools. The rest produce victims, eccentrics and monsters.'

'Really, Raffles? Which are you?'

He ignored that completely. Eccentric I would have thought, probably. I hoped I was too. The alternatives were altogether too alternative.

'That's why you did what your family expected of you and joined the Army. A final chance to join the ranks of the Establishment?'

'Wrong again.'

He was right, but I wasn't going to give him the satisfaction. I diverted attention to discuss the Tour Manager.

'Jerome says he's been trying to win this match for us, by "sitting up all night in front of the blinking lights of a TVP". What exactly is a TVP, Raffles? Some sort of viewing panel?'

'Why didn't you ask him?'

'I would have done, but he speaks so fast it hardly gives anyone time to jab in a question.'

'Good for him. I would say it's another kind of psychology. He would like people to think he knows so much about his job that no one should dare to challenge him. Therefore, he'll rely on corporate buzz-words to fill up sentences, whole speeches, when in fact he has nothing to contribute. Perhaps you've noticed the way a poet or songwriter can make an awful lot out of a tiny idea or a figure of speech? It's trick of the trade. The use of acronyms is a bluff along the same lines. They might as well mean nothing if no one understands them outside the privacy of the Tour Manager's head. Of course, he'd like you to ask. He'd really like you to concede your lack of knowledge.'

'TVP?'

'Texturised vegetable protein? A soya-based food substitute for meat. Unlike the meat, it has never blinked.'

'So he's up himself?'

'Anyone who employs unidentifiable acronyms to make themselves look superior is more than likely a JID.'

'What's a JID?'

'I was kidding, Bunny.'

I wish he would tell me when he was kidding before he did it. That sort of thing could easily make me look stupid.

Letting me off the hook gracefully, Raffles speculated instead on the rising influence of Tour Manager.

'I wonder how this Jerome person reached his elevated position within the regime. Highly qualified, they said, but I've seen the intelligent, hard-working, type before and he doesn't seem to be one of them.'

I decided to blind him with one of my clever insights.

'Could it be a case of transposed marks?'

'What do you mean?'

'In my college it happened all the time. All marks were compiled by individual lecturers on their computers and then they were supposed to adjust them with penalties for late submission, then type them all into the permanent central database, which resolved them all into alphabetical order. Of course, with hundreds of students to keep track of, the lecturers found it easier to keep their records in alphabetical order and then 'cut and paste' the whole column into the central record.'

'So?'

'The central database had a glitch. It resolved all the surnames into alpha-order alright, but it had a blind spot for initials! If several students had the same surname, with the initials A, K and W for instance, they might appear in any order within their surname group. When the column of marks was pasted across, W could easily graduate with K's marks!'

'Well, that does explain how every member of the Cabinet with a common surname has risen faster than whale spume: Brown, Cook, Smith, Roberts and Williams. I suppose, sometimes in life, being in the right place at the right time and having a random slice of luck blesses your entire destiny' he added philosophically. 'What happened when they discovered the situation at your college?'

'It was too late, I think. The University tried to save face by pretending it hadn't happened. I'm fairly sure G got either P, D or N's marks, probably N (no relation) as he was top flight, otherwise I have no way to explain how 'Thicky' G got that job as under-secretary to Pensions in the Home Office. I really don't think it's going to help resolve the pensions crisis, but G has certainly done well for himself. Of course, that's no consolation at all to poor old Bichlenfasselweisser N.'

'The ICC will send an anti-corruption representative to dog the tour' said Raffles unexpectedly.

'Is that a problem?'

'Perhaps. He's a friend of mine, which means he'll get in close. It wouldn't do to let the guard drop.'

'Can you tell me about him?'

'On the pitch or off? Although, the one is often a guide to the other. Actually, I've not encountered him in his civilian capacity before and it's hard to think of him as anything other than an unduly immovable lump preventing me from getting at the stumps.' A.J. smiled warmly at the reminiscence. 'He doesn't know it and never will, but the ICC asked me to referee his application. I recommended him to appointment with the Anti-Corruption Unit ahead of all other applicants. Wouldn't it be poetic justice if he became the one to turn us in?'

'Would he?' *Turn us in?* What was Raffles planning?

'He's honest. He gives himself out when he's edged behind and walks off the pitch before the decision. If they were all like that, the game wouldn't need umpires. Yes, he'll do his job and I would never ask him not to. Is he an adversary? I don't know. He could be.'

I had a worrying vision of Raffles preparing a list of who he'd prefer to be caught by. Controlling to the last, even unto who got the credit. It was a worrying thought, his enjoyment of risk.

'He was always a heavy man with a heavy bat. In the old days, he paid no attention to field settings whatsoever. Wherever the players chose to stand, he just cracked the bat like a barn door slamming in the wind, the stumps shook, players flinched and the ball soared over all of them. I once saw him lean into the block and he pushed the ball up a tree at long-on. A blocked six, Bunny! No one has ever seen the like. I think we'll have to get on his good side.'

'How do we do that?'

'That's easy. He's a Zimbabwean. We'll take him to the pub.'

Raffles went silent for a moment, as if still thinking about it.

'There is, of course, the issue of liquid capacity. We'll probably have to get him drunk in shifts.'

The atmosphere changed. Sometimes that's a good thing, but this time I wasn't sure. Why were hotel staff hurrying to the breakfast room and all but standing to attention? I looked to Raffles, but he seemed not to have noticed. Then the wave struck. England player after famous England player poured through the doorway and spread out to the tables. The Vice Captain surveyed the room, smiled a smile of painful duty and sought out Raffles.

'Hello A.J. It's good to see you're up and about. Did we forget to mention there's a match today? I don't think you favoured us with your presence at this morning's team meeting, did you? I had to lie again for you, Raffles. I had to tell Jerome you were feeling a little off colour, but not sick enough to be unavailable. It's a very fine line, don't you think?'

'The man's an idiot. You can see it too.'

'At least make the pretence. What's the harm in turning up at meetings? I can't cover for you all the time, can I? What am I going to do for a demon spinner if you're dropped? Just think back to Lewis. Sometimes people don't turn up for net practice and we never see them again. Come on, A.J. Do it for me.'

'Okay. I'll be at the next one.'

'Good man. Thirty minutes for breakfast, don't forget you kit and the coach leaves from the main entrance at ten.'

'I'll be ready.'

●

I hitch-hiked to the ground. I'm not proud of it, but there it is. I didn't know how to get to the place and there simply weren't any taxis. If you had any better solutions, I wish you'd mentioned them at the time.

"The last bloke I gave a lift to wet himself in my car" said the driver, putting a newspaper on the seat as I got in. I felt obliged to sit on it throughout the journey and found conversation uneasy. When I mentioned I had come all the way from England, he made no mention of removing the newspaper.

President's XI matches were the first warm-up games of a new tour. The thought was to give the touring team a good workout and acclimatise them to the local conditions. However, as Raffles told me, they rarely ran them like that. Test teams received no quarter.

'They will do one of two things' said A.J. 'and you won't know which until they announce their team in the morning.'

'What do you mean?'

'It's the opening skirmish of the campaign. On no account do they want to prepare us for the Test Match. Therefore, they will either put out a very weak side which bats first, to give us a swift victory and no chance to practice batting, or, they'll field the strongest side they've got and try to beat us hollow to crack our morale for the First Test.'

As soon as Raffles saw that it was the former, he visibly lost interest in the game. I expect he thought the quicker bowlers would blow them away before the spinners got a go. As it turned out, he bowled one over and took one wicket with an off-break that jagged back sharply and displaced the stumps of an amateurish defence. England were left with 129 to win and the writing found itself firmly daubed to the wall.

The England Captain, bless him, decided he'd use the opportunity to give his middle-order batsmen some practice chasing down a target, so he opened the innings with a man who usually settled at number five. His name was Garrett. Meheux was up the non-striker's end at six and that meant Raffles would come in at the first wicket down, as he usually played at seven.

The fielding tactics were strange. They brought the field in and gave nothing at all to Meheux, but then relaxed the grip and seemed to bowl loosely at Garrett. It almost seemed as if they wanted him to score freely. Why did they have such a heavy leg-side field if they kept bowling on the off? What was the point of the long-hops and full tosses? It didn't make any sense, unless they wanted to get the match over quickly, as Raffles had predicted. If so, why weren't they giving any freebies to Meheux?

Garrett had thirty to his name before Meheux scored. Garrett went to fifty when Meheux was still in single figures. The second string bowlers seemed to be under instructions to bowl consistently wide of Meheux's off-stump. One, two, three, four – all out of reach. This tactic was never going to get him out. Then, just as I was getting bored with it, Meheux got restless, lashed loosely at a distant offering and only succeeded in edging it to the fielder at point. "Atherton did the same at Barbados" chirped a spectator. Raffles was in.

There was plenty of time left to get the remaining runs, but even so, Raffles appeared in no hurry. Much to the consternation of the slip fielders, he ignored the first four balls and let them fling through harmlessly to the keeper. One of the President's XI players decided to barrack him.

'Get on with it Raffles. This isn't a Test Match, you know.'

'I can see that. You're here.'

The close fielders fell about laughing at the expense of their own player.

Raffles' innings after that was worthy of little attention. He scored fourteen hard-fought runs in a partnership of forty or so and then Garrett called for a single which wasn't there and ran him out. The funny thing was, the obvious end to throw the ball to had been Garrett's, but they threw it to Raffles' end anyway. I made a mental note to ask him about that later.

Fordyce came in next – a bowling all rounder. He hit the shot of the match and between them, they wrapped up the game with twenty one overs to spare, leaving Garrett not out in the nineties. The crowd went home early, feeling mildly short-changed by the one-sidedness of the spectacle. Simon Quince, England's opening batsman, launched his bat at a chair in frustration. It splintered across the edge and Quince discarded it, broken. I wasn't allowed to cross the little fence separating the crowd from the players, but I watched as Raffles collected it and went in to say a polite farewell to the scorers.

Raffles emerged a few minutes later with bat-protecting tape, a marker pen and a small pocket knife, with which he split open and hollowed out a cavity in the bat, then taped it closed. 'A.J. Raffles' he wrote across the face of the implement and threw it into one of the trunks of England team equipment.

I caught up with Raffles as he threw his coffin bag into a locker beneath the team coach.

'Raffles, Raffles!'

'No, don't tell me. Just let me guess' he said, holding up a finger. 'You're so excited that you just can't hide it. In fact, I'd go so far as to speculate, you're about to lose control and you think you like it.'

'Stop being facetious.'

'Well? What can I do for you?'

'They weren't trying to get him out!'

'You noticed that, did you?'

'I couldn't help noticing, but why?'

'It's called 'The Somerset Method'. When Australia played a warm-up match against Somerset some years ago, they came up against a player called Laidwell. They could see a weakness in Laidwell's technique, one so fatal that the Australians knew they could get him out cheaply anytime they wanted. So, they selected him for England.'

'They did what?'

'They allowed him to pulverise their bowling and score a couple of hundred easy runs, to ensure he got noticed by the England selectors, who duly included him for the first three Tests of the Ashes series and then they accounted for him quickly in every knock.'

'The cheeky sods!'

'The South Africans were under instructions to allow Garrett to score heavily, precisely and surely because they know how to get him out quickly. They've identified the weakness, but won't use it. They'll deploy that in the Test, where it helps them most. Of course, it's no use if he isn't selected.'

'Do the England selectors know this?'

'They weren't here, were they? They'll just see the score in the book and pick the man in form. That man's a walking wicket. The British press will demand he plays. The managers will consult their little statistical projections on their skinny laptop computers and the numbers will demand he plays. Their will be voices, Bunny. Powerful calls from powerful names insisting the walking wicket takes the field in the opening match, but he can't. He can't be allowed to play.'

'You put the diamonds in that bat, didn't you? I can't believe you brought them here!'

'Of course I had to bring them. I even batted with them. You can forget about those beauties now. They'll go all the way back to the Albany without any bother from customs.'

With that, Raffles boarded the coach and we travelled back separately.

Cricket is life, they say. All the risks, the bravery and shame, the delusions of failure and glory. In playing the great game, you submit to the randomness and chaos, praying your timing and reactions might give you enough advantage to change the flow of the game. For cricket works in flows, in tides, and when they run against you, it takes strength of mind or you're battered down. Sometimes, as in life, playful chaos lets the worst man win and the talented fail. Life itself isn't fair when the criminal enjoys more than the honest man. Life isn't trying to be unfair. It is just a feature of random possibilities, of chaos. In a game which opens itself up to as many possibilities as there are, I no longer see fair and unfair. I see random neutrality. Raffles wouldn't say that of course. Raffles would say I'm talking bollocks. Cricket is life.

I found Raffles that evening sitting on a sofa in the hotel corridor. He'd borrowed Jerome's computer from under his seat on the team coach and appeared deep in thought, or maybe just trying to work out how to move the mouse.

'What are you doing? I thought you'd slunk up here to break in!'

'I don't need to. They've each got a laptop on a wireless network.'

'Each?'

'The Coach, Captain and Team Manager.'

'What?' I flummoxed. 'What are you doing?'

'The ECB computer infrastructure is like… Imagine the scenario of building a house room by room. You can wander around the house at will, but sometimes you open a door and there's an empty space behind it. There isn't really an empty space, but viewers with the wrong level of access can't see anything in there because that room isn't compatible with their log-in. Understand?'

'No.'

'Good. Now you know how the players feel.'

'Sorry?'

'Didn't I explain? If I can access one machine in a signatory group, it should update all the others. Common databases. Here we go. Local area network active. Input email address. All ECB email addresses are in the same corporate format: Surname followed by first initial. I know. I've received enough of their ultimatums over the years. D-E-Z-E-M-A-N-T-A-L-J. Next, the password.'

'Hang on a minute. Why aren't you using your own log-in? How can you possibly know his password?'

Raffles stopped what he was doing. He did it purposefully, in much the same way as an engineer designing something vital to the future of millions might fold up their plans, count to ten, then go and help his child look for a missing crayon.

'OK. I'll explain. I've no need to rush this, anyway. When they announced the players who would be coming on this tour, we were each issued a password to the ECB network.'

'So what's your password?'

'Lucrezia.'

'You're actually telling me your password?'

'It was originally 'Marconi', but Willets asked me if I wouldn't mind swapping because there's no chance he'd ever be able to remember how to spell Lucrezia. I can't think of a single circumstance where the knowledge might be any use to you, so take it with my blessing.'

'So, you've got access anyway. What's the problem?'

'I need higher level access to do what I am proposing to do. I need access at team selector level.'

'How do you intend to get that?'

'Think about it Bunny. I asked myself what have Marconi and Lucrezia Borgia got in common? That's when I realised that the player's group of passwords might all be 'famous Italians'. I spent a highly instructive evening tapping in the England players' names and trying to match people to passwords. I think I did quite well.'

'Very well, by the sound of it.'

'There's more. I then opened the ECB site's telephone and contacts directory.'

'Clever.'

'No, that's easy. Anyone can do that.'

'Sorry, carry on.'

'I printed out the names of the clerical and administration staff. There are lots of them, so I assumed it must be a large password group. After a dozen attempts, I discovered that the clerical password group are all famous French men and women. They're all there: Cardinal Richlieu, Brigitte Bardot, Napoleon, Jean Claude Quillici.'

I heard a door open further down the corridor, so looked back to see if it was anyone we knew. Not this time. I turned back and nodded, encouraging Raffles to continue.

'Then I had a cynical thought. They'd never be able to use 'famous Belgians' as an ECB password group as there are only a maximum three and one of those is fictional!'

'Of course.'

'When I was shaving this morning, I made a cognitive leap.'

'Good Lord! Is that safe?'

'For those of us who've done it before, yes. I thought they wouldn't be able to use up the password group of three, so they'd hold it in reserve until a signatory group of three came along.'

'Ah-ha.'

'Aren't you going to say 'Clever'?'

'Um, yes, most clever. What?'

Raffles re-opened the lid of the laptop.

'Well, the management on this tour, also comprising the team selection panel, are a group of three. There are unlikely to be any other groups in the ECB as small as three, therefore any password list by nation with only three available options would most likely be assigned to them at this opportunity. Otherwise, of course, they'd never use it up. Ergo, I'm betting on 'famous Belgians'. It's a safe bet that if I type in Poirot, Eddy Merckx or Van Damme, pairing the right official to the right password, within three goes I should be in. Now, let's test the theory. H-E-R-C-U-L-E-P-O-I-R-O-T click enter... and there we are. First time. Predictable as the dawn.'

'That's great, but why?'

'De Zemantal walked off with my gold pen. I've got half a mind to offer him the lid to go with it.'

'Seriously?'

'No. It's all about Garrett. The man's a walking wicket and South Africa sense it. If he's selected for the First Test, we'll have to carry him. He's in the squad, which I can't do anything about, but I absolutely can't allow them to select him for the team.'

'Can't allow? You keep saying that.'

'You do ask a lot of questions, don't you Bunny? I'm adjusting the batsman's average downwards on the database to make it appear as if he's easy game on a bouncy wicket. They'll input pitch and weather conditions into the computer model and it will throw up a list of names based on these statistics. Influential things, statistics. You can prove anything you need with them. Rounding all fractions downward instead of up, round down the cumulative values... Now, when I hit 'save', like so' he depressed a button and, at another level, my faltering trust in the world 'it updates all other management and coaching laptops in the sub-group automatically over the wireless net.'

'Hang on. You've just picked England's team for the First Test? That's despicable.'

'Quite. You do want England to win, don't you? Anyway, I've only changed the career of one player.'

'Do you honestly think the team management rely on computers to pick the starting XI?'

'I don't know, but I suspect. If not, why did they drop the spinners for that fiasco at Adelaide? The Captain probably uses his instinct, but the other two outvote him, even on the best spinning wicket in Australia.. We'll wait and see, shall we? Do you by any chance have a small magnet with you?'

'No. Should I have?'

'Pity.'

As a matter of sporting record, Garrett did not make the starting XI of the First Test against South Africa. I secretly hoped I'd never, ever, have to meet him. Conversation would be impossible.

'Raffles?'

'Yes?' said A.J., setting the mouse speed to slow, then powering down and folding up the computer.

'I don't mean to labour the point, but I've just been thinking. The Chairman of the ECB must be a signatory group of one, so...'

'Bjork.'

'Oh.'

125

Chapter 9

Our Man in the Bush

'Ring-ring-ring-ring' I hauled my head off the pillow. There are special winches that do this to logs.

'Whu?'

'Bunny? Raffles.'

'Whut?'

'Bunny, it's 8am and you are in a definitively pleasant hotel in South Africa. I am at the reception desk of the same hotel and would like you to come down here now.'

'Is it a fire drill?'

'No, would you like one? There is a letter.'

'A letter about a fire drill?'

He hung up. He does that. It's really annoying. The thing that really gets to me is when I'm left with the impression that he's to busy to waste time speaking to me, when *he* made the telephone call. Now I'm supposed to rush down and beg him to reveal the mystery of the letter he's so worked up about. Only, now he's distributed all his worked-upness onto me, he can therefore appear very relaxed about it himself. I sometimes wonder whether all this bilge isn't finely calculated.

I washed, changed, brushed a few teeth and went out. I went back in again, just before the door snapped shut, and gathered up my collection of keys, coins and cards. Still groggy then. I suddenly had the vision of my playing the fool to Raffles' Lear. You know the form. Running around his ankles, with a sort of bathing hat with bells on. How utterly, utterly excruciating. I'd better not say that sort of thing out loud. It might get into print and, boy, then I'd look stupid. Alright then. One image to be dispelled. No wind here? Check. Any cheeks cracking? Nope. Do I see any cataracts about the place? None in evidence, although it struck me that it would be pretty difficult to see anything much with cataracts. Okay then, what about hurricaneos roar? Not a sausage. Did someone mention sausages? I flopped down the stairs in the approximate direction of breakfast.

'What do you mean we don't have time for breakfast?'

'Just that. I'd like to get going.'

'How about a bacon toastie?'

'We have an appointment.'

'A cup of tea then.'

'Don't you want to hear about this appointment?'

'I'd understand it much better if I had a cup of tea in front of me.'

We had tea. It was the first small victory in my rise through the theatrical company of Raffles' control. I wouldn't like to be Othello though, I'm not the jealous sort. Antonio? No, too Calvinist. Toby Belch? No, I have an uncle like that. More than one in the family and it would look like a case of the Fergies.

'Right. You've got your tea. Satisfied? Don't need the chamber-maid to draw you a bath? Good.'

He banged the tray in front of me and I returned to Earth like Puck in a sandstorm. Raffles extracted something, a small card in a torn manila envelope.

'I thought you said it was a letter?'

'Do you seriously think I could have dragged you out of bed at eight in the morning for a small card?'

'Um, no, sorry.'

I'd done it again! I'd apologised to him. In my hind-brain distant bells jangled. The card transcended the table.

'Tickets for a bush safari?'

'Yes. Left at the hotel desk in my name. Turn it over.'

Intrigued, I flipped and read the tantalising inscription 'We hope you can come.' I'd always wanted to go on a safari. Cool! A freebie! Sir Toby it was then. The tea was horrible, so off we set.

'This is going to be pivotal, Bunny. Absolutely pivotal' said Raffles as the coach pulled up five minutes later. Ah, so that explained the rush. Would he have gone without me? Yes, I realised. I could only assume I wouldn't be doing a lot of actual pivoting personally, but Raffles seemed pretty keen to give it a go. I tagged along. After all, that's what I do best. We spent forty minutes collecting tourists from other hotels around the city, which dampened the thrill somewhat.

As the coach took us away from the last hotel and out, I stared through the window and soaked in the living sights and sounds of the city. The smart, impenetrable homes in the streets of the centre-dwellers soon gave way to leafy middle-class suburbs, their roads festooned with red and yellow trumpets. No, they were flowers. How strange to see them in the city. Then, inevitably, we passed the further settlements, depressing shanties of the poor. These places seemed quieter than the central zones. Perhaps they'd all commuted inwards to do a day's work? Then their frothing tide of humanity would return, as it always did, before nightfall. Only in the night did the wealthy have their comfort and segregation.

Then, the freeways and shanties and trumpets and all were gone. Fell away, blown away behind us by the wind of our passage. Hurricaneos roar. This, at last, was the country! I looked for wild animals, but saw only a dog. Pity. Safaris have come down a peg or two, haven't they? It was after a couple of hours on the coach that I began to tune in to the vast scale of this country. Why had I thought the safari would be just outside the town? This was typical of my modern 'convenience' mentality; until now, I'd thought Marwell was a long way out in the sticks. The coach trundled on. I saw impala. Yea! A real wild animal. I wasn't overly excited though. They have those at Marwell too.

Something tapped on my shoulder. I'd quite forgotten about Raffles sitting quietly behind me. He must have had a great view of my neck. I wondered if the fluff needed shaving. Of course, that's not the sort of thing a bloke can ask another bloke. I'd probably have to resolve the issue, I decided, with a triangulation of mirrors. He tapped again.

'Hi, yes, what is it?'

'There. A big cat.'

I looked. A few of the other passengers had seen it to, snuggled down in the grass and watching the impala. It didn't seem in any hurry. Was it a cheetah? I'm no expert. Well, I don't have to be, do I? I'm not an impala. Did that mean the safari had already started?

'Bunny' said Raffles, moving up one place to take the vacant seat next to me, 'Do you know why predators are fast?'

'To catch stuff?' I wondered whether the questions were always going to be this easy.

'Yes, it's a kind of arms race. If they aren't faster than their prey, they vanish. Genetically.'

'Seems obvious.'

'Do you know why the prey are fast? They have to out-pace the predators or they won't survive.'

'So?'

'So, natural selection ensures that only the faster and progressively faster genes continue to survive. That's a waste of resources, in terms of biological efficiency. Genes need to replicate to persist. All this resourcing of athleticism reduces the capacity, the efficiency, to make babies.'

'Is there an option?'

'Applying the level of intelligence enjoyed by our species, yes. We would sign a treaty. Don't run after us. We won't run away from you. When we need food, we can fill our boots, without having to look up for danger all the time. When you need food, we'll draw lots and sacrifice one of our number. Tough on them, but the rest of us will get fat, old and increase our numbers. Okay?'

'Deal. Yes. Good idea.'

'Would it work?'

'Yes.'

'No. Natural selection, you see. One day, someone would draw the sacrifice marker and they'd say 'stuff that' and run away. They'd cheat. The others would be too fat and slow to catch up with them. The system of society will always fail the majority of those who obey it, who behave by the rules, and then natural selection will favour the genes of those who cheat. They will *become* the surviving strain.'

'I see. So?'

'I believe that's where society is now.'

I mulled it over for a mile. Huh, I concluded, try telling that one to the Inland Revenue.

Not long afterwards, we arrived at a sort of game lodge affair. Very Hemmingway. Old photographs on the walls, colourful paintings of elephants and a veranda with a beautiful panoramic view of a muddy water-hole. When I say 'water-hole', that doesn't complete the image. If it were in England, it would be called a lake. Actually, it was lucky not to be in England. It would be drained, the animals poisoned and the whole site property-developed before the leaves changed colour. Reality aside, this was Africa after all, it veered more into the lakeish category than what you might call a hole. Oh look, there was a framed picture of Hemmingway. What a surprise. My attention was being attracted. Thank you. I'll have a gin.

We had a light lunch, which included thin slices of the local wildlife, aimed at the connoisseur. Well, I suppose someone had aimed at the local wildlife, but the gist and/or nub is that they intended to add it to our experience of safari life in Africa. The sights, the sounds, the smells, the tastes and the tourists. Perhaps they could shuffle those behind some sort of screen? I realised I might be one of them. Raffles wasn't. He looked like the owner. I think a couple of the tourists asked him for directions. *Typical.*

After that, and one complimentary drink per ticket, Raffles got two on account of being a cricketer, we slotted into a fleet of land rovers and chugged off into the veldt. I saw a lot of scrub. I saw a lot of interesting creatures, more birds than I'd expected and a lot of herding animals. No lions or elephants though. I was quite disappointed about that. Giraffes! I forgot to say we saw giraffes, even a little one. I wondered how it reached enough leaves to grow tall enough to reach the leaves? Perhaps somebody will explain that to me some day. At this particular moment though, discussion was not forthcoming. I was sitting next to someone from Frankfurt who was no fun at all, in a constipated sort of way.

Three hours had passed before I finally saw a zebra. A day, little different from any other in a zebra's diary, but to me... wow! Amazing things, in the wild. Who needs unicorns when you've got zebra? I wish I could take one home. Deborah the zebra, I'd call it. We go for walks in Hyde Park. Maybe sophisticated parties. Lucky I wasn't sitting next to Raffles. It's daydreamy moments like this when he usually interrupts me. Oh, we're turning back. Bye-bye veldt. Bye-bye Deborah. It might have been, but really, try to forget. It never would have worked between us. Keep your mane up.

Once I'd been extracted from the vehicle, I'd been sitting down a long time, I wandered back into the lodge and noticed a kiosk. 'I'll have these postcards please' I asked, fidgeting around for money. Okay, good stuff, because I hadn't brought a camera.

Raffles had already secured a table overlooking the waterhole and appeared to be enjoying the sunset with drinks and one of the other tourists whom I hadn't noticed before. Perhaps this one had come along later? I expect he probably had to go to a theatrical casting for Khrushchev look-alikes first. Oh, how stupid, he'd be the match-fixer, wouldn't he? I crossed the room and barged into the delicate negotiations like a buffalo who isn't about to let a few technical flamingos get between him and the good stuff.

'Hello Bunny. What did you think of all the lions and elephants?'

'Oh. I didn't see any. Were you with the other group?'

'Yes. We went into the sun and your lot ventured away from it. It's all pot luck though, really.'

'Yes, isn't it? We saw a baby giraffe.'

'Really? I'm surprised you didn't ask to take it home!'

'Don't be silly. What would I do with a giraffe? Walkies in Hyde Park or something!'

We all laughed. Was I really so predictable?

The introductions were brief and incomplete. This was a business meeting after all.

'Call me Ivor.'

He knew who we were, but I wasn't going to bother asking his full name. He'd only have told me it was Uncle Ivor Bulgaria or some equally devious tripe. Short and devious then. I don't know why I thought of Uncle Bulgaria at that point. Subconscious whirrings, probably. I needn't have worried. He certainly had a lot more fluff on his neck than I could ever have accumulated, even given a year's preparation for a major competition. I must say it did put me in mind of a missing link between Man and Womble. Okay, I'm not being anti-Womble as such, but if you can't take a swipe at old fashioned bounders like that, what have you got left?

I listened to the match-fixer set out his stall. Some of it was really interesting, enough so to make any cricket historian sit up and blink. That wouldn't change anything of course. When cricket historians do sit up and blink, it's usually the sign for some kind nurse to bring their cocoa.

'Then there was the last match of the India tour' he told us. 'England's reserve wicket keeper returned home for family reasons, so only the first choice keeper was available, without back-up. That isn't ideal, but would normally be fine. Our clients rather hoped that India would win, so asked us if we were likely to surprise them, in the next two weeks, with news of a tragic food-poisoning incident affecting this player. India would win, although obviously they would be grieved to make money in that manner, but everyone would take it on the chin and accept that the game must go on.'

'Obviously. Decorum est.' agreed Raffles.

'We advised them that, sadly, that sort of thing was always a possibility in the sub-continent and hoped they would be able to take steps to cover their position in the event of such an inconvenience taking place.'

I though A.J. was taking this rather well. After all, he must have been playing in the affected team.

Bulgaria, or whatever he was called, continued his explanation to me 'The player concerned was famous for a certain food-faddishness, which minimised the chances of becoming ill on tour. The England wicket keeper...'

'It was Rickley' supplemented Raffles.

'... firmly believed that performance at the highest level could only be maintained by surviving on a diet of tinned beans, hob-nob biscuits, bananas, raw jelly and boiled water. He took all of his food supplies on tour with him, which brought smiles to team-mates' faces and tears to hotel porters' eyes. Of course, he got food-poisoning on the first evening of the final Test. That sort of thing was always a possibility on the sub-continent.'

'Ordinary bad luck, we thought. For once in his career, the fool must have eaten something at the ground and not remembered it' remarked A.J.

'Yes' agreed the devil's womble 'The alternative theory is most unlikely: that someone bribed a member of the hotel cleaning staff to remove one packet of raw jelly and a half-eaten banana from his room, took both of them to a university teaching laboratory, fed the oral bacteria from saliva on the banana into a dish containing a colourless, tasteless, jelly derived from sea-weed, supervised the cells at ambient temperature as they doubled their numbers every ten minutes, tested the culture growing on the substrate for endotoxin and exotoxin saturation to ensure it had reached a poisonous level, dissolved the stolen fruit jelly and combined it with the tasteless seaweed jelly, reformed it into a mould, placed it back in the jelly packet and heat-sealed the wrapper, had it returned via the cleaning staff to the bedside of the cricketer, who returned home after the first day's play and ate it. Of course, there were no facts at all to support a ridiculous hypothesis like that.'

'Your clients must have won a lot of money' said Raffles, holding his temper well.

'They almost didn't!' He again addressed me, 'Not when your friend here plugged away and went through the middle order! It was a great victory for India. A memorably close occasion.'

'The capacity to entertain' drawled Raffles, his emotions once more under iron control.

'Our clients have been very generous to us over the years. This, I think, is the most reassuring feedback for the service we provide. Whenever we think a million-to-one event just might crop up, we try to warn our friends so they can enjoy their sporting occasions without suffering undue stress. I see our role as helping to remove the worry that comes from betting on a sport and not knowing what's going to happen. We like to think our clients are left feeling 'comfortable'. I am sure this is currently the case, to the extent that they've formed a sort of friendship club, a syndicate if you will, to enjoy following their sporting events together.'

'This syndicate then. Do they welcome approaches from the players?' Raffles was trying to push things along. When were we meant to be on the coach? Get on with it man.

Clumsy as ever, I barged in. 'How long will this take?'

The match-fixer had had quite enough of me.

'I'm sorry; I'd forgotten you were here. You can go now if you like.'

I sat back and shut up.

'It is my fond wish to extend my organisation's service to some of the more discreet players themselves. Perhaps those nearing retirement, who might welcome a little more support for those long years after they've stopped playing the game. Did you know that the average fast bowler finds their contract will not be renewed beyond the age of twenty-eight? If they pick up an injury, it's sure to be sooner. Spinners, like your good self, can go on for a few more years than that if they stay in form. Perhaps even into their thirties. Mr Raffles, I don't mean to give offence, but I notice from your entry in Wisden that you'd be nearing thirty-six now, wouldn't you? That really is a tremendous effort on your part and I applaud you for it.'

'Thank you. On some occasions I never thought I'd live to see thirty six.'

'Oh, Mr Raffles, you'll be a ripe old age! You just need to take the sensible path, that's all. I could tell you some amazing things about the wear and tear on first-class bowlers' knees, not to mention the spine and the lower back. Do you know the cost of even the most straightforward operations? The subject fascinates me. Are you aware that, by the age of seventy, most international fast bowlers can only get about in a wheel-chair? Of course, you'll already be aware that medical insurance premiums for cricketers are second only to those of heavyweight boxers. I mean, for heaven's sake, you fellows can be killed outright in a fraction of a second! The risks players take nowadays, with very little reward other than the knowledge they've served their country.'

'Noblesse Oblige' acknowledged Raffles. I really do wish he'd stop speaking in Latin all the time.

'It's saddening to relate, when the players retire from the game, they seldom have training or professional careers to fall back on and the going can become a little rough. I'm sure you'd be as upset as I if I were to tell you what's become of the great names now, after their wages stopped rolling in. What happens if all the commentator jobs are taken? How can one maintain the lifestyle? Women are such fickle creatures. When the funds run out, what does one say if their marriage should... weaken?'

What a complete shent this man was. I so hoped to see the day when we'd give him a hiding.

'Now Mr Raffles, you must realise, we're all part of this great game together. We are brothers and as such we should look after each other's interests. Just consider, hypothetically, how many times could you fail with the bat or ball and expect to retain your Test place? You're a great player, so reputation counts for something. The British newspapers, I'm sure, would help. As they do... sometimes. Still though, on how many occasions could you be dismissed cheaply before feeling your position in the team had become... vulnerable. Five? Six, or seven perhaps? My colleagues and I all are keen followers of the game and we enjoy encouraging our great players, as any loyal fan should. Of course, we have a little more funding available than ordinary followers, so we can show our appreciation in so many... so many *practical* ways.'

'Practical ways?'

'Are you afraid of failure, Mr Raffles? Failure at international level? Wouldn't it be reassuring if you had a kind of insurance policy on hand for such an eventuality? One where you never have to pay a premium? For example, in the upcoming Test, if you were to get out for less than, say, ten runs, you could be safe in the knowledge that £30,000 would be transferred to the account of your choice as a gesture of compensation from loyal brothers who share in your misery. Of course, to the man who bowls 'the most puzzling ball in England', wouldn't it be a disaster if you weren't to take a wicket on the fourth and fifth days? What if your bowling conceded more than seven runs an over? I think you'd need some compensation to get over the trauma. Shall we say £3,000 an over? Surely it would help England immensely if you were to recover from the obvious depression quickly. Consider it... for England.'

I finished my glass. Oh, it wasn't a toast.

Raffles cross-examined: 'If the 'insurance claims' came to light, it might look a little inappropriate to the uninformed observer. Perhaps even the ICC might view non-declaration of the income as being unusually casual. Forgive me, since I'm new to these things, but what should a player say if the matter came up?'

'Well, the first thing is not to say anything to anyone until you've spoken to us. Do you remember Dajvot Singool, the hero of the All-Asia Championship? There were rumours he'd been talking to the ICC anti-corruption unit. I can't imagine what about. Wasn't he on the winning side after all? Then he had some kind of domestic accident. I think he was charged with killing his wife. Awful business. I don't think he ever played again. The strange thing is, these unpleasant incidents always seem to happen to people who talk. It's almost as if they attract bad luck. Really, I've seen it time and time again. When I hear they've been talking, the hairs stand up on the back of my neck and it's almost as if I know what is going to happen next. It is a very sad thing.'

If this job fell through, he could always find work as a clairvoyant. The star of staged screens, or something.

'So, you think it was a matter of poor judgement?'

'Oh yes, most accidents happen in the home. You're never completely safe. Let's say, if you want to avoid million-to-one risks, that's our business. Always call us first and we'll manage the situation.'

'I'd just like to be sure, in terms of your coaching of media skills, how should a player, if they were to accept your generous assistance, be equipped to explain it?'

'Come, come! You're thinking of the worst eventuality! It is just this sort of negative play that earns your team so many draws. Oh, alright then. There are various ways. A couple of the Australian boys were had-up in the 1990s. They were accused of taking bribes, of all things! That's Australia for you. They just come straight out with such insults. Well, they were most offended, but then took some good advice and admitted that an Indian bookmaker had indeed been paying them sums of money for 'a weather report'.'

'All very crude that' said Raffles. 'It sounded a bit spur of the moment to me.'

It seems the bookmaker could easily have got the weather report from the nearest television, but the people he represented much preferred to hear about it from the players themselves. It's a confidence thing. For the sort of people who'll only buy their breakfast cereal if a famous player tells them it's good. Explanation accepted, players cleared, life moved on.

'You could say we're hiring you to play in a benefit match and you haven't got around to declaring it to the tax man yet. I'm sure we could set one up if it came to it.'

'I'd like that, come to think of it. Do you know my county's never given me a benefit season?'

'Yes, I'm aware of that. They awarded a benefit season to Wren Cooper the previous year. Loyal to the club, I'm sure, but hardly the greatest player of the era. Then, they say, a private accountant embezzled all his money and, even though it was gone, Cooper was still asked to pay tax on it. Very nasty.'

'Correct, as far as it goes.' Raffles added. 'The accountant had to replace losses he'd made to another client's funds, an account he'd personally underwritten, and thought "Hello! I've got another client account here, choc-full of money, so I'll just switch it across to fill the hole." Wren lost the lot.'

'I heard the accountant committed suicide and they couldn't recover anything from the estate.'

'Not exactly true' said Raffles. 'They could, but I believe there were children involved. So, as you've guessed, Middlesex have awarded him *another* benefit year out of sympathy. In fact, Middlesex have awarded him *my* benefit year.'

'That's rough' smiled the match-fixers' agent. Somewhat duplicitous, that. He said it with all the sympathy of a hitchhiking leech.

'I've always led the club to believe that I had enough private money, and I love my cricket so much, that being paid to pitch up and perform was an insignificant detail. In hindsight, leaving that impression may have been a misjudgement. Yes, I'd like a benefit match. One with some serious opposition. Could you arrange it?'

'Why not? We'll sell it to the television networks. Glad to have you on board, Raffles. Here's my mobile number and an email you can leave messages on. I don't have a card as such. I'm saving trees. Well then, that's quite a thing. A benefit match. You are a surprise, Mr Raffles. Here's to a comfortable retirement!'

Understanding full well the reason for this morally-bankrupt exchange, but feeling disgusted by it anyway, I walked out leaving A.J. at the table and the amazing clairvoyant bookmaker to settle our bill at the bar. After all, he was going to make enough out of us. I needed fresh air. Possibly a shower too, I thought, to wash off the stink of corruption.

As the first outside, I saw a strange scene. The owner's dog (I presumed it belonged to the proprietor), a full grown Rhodesian Ridgeback, Zimbabwe now, or 'lion dog' as they called them here, had reached the end of its chain in a fit of exuberant frustration. Why? I'll tell you why. A nocturnal bush-baby, one of the most widespread mammals in Africa, had been cornered. I could easily see it clinging on, in broad daylight, to a lower branch in the sparsely boughed canopy of an old tree shading the doorway. It looked exhausted and injured. If it dropped, the dog would surely have it.

Oh hell. As if I hadn't got enough to worry about. I climbed. Slowly at first, then with increasing confidence. The spiny bits on these African trees seemed to grow fairly high, up by the leaf canopy. Presumably that was all part of the plan to make the edible sections out of reach and unattractive. I climbed.

I edged out across the bare and twisted branch, gripping with my right arm and reaching out with my left for the surprised bush-baby. It could see what I was doing, but moved outward too. This wasn't going to be easy. The dog snarled beneath us. I snarled back, which didn't work at all. This dog had clearly never backed down in a snarl-off. Pushing my body as far as it could safely go, I hung in the air ever closer to the tin roof of the lodge. The bush-baby saw it too and, moving a little faster than I, flopped lightly down and scampered away to safety amongst the overhanging fronds of denser vegetation. Oh great. It could have done that without me, couldn't it? What was I supposed to do stuck up this tree?

Beneath, a door opened. I had a ringside view of the top of some-one's head. They drew out and tapped at a mobile phone. Could they really get coverage out here? Perhaps it was a national priority or something, for safety. I kept quiet, for once, trying as always to avoid the embarrassment of *explaining*.

'Hey! It's Bryce from *Sporting Outcomes*. Is Sugarman there? Put him on then.'

You've realised who it was by now. Well, so had I. I'm not completely thick you know.

'P.J.? Yes, fine. Yes, not a problem. I've hooked the mark, but there are a few complications. No, I've got to think about the set-up first. It's going to be a big one, but he wants it bespoke. No, bespoke. He wants us to arrange the match he plays in. Why can't we? No, I don't see why not. This is A.J. Raffles, we're talking about! Yes, *the gentleman* cricketer. You can't put anything further beyond suspicion than that, can you?'

Raffles was right. People seldom look up.

'Right. Then we've got an exchange. I'll come in and we'll brief the members. You'd better give Gus my thanks for the lead too. Right. Bye.'

So it was Hedges! Raffles thought they were connected to Khalife. Excellent, I actually knew something he didn't. I watched as he threw a stick at the dog, clambered into his car and accelerated away through the flyblown dust of Africa.

My thoughts turned to getting down. Hardly a funky thing, I tried pushing myself along the branch backwards, which worked to some extent, but probably wasn't the most efficient method listed in *The Boy's Book of Treemanship*. That's something I've just made up, in case you were wondering, but it would have been handy at that particular moment. Thoughts ran through my mind, some of them involved words like 'headlong' and 'multiple'. Nothing 'multiple' could ever be good. No, don't write in. Plummet; now there's a lovely word on the lips, usually followed by a nasty crunching sound on the path. I backed into the broken end of a side branch which entirely spiked my trousers. 'Ouch' I exclaimed and meant it.

'Has the nasty horrid dog chased you up a tree, Bunny?' asked Raffles, walking out and patting it. 'Never mind, we'll soon have you down.'

There were times when I hated him. I fell off the branch, just to show how easy it was. Landing wasn't easy at all, but these things have to be done. At least I'd entertained somebody.

'What did you think?' asked Raffles as we walked/limped away.

'He looked suspiciously normal. Although, he did walk with a scrape, which certainly indicates something.'

'That's it? It's a big day for limpers, isn't it? So, you noticed he's a bit of a scrapey walker?'

'Pretty much.'

'Where would you say his accent was centred?'

'I don't know. It sounded sort of international.'

'South Africa, although his shoes were Dutch and he pronounced his Rs like a French-Swiss or Belgian. Intriguing, isn't it?'

I agreed that it was intriguing and wondered what else he'd noticed that I hadn't. Probably nothing. Hey, ho. Back to the coach? Oh yes, hold your horses, there was one thing.

'Bryce drove away in a car without number plates.'

'Don't you mean Ivor?' asked Raffles.

'No, his name's Bryce, from *Sporting Outcomes*.'

I'd earned an 'I'm impressed' expression Mark III, which is like a Mark II, but with higher eyebrows.

'No plates means it isn't used on the public road, so it must be kept on one of the private estates. I expect his end of the syndicate might be operating out of one of these huge South African farms. No better place to avoid prying eyes.'

Clever bloke, our Raffles. It's best to ignore it though. It wouldn't do to acknowledge the fact or we'd have to get the national grease pot out to squeeze his head through the door.

'It was Hedges. Gus Hedges.'

'What?'

After all these years, I had finally surprised him. I trod my carpet of smugness all the way to the coach.

On the return journey, I looked out of a smeared plastic window and allowed my thoughts to wander. I thought of how Raffles compartmentalised his life. The people he knew through cricket never got to meet the people he knew through his family, or those he knew in the North-country, or friends in the charities, the mysterious folk who asked him to play amateur cricket at weekend house-parties or those he knew through sailing or The Guild of Engineers or obscure researchers in cobwebbed and forgotten departments of the museum service. These groups lived in strictly defined pigeon-holes in his head, the edges of the boxes never blurring. The contents never mixing or sharing their knowledge of him. If they did, they were cut. It was how Raffles maintained his privacy. How he kept control.

I realised I inhabited a compartment all of my own. A dark and secret box marked 'known through crime'. I lived on the margin of two other boxes, 'known through school' and 'world of cricket', but I knew, I just knew that discussing Raffles with anyone from one of the other boxes would be the end of our friendship. In consequence, the end of me. Raffles would withdraw all assistance and step behind that fortress door of the Albany. Not at home, when I called. Not at home, with rending cries down the streets of the wolves after me.

Okay, so that was an exaggeration.

Chapter 10

Strange Events of the First Test

I woke the following morning and thought for a moment I was back in London, but I wasn't so that was the end of the anecdote. Sleeping late also meant I was too slow to catch up with Raffles before his compulsory attendance at that morning's team meeting. The England squad used to gather for a road run on days when they weren't playing and sleep for an extra couple of hours on days when they were. On reflection, you'd think it would be the other way around. However, all that had changed with the Tour Manager's schedule of TAMs or 'Team Awareness Meetings', in which the team itself seemed to do nothing but provide a star-studded captive audience for the Tour Manager to indulge in the sound of his own voice. I'm sorry to say it, but that's how it seemed to me.

I spotted A.J. briefly in the corridor beyond the conference suite, but he was already looking for a chair and deep in conversation with one of the other players.

'Your eyes look glazed. What's the matter, Lampers?'

'To be honest Raffles, I'm in love.'

'How much?'

'Completely head over heels, I'd say.'

'How do you find it affects your game?'

'My timing's gone. I can't move my feet in the crease.'

'The balance of your mind?'

'Well, getting out doesn't seem to matter as much any more.'

'That's a bad case. You shouldn't be playing.'

'But Raffles...'

'Seriously, just think of your average. Think of your country.'

'Yes, I suppose you're right. I'd better tell the captain I've caught something.'

'You've made the right decision. Tell him it's irritable bowel syndrome. The effects are much the same and no one will want to see the evidence.'

'Thanks A.J.'

'Budge up, budge up' said the Vice-Captain, taking a seat next to Raffles. 'What's young Lamprey doing?'

'Medical problems. He's going to sit this one out.'

'Oh, okay. That's a shame.'

'No it isn't.'

'Isn't it? Alright then, I'll take your word for it.'

From an unseen entrance at the back, something bounded along the room with a black plastic microphone attached to its face.

'Hi Team! Welcome to all the new boys! As I'm sure most of you know from my emails, I'm Jerome, the Tour Manager. I will be facilitating your briefing today.'

Raffles gazed at him with the clouded dead eyes of a deepwater fish as yet unknown to science.

'I've emailed you all a front end process chart with flow diagrams of the way I think the first match should go. Which of you have only got black and white printers?'

Everyone's hand went up.

'It doesn't make sense if it's not in colour.'

Birds sang. Minds wandered.

'Okay, well this is it Team. We've got five matches here guys, but this is the first fixture, so this is the one we're going to look at first.'

'Oh God' said Raffles.

'I've been headhunted from the business side everyone, so it's a bit of hard-headed no nonsense strategic thinking you're going to learn today. I'm not saying learn from me, I'm saying learn *with me* people.'

The cricketers stared at him blankly.

'Remember, people, admitting to your weaknesses is a strength!'

He reclined against the whiteboard and braced himself for the wave of approving nods he'd expected to see from this comment.

No, nothing. Tough audience. This was shaping up to be an even harder sell than his famous *Shake 'n' Vac* campaign.

I must admit, I'd set my mind very much against this Jerome fellow from the start. I know it was unfair to him, but Jerome reminded me so much of a market trader from Essex I played golf with on occasional occasions. They couldn't be occasional enough for me, but I'd made the mistake of giving my phone number.

This individual, I think his name was pronounced 'Mike-E', believed himself to be very clever indeed by applying his little dodges to relieve people of their money. If anyone appeared to be in a hurry to catch a train, he'd slip a foreign coin or two into their change. If any customer asked for directions, he'd deliberately short-change them on the reasonable grounds that they were not from around here and, if upset, wouldn't be a repeat customer anyway. He once boasted of his greatest accomplishment: On a visit to Spain, he'd taken two hundred empty plastic bottles labelled 'Amber Sol' which, on arrival, he filled with cooking oil and sold on the beach as if they were sun-protection lotion. "What have they got to complain about? If they don't go brown wearing that..." he'd said.

Jerome interrupted my train of thought. He had the rare knack, prized amongst salesmen and dictators, of mesmerising his audience to the point where they almost stopped thinking for themselves.

'Look, fellas. I have this pencilled in as an "improvement session", so that's what we're positioned to do.'

Had he really just mimed inverted commas with his fingers?

'Do you know what a Guru is? Well, look upon me as your Strategic Performance Guru. Guru Jerome, okay? That makes you guys *The Beatles*! If you aren't quite with the band, if you don't want to leave Liverpool or have any issues around your commitment to the "I am a player" concept, bring them straight to me and we'll solve them or send out for a new drummer. Yes?'

The possibility seemed remote. It had also seemed remote on the multi-million pound *Consignia* rebranding project, but his ideas had won through in the end. He had earned a lot of money with that one, then moved on. Jerome's microphone whistled, so he hurriedly spoke over it.

'Look, Guys! This isn't some village cricket match with one old man and his dog watching! This is the big time! Razzmatazz! Let's hit 'em with lights! Action! The best show in town!'

That took me back. Right back to my youth, to the perfect summer when I made up the numbers in our village cricket team. I could never match the achievements of others, but I made up the numbers nonetheless and tried to hold my catches. I remember saying I'd noticed that every time and wherever we played our only spectator would be a black & white border-collie dog, which would sit patiently on a distant boundary and follow the match with rapt attention. To this day, the phenomenon can still be seen in all the leafy shires of England and Wales. "Why is there always a border-collie watching us? It doesn't even seem to belong to anyone" I enquired of an elderly member. "Be careful, lad. Play fair. That isn't a dog at all" he explained, "That's the Supreme Being."

Jerome spoiled my reminiscence with his never ending stream of self-importance.

'If you're competent, if you're doing a good job for the team, you'll probably think the people around you are doing their jobs properly too. That's workflow.'

He mimed a sort of wanky wavelet with his hand.

'If they're not, then you're working in a silo with great voids and black holes on every side of you.'

He mimed that too and it resembled a man walking in wet trousers pointing to a couple of shopping bags.

'So when you rely on the co-workers to the side of you, whatever gets passed that way falls down a hole! It's like a ball kicked around on the field, people. None of us has got to drop the ball or the referees are going to rule us out and send us off. Okay?' He paused for effect. 'Do you see where I'm coming from?'

By now, most of them could see.

I guessed Jerome knew little about cricket. Perhaps he thought sports were all the same, like different types of production from a factory. In the highest circles of management, it doesn't matter what the units sold per month actually are, does it?

Simon Quince, the opener, obviously had a lower threshold for suffering his fools gladly and murmured something that I didn't quite catch. The Tour Manager missed it too, so could only frown in his direction and continue, something about a learning curve, until the opener's voice could be heard again.

'More of a learning plummet.'

Jerome heard that one and immediately rounded on the player with the intention of bowling him out. This would be an interesting confrontation, I thought. Quince, with his three and a half thousand Test runs for England and the Tour Manager with his Shake 'n' Vac, Consignia and some pointless shampoo that made impressionable teenagers look as though they'd been electrocuted.

Now, let's see, which one of them would England protect? It was sad to think that, in the present climate, this choice was no longer obvious.

I laughed. Unfortunately, I think I did it out loud.

'Hey, who's that?'

I turned around to see who he meant. There wasn't anyone behind me. Oh, I could see now, he meant me.

'Yes, you. You're not with The Team. Get clear of the doorway. Leave the room completely please and don't tell anyone what you've heard here today.'

As if I would. As if they'd listen. I walked away, but could still hear his voice droning along in the background.

'Listen up guys! This is going to be tough, but I'm a tough guy and we've got ourselves a tough team. When I introduced the UK market to *Nutrithreat* the shampoo for dangerous people...'

Perhaps it would have been worse if he'd asked me to stay.

Ah, a restaurant!

Pah, a closed restaurant.

I nosed in at The Morning Room, which rather confusingly stayed open all day, managed to order a cup of tea, foul as always, paid up, thanked them from the bottom of my heart and made my way to the ground.

When the England coach arrived, I still stood in the queue, so watched as they all trooped out and a small crowd of barely dressed well-wishers welcomed them. Raffles emerged, looking sprightly. He shook a few hands, signed score cards for the children and then found himself in earnest conversation with a keen supporter who apparently had only half the entrance fee to his name. Raffles walked nearby, so I managed to overhear some of the conversation.

'The tickets are one hundred and thirty rand, but you've only got sixty five in cash?'

'That's right. It's a long way to come not to see it.'

'Well I'm playing, so I didn't have a reason to bring any. The standard child's ticket is half price.'

'So?'

'Did you know, today they're letting in children under fifteen for free, if accompanied by an adult?'

'How does that help?'

'Find an un-accompanied child who would have paid for a ticket anyway, go through the gate with them and charge the child half the joint entrance fee.'

'Thanks! You're a star.'

'Yes' confirmed Raffles as the spectator moved away 'Pleiades Epsilon.'

Sighing inwardly, always an awkward sigh to master, I ploughed through the turnstile and located my seat. Some of the locals were already preparing a braai, the traditional regional barbeque. Beers chilled on heaps of ice and thousands of suntans settled into place for a five day roasting. Only it didn't go five days, did it?

On the first day, there was the word and the word was 'Tails'. The South African Captain chose to bat.

The first innings was exciting, but of little concern to historians of the game. Their openers ploughed into an ill-prepared English seam attack and racked up the runs at an alarming rate of 5.4 an over. Half way through the first day, I would have told you the Proteas were favourites. Smack, clack went the boundary boards as another tired English bowler left the pitch. We had a little hope at 150 for two, but when they took the game away and forged ahead toward three hundred and I assumed the worst.

The England Captain signalled Raffles to move in close. This seemed a little strange as Charl Pretorious was close to his hundred and playing magnificently.

'Do you mind me fielding this close?' asked Raffles.

'Nah. No mon. You field where you like.'

The bowler bowled.

'Are you sure you don't mind me in close?'

'Nah. It's fine.'

'Good, good' said Raffles.

'In that case, let me tell you about Jesus.'

The bowler bowled him.

As a reward, the Captain brought Raffles on a few overs later and he took three wickets for thirty nine in an economic spell that lasted the rest of the South African innings. They fell at the close of the first day and had scored at least a hundred runs less than expected.

Day Two.

'It looks like Andre Tudjman will open the bowling for the host nation. No surprises there Peter.'

The voice of the one called Peter came from exactly the same direction, but there were no surprises there either as both spoke from a spectator's radio. The owner seemed unaware that, at this volume, no one could escape hearing it. He carried on drinking from a bottle and waving a large flag on a pole which he'd also brought along to the match with him. I wondered whether I should ask a steward if there might be somewhere less annoying to sit, but decided in the end it was another facet of the carnival atmosphere.

The first over was a tidy one. No runs and every ball on the spot. Quince, for England, looked good for a long innings. The choice of bowler from the other end seemed a hot topic to the commentators.

'Who's this? They've put Lelling on at the Pavilion End! That's a strange decision.'

'Oh, I don't know. Ritchie Benaud opened with spin back in the season of '54. Maybe it's a tactic? You're right. It is Lelling. I remember he played half of an English county season two years ago.'

'Really? I must have missed that, Peter.'

'Oh, yes. He was absolutely pivotal in helping Derbyshire to the title.'

'Remind me Peter, how did he do that?'

'He bowled for Warwickshire.'

'Oh, I see. Not your first choice then?'

Lelling seemed to get away with the first over, but his second went for a leakage of runs.

'The Captain's had quite enough of that experiment.'

'You're right, he's taking him off. Well, well.'

Tudjman wasn't faring much better. A four of wides followed by a couple of full tosses, the second of which thudded irregularly into the splice of Quince's bat.

'Is your bat broken? That sounded like an E-flat' observed a South African short leg.

'Hey, listen' said Quince, 'if you've got perfect pitch, for heaven's sake don't pass it on to your bowlers. They might try line and length.'

When Quince finally departed, leg before, a few overs after lunch, the opposition assessed the weaknesses of the England number three, forgot their plans and lapsed into simplistic sledging:

'Hey, Ump! He reckons the other batsman's nose is obscuring the bowler's action.'

'Play on.'

'Hey fellas! Don't let him hit my helmet on the ground behind the keeper. Hey, Umpire! If the batsman hits the ball with his nose, do we get five penalty runs? Only fair.'

'Play on.'

A few hours, beers and wickets later, England were edging ahead in the hunt.

'That's an unusual number of runs for the first two sessions' said the commentators and they were right.

'Too many loose deliveries, old man. Too many extras. Oh! What a ball! That's cut him in half!'

Raffles was in.

A strange thing happened, as Raffles told me later. When he walked out to the wicket, a South African bowler jogged up to him and said:

'You haven't played Tests for a while, so the first ball's going to be an easy half-volley. After that, you're on your own, okay?'

Naturally, Raffles didn't believe a word of it and missed out on an easy half-volley which he should have put away for four.

Curious and curiouser. Raffles nudged a single to get off strike, camped up the other end and tried to think through what had just happened.

Over... and it nearly was.

Raffles had barely occupied the crease before he perpetrated the most ridiculous shot I've seen in his entire career and slung the ball straight up into a cloud that had selected that moment to hover above mid-wicket. Three highly-professional fielders converged beneath.

There is an old theory of cricketing captaincy. When multiple fielders run under one ball, the Captain (or one of the catchers) must nominate who should be the one to take the catch, so the others can back off and *stop crowding him*. Let's say the fielder to be nominated is named Douglas Marmoset. If the ball is hit up in the air and the Captain calls out the fielder's surname to take the catch 'Mr Marmoset!', he is much more likely to drop the ball than if the Captain calls out his first name, 'Dougie's ball' or 'Dougie's go it'. The use of the first name inspires a warmth of confidence in the player's ability. The use of the surname cools and formalises the event so much that it tips some minds into self-conscious and nervous unbalance. Suggestion is a powerful thing. Hypnotists base their whole profession on it. Do you believe me? No? Look into my eyes...

Raffles, being Raffles, had another twist on this. If the ball is hit up in the air and the *batsman* calls out the fielder's name, it will definitely be spilled.

This is exactly what happened.

Plonk.

Raffles had another life.

Yorkshiremen everywhere groaned and tut-tutted, but only one of them held a convenient microphone.

'He won't catch much like that. Look at him. He's flapping around like a girl.'

Not letting a good subject go, the unappreciative airwave reeled off a catalogue of lapses from the fielder's career.

Interestingly enough, as any sporting journalist will tell you, the word 'Yorkshiremen' isn't recognised by the modern spell-checker. The options it will present you with are 'Yorkshire men', 'Auto-Correct' or 'Ignore All', which is tempting.

Dying with your boots on, with tens of thousands watching, is as soul-destroying as it gets for any sportsman. One fielder, at least one, prayed that nothing else would come to him. Raffles deliberately sliced the next ball just beyond his reach, which made him dive into the dust and look even more useless. One run. I noticed the South Africans were trying not to look in their own player's direction. The focus was well and truly off the new batsman. How strange. It was as if Raffles had been out there *for ever*.

Half an hour later, Raffles still occupied the crease and looked as classic and composed as a portrait of Wellington and his horse or the heir to the throne and his wife. He angled a straight ball down to deep fine leg seventy yards away and made an easy couple of runs. As the bowler trundled in and bowled exactly the same ball as before, I noticed something Raffles hadn't. The deep fine leg fielder, positioned behind Raffles' back, came forward a couple of strides. Raffles angled another easy two and chatted amicably to the bowler, who tried to keep him facing forwards.

Step, step, step went the bowler's feet, running in, running in and … lunge.

Another ball, exactly the same as the last, sprung into existence before him. What Raffles couldn't possibly have seen was the subtle way in which that deep fine leg fielder moved in for the kill by half a dozen paces. Sixty four yards, ish? Oh hell! Colin

Bland's ploy. Two runs wouldn't possible now. It would be a run out for sure!

Raffles weighed up the odds and purposefully chipped the ball behind in the air, up and straight over the fine leg fielder and down onto the spot where he used to be standing. It rolled away to the boundary and half of South Africa groaned at the fielder. Oh, of course. Raffles knew that one.

For the record, A.J. didn't make it to fifty. He did well though, propping up his end and giving the others the freedom to have a bit of a slog at the part-time bowlers. He could have joined in by hitting the ball in the air, but it wasn't really his modus operandi. "When I learnt to bat, we had a low garden fence with the Alsatian breeders on one side and the Adams family on the other. That taught me to hit the ball down."

England drew level, then A.J. edged an out-swinger and the tail fell apart in a nervous shambles.

Day Three.

South Africa took the match by the scruff of the neck and attempted to blast England out of it. They scored swiftly, decisively and with irreverent aggression. One hundred, two hundred and up.

At the tea interval on day three, the South African Captain did something quite remarkable.

He declared.

'What?' said the English Captain.

'What?' echoed everyone. Let the good times roll! Well, perhaps they weren't quite rolling yet, but at least they appeared to be creeping off the slope in a more or less downhillish direction.

'Do they have enough lead?' asked the radio. 'An unbelievably sporting gesture, wouldn't you say Peter? He's showing great faith in his bowling attack to defend such a nondescript mark.'

Raffles left tea early and made his way across the field to a boundary board in front of my area of seating.

'Would you believe it, Bunny? He's giving a speech in there about having absolute confidence in his bowlers and needing to leave a tempting target that England would risk wickets for. He wants to give the crowd some entertainment - avoid a certain draw. Utter drivel of course, a draw is the least likely option, but it's their funeral. Get your money on England!'

What money? How? Oh, I see, a figure of speech. How strange.

The radio agreed with me that it was strange. The owner of the radio, the by now badly inebriated man with his flag on a stick, closed his eyes and allowed his flag-pole to dip at an alarming angle. Ahead of us, members of the crowd turned back in irritation as the flag draped across their heads or tapped down on unsuspecting shoulders. Some kind soul relieved him of it, which he wasn't in a position to notice.

Simon Quince, the England opening bat, was first up. I can't remember who the other batsman was, but I'll do my best to tell you what happened anyway. The first over was a welcome surprise. The bowling had good pace, good rhythm, but was so far wide of his stumps that it posed no threat whatsoever. Quince watched the first six sail past. The over done, his partner wandered down the pitch to compare notes.

'I suppose it helps you get your eye in' he'd muttered, 'but what's the point?'

The second over covered much the same ground, it went for two, and the batsmen compared notes again.

'Remind me Simon; this is supposed to be a Test Match, isn't it? Only, I don't think either of these bowlers use *Nutrithreat* shampoo.'

Both bowlers then aimed straighter, but leaked runs consistently without posing much threat. The odd thing was, the Captain kept them on.

The other England opener lost his wicket on sixty, caught pulling a freebie through mid-on. It didn't matter much as the visitors had rattled up one hundred for the score board already.

For a team regarded as the best fielding side in the World, the first over to the new man was a comedy of errors. 'Sunny' Holliday, a cheerful bat, watched his first ball swing away through leg and run down to the picket fence for five wides. 'Okay. Treat every one on its merits' Sunny breathed deep and steeled himself as the bowler looked to make amends. 'He won't try to swing it. Not until he's got control. Not until he thinks I think he's forgotten he's a swing bowler and then it will swing, but not *much*.' He was right. The next was straight, gun barrel straight, as Sunny met it with straightened bat and twisted logic.

The third, he dabbed through a gap and called for a single. A loose mid-off tore after it and completed the interception. Just as Sunny made his ground, when there really was no longer any point throwing, the breathless fielder hurled the ball at the bowler's end where no one tended the stumps. The returned ball flew over the stumps and skimmed away down the ground for four more.

'An amateur mistake', 'Very much village green stuff' tut-tutted the commentators as another radio gargled away to itself in the stands.

Seeing no one attending that boundary either, the guilty mid-off crossed the cut-strip and jogged the length of a lawn to the fence after it.

The radio became ecstatic:

'Just like the day Pheidippides ran from Marathon to Athens and then had to run all the way back again because he couldn't quite remember what the bally message was.'

'One for the record books' warbled the radio, for the fifth time in the match.

After that, the passage of play veered into something recognisably English. The ball bobbling, the batsmen nurdling, the advantage tilting. Before long, all the nudging and wobbling had edged the advantage into England's favour. South Africa's new tactics, to move all the fielders up and force the batsmen to chip over the top, just seemed to hasten the inevitable. Wepper looked as though the fight had gone out of him. The batsmen sensed it too and assumed the ascendancy as their run rate accelerated.

England should have won it with five wickets to spare, but they didn't. Some appalling shot selection by the fourth and fifth batsmen meant Raffles would get a go after all, but with just fifty runs to win it looked like a caretaking job.

'Wha-ooo, we're half way there' sang the home team's supporters.

'...and you're also living on a prayer' quipped the radio.

I couldn't work out what Raffles was doing at the time. He just kept looking about at fielders and flexing his legs a lot. There's no point in me describing that, so I'll tell you what he said afterwards.

During the evening, quite without prompting, Raffles explained to me about the bowler who seemed to hand out runs, the bowler which the Captain had *kept bowling*. He explained about the batsman who twice seemed to make a solid start and then deliberately guided the ball away to be caught in the slips. It took me hours to get an explanation out of him about the knees though. I'll be dreaming about those dratted knees. Apparently it's another trade secret.

Raffles has a proven theory from the Test arena to help your fielding. It originated in South Africa, so it wouldn't surprise anyone to hear it in this neck of the veldt.

Picture this: You are a fielder standing at square on either side of the wicket (it works equally for both). The bowler bowls, it's in their nature to do so, and the batsman, as accustomed, prepares to strike the ball. If the ball is pitched short of a length, the batsman should flex the right knee as he leans back. If the ball is pitched at full length, the batsman should bend the left knee as he leans forward into the shot.

If the batsman is playing back, the ball is much more likely to be angled behind them, behind square. If playing forward, the ball is much more likely to be hit in front of the batsman.

The practical upshot is that a fielder placed to the side of the wicket can look to see which knee bends and then set off in the right direction, to intercept the shot or take the catch, *before the ball has been struck.*

You can do a lot, in a Test Match, with a half-second advantage.

Alright, we all know that first class cricketers have tricks that club cricketers never hear of, unless they run across one in some crazy old ex-player's book, only that wasn't Raffles' observation. Raffles never appreciated being caught at square, or point, or anywhere. Let's face it, Raffles *hated* being caught.

Raffles watched *them* watching his knees. Raffles' knees didn't betray him. Raffles' knees told lies.

During his second innings, as in many others, he'd reserved a corner of his vision to see if the square fielders would move early when he played a shot. It confused the bowler no end, when he bowled wide of the stumps, to see Raffles play at thin air and miss as if receiving a completely different delivery all the while looking elsewhere.

'Had he even seen it?' thought the bowler. 'He's up to his tricks again' thought the umpires. Raffles didn't care. If the fielders moved, they were knee-watching. If so, he could direct them left or right any time he pleased with the mere flick of a knee. *That was control.*

In the nets, Raffles even practiced exceptions to the forward/backward rule: going forward to cut the ball behind, standing high on a straight leg to backfoot-drive a ball through cover point. In so doing, he learned to clear fielders from the paths of his strokes. Wrong-footed, he took them out of the game.

Today had been odd. He'd spotted the watcher and sent him left, as usual. Only, this time, the fielder went right and couldn't help cutting off Raffles' shot.

The batsman tried again, directed him right and he instantly set off to the left, into the path of the ball.

Raffles sighed and counted his years. They'd clearly solved his double bluff. The technique was no longer working. Switching back now, he played conventionally and found the ball angled square always pierced the field. Really, the player always set off the wrong way. They were clearing a path for him! This stank, but Raffles was the only one who noticed the smell.

'Okay, I don't understand this, but if they really want me to look good, I'll oblige them' he thought.

Van Jalk, a gigantic quick bowler, was the unfortunate man to come on as Raffles slipped his chain. I saw a Raffles that day who hit the ball cleanly in the air with a freedom unknown since the early days, batting on the beach with his father.

Van Jalk bowled the third ball fast and short.

'Fetch' said Raffles and smashed it over the three-tier stand and away to the deepwater harbour.

In the air and out of character, Raffles rode his luck and the crowd rose to him. That set the tone. England raced up to the total and won by five wickets.

One spectator, quite near me, nudged another.

'That's the most misjudged declaration since Gary Sobers cocked-up the England series in the '60s.'

As Raffles walked off, unexpectedly ignoring his own team's cheers and jubilation, he looked concerned and pensive. An ECB man was the first to reach him.

'Well done! That's the spirit! Open the tour with a win!'

'We didn't win that match. They lost it.'

Chasing him back to the pavilion, the ECB man pressed on with the matter.

'Do you mean you suspect the result was arranged, A.J.?'

'When no other explanation covers it...'

'Hmm. I never though it would reach the Tests. They're too important, Raffles. Should I refer your suspicion formally to the ICC?

I would do it, for the sake of the game, but it'll start an awful fuss. Raffles, Raffles? Are you sure though? They only declared the innings too soon.'

'There was more to it than that, Michael. You didn't see the knees.'

'What knees. What did they do to your knees?'

Chapter 11

A Friendly Face from the ICC

An attractive member of the all-girl reception team dodged neatly through the crowded bar as a broad Zimbabwean voice boomed above the din. Raffles' head went up instantly in recognition.

'Young lady, can I ask you up to my room?'

Variations on the theme of 'phwoaah!' and a gaggle of chuckles emanated from the herd around the water-hole.

'And why would that be, Sir?' said the girl.

This Zimbabwean had an answer ready, as always.

'Last night I had a dream that I was eating an *enormous* marsh mallow and when I woke up this morning, my pillow had gone!'

'Well Sir, I'll ask the domestic supervisor to replace it.'

'Ah crap' came the voice again as she moved away.

'Hey, Dale, over here you reprobate!'

'Is that you, Raffles? Of course it's you. Nothing else in the country's that ugly.'

'Have you time for a drink?'

'I'm a volleyball for that!'

An unusual person made his way up to our table. Not as unusual as the last time, but still... I won't discuss the tropical shirt. I'll try not to mention the sandals. Suffice it to say he had a face which glared like the sun through a cloud of rain and black-haired hands so broad they could juggle cannon balls.

'If you're quite finished spooking the staff...'

'I was just checking the location of her room in case of inflammation. Precaution is my watchword.'

'Dale, you were trying to give her shots.'

'Me?' said the big man, feigning innocence. 'Anyway, it's called strokes, not shots.'

'Dale, you've got a one track mind and that's the dirt track.'

'Hey! Hands off my sayings!'

'Me?' Raffles mimicked.

'I am warning you Pal; my lawyers are *poised*. One word from me and *Fwoah*, there'll be ink everywhere.'

'It beats me how you ever manage to entice ladies into your... what would you call it?'

'...into my fart sack?'

'You don't change much, do you Dale?'

'Why should I? I'm lacquer!'

'Does that word really have secondary meaning? I had no idea. Dale, why don't you have a regular wash, smarten yourself up and try to act civilised? You must be in your forties by now and that really is the age when you should consider the habit of a good regular scrub.'

From Raffles' tone, I formed the impression that this was a little like explaining the concept of altruism to a crocodile.

'Raffles, you'd better start buying drinks soon or you and me are gonna clash.'

A.J. signalled and, despite the baying crowd at the bar, the bar staff came to him. Amazing.

I developed the dual impression that a) we were in a bar and b) we'd tracked down a strange animal to its natural environment.

As a group of Englishmen vacated a neighbouring table, Raffles leaned across and lifted their paper, the Times I think, or maybe the Telegraph. He asked for a pen and leaned into the cryptic crossword. I thought he was being rude, so stared at him for a while and wondered if he was going to rejoin the party.

'Oh. Bunny, I'd like to introduce you to Dale McKenna, ex-player, ex-heavyweight boxer, an all-round has-been and able to perfectly recite the labels of any brand of vodka you care to mention. We go way back. Dale, I'd like to introduce you to Bunny Manders, student of the game, who's on holiday getting over his drippy girlfriend.'

We shook hands. His were twice the size of mine.

'Women, huh? Hello-hello, don't mention women.'

I didn't. Raffles had and then, without looking up, hijacked the conversation.

'So you're not with Sheryl then?' he asked, quick on the uptake.

'Nah, that was a long time ago. Months.'

'I thought she was good for you.'

'So did I. Then the big hand went past midnight and her horns came out.'

'Oh dear. Can I get you a drink? You seem to have accidentally finished your first glass in one.'

'I like this game!' said Dale, perking up, as Raffles ordered a bottle.

'So, how's it going back home?' I asked Dale, not knowing much about Zimbabwe.

'I'm not sure where home is now. Capetown, for now. Maybe the UK eventually. I can't go back to Zimbabwe until the old loony dies.'

I guessed this to mean the notorious Robert Mugabe. Not a fan then.

'Did you have to get out in a hurry?'

'Yeahup. I only stopped to bury my savings and now they've cancelled my passport, so I can't go back for them.'

'You buried your sayings?' asked Raffles, having missed the first half of this topic.

'My SAVINGS, you duhrse.'

Dale looked around the room carefully, in case anyone had heard. They hadn't.

'Alright, we've got a week with nothing to do. How about we go and retrieve them for you?'

'Get lost, Raffles. I'd prefer to wait twenty years than leave it to you.'

'Okay then. Why don't you slip into the country over the border with Zambia?'

'I can't make trips like that. I've got this bone in my leg' Dale explained, clutching his leg.

'Dale, be serious. What's the real reason you can't go back to your farm?'

He looked hesitant, gulped down a second glass and lowered his voice.

'Well, there might be a couple of, quite small, land mines.'

'What?' I yelped.

Raffles put down his paper. He'd finished the crossword.

'Well, the other farmers with eviction orders were burying them and I'd had a few drinks and then I went to see a mate from the old days who had some left over and it seemed like a good idea at the time.'

'So you can't go back because the Police might want to ask you about that.'

'They might have had some complaints.'

'Where did you plant them?'

'Just by the gate. I think there might be some on the drive and one under the kitchen window.'

'That's it?'

'Yees. Apart from the one in the lavatory cistern and another under the loft ladder. Maybe there are a couple more, I don't know. They're olive coloured. I do remember that they're olive coloured.'

'Why did you put a landmine in a lavatory cistern?'

'I figured that whoever turned up to steal my house would need to go for a crap sooner or later.'

Raffles, despite a moment of interest, looked to have re-considered the mathematics.

'You're right not to go. If you can't trust anyone locally to collect it, you should drop the idea for ten years at least.'

'That's a long time to do without. Yeah, you're right. There's no one nearby. They've all emigrated or been murdered. Officially, that's the same as emigrated, but there's no forwarding address.'

'Ah. I see. However, if you could get into the country, perhaps cross the border in the night... If you came back, even for a day, do you think you'd be noticed?'

'I played cricket for Zimbabwe for five years. That's pictures in the paper, Brew. Of course I'd be noticed. Gees, it's a wonder you've got the brains to get out of bed in the morning.'

'You know I never get home before morning' replied Raffles casually. 'What are your savings anyway? Did you convert everything to dollars?'

'Hey, hey, hey! You're nosey all of a sudden. I'll have to watch you. No, nothing's in currency. When you've got the worst inflation rate in the world, you learn not to trust cash. There's some in gold dust and there's African art as well.'

'Art? You? You're kidding. The last time you thought something was artistic, it was a stripper.'

'You're getting me confused with someone else. I am the *epitome* of culture. That's Culture, Raffles. With a capital K.'

'You're going to have to watch those long words, Dale. Sooner or later someone's going to ask you to explain one and then you'll be stuck. What's the re-sale value of African art nowadays?'

'Raffles, you're a horse's arse. This isn't *modern* African tribal tat you know. It wasn't knocked out by some Mumbo in a bike shed with a tub of clay and a paint brush.'

'Okay, blow me away. What is it?'

'Benin leopards. A pair.'

Raffles' intake of breath was audible. He was re-calculating.

'Replicas of course.'

'No. Genuine top notch iron sculpture from the greatest civilisation this continent ever produced. I traded it with the Nigerians for my brother-in-law's farm. He knew he couldn't sell it, so signed it over to me when he walked out.'

'Where did he go?'

'Australia I think. I haven't heard a thing from him though. I'm not so sure he ever arrived.'

'Won't the new owners have to hand the farm to Mugabe?'

'No, he only hates whites. They'll be okay.'

'So, what are the leopards worth?'

'Maybe two hundred thousand the pair.'

'Rand?'

'Sterling. The gold's enough for travelling expenses and the rest's just sentimental.'

'That was quite some farm' said Raffles.

'Yees, it was. They both were. I worked my ruddy guts out for my place and then I got a cop at the door issuing the notice to quit. I went out and met him, wearing my Zimbabwe cricket shirt, but that didn't cut any ice. I had planned to take everything I could out by land through Mozambique, but the armed gangs turned up at neighbouring farms sooner than anyone thought.'

'So you ran?'

'I never run. Alright, I did then, but just the once. I went out the back before they came and slogged it down the track for fifteen miles and then hitched a lift to the airport. They won't take Zimbabwean currency for flights nowadays, so you have to have foreign money or a credit card. I was lucky, I had one. There were a lot of my mates who didn't and they had to stay.'

'They aren't any mates there now?'

'No. They weren't allowed to stay or to leave, so I don't know what happened to them. They're not there now.'

'Maybe they've been arrested for setting landmines' I speculated helpfully.

'If the ICC find out I've been involved in anything like that, I'll be up to my neck in kack.'

'Seriously though, you played for your country. They can't do anything to you without a trial.'

'They won't catch me. Do you remember the team of '91? Most of them aren't allowed to play cricket. They've all lost property. Some have stayed, but not many. Most got the cops at their door demanding they sign pro-government statements.'

'Could the ICC help?'

Dale laughed miserably.

'They already have. They gave me a job and sorted me out. That's why I'm going to do my best for them. Do you know how I was living in England? They put me on social benefit. Me! I've spent my whole life doing enough work for four men and they tell me I'm incapable.'

'Why exactly?'

'Poorly-sick-ill'

Raffles stared levelly at him.

'Okay, broken spine. I slipped down some stairs, but that's not the point. The point is they wouldn't let me play cricket because that's evidence of being physically alright, which means no money. I played anyway of course.'

'With a broken spine?'

'Yees. Dosed up on Pethadine and boy, did my back pay for it.'

'God, you can't leave it alone, can you? How did you get away with it?'

'A fake name in the book. Pepi Steinberg. That bloke's got the record for most sixes in a league season and I'm pleased for him. It's enough for me though. I'm hurting.'

'So you just got pulled out of retirement by the ICC?'

'Yees. It's funny, but some of the lads must have put my name forward. They said I knew everyone in Africa. That's a bit of an exaggeration. For instance, I don't know a bloke called Chuddy Woodruff from Botswana even though we did go to different schools together.'

'They meant you know everyone in African cricket. That's probably accurate. You also hear all the stories, which is really valuable.'

'Yeah. Pollock? I remember his father. There was a man who could hit the ball hard' he gestured unexpectedly with the swipe of a paddle. 'Fwoah! The boundary fence rattled and none of us okes had moved a muscle.'

The night was wearing on and I began to tire of all this.

'So, you're the continental representative on the ICC's anti-corruption unit.' I stated it plainly as Raffles had already told me what he did.

'Yees. The one thing the ICC never got was good information. They're mostly business-thinkers in that office down in Jo-burg. When they set up the Anti-Corruption Unit they put a cop in charge and he hired policemen, 'cos that's what he knew. They don't know how to speak to the players. Who's going to tell 'em what's going on. So, I got a job. A genuine cricketer - for a change.'

'Is that why you're here? Corruption?' I asked.

'Yeas. I was having a good time, 'till I ran into Raffles. Some players get jobs as commentators. I got to be a full-time stink-sniffer.'

'What does that involve?'

'Put it this way: If you want to play cricket for Zimbabwe, you've got to move to Mashonaland. They missed some great players who wouldn't. If you want to work for the anti-corruption guys, you've gotta move to where the stink is, so I guess I've gotta sit next to Raffles. Hey, it's getting like a desert in here.'

He ran his finger round the rim of his glass and Raffles gave a thin smile.

'Do you think the First Test was fixed?' I asked, 'Raffles does.'

A.J. scowled across the table, not for the first time regretting his decision to bring me along.

'Does he now? The declaration? That's good, 'cos so do I.'

'You do?'

'Yeas. We've had accusations about Wepper before, but not enough dirt to make a case. This time might be different. He's a very greedy boy. Pious too, which makes me sick. More greed than caution, I reckon.'

I pressed further, asking 'What about the World Cup?'

'Can't prove anything. If there were any fixes, I'd say they did it on the run rates. It isn't like boxing; you don't have to take a fall to fix a match now. Do you know you can bet on which team will have the most runs after six overs? Who will be the top scorer? A player can score slow in the first six, then get a good score, or make sure he isn't quite the top scorer by a run or two, and then his side can still win the match without upsetting the fans and *someone* gets rich. It's a crazy game now.'

'I see the logic behind your appointment. At least you might be better at this job than batting.'

'Hey, hey, hey! I don't see your batting in any record books pal.'

'That's because I'm a bowler'

'Oh, that's no excuse buster. You've still got to hold a bat. I heard you got a fifty last season. What do you think you were doing, playing the blind school?'

'Bunny, here's a man who built a career on being hopeless at batting. Dale can't even play the basic forward-defensive shot.'

'I blocked once! At Arundel!'

'Yes, you blocked it for six, up a tree. That's rubbish. The forward defensive shot is supposed to leave the ball puttering around on the deck, completely uncatchable. Look it up in the MCC coaching manual if you don't believe me. Leaning into the block should never, ever, result in the ball being smothered straight up a tree on the long-on boundary.'

He had a point.

'Yees, well my play wasn't very *English*, but…'

'Quite. If you'd learned to bat properly, you would have respected the good ball and hit the bad one. You wouldn't have just turkey-slapped everything that came through. Disrespect is even more oafish in white trousers '

'You've got the ball, I've got the bat, pal. If the little red thing comes anywhere near me, it gets klunked!'

'Fielders?'

'Put 'em where you like, I don't care. If I take the aerial route, it doesn't matter where they're standing.'

'That's Neanderthal.'

'You mean it's not very *English*. You're just sore about that Middlesex Northants match aren't you?'

'No, I'd quite forgotten it. Anyway, I bowled you.'

'Yah! With a full toss that should have been no-balled, when I was on about twenty hundred and seventy eleven.'

'You were dropped twice and should have been LBW in the third over!'

'So you'd forgotten it then?' asked Dale, almost laughing in Raffles' face.

'Anyway, look it up in the book. Out, bowled Raffles.'

I tried to change the subject. 'Shall we go somewhere to eat?'

'You should never, ever, eat on an empty stomach' asserted Dale, his eyes sauntering to the bar.

I thought to leave them like that, back-to-back affronted, but I found my exit blocked by a squeeze of other rowdy sports pundits.

'Hey, Raffles, if you're so ruddy *English*, I've got a grammar question for you.'

'Okay, fire away.'

'Right then. You can tell me which one of these is right: Seventeen and sixteen IS thirty one, or seventeen and sixteen ARE thirty one?'

Raffles didn't pause before answering 'Seventeen and sixteen are thirty one.'

Dale sat back in his chair, then bulged and howled with laughter.

'Ha! Monkey-boy here says seventeen plus sixteen makes thirty one! How do you spinners ever count six balls in an over? Gee, it must be shit to be thick!'

Raffles made a face you might have comfortably squeezed lemons on and some customers were edging out of the bar ahead of the volcano erupting.

I tried changing the subject yet again.

'Did you see Westlicott's long straight six in the warm-up match?'

'Oh yeah! What a shot! It reminded me of me.'

'He has a good yorker too' I added.

'Rot! There's no such thing as a yorker! Step up the pitch and it's a rank full toss. I am telling *You*.'

'It's still a good ball. Did you try to hit everything for six?' I wondered.

'Yes. That's why he didn't last five minutes' confirmed Raffles.

'Dog-coils' summarised Dale, with the emphasis of one who knows. 'Count the centuries.'

Raffles glanced over his shoulder.

'Do you know any of those people on the terrace? I don't think they're to do with the cricket.'

'Cricket?' said Dale, 'Did someone mention cricket? I give lessons. Tuesdays and Thursdays two 'till four. I warn you Raffles, they get booked up. A thousand rand an hour, but as it's you, two thousand. Don't worry; I won't make you count anything, 'cos I wouldn't want to embarrass you.'

'Alright, you got me' said Raffles.

'I always get you!'

'So you'll be buying the drinks then.'

'Hey, hey. It's your turn at the bar pal. They already know me there. Get spans*, while you're up. It's economy - saves on shoe leather.'

Clearly the whole evening was going to be like this, so I tried again to take my leave before the pair of them flushed any more double vodkas through me. It wasn't easy. Dale didn't approve of people leaving parties and every night was party night.

When Dale eventually bought a round, I picked up the paper, read 'Blodgers', 'Landlubber', 'Snood' and 'Ekranoplan', then asked a question that had been bothering me.

'Raffles? How did you do the cryptic crossword in six minutes?'

'Easy. Without looking at the questions.'

'Sorry?'

'I just fill in whatever words fit the grid. One-upping on Dale, you understand?'

'Oh. I don't think 'snood' is a word, actually.'

'Yes it is. My Granny had one after the war. However, the same could be said about Blodgers, but Dale doesn't know that, does he?'

Raffles and Dale both started at the same time in village cricket, thousands of miles apart. They'd come a long way from there to drinking toasts in South Africa, but that was how I'll always remember them:

'To village cricketers everywhere!'

'To Dave Tinsley who died playing cricket for my team.' 'To Dave!' 'Mr T!'

I suggested 'To John Howard-Whitehouse who died playing cricket for our old school' (before our time, we hadn't met him, no one cared) 'To John!'

'To that chap from Sarisbury Green who died playing against us' 'To the chap!'

'It's a noble fate, you know. Frederick the Prince of Wales and heir to the British throne was killed by a cricket ball, back in 1751. It was the first case of reign stopped by play.'

---

* Lots.

'Yah. Raffles was quick in those days. Hey Brew, how come you're still playing?'

'So someone will know what to do if you old-timers make a comeback.'

'To the umpires' fingers!'

'To the groundsmen of every pitch in the world!'

'To the batmakers!'

'To the ball-stitchers!'

'To the scorers on the village green!'

'To the wickets!'

'To the cut strip!'

'To the middle!'

By this time, people lounging at the bar vaguely realised that toasts were being proposed and had more or less tuned in to the last one. Along the bar someone took up the chorus 'To the Middle!' and downed their drink mechanically. The sunburned faces of their friends echoed the sentiment and ignited a chain of 'To the Middle!'s which plagued the team hotel and stretched 'till sunrise.

Unbeknown by us, yet worthy of a footnote, the now-famous cricketing toast 'To the Middle' was proposed many decades later at a dinner to mark a re-union of this tour, although none of the wizened old players could remember what it meant.

'Do you think we should order again or maybe find another bar?' said Raffles and I do believe he slurred. 'They're looking at us strangely here. They're looking at you strage-lky. Not me. I'm a genelmen.'

'Difficult.'

'Hmm. Still…'

'Hannibal crossed the Alps.'

'Nixon went to China.'

'Steven Fry went to Belgium' I supplied, with my usual enthusiasm.

Then I realised it was probably my turn after all to get the drinks.

Raffles didn't show his face the following morning. The England physiotherapist seemed in command of the facts, so I asked for an update.

It seems that Raffles and Dale left the bar quite late, then went about knocking on doors until they'd collected an armful of complimentary oranges. Dale set up an electric fan at one end of the third floor corridor and Raffles bowled great squashy orange leg-breaks at it from twenty two yards. Other cricketers came out to see what the noise was about and a round of betting ensued to see whether they could pick his googly from his leggie and also whether he could hit the fan with either. Whenever he managed the feat, cash changed hands, a drink was the forfeit and the stakes went up.

As the above entertainment found itself closed down and dispersed by the management, our pair of middle-aged hooligans found themselves pushed into the street and proceeded to the nearest open doorway in hope of making a rescue telephone call. The doorway just happened to be that of a bar, which was unfortunate. Dale had won a lot of cash, which was more unfortunate still. "If you don't spend it, the damn stuff depreciates. I'm from Zimbabwe. I know these things." Someone showed Raffles a photograph of himself in a newspaper, which he declined to sign, strangely insisting "It doesn't make sense if it's not in colour." From there, the evening turned into quite a festival.

It was only when they were walking home in the early hours that someone stood on Raffles' hands.

Unfortunately, that's bad news for a spin bowler. Just ask Phil Tufnell. The England Physiotherapist was called, but arrived predictably unimpressed. "If you wouldn't mind helping me take these skates off" said Raffles. The Physio informed him that he wasn't wearing any skates, after which the patient appeared confused and asked whether someone might pour him "a large Mutt." Doing his best, he patched Raffles up and gave him something to knock him out. Probably the bar bill.

It was lunch on the following day before I caught up with A.J. again and heard his report of the rest of that night.

It seems I missed an anecdote about Dale's drunken pal in the old days who left a party and climbed up on the roof, waiting to jump down on some poor cricketing acquaintance as they were leaving. Unfortunately, he went to sleep on the roof and his intended quarry escaped undetected. As morning raised its clothy head, the madcap assassin woke up, having forgotten he was on a roof, stepped off, broke both his legs and never played first class cricket again. The Zimbabwean element thought this was terribly, terribly funny.

I'm not sure if Raffles might have been exaggerating, but apparently Dale attempted to introduce the hotel's guests to an old army game called 'Spots' and was nearly thrown out for his trouble. Allegedly, he was ejected from the Ten Thousand Horsemen Hotel in Zimbabwe in about 1972 for trying exactly the same thing.

The rules were simple enough: Make a mess in the middle of the table, encourage everyone to lean toward it, slap down on the sloppy pile with a cricket bat and the winner is the one with the most spots on their face. The winner buys a round of drinks, needless to say. What wasn't anticipated was the choice of material from which the pile should apparently be constituted, the nature of which contravened the broader human race's acceptable health and hygiene conventions.

It had probably taken all Raffles' diplomacy and charm to save the pair of them from global attention that night, but save them he did. I believe, in the end, he had to set Dale's trousers on fire to stop him. The big Zimbabwean had hesitated for over twenty seconds before using his vodka to put the flames out, but then again, he was like that.

You'd think that would be the end of the evening, wouldn't you? Well, no such luck. The nights in Africa are long indeed and some-times the most useful conversations are reserved for those with enough strength of mind and width of bladder to hear them. So it was that A.J. caught the big man in melancholy mood and heard tales of the abandoned lands.

He heard stories of the impotent dictator, whose wife unexpect-edly fell pregnant. His brother in-law co-incidentally died the very next day, found floating face down in a swimming pool.

He told of the Grain Board using road blocks to seize food for the cities and leaving people of the countryside to subsist by foraging. Some chose to eat animals from the National Parks, with their zebra-snares and spiked pits. All that was once protected now seen as a great larder with only the big cats for competition.

Unfortunately for the rest of the public, the removal of all the country's working farmers did little for food production. So, the masterstroke came. The captured lands were awarded to goat-herding squatters, seventeen year old veterans of the civil war that ended thirty years before. The war from which a penniless Marxist President had taken power of the third richest nation in Africa and transformed it into one of the poorest, whilst himself joining the elite of the richest men on Earth, in the name of the people.

The trouble with herding goats on arable farms is one of sustain-ability. When the goats have eaten all the crops, there's nothing to plant next year. Nothing to sell. The nation becomes a goat-only economy.

Raffles heard all these things and wanted to help. He had no suggestions though, nothing at all. Dale would just have to wait until the old man died. Dale would throw himself into his job and hope no one made the connection between an old soldier of the great game and a lavatory tank in the lost end of Africa.

I was relieved to be wrong this time. I would have bet my shirt and shoes on Raffles going.

Chapter 12

The Investigation Turns Sour

I'm not quite sure how I lost Wednesday, but I did. These things happen. I know it sounds odd, but there seemed to be only about two hours of daylight in the whole damn thing - a strange astronomical fact which no one but me noticed. Someone even tried to clean my room and then rushed away again as I surfaced from my mound of pillows and blankets to see what it was they wanted. "Should I come back later, Sir?" "Eh? No thanks." Then it was Thursday, the day the outlands opened and the circus came to town.

The first indication that something was up had arrived with the morning paper. International English language news is apparently a lot easier to get when the Test matches are on, so I'd taken advantage and ordered early. I disregarded a selection of clearly fabricated stories on the back pages (they claimed that all sorts of different things had happened on Wednesday, which I happened to know hadn't been long enough) and tossed the paper onto a chair at the call of a toothbrush.

When I returned from the bathroom, I noticed that I'd left the newspaper the wrong way up and the front page was showing.

Hansie Wepper. The repetition of the same name caught my attention. Wepper, Wepper, Wepper, in as many typefaces and headline sizes as my pre-breakfast mind could cope with. I wasn't prepared to believe he'd hit six sixes or something the day before; there hadn't been enough light. No, it looked like he hadn't done that. He'd done something most unusual instead. I woke up.

As anyone can tell you, summarising isn't my style. I prefer to explain things the long way around. However, the newspaper, with its finite allocation of column space, did it for me.

- South African Captain questioned over taking money from a bookmaker to lose the Test.

- The Public ask: What is Wepper playing for?
- Were players paid to drop catches and concede nine runs an over? The FACTS!
- The history of generous cricket declarations. From Anjab to Sobers to Wepper.

It was a mess alright. It seemed that once before a South African Test batsman had admitted accepting bribes to under-perform. They forgave him because, at the last minute, he found himself unable to go through with it. That man is still playing. The public mood was different for Wepper though, less charitable.

I showered and changed alone with my thoughts and my thoughts were bone-shakers. To me, it seemed the whole thing had been blown wide open. Bewildered, as usual I was, to see where the sticks and facts and fragments would land. I mean, would this knock confidence in the game? Would it place all of us under scrutiny? Would they arrest the bookmakers who'd then give up Raffles' name? Yesterday must have been excruciating for Wepper. I wondered what new victims today might bring.

I locked the door, walked downstairs and spent the next ten minutes totally failing to get through to breakfast. There seemed to be a press conference going on. One of the media people approached me.

'Excuse me, but can you tell me which one is Mr McKenna?'

I looked at her blankly.

'You don't follow cricket much, do you?'

'Not really. I'm usually assigned to the crime desk in Liverpool, but this story has a lot of crossover.'

'Yes, I suppose it has. Is there a lot of crime in Liverpool?'

'You don't follow crime much, do you?'

'Touché. Welcome to South Africa Miss…?'

'Boyd. How do you do?'

'Let me introduce you to the local landmarks then. In that direction is Table Mountain' I gestured, 'over there is the National Parks Game Reserve, that's the station for the Blue Train, one of the greatest railway journeys in the world, just to your left you'll see the towering hulk of Dale McKenna, over there you'll find the Cape and just beyond it live the coelacanth.'

'Thanks, although I think you'll find those particular fish live much further along the coast.'

It was only when she'd been gone for five minutes that I realised she hadn't bothered to ask my name. I don't mind when my chances fade out with a pop, but it would be an encouraging thing to believe I had the ghost of a chance in the first place. Oh well. How could anyone hope to compete with the steamy attractions of crime-scene reportage in Liverpool? Call me weird, but I couldn't think of anything worse.

'Surely he'll defend those charges?' said one of the passing newsmen.

'What's the point? He's already admitted most of them. He's even added some more of his own. Do you know anything about last year's one-day matches in India?'

'Not me Guv. Why, what have you heard?' replied Raffles, arriving on the scene with his usual off-hand theatre.

Half a dozen reporters rounded on him like piranha on a sunken breakfast.

'Ah, Mr Raffles! Would you like to say a few words?'

'Sure. I've just turned up here today to see if anyone can possibly believe him.'

'I'm sorry? We don't understand what you mean.'

'When the English team are rubbish, you wouldn't believe us for a minute if we came up with some lame excuse like we'd been paid to chuck it.'

'Thanks Raffles. Great quote. A little birdie tells us you're mates with Dale McKenna from the ICC Anti-Corruption Unit. What's the connection with your damaged hand?'

'As you know, Dale is allowed to give all the players Chinese burns until they admit everything.'

'Of course. Thank you for your time, Mr Raffles.'

Raffles shuffled through the room and joined up with Dale, so I made headway and tagged along.

'Ah spit. I wish I had a clue what he's going to say before he says it. You see, we're planning a major enquiry. I mean major. Nothing like this has ever happened before. Organising that's going to take more time and resources than we've got. If anything else happens, I'll have to follow it up without support.'

'Dale, why not just interview him and the other two then hand down a suitable punishment?'

I wasn't sure what Raffles meant by 'the other two'. I felt like I might be a chapter behind everyone else.

'That's not root & branch, is it? What about public confidence in the game?'

'They'll be caught and punished. That's enough, isn't it?' I asked, since no one had spoken to me yet.

'We're not so much after the junior players he's corrupted. The ones we really want are the bookmakers who paid the Captain. He wants to tell us quietly, over lunch somewhere, but what's the use of that? They'll say we hushed it up. No, we have to do this out in the open. Proper procedure and a proper legal defence for the players. Being public, honest and embarrassing is the only way the ICC can think of scaring anyone else away from accepting these payments.'

'You're very serious all of a sudden.'

'Yeas. Play time is over' confirmed Dale.

'So what are you going to do with him?'

'That's my problem for today. We can't stick him in prison. He hasn't broken any civil laws. He can't stay in the hotel. He can't speak with the team. The only thing we can ask him to do is piss off back to his place at Stellenbosch and drink himself stupid until we're ready to call him back. One thing's for sure; you won't be seeing him turn out for his country again.'

I looked at Raffles in earnest, but he didn't even blink.

At that point an ex-England Captain, now working for a satellite television broadcaster, spotted Raffles and Dale in the crowd and budged into our conversation.

'It's not on, is it? All this bribery and whatnot. I remember the days when cricket was cricket. Whacking great leather bowling boots. Bats that don't split to shrapnel every time you use them. Magical days in the West Indies, where the ball always seemed to bounce too high for the wicket, fifty was on for the good back-foot player, although they were never England's back-foot players, were they Raffles? D'you remember? Gravy danced in the stands and Blue Food blew the conch. We ate fish cutters, drank rum or bottles of beer in the Ship Inn, played moonlit cricket on the beach 'til late and couldn't get a wink of sleep for the sunburn! Lads, you haven't lived 'till Jumbo's thrown nuts at you and had a slap up seafood dinner at the Strawberry Mountain. Great days, hot nights.'

'I remember you spoiled it' said Raffles.

'Sorry?'

'You told that sadistic coach to ring us up first thing in the morning, every single day of the tour, requiring our supremely uncommitted presence on the morning training run.'

'Me?'

'Yes, you.'

'Yep. We did that' said Dale, to the surprise of Raffles.

'I thought you never toured the West Indies?'

'No, in Pakistan. It was the same, only different.'

He stared, challenging us to pursue the matter.

'Is it your turn to buy the drinks? Phew, it's like a desert in here.'

'I'll get these', said the England Captain, resuming his tour of the room and looking for a bar that wasn't there.

'Hey, Dale. Did you know where they sell that beer called 'Mutt'? You know the one. "Pint of Mutt please barman".'

'Yah. It was the bar with the funny sign. There's another one they have called Tug.'

'In Elizabethan England the most popular beer was called 'Left Leg' ' I mentioned, helpfully. That permanently extinguished the topic of conversation.

Dale picked his nose with care, seemed to remember something important and voiced it to Raffles.

'There was that one time at Headingley, d'you remember, when you came in to bowl and I had to walk away?'

In between the smiles of recollection, Dale turned to me.

'This bloke, right behind the bowler's arm, stood up...' A.J. was already smirking 'he only stood up to feed his whippet!'

Raffles was simmering with amusement 'He held up the whole Test Match. Still, I expect he named the puppies after us.'

'Hey, hey, hey. There was only one good looking puppy and he named that after me.'

'Ah, yes, but I expect he named the clever one after me.'

'Ah, trash mon. He named the annoying little wrecker after you. I bet he put an MCC dog collar on the damn thing and kicked it right out the front door! Come to think of it, I reckon I saw that dog the other day. Did you see him? A useless stray still hanging around the tour, proud of its own coils?'

Raffles took it well and acknowledged it was his turn to bring the drinks. He went off in search of the bar that never existed.

A waiter ambled past, slowed down in recognition and approached me conspiratorially.

'Garden of Proteas, Sir?'

'No thanks. Not just now.'

Dale looked around, shocked.

'Did you just refuse a drink? Hey, you English have got a lot to learn.'

'British.'

'You refused a drink! That makes you English. Look it up' and with that he headed off through the press of the Press and on toward the rostrum.

Before he made it through the last lines of the throng, a journalist with an identifiable Aussie accent budged up to him, angling for a quote.

'Hey, big man, you're not mates with that washed-up old lobber are you?'

Dale's expression changed and he answered with a controlled ferocity I hadn't witnessed before.

'How about shutting up, you little creep? I have *never* seen *anyone* move a ball further than A.J. Raffles. He can make those ruddy things *dance*. You'd better watch out 'cos he's got more to his game than that entire so-called bowling attack of yours. Oh boy, I'm gonna *enjoy* watching him cut you up in the Ashes. Most of all, I'm gonna enjoy reading what you've got to say about it. Was there anything else?'

The Aussie backed off in a hurry.

Dale seemed to think of something and leaned back into the throng to speak to me.

'Hey Mon, Bunny is it? For God's sake don't tell Raffles I said any of that, will you?'

'No, I'll tell him you said he was crap.'

'Yeah, that's right. 'Cos he is, officially.'

The room quietened in anticipation as Hansie Wepper, the (by now) ex-Captain of South Africa, slid out of the wings and sat down behind the raised table. He tried not to make eye contact, but seeing a few hundred pairs of eyes exclusively focussed on his, Hansie gave in and faced the music.

That was odd - one of my most uncomfortable moments. I hadn't expected to, but I felt sorry for him. I mean to say, there but for the grace of Raffles, go I.

Watching Wepper make his tearful confession, I could only think of my own courts-martial and how narrowly I'd escaped it. A trial that might not now happen, but if it did, one I unquestionably deserved. Wepper stood before the media. The same reporters who'd built him up and now gloried in his betrayals. My jury would have been soldiers, uniforms that insisted upon discipline and honour; uniforms that once would have died for me. Now, they might snip off my buttons and leave me for dead without a backward glance. Was I still on unpaid leave of absence? Was I cleared? I had no appetite to ask. I had hidden my crime and I did not know what would happen. Wepper had taken a braver path and I applauded him for it.

The irony of the situation struck me. Raffles had shielded my dishonesty and made my life horribly complicated. Wepper, with no such Raffles to save him, had chosen the honest route and a future of simplistic direction. I wondered what it would be like to swap; to own up and put one's relieved life in the hands of others. At least then, after the judgement, there would be no more worry.

I imagined Raffles hearing some of that and fetching me a look, the look he usually reserves for people who think cricket's boring and aren't ashamed to say so when they're wearing white socks and sandals.

Wepper spoke. Wepper confessed. I suppose he must have thought that by doing so the whole idea of a trial would become unnecessary. Various ICC representatives looked uneasy – they'd wanted a trial, hadn't they? They could still have one too, if they pushed for it. Wepper stepped away and left the room as the pack barked their questions after him.

When I finally fought my way out of the mosh pit, I cleared the corridor and spotted Raffles and Dale in the palm-fringed breakfast room ahead of me. How the hell had those two got out of the room first? Ah, I began to see. They must have, as VIPs, been let out through the wings at the front with Wepper. So, I concluded, fame opened doors.

Barely noticed, I filled a chair at their table as Raffles chatted away.

'What do you do when you're in London? I didn't notice you trying to get in touch.'

'For what? You know that last England coach, the one who came from Zim? He said blokes from the old country turning up at matches all the time and trying to be his best mate were a ruddy nuisance.'

'Good point, but in this case, you're invited.'

'Raffles, you're a horse's arse. I'd rather sit in my hotel room all day watching TV. It's more hygienic. No, as you were, that British television of yours has got so bad, I'd rather sit in front of the washing machine.'

'I thought you lot stayed at the Savoy? They must have palmed you off with a very cheap room if you've got to share with a washing machine. Seriously Dale, do you think you can remember a simple address?'

'Me? You're asking *me*? You can't tell me anything about memory. Geesh Raffles, you're so crap at that game, you can't even remember what mnemosyne means.'

He had me there.

'Come on, Dale. I'll have all your favourite drinks ordered especially.'

'All of them? I won't get slung out of that stupid club?'

'Not if you're good.'

'I am always good. I'm lacquer! Alright, I'll be around in October.'

That was quick.

'Excellent!'

'I'll enjoy it more if you're out.'

'Of course' waved Raffles, always the genial host, 'I wouldn't want to get under your feet. I'll just go out to a nightclub every evening'.

'Hey, hey, hey! I'd better come along. Someone's got to keep an eye on you.'

'Why October?'

'We're launching a *Purity of Cricket* campaign right around the world and that's when it begins.'

'Where are you starting?'

'Hove.'

'Good choice. They really are dreadfully impure down there. So, you're definitely dropping in then?'

'To talk and drink, mind. I don't want to see any TV shows with you in them.'

'No masterclass recordings, check.'

'Just vodka.'

'Vodka, check. What about beer?'

'... and beer.'

'Food?'

'First rule of life: Never eat on an empty stomach.'

'Dale, if you don't mind me asking, how are you still with us?'

'I'm a rufty-tufty-Rhodie.'

'That's the cause, not the explanation.'

'Raffles, you really are a duhrse.'

The invitations complete, 11am notwithstanding, I edged out to update the drinks order.

On the way to the bar, I thought at length about the 'watching videos' comment. Where had I encountered that before? Then I remembered. It was Cowes Week in about 1988. I'd spent a few days slouching around town in the disreputable company of society's teenagers - those Evelyn Waugh would once have termed 'bright young things.' The previous evening we'd gate-crashed a private party thrown by the drummer of a well known band. He knew we'd hopped the wall, but was still surprisingly welcoming, under the circumstances.

That night, we hadn't much to do. The Royal Corinthian Yacht Club ball began later, but none of us happened to be members of that one, so we gathered in the marina and soaked up the fading sunlight at one of the long crew tables overlooking the multiply-pontooned harbour. The nomadic wasps and the pervasive smell from binloads of warm plastic lager mugs weren't enough to spoil our and a thousand more summer daydreams. Ah, this was Cowes Week up-market. Cowes of the summer balls, before they retired the Royal Yacht Britannia. Cowes Week in the years before they scrapped 'Society' itself and it all went so hideously wrong.

One of the girls in our loose association popped up, appearing excited and breathless after an absence of an hour or two. Hey, she said, could we look after her bag and sunglasses? She'd met Simon Goodboy, the lead singer of the most successful band of that time, and he had asked her up to his hotel room. She was going. The tabloids of my memory kicked into gear. "Isn't he already engaged to... some model or other... oh, um, never mind." Okay, fine, I thought; what a fascinating sex life other people seem to have.

Two hours later, she came back. We didn't have to pry. "You won't believe what he did!" We leaned closer, whist at the same time trying to maintain that intangible air of sophisticated disinterest. "We went up to his room."

"Yes?"

"He fixed me a drink..."

"Yes?"

"Then he sat in a chair and showed me videos of himself! For God's sake, someone get me a punch bowl."

"Full or empty?"

We did. Closer examination revealed little more than the fact she'd seen all of his pop videos and most of his mid-Eighties hair-styles, some of them three times over with different edits. Too much fame can be a terrible thing. Clearly, in his case, the only person he really, really, wanted to sleep with was himself.

That's the trouble with presumption. I'm sure you'll remember it was years, decades even, before we found out that prawn toasts are eighty percent pork fat, Bombay Duck is a fish and corned beef isn't *really* made from cattle.

Chapter 13

Unpleasant News From Georgeives Mountain

The following morning was bright, cheerful and rife with rumours of match-fixing. When I was young, some friends had a band called 'Oblivion'. Electric guitars and whatnot. They practiced secretly in an old mechanical workshop in the village. There were rumours they were really good. Then they had a concert. They weren't. The point is, sometimes the rumours sound better than the real thing. I went to the nets.

A.J. was already there, watching some ground staff kicking the bowling machine.

'It's useless. A heap of old tins. Push it in the sea and we'll have throw downs' advised a waiting batsman.

Raffles took on the challenge 'I'll have it working yet.'

'That would invalidate the warranty.'

I don't think A.J. even bothered to register sounds on that wavelength.

The two great wheels that were designed to clutch the ball turned aimlessly.

'What's that latch for?'

'That's where you pop the hatch and raise the wheel to feed the hamsters.'

'No need to be sarcastic.'

'Why don't they replace it then?'

That was Mercer, touring for the first time. His illusions of technological, managerial and medical support would soon be dispelled by a frustrating month on the veldt. A small crowd had gathered by now, mostly to watch Raffles work. It was a novelty. They'd probably though that his type never had to.

'Oh, they're too tight, as usual. Okay, so a modern one's expensive, but they can't say they haven't got the money. They'd just prefer to spend it on some new PR agent or pour it away on another round of hospitality. Do you know how much they spent on that kids' cartoon series about lions playing cricket?'

'Careful now, that sort of talk will get you vaporised... or is it liquidated?'

'It's a lot easier to vaporise something if you liquidate it first' said Raffles, pitching in as a ghostly echo from the thorax of the machine.

'Good point, good point' said one. 'Naturally Raffles, we don't have your advantage. All those hours you spend at your posh club, swapping notes with Davros.'

'What would happen if this thing broke?' asked Mercer, tapping it with a helpful boot.

'Then we might get it replaced. Half-working though, they'll just keep it flogging along and pay a stack to lug it round the world so we can enjoy watching it break down just before the first Test in every major cricketing nation.'

'Oh, back to your marks gentlemen, it's a stuck cylinder. I've got it now.' *Whhrrrrrrrrr.*

'Just a sec, Raffles! You're supposed to switch it off from the mains before you do things like that.'

I could have told them, I really could, but it would mean upping the insurance. Raffles was always clever at mechanical engineering. Less so at safety. I know for a fact that the young Raffles used to saw down council signs that read 'no ball games on this public common', partly from protest, but more often because he liked to see cars parked illegally on the grass getting their windows smashed.

Wheels revolved, a mild hum turned into urgent susurration and they poured a bucket of balls into the hopper. '*Thwang - Kapuck*' said the cricket ball in a fit of healthy playfulness.

'Cheers A.J.'

That concluded Raffles' net practice. Not because he'd lost interest. It was just one of those times when the rumbling snore of history woke enough to take a turn. Sometimes I think we all forget that we're living in history. We didn't then.

'Gather round, everyone. Please, gather round. I have some news which will affect the tour.'

This was the first occasion on which I'd heard James 'Mr Pye' Thurston, the England Captain speak. His nickname originated as a university joke, probably referenced to a book by Mervyn Peake, but no one using the nickname today had any idea why 'Mr Pye'. Still, they used it anyway and he never seemed to mind. As Captain, Thurston had always delegated the trivial administrative announcements to the Tour Manager and Coach, so the players spilled from the nets, sensing this could be something serious.

'I'm sure I can say openly now that, in the First Test, the South African Captain made what turned out to be a terrible tactical mistake. The declaration policy of opposing teams is, of course, an internal matter for the opposition. We can only be expected to tackle the tactical situation we have been presented.'

The players nodded and murmured in agreement. Thurston paused, as if running through the words he could or couldn't say.

'For a few days now, the Press have been saying that we didn't win that match after all and yesterday's announcement by Hansie Wepper adds a great deal of weight to that opinion.'

'That's an insult! You should make a public statement rejecting it' interrupted Mercer.

'Mercer, I take it that you are not fully aware of the statement made yesterday?'

'Not really. I was busy practicing.'

'No one told you?'

'Um, no. The people I was practicing with were busy practicing.'

'Do be quiet then. For anyone else who's been on the Martian surface for the preceding twenty four hours, I'm afraid it's much too late for firm rejections. Events have now overtaken us. As everyone else seems to know, an enquiry has been opened and adjourned to investigate the very serious allegation that the South African Captain held a close association with a bookmaker who may, or may not, have encouraged him to affect the course of the First Test match.'

'For cash' said Quince.

'For cash' Thurston confirmed.

'Surely, that's their problem? It's going to trash their morale for the Second Test!'

'Enough. Mercer. Alright? Please listen to me.'

'Sorry Captain.'

'Yesterday afternoon, a South African seam bowler presented himself at the ICC building in Cape Town, in the company of his lawyer. He then volunteered a written statement in which, I am told, he claims that Wepper instructed him to concede runs in his bowling spell on the final day.'

With that, everyone knew exactly which bowler he was talking about.

'At the same time, representatives of the Anti-Corruption Unit were interviewing the South African Captain at the Central Police Station. Faced with this development, Wepper abandoned his defence and admitted not only his association with more than one bookmaker, but also that he had previously accepted free accommodation, holidays and a separate payment to influence a one-day international fixture in India.'

This was news. With the Wepper confession, the Anti-Corruption unit must have had a field day, which would have been quite an unusual event in itself. As Raffles said, they rarely found any reliable sources of information. The great thing was that all leads went through Wepper. The bowler reported to him and he had spoken to the bookmaker. With him as a co-operative star witness, the betting syndicate might even be done for... which would perhaps let Raffles and I off the hook!

'Thanks for telling us early, Skipper.'

'I haven't finished. This isn't easy, so please bear with me. In the last hour, I have received a telephone call from the President of the ICC. He has considered it his duty to inform me of the events of yesterday evening, about which a public announcement will be made shortly.'

They were all listening carefully now.

'At 5pm, after Wepper agreed to cooperate with the investigation, the Chairman advised him to go home and make his legal preparations. Clearly something of this magnitude would take a couple of months to set up - the paperwork, briefing defence lawyers, that sort of thing and as Wepper was about to tell them the names of all the people he'd been paid by, they wanted a show. They thought they'd won.'

This perplexed us a little. I mean the unexpected use of the past tense.

'Trying to avoid the media, Wepper left immediately for the regional airport, intending to travel back to his family home in Stellenbosch. It seems that, when he arrived at the airport, he discovered that there were no more flights that day and so he found himself stuck. Deciding not to return to a city full of reporters, he spoke to the crew of a cargo plane which happened to be heading to his local airport. They offered to take him.'

'How does any of this affect us?'

Thurston closed his eyes and counted to five, struggling to stay calm.

'It affects us, it affects our very presence in this country, because, just after 8pm, the cargo aircraft that Hansie Wepper was travelling in impacted against the Western slope of Georgeives Mountain.'

'Survivors?' asked Raffles.

'No one survived the crash.'

A whacking great mountain. Who'd have thought it? Bam! Cancel the inquiry. Sorry – poor taste.

We stood in silence.

'Poor beggar' said Mercer.

No one had the stomach for practicing cricket after that. Familiar faces drifted away in respectful contemplation. Apart from A.J., who changed his mind and had a batting net all to himself.

To this day, the air crash investigators believe this accident was the result of poor visibility. I must say, I used to think that planes were comparatively safe. Still, hard things to see, mountains. Invisible to radar. Not always clearly marked on the map. With the South African Captain on board, I thought this might just be one of those million to one chances that the man from the betting syndicate had warned us about.

Chapter 14

Tennis Ball Bounce

Raffles exited the team meeting early. This was rather unexpected, so I had to step back from the door. As he passed through, I could hear the end of the Tour Manager's briefing.

'Now you've all got your strategic flow diagrams with process notes on the back?'

Some players waved the bits of paper they'd been issued with.

'Sorry about the hotel's black and white copies everyone. It doesn't really make sense if it's not in colour.'

Good start.

'That brings me on to my first point. How does everyone feel about interactive role-play? What we're looking for, people, is colour, inspiration, out of the box thinking! Now come on guys, let's get the wagon rolling. Hit me with something wacky! Right out of left field! Come on people. There's no such thing as a bad idea.'

'Hiring him was a bad idea' said Raffles as he joined me in the corridor. He doesn't know the difference between affect and effect, so he uses 'impact' all the time instead. One of these days, I'll give him impact.

'Would you like to hit him with something wacky? I've heard you can have people professionally murdered in this country for as little as three hundred pounds.'

Raffles thought over the implications of that, staring all the while at his black and white photocopy with incomprehensible flowchart bubbles plastered all over it. He folded the pointless thing carefully into a sort of origami admiral's hat and deposited it on one of the hotel's pot plants. We began walking.

'Dropped' said Raffles, succinctly. We continued in silence down the stairs.

'Oh, I see. So at last you've been cast into the outer darkness.'

'Outer darkness isn't a problem. It's inner darkness that worries me.'

That morning's breakfast was a tortuous one. The mood wasn't lightened by a sunny egg. The wide smile of melon had little effect on us. Even the 'tree of happiness' in the middle of the table failed to raise a chuckle.

Then, just as we thought it couldn't get any worse...

'Hi Phil' said Raffles. He'd broken the silence after a dozen minutes, but only because the bowling coach had plonked down next to him.

'Mind your back, Raffles. Our favourite latté-fuelled idiot is looking for you.'

'Jerome De Zemantal?'

'Of course. He thinks he's going to come over and talk you round to the team ethic with his award winning conversation, but he wants to finish his panini first.'

'I don't need this.'

'Of course you don't. What you need is an old-fashioned bacon butty. That's what you need to put you right.'

'No, I mean I... oh, never mind.'

It was true; he didn't. None of us did. Unfortunately, the Tour Manager noticed us across the room and kept a close watch in case we made a run for it. I could see the panini disappearing, chomp by chomp, like one of those string fuses they used to attach to the sticks of dynamite beneath Penelope Pitstop.

'Raffles?'

'Yes Phil?'

'Jerome sent you an email about a performance analysis, which was copied to me. Do you remember?'

'I recall something of the kind.'

'Only it didn't have any spelling mistakes.'

'No?'

'No, but when you replied and copied it to *everybody*, you accidentally included Jerome's original email to you, only this time it had about ten spelling and punctuation errors and made him look like a fool.'

'How awful. Is there a problem?'

'I just wanted to say that the coaching staff think you're a bit of a legend.'

'Thanks Phil. Could you distract the fool when we slip out?'

'My pleasure.'

Whatever he did, it wasn't enough. The Tour Manager dropped the end of his panini, sprang out of the breakfast room, changed to the stroll of someone who just happened to be passing and intercepted A.J. in the corridor. It wasn't as nonchalant as he'd planned. Jerome almost had to trip A.J. up to stop him.

'Raffles, Raffles, my man! Hey, hey, hey, whoah there bronco!'

'What?'

'You left the briefing early today. I'd like to think we haven't got off on the wrong foot.'

'A cricket expression?'

'Was it?' That threw him. 'Um, trust me, Raffles. I do know my cricket.'

'If you're a selector, the reasoning behind which I am not, why did you originally select me for the tour?'

De Zemantal seemed un-phased by the sentence.

'Fuzzy logic. The software came up with your name as someone the South African computers wouldn't have flagged their coaches to prepare their players against.'

'That's ridiculous.'

'It's only temporary. We will soon be delivering electronic market-place functionality to the team selection process.'

'I thought you'd already persuaded the ECB to pay for expensive software to do something like that.'

'Yah, yah, but the software's not out of the implementation transition phase.'

'It's broken?'

'It's resting and will be back online as soon as we've refreshed some bad clusters in the code. It's all good.'

'It's broken.'

'Resting' insisted Jerome, which earned a pitiful stare from Raffles.

'Perhaps you could stick to managing the tour and let the Captain pick the team.'

'Why would we want to do that?'

'He's a cricketer.'

'So he's never had a real job? He knows nothing of business process? I'm here for you guys. We're just repurposing the team learning activity to position our talent-base for the push to the back line.'

'You're doing what?'

'Repurposing.'

'Are you on our side?'

'A.J., can I call you A.J.? I understand the game and I really appreciate the cards you're bringing to the table. You know where I learnt to think 'Team'? Barbados, man. I was touring with my team, my willow, learning, paying my dues. First shot at captaincy. Playing against the Shield sides all day then beach cricket with the Rastas and crack-dealers on the sand at night, until we couldn't see the ball any more, man! Then we went to The Village, it's a hard Rasta ghetto where they respect real cricket. They just live it. That's where I learned to crush up aloe vera leaves and soak them in rum to get the sunburn out. I was the only white guy there, man. They taught me how to play the conch! D'you see?' he pointed, 'I got this scar on my eye that night. A bouncer. I didn't see it off the beach and the seam cut me. That's my dues paid, Raffles. I know cricket. Trust me. I'm in your corner. I'll speak for you. This is a team, Raffles. You've got to lay down your life for the team. That's respect. This team's looking at you. This team's thinking 'winner'!'

He gave a thumbs-up gesture, smiled artificially and got in the lift. In the fond hope he'd vanish up his own lift-shaft, I sighed and turned to Raffles.

'You don't look convinced.'

In fact, A.J. looked more isolated than I've ever seen him. No, there was more to his expression than that. He looked both deadly serious and somehow betrayed.

'Tennis ball' he whispered.

'Sorry?'

'In the West Indies, they don't play beach-cricket with a cricket ball. It doesn't bounce off the sand.'

'Ah.'

We looked silently across as the lift doors closed.

'Where did you learn that?'

'Oh, a long time ago, in the Caribbean. It was quite late in the evening, on a beach, just walking distance from The Village in Barbados. A few years ago I mentioned all this to an office manager at the ECB.'

'You weren't cut by a tennis ball too?'

'No, my story didn't have a scar.'

'What a strange co-incidence that both of you should have done the same thing.'

'Yes, most unusual. That piece of slime has just told my own anecdote straight back at me.'

I couldn't find anything to say for a minute or two, so we stepped through the hotel in near silence.

'Raffles?'

'Yes, Bunny.'

'Do you remember the bit in Genesis about bringing forth the creeping crawling things that creepeth up upon the Earth?'

'Yes?'

'Well, I think he might be one of them.'

Raffles normally had an excellent way of getting rid of people politely. He just repeated 'Oh, really. How interesting' until they became nervous from it, gave up and drifted away. Simple, polite and effective, leaving very little room for complaint. Unfortunately, since Jerome had no intention of drifting away from the very management of Raffles' workplace, this method would never be enough to dislodge him.

They'd reached an impasse. Raffles wouldn't respect him and yet Raffles wouldn't rebel. Jerome wouldn't change and enjoyed the comfortable protection of a signed three year contract. Could the Tour Manager alone arrange for Raffles to be dropped? I wasn't convinced. For the time being, they'd just have to avoid each other. Anyway, I'm sure Jerome would find a way to get the flow diagrams to Raffles.

The best method of getting rid of people that I can report wasn't the 'how interesting' or even the other extreme, as traditionally practiced by our colleagues in Sicily; it was 'the hive scenario'.

In our schooldays, as A.J. could confirm, we had an old biology master who used to keep bees. I think it was a hobby to pass the evenings when he wasn't lecturing or pickling occasional amphibians. When he felt like shaking off over-zealous students trotting around after him, insisting he provide a timeframe by which whales lost their legs and ceased to be classified as land animals, he'd simply walk into the lavender gardens and stand silently in the middle of a moot of five or six working bee hives. The enquirers never stayed long.

We walked out to the nets, alongside the hotel complex. Raffles wanted to bat, to take out his frustration on something, and with most of the players still inside, this looked like a good opportunity. At least, it did until we saw who was there already.

'Morning Dale' said Raffles, dumping a bag by the net.

'Morning Dog-Ball. Hey! Who told you that you could bat? I don't believe your gonna try! Pull up a chair folks, this is gonna be funny!'

'Give him a break today, Dale' I said. 'He's been left out of the eleven.'

'Ah, nuts. Forget it, Brew. You haven't a chance bowling spinners on that pitch. It's flatter than Keira Knightley.'

'There's such a thing as flight, angle and change of pace, you know' said Raffles.

'Man, let it go. Hey! You should listen to me. I never bear grudges!'

'I think I know this one. "In South Africa a grudge is somewhere to paok your coah", yes?'

'Raffles, you are a horse's arse.'

'Just because I'm better than you at everything'

'I'm better than you at batting!'

'Batting isn't everything.'

There was a pause as Dale worked this out in his head. Had someone just scored a point?

'Well you've got no ruddy timing. Just look at your hook shot.'

'What hook shot?'

'Exactly. If you listened to me a bit more, you might get the ball off the square. Then they *couldn't* drop you 'cos you'd be the only England player who can.'

'Au Revoir Dale' replied Raffles, deciding he'd prefer a short walk than to bat under these conditions.

'Sod *right off* Raffles!' replied Dale cheerfully 'I hope a sandpaper company sponsors your jockstrap.'

'Jolly good. See you on Wednesday.'

'Not if I see you first. People might think we know each other.'

More players arrived, some nodding to Dale and Raffles as they set themselves up. The regular klunk of cricket balls being hit blended into the backing track of the living city.

With the confidence of a factory owner, Dale walked amongst the nets where a dozen household names were now practising. A streak of red shot out of one enclosure and 'Like a panther!' came the cry as Dale tripped up and fell on the ball, effectively arresting its progress. He then stood up, looked contemplative, released the most appalling tunnel of wind I've ever witnessed and announced to one and all 'Breathe deeply children! There are vitamins in the air.'

A few people stared at him, but most tried not to think about it. Dale looked for a moment like going into the nets himself, but then passed up the opportunity and distracted himself for an unnecessary amount of time discarding and clattering through a heap of bats as he tried to find 'the heavy one'.

I suddenly realised what had been bothering me all along. Raffles wasn't at all interested in the game now that he wouldn't be able to affect the outcome. That was it, wasn't it? The selfish little oaf! It was on this day, the nth of the nth, that the feeling crept up on me that I didn't really know this person at all.

I don't know what I'd expected. Alright, I do know what I'd expected and it wasn't this. What I'd expected was a sudden image of him in RAF uniform, chewing a pipe, watching the symbols moving around a war-room map and muttering 'God, I wish I was up there with them'. Nope. Not a bit of it. When Raffles wasn't needed, Raffles bogged off down the beach.

I had a sudden image of the 12th Man, a position in the squad and yet not playing. There he'd be, sitting pointlessly on a bench for five days and wondering how A.J. was coping with all that trouble-some sand on a beach speckled with a bunting of bikinis, suffering all those horrendous interruptions from waiters with trays of snacks and cocktails. 'God I wish I was down there with him'. Well, you can't be. Your job's to sit here for five days in case one of the batsmen calls for water or new gloves or any number of other things they could get for themselves. Oh, by the way, tighten my spikes would you?

To fully appreciate the advantages of being a senior player, it is best to make a list of all the disadvantages of being a junior player. Sharpen your pencil. Now cross them all off. Isn't that satisfying?

I broke into a trot and caught up with Raffles. He looked as if he didn't care if I spoke to him or not.

'You absolutely don't give a damn about this match, do you? You aren't even interested!' I was fraught.

He shrugged.

'Is this just a job to you? Just cover for your other life? Tell me once and for all, Raffles. Do you even like cricket?'

An old bowler pretended to search his soul.

'I refer the honourable gentleman to the popular answer by Dreadlock Holiday.'

Alright, so I fell headlong into that one. In fact, in the long history of jockeys pulling twigs out of their hair at the bottom of that godawful ditch at Beechers Brook, I doubt anyone pitched into an obvious one as blindly as I did then. I tried making the same point in a different way.

'Raffles, I hope you don't mind me saying to, but you don't act much like a team player.'

Raffles fixed me with something I'd rarely seen before, his 'I'm impressed' expression. You know, the full attention variety he reserves for those rare occasions when one of the assumedly negligible suggests a cutting insight into something like the behaviour of the thermic cascade in supra-molecular chemistry. Okay, so I don't know anything about supra-molecular chemistry, but I was on a roll here, so I made do.

'Bunny, in this world, variance is as important as the mean.'

I ignored that, mostly because I didn't understand it.

'Only, they always say cricket is a team game and it occurs to me that you play it very much alone, which doesn't seem to make much sense.'

I had earned his 'I'm impressed' expression Mark II, which was very rare indeed and I think he gets them especially from a private catalogue.

'Which means, I can't help thinking, if you were a soldier under my command I'd have to promote you or shoot you or maybe both.'

Raffles laughed. I smiled back and wondered if he was going to explain anything at all. Raffles almost certainly also wondered whether he was going to explain anything at all. In the end, he must have thought 'why not?' The lancing was true enough and out the poison came.

'Alright. Where shall I start?' His eyes toured the room as if for inspiration. 'Do you understand the thinking behind a collapse of batting?'

'I know they drop like a line of dominoes.'

'Yes, but why do they get out?'

'Is it because they're not accustomed to the conditions at the start and it makes them vulnerable?'

'Good try, but not the whole story. In any batting order, the players at the top of the list are perceived to be better than the players coming in after them. The players at the very end are normally bowlers, who tend to be unaccomplished batsmen, sometimes called 'rabbits', Bunny.'

Did he drop that in deliberately?

'Okay.'

'The last one has sometimes been referred to as 'the ferret', because he's so bad, he comes in after the rabbits.'

'Ah, right. Um, I don't see your point.'

'That's not my point. The point is that if someone at the top gets out and then the next man gets out straight away, the players after that panic. They will think 'Those two batsmen are so much better than I am, there's no chance of me lasting more than a few balls out there.' So, they aren't concentrating and they get out too. The next player comes in and thinks 'Ah, hell, those three batsmen are so much better...' and it just gets worse and worse until all the rabbits are back in the hutch. So, my question to you is... why?'

'I don't know.'

'It is because they are team players. Lemmings are team players. Fish in bait-balls in whales' stomachs are team players.'

'What do you do then?'

'In a collapse? Easy. I have an entirely different view of the matter. In my mind, I am in competition with the opposing team *and* with my team. I aim to be the best player on the pitch every time I step out on it. Often I'm not, but that shouldn't affect the psychology. If my team is surrendering pathetically, I ask myself 'What's the top score so far? Eleven? All I need is to make twelve runs and I'll be the top scorer! If my team look like being cleared in half a day, I think 'This is great! I've got all the time in the world to make a big score! No pressure!' After reaching the first twelve or whatever it is, I'll set a new target: 'If I can make forty, I'll have more runs than the rest of the team put together!' Then I might move on to 'If I can make double the rest of the team, I can really embarrass them! What's the highest score made by the opposition? Eighty three? I wonder if I can beat that...' and so on.'

'What happens if you're team's definitely lost and you're still batting?'

'That's when I get bloody-minded. The opposition will know they've won and it's just a matter of time, so I try to frustrate their celebrations. I'll say to myself 'We have one wicket left, but there are eleven of you standing around out here. If I can bat for one hour, I can keep you lot running about in the noonday sun for eleven hours! If I can string this out for two whole hours, I'll keep you here for the rest of the day. Then we'll see how much energy you've got for the next match. Perhaps one of their key players will pull a hamstring or something. Yes, let's try and win the next match right here. I've got nothing better to do.'

'Does it ever work?'

'Historically? Once upon a time, there was a Test between Australia and South Africa. The last two Australian batsmen were at the crease on the evening of the third day, with four overs remaining. They'd followed on, had hundreds to make and were surely about to lose. 'Listen Mate' said one to the other, 'Let's have a slog and get out now. I can't see the point of coming back tomorrow', which is what they did. South Africa won the Test that night and they all went home.'

'So?'

'For the next two days it rained solidly and no play would have been possible. If they'd survived those few overs, they wouldn't have lost.'

'I'm beginning to understand. In cricket, as in a battle, you can win, lose or draw. If a side can't win, they should try to hold on for a draw and give themselves a chance to win another day, even if it looks unlikely. Your personal tactic is that if you can't win and can't draw, you try to damage them to give you more chance in the next encounter?'

'Essentially.'

'In essence then, you're also saying that when your team has collapsed and you're not out, you weren't part of their failure, so you've won a sort of victory?'

'Not just that. I can actively stop the collapse if I refuse to let my team's failure upset me. If I ignore them, play in my own little world and hang around, the other players will realise the bowling is playable and scoring runs is possible after all. Their perspective changes and there isn't a collapse! The scare evaporates and balance is restored. Then, you'll usually find they have the confidence to score a few runs too.'

'Do you share in their successes?'

'No. That would be unconstructive. If the team has won and I have performed badly, I brood on the matter, identify the weaknesses in my performance and arrange practice to restore those skills. If the team has lost, but I've done something exceptional, I'm delighted. I go to parties.'

I wondered how that logic would go down in the Army. At the first opportunity, they'd shoot him in the back. Perhaps *before* the first opportunity, just on reputation.

'Unusual. You aren't egotistic though. I'd have expected the two things to go together.'

No comment to that one. I lured him experimentally toward an unseen net. I once did that to a brown trout in Tobermory Bay, something you have only my word for. Ooh, it was about *that* long.

'I am just about following this reasoning so far. You're saying that playing for yourself, in competition with your own side, indirectly helps the team?'

'Yes.'

'So, by association, you'd justify greed by saying the wealthy pay more income tax, which piles up a bigger war-chest to spend on the poor?'

I'd carned one of his 'I'm not impressed' looks and the conversation dried. Obviously not a classic social idealist then. Cambridge must have changed.

I remembered annoying my father, just for the sake of it, with entirely the same sort of comment. He called me 'a radical' and stopped my pocket money. I don't know why I say these things. I suppose I just can't help it. In a previous life I was probably a downtrodden Peruvian, although no, probably not that. I couldn't get used to life in a bowler hat. In that case, I might have been one of those chappies who threw spanners into Spinning Jennies and other roomfuls of expensive machinery in the cast-iron belief that this sort of action would stop them losing their job.

I thought I'd go for a coffee, if only for the sake of something to do.

'Bunny' he called after me.

'What?'

'It is your left wing nature that notices the unfairness in life, but it's your right wing thinking that suggests the solution is to knock down the offenders. You wobble, Bunny. You are a wave, not a particle.'

I rolled away and left the particle stranded on the beach of its own superiority. If that doesn't make sense, you'll at least know how I felt about Raffles just then.

He followed me, so I ditched the idea of a coffee and turned out toward the nets.

'Leave me in peace for a moment, would you?'

'I need to be sure you're alright.'

'I'm alright.'

I had turned back, but then thought 'why?' I honestly didn't care if Raffles talked to me or not. Actually, I preferred not. I could wander around this country quite happily without towing a thundercloud.

Taking in the sights and sounds of my privileged access to the practice areas, I found myself distracted by the increasing volume around one cricket net, where an elite clamour of the most respected international bowlers seemed intent on drawing lots for the honour of blasting Dale's supremely annoying head off. Yes, it was definitely Dale. Nowhere on Earth is there another silhouette like that. Actually, I suppose if you lifted a garden toad up by the ears and viewed the side-on profile. No, sorry, that's too cruel. You shouldn't do that to toads.

I watched with morbid fascination as one of the fastest bowlers in the sport steamed down a long runway and launched a lightning quick delivery aimed at the loudmouth's ribs, which Dale instantly stepped forward to and pulverised back over the bowler's head, followed by a call of "You've gotta be faster than that to be a Roebanker, Pal!"

So, this was Dale. I don't think I could improve on that character study if I had all day, which I hadn't. It was time to go.

Chapter 15

Good fer Now't but Bowlin'

For all these years, the overriding impression I've had of an international cricketing tour was the cricket. You know the form – whites, padded up and trying to survive a testing spell in the middle. Having now experienced tagging along on one of these campaigns, my impressions are of waiting, the local distractions, avoiding photographers, internal politics, lots more waiting and then the endless rounds of net practice. When the schedule clears and the players are actually allowed a go at the opposition, it's a genuine change of scene.

The endless net practices had at last worn down the resistance of Raffles to the point at which he took the almost ridiculous step of inviting me along to one. I hadn't batted in years and my bowling was unlikely to fall on the cut strip, so I supposed I was there for little more than entertainment.

Concerned that I might embarrass myself, as usual, I turned up early and hoped I'd have time to remind myself of how it was done. I knocked the ball around for a while, patiently coached by a club pro, but just as I began to enjoy it and my defence was holding, a familiar voice quite put me off.

'No, no. no. Get up the track to the spinners! Knock them the feck back over their heads! Spinners should not be on the same field as you. Spinners shouldn't be bowling! If you give a spinner respect, you should quit right now before it gets *embarrassing*.'

'Hi Dale. I'll tell Raffles you said.'

'Yeas - and he's the worst of them, that blue eyed son of a hyena. I don't suppose you've noticed, but all the other devils have got black eyes, black as toddy bricks, but not that one. Oh no, he's got blue you see, 'cos he's in *disguise*. He still stinks of sulphur though, that Raffles. If you're ever at Lords, check his locker. I bet you it's got a ruddy pitchfork in it.'

My mind cast back to the inter-school matches, so many years before, in which A.J. had taken enough five wicket hauls to beat the county record. Thirty, at least, of those occasions had been on our school's main pitch, flattened and compacted as a tank-drivers' training ground in the wars. Different wars were fought there now; wars of grace and timing. There was never much there for spinners, but when Raffles couldn't blast them out with pace, he lured them out with spin. It was an amazing thing to watch.

Whoosh!

'Sorry, I wasn't concentrating' I explained to the bowler who'd grazingly missed my nose.

'Don't do that. You'll lose your off-peg' chirped Dale.

'That was nowhere near my off-peg.'

'Pardon me. I didn't realise you had it under control.'

I concentrated and concentrated and tried to block out all the advice he was giving me. I thought I was doing well, right up to the point where the club bowlers stopped giving me practice because they didn't want to waste all their energy on such an obvious amateur. I called it a day and handed over my net.

By now, the real crowd-pleasers of the game had arrived. Quince, with his beautifully timed cover drives. Mercer, with his elegant leg-cutters that made fools of fine batsmen. Westlicott, ah yes, I wasn't the only one interested to see the county 'big hitter' practicing. He'd just flown out to join the squad after touch-and-go medical clearance. Something about recovering from torn intercostals, which had kept him out of the early matches. Westlicott was a name. Westlicott was a reputation. Actually, I'd never seen him bat, except on TV, where everyone seems older and wider and somehow more capable.

Watching him warm up was a little dull, but quite a few spectators had gathered around to see him do it. Quality bowlers too, watching, waiting to see which net he'd go into for their chance to take a scalp worth bowling. Pat, pat, pat. He took throw-downs from the England coach. Ah good, he'd had enough. Now we'd see some fireworks!

Westlicott walked past net after net, oblivious to the queue of bowlers that were stalking him. Right to the end, in fact, where much to the chagrin of the professionals, he faced a hundreds of seemingly identical deliveries from the bowling machine. To the further exasperation of the crowd, he then spent an age repeating much the same sort of shot.

Club bowlers aplenty asked other England players if they'd get a shot at him. The wicket keeper put them right, although he didn't enjoy doing it.

'Sorry lads, but he never takes normal net practice because he doesn't like the inconsistency. He doesn't care much for local lads dropping short or firing the ball down the leg side all the time. He just practices against perfect line and length.'

They didn't seem impressed.

'He's an arrogant one, since he left the academy. What's his Test average so far? Zero?'

'Don't worry mon, that will soon go up' said a Durban professional.

'You reckon?'

'Yeah. Sure. As soon as he meets a team of eleven bowling machines. Until that happens, he's stuffed.'

'Sorry lads. You can't tell him' consoled the keeper. 'Have a bowl at me for a while. I need the practice.'

'Cool mon.'

They seemed placated.

Raffles arrived without even looking about and threw his kit, stumps and things, into the back of a pick-up truck. Soon after that I noticed two locals who'd been following close behind with cardboard boxes. They formed an impromptu human chain and handed ten or more six-packs of beer along to the harassed driver, who then brightened up considerably and seemed on very relaxed terms with Raffles.

A.J. pulled a heavy cricket hold-all across the grass, an old fashioned canvas 'coffin-bag' though hugely overloaded, and heaved that into the truck too. He paused to slide out a single bat and trotted with it over to Dale, who was by now holding court as if he owned the place.

'You've brought the heavy then.'

Raffles handed it to him, said something I was much too far away to pick up, turned on his heel and left the ICC rep standing bereft.

'Aw, come back Raffles! I want to see you get injured. Where are you running to?'

'Raffles, I don't know if you've noticed, but the nets are that way' I reminded him.

'The team nets are that way, yes. *My* nets however are *this* way.'

We drove off and left the team to it. Dale shouted something insulting and Raffles waved regally.

During the trip, through roads lined with box houses and tattered shops, Raffles introduced me to the driver who helped him do the same thing on this very tour six years before. Raffles spent the journey telling us many things. I can't remember all of it, but I know he said that in a Test match it's lack of concentration or the unexpected ball which gets you out. Apparently, orthodox players don't spend long at the top level due to the obvious handicap that everyone's spent the last three hundred years learning from each other exactly how to get orthodox players out. Then there was something about de-hydration, which I'm afraid I didn't listen to.

'Bunny, do you remember when we were chatting to that detective? Well it reminded me of something I heard a long time ago. Do you know how Zulu justice works?'

'I don't think I do, no' I answered, preparing for further and better useless information.

'Sometimes, when they collar the condemned man, they discuss him for a while, just to put the fear up him, then make an offer he'll jump for. One last chance and such a simple thing, when all's said. The criminal is offered freedom if he can follow a five year old child for a day and do everything that the child does. He'll take it, Bunny. Then he'll lose and be put to death.'

'Why?'

'The young are so much more active, pound for pound. As we get old and wise, we also get slow. We can't keep up. Should I wait for England to tell me I'm over the top? No, I won't let it come to that. Sometimes it's wise to pit yourself against the fit and young. The amateur assassins. The ones with raw energy, wildfire in their hearts and absolutely not one damned ounce of respect. The untrained, the unrefined who deliver the unexpected. I won't learn much against the bowling machine, Bunny. I prefer to be kept sharp with a challenge or two. I need the mental discipline to survive an unexpected delivery or unfamiliar thinking when I'm at my most exhausted. Can a bowling machine give me that? I don't think so. I don't think I can practice for the randomness of life against a routine because life doesn't have one. I need chaos, lack of respect. I need to run for a while with those Zulu kids.'

'They're not Zulus mister. We're in the wrong province' pointed out the driver, but I think Raffles had made his point.

So he did. Hours and hours in the baking sun of the public recreation ground. He wore no pads, just as he hadn't back in the old school. "A few bruises, but it certainly teaches you to get some wood on the ball" he'd said – a lesson which later reflected in his international statistics. Raffles, the first class player least often claimed by the dismissal known as 'leg before wicket' was publicly inviting them to bowl at his legs! As hard as they liked.

Raffles the showman, Raffles the masochist. England's Aunt-Sally in an old powder-blue touring cap. Strangely enough, the more they bowled at his legs, the more the old player seemed to relish it and then, at last, I could see the reasoning, for the better he became at intercepting them.

When Raffles began to tire of this, he did something I've never seen before or since. He took out three golden sovereigns and placed them one each of three stumps in place of bails. The implication was clear. 'Hit the stumps and they're yours.' In a township of Southern Africa, this was a coconut shy of note.

The bowling got faster. The bowling got straighter. Raffles got in line and used the bowlers' energy against them with subtle deflections and wristy turns of his creaking bat. Some bowlers tried too hard and over-pitched their full tosses straight into his rib cage. Raffles pulled and hooked and punched these balls off the back foot and through the petrified strings of the netting. New bowlers joined the pack, awaiting their turn. Word had clearly travelled and the better club players were tumbling out of their dwellings and getting down to the nets. I could sense the tension rising and the bowling became serious. For once, I learnt what it means when they say 'the bowler steamed in'.

Raffles was exhausted when they got him. He'd just faced a dozen superbly testing deliveries, which he'd got into line behind perfectly. A genuinely talented swing bowler from the Orange Free State Under-19 side had swished the ball all over the shop without having much luck beating the old boy's defences. Raffles had played and missed the out-swingers half a dozen times. Then, surprisingly, it was all over.

A youth, a no-account lad in hand-me-down clothes and a French tee-shirt he surely couldn't read, bowled a delivery of such medium paced rubbish that I winced to watch it. So painfully off-line, it smacked into the edge of the coconut matting at the side of the pitch, an area secured with hammered steel tent pegs, deflected at right angles back onto the wicket and took down Raffles' stumps. Coins span. It had gone *around* him. Amused, the sun sank lightly into the sea as seventy men rolled their eyes, a batsman smiled a warm and encouraging smile and a beaming no-account lad rolled home in money.

As we packed up to leave, Raffles handed out the beer tins, shook lots of hands and had time for anyone who approached him. I wondered idly what the Embassy thought and had to settle instead for one of my visions – "A.J.Raffles? The best of us. Worth a battleship for our image here." If only they knew.

Towards the end, before we drove away, I saw him share a beer with the tall bowler who perpetrated the alarming swing and I know for sure that Raffles asked his name.

'I was sure I'd nail you man. What's the one thing I could have done to get you out?' he asked the more experienced player.

'Here, take a look at my bat.'

The bowler took the old monster and stared closely.

'What am I supposed to see?'

'How wide is it?'

'Oh man, that's easy. It's the regulation width. Four and a half inches across the face.'

'Then think: I want to hit your bowling with the middle of my bat and you're after the edge. How far's is from the centre to that edge?'

'Two and a quarter inches mon.'

'Two and a quarter inches. The margin of error.'

'Yah, so?'

'So, why are you swinging it three and a half feet?'

Light dawned.

'I only have to move it two and a quarter inches?'

'Provided they don't notice, yes. It works best if you move it late so the batsman doesn't have any time to adjust. If it moves as much as it did today, you'd better get the ball dirty to reduce the effect, or just try bowling a straight one. If they play for the line they think it's swinging onto, that's as good as getting one to slip back the other way.'

'Thanks Mr Raffles.'

'Good luck. I'd be honoured if you'd keep the bat.'

'Ah man, you're a treasure.'

To this day, it beats me why we bother with Ambassadors when people like Raffles are roaming the planet. He was a good judge of a cricketer though. That swing bowler, no longer alarming and no longer brash, walked out of the baking recreation ground that day and into the papers. The Antipodean and Caribbean papers too, for a while.

For decades, the game of cricket was run by the cricketing Peers of the Realm, who gathered at Lords Cricket Ground, St John's Wood, London. Within sight they were, of the immaculate green turf of Lords. A sight to make men freeze; no less than a concept. For those wickets, those twenty two yards of sloping lawn are the very centre of the civilised Universe.

Like great leviathans they came, rising up from the counties of England, sometimes roaring, sometimes snuggling under the cheerful cloak and colours of the MCC. Lord Harris was most likely the greatest of them. One of life's generals, ruthless, hardly a man to spend his wars in India playing tennis. He neither snuggled nor snoozed when there was a good night's scheming to be done. Harris introduced cricket to India and then pushed the game to the Empire and the wider world. Notoriously, he sanctioned Bodyline strategy and mentored a captain that used it to tear and rape the Ashes from a stronger side.

Lord Harris's smoky, archaic and octogenarian, councils of war are far removed from the management of cricket today. The Lords who come are powerless. Members of the Upper House are no longer hereditary, highly educated, deeply experienced and free-willed experts. Alternative opinions, checks and balances, are hardly what the Prime Minister wants in his personal version of democracy. No, his Peers are selected from lackeys and donors, sometimes favours, sometimes titles allegedly sold to shadowy friends. They owe their titles to him and will vote in the House as he commands them. They have no interest in cricket.

Political contamination isn't cricket, as they say. To its credit, the Marylebone Cricket Club has acknowledged the changing times and the worldwide ownership of the game's future. Control of the sport has been passed from one private members' club to the modern offices of the International Cricket Council, headquartered in South Africa. To everyone's surprise, in 2006, a convoy of diplomatic vehicles rolled up outside their building and The People's Republic of China asked to join. As dominance of the game flows inexorably to Asia, many thinkers predict the pattern of command may slip, slide and transform again.

I thought, briefly of Jerome De Zemantal and his type's place in the brave new ethos. How much influence did he have in their decision to drop Raffles? I couldn't imagine Lord Harris would have suffered the man for a moment. Would the old war horse, with England one match clear in the series, have pitifully squandered the Second Test and allowed South Africa to draw level? I doubted it. Did they lose as casually as the papers said or did they put up a fight? I don't know. After day one, I couldn't watch. It's like that week never happened.

Someone, somewhere, believes they control cricket because others will pay them money for it. Is 'control' of a sport a delusion for sale to the deluded?

These are the other voices. Sounds to be heard in the roots of the grass and whipped by the breeze on your village green. Whispering now in the drifting dust of the Punjab or the sharp chill-air of South Island. How can cricket be owned, controlled? It is *our* game. We can play it without you. With my bat and my ball, my arm and my timing, I own this game as much as you. I certainly play it more often than you. I know the old laws and I know what's fair. All else is chaos and freedom.

Go run a business, if you must. Cricket doesn't like control. Control isn't fun. Has no one explained? Cricket is Life.

'Life?' The paperclips reply, 'We understand'. 'Fine, tell us, how do we sell advertising space on it?'

Chapter 16

Dapplewood Park, Fair and Square

I surveyed the ground on the eve of the Third Test. What would happen this time? What would they see from those proud crenulated stands of the members or the relaxed picnic tables under the clock tower? What would they chant from those uncovered white plastic seats glaring angrily in the sunshine? Members called them 'the bleachers' and never sat there. I wouldn't be there either, not alongside the lads of The Barmy Army.

I had nothing against them. To be fair, they were an asset to the atmosphere of the game. Can you even think of Port of Spain or Eden Gardens without the wall of noise? Can you imagine the famous West Indies grounds without atmosphere? Oh, sorry, I forgot you saw the World Cup. It was just sitting in there I couldn't imagine. Not with the chanting. I remember one incident where the tannoy announced "Is there a doctor in the house? Could a doctor please attend at the West Indies dressing room?" and three doctors clambered over the boundary boards to help; all of them having spilled out from the Barmy Army section. I'll never be sure if that reveals to us more about The Barmy Army or more about doctors.

I wasn't going to be in the bleachers, no. I was due a loftier perch. Alright, I'm not being pompous. I'll explain. After a pretty decent hotel breakfast... I had bacon and eggs by the way. Usually in South Africa they try to palm you off with some sort of mucky chopped fruit nonsense with fruit juice and a side order of fruit and then they come round to see if you'd like grilled fruit with that. "Maybe some tea?" you enquire hopefully, but that's too much. It's like Percival asking whether anyone happens to have a Grail about the place, 'About yea big'. "We have many kinds of fruit tea, Sir. There's apple and berry, mango and..." Okay, shoot me in the head. Well, no, not this time; I want to see how it all turns out.

We were in a quality hotel which really did have bacon and eggs, tea and toast, beans and black pudding. As my first proper breakfast in months, I should have been in my element. Come to think of it, I was. The black pudding turned out to be boer-worst, which tasted quite good anyway and so, despite that brief totter, I fell back into my correct box on the elementary table and sighed in satisfaction. Good hotel.

After regaining my feet, I slugged through to reception, cradling my stomach like a sleepy child, and dropped off the key. They gave me an unexpected envelope, which I opened with the same sort of curious lifting action that the Aye-Aye employs when exploring under loosened bark for weevils. This time it wasn't weevils. It was a press pass for the entire Test Match. Good old Raffles. Although, it occurred to me that I'd better invent a newspaper to be writing for. I scrabbled around. Dominic Egg reporting for *The Evening Bacon*. Probably not then. Roving reporter for the Sports Overfeed on *The Cricket Digest*? No. How about *Readers Digress*, books that go off-topic and completely miss the point? Alas no. I suppose it had better be the BBC. At least then none of the other hacks would question it if I wasn't doing any actual work. Manders of the BBC. Yes, I liked that. It explained the belly and the top hotel too.

I settled into a taxi outside the team abode and sensed a degree of annoyance from the driver.

'Is there any problem? I can get out if you like?' I asked when he'd safely negotiated the crossing traffic beyond the slip road.

'Nah Mon' he explained, 'I just thought, bein' the team hotel, I'd maybe get to drive one of the players. Goin' to the cricket ground and it's not one of the players is a big drag. Now I gotta fight the traffic and go around again and tag onna the back of the queue.'

'Sorry to disappoint you, but they're all in a coach.'

'You Press wit' that badge?'

'Yes, I am.'

'You know any of 'em?'

'I know Raffles.'

'Aaah, he's a good bowlin' man, but he gotta work on his battin'. You tell him I said so.'

'He has been, but I'll be sure to tell him.'

'He is a has-been?'

'No, he has been. Working on his batting, that is.'

We arrived quicker than I thought, so I paid off the driver and he accelerated away with undue haste – presumably in case there was a chance I was wrong about the coach.

The grounds filled up quickly over here. I suppose, back in England, people are kept waiting, filtering past all those anoraked jobsworths checking all the bags and confiscating whatever they fancy. With my press credentials and absence of baggage, I avoided all that fuss by taking another entrance leading up to the Press Box. This was an eye-opener. Faces I could put a name to, voices from the airwaves. A room full of them. Punditry; what a wonderful job. If there weren't already enough oars in the water, I could have easily added mine.

I spotted Jonty, the rubber ball, the best fielder of all time in most people's opinions. I once saw a match where he sprang into the air, clawed down a catch, returned to the ground and then appeared to bounce straight up his own trouser leg. Marvellous.

Some of the TV people were ex-players I never thought I'd meet. There was Angus - as Raffles said, a real bowler's bowler. I recognised one tall left-handed Warwickshire batsman who'd temporarily lost his England spot after a finger injury. The temporary drifted into permanency when the selectors forgot all about him. "Stand by your beds lads! New boy!" said someone with the fruity voice of an old ham actor. The atmosphere was convivial as various hacks stood up and shook my hand. A few took time to introduce themselves.

'Hello', said one as he offered a hand 'Agnew of the BBC.'

'Oh. Manders of *The Evening Bacon*'.

After that sorry passage of play, I decided the Press Box wasn't the place for me, so I went and sat by a window in the Media Centre. That was even better as I found myself within range of the live feed from the stump microphone. I must admit, I still went for the buffet lunch with the press though. At one point someone sent a waiter over to my table with a drink they'd bought for Mr O'Manders, which was kind.

Okay, so I'm not cut out to be a journalist. I suppose I knew that anyway, being more of an outdoor sporting type and I must admit this wasn't the first time I abandoned the idea of a writing career; oh no. There was a period where I decided to make it as a light-hearted, romantic novelist. No, honestly. Not quite Mills & Boon, but just enough to make the misty-eyed female readership post me those longing fan letters… and photos. I seem to remember that photos were part of the plan. Badly frustrated single young chaps come up with plenty of schemes like that, but rarely make the effort. Unless it's just me. Well how would I know? It's not the kind of thing we talk about. Oh, don't look at me like that. After all, didn't Terry Pratchett write a Mills & Boon?

Anyway, I cranked up the old typewriter, as I'd promised my yet-to-be-appointed social diarist, and smashed my way through the opening paragraphs before noticing the ribbon had dried up. It was an old type-writer after all. An Imperial, I think, and so was the paper size. I went to buy a ribbon and learned that respectable stationers no longer stocked them. I went to buy a new type writer instead, but found they'd been consigned to history. "Ooh no young Zir. We aint got no call fer typewriters. What you need is one of them computer things." So, I bought one of 'them computer things' and spent most of the evening fiddling with cables, installing whirring noises, getting through to people on the phone and then another good couple of hours enthusiastically kicking the back off it. When I finally got the hang of the ghastly bleeping monolith, I bashed out some text in a storm of rapid stabbing movements and, frustration exhausted, collapsed into bed at five in the morning.

When I read through my light-hearted romantic novel the following day, I couldn't help spotting the seven murders and a near-fatal lynching in the first two chapters and I hadn't even managed to introduce the characters yet. Coincidentally, most of the slain had worked in the computer industry. No, writing wasn't for me, so I went out to throw a rugby ball around.

In PC World.

Catherine Cookson didn't know it, but that was the day she escaped some unbelievable competition.

There I go again. I've mentioned lunch on the first day without a single word about the cricket. I can probably put that down to the way the mind blots out painful memories. Yes, you've guessed it. England batted first.

The first session can only be described as attritional cricket. England lost the first two wickets for eleven runs to a battling attack of good cutting and swinging bowling. Just when they had re-grouped and got the hang of that, they lost another batsman leg before the stumps to a wickedly unexpected ducking delivery. The fourth man hung around for forty minutes, but hardly troubled the scorers before a ball scuffed his glove and was caught expertly by the keeper. The players left the field and England had clawed their way to the lunch interval at 40 for 4, in a bad position.

When lunch ended, the spectators were in for a small surprise. Westlicott, expected to make his debut at number six, didn't take the field after lunch, presumably so as not to expose his mighty ego on debut to the last spell from the opening bowlers. No, he stayed put and the crowd had to wait a wicket longer.

It was Raffles who trotted down the pavilion steps and opened the little white gate onto the playing field. Raffles, the hand of experience, sent to steady the ship.

One of the South African fielders launched into his confidence immediately, calling out:

'Don't bother to close it. You won't be out there long enough.'

I edged closer to the feed from the stump microphone, trying to make out the words as the fielders tried to put the batsmen off.

'How's your wife and my kids?' a short-leg asked of Raffles as he faced the first delivery.

His defence was immaculate.

'My wife's fine. The kids are retarded.'

Raffles wasn't the only wit on the field. Barney Batterson, the number five, had heard it all before.

'Hey, Batterson, why are you so fat?'

'Oh, that's easy. Every time I see you get out for nothing, I have another biscuit.'

That really set the fielders off. They went through their whole repertoire.

'How do we tempt this fat lump out of the crease then lads?'

'Dunno' said another. 'I suppose we could put a Mars Bar on a good length.'

'He'll never get there' commented Raffles. 'Van Royden will be onto it before Barney blinks.'

Heads turned to the South African bowler, who had indeed grown a paunch. He tried to hold it in.

Barney 'Barnacle' Batterson had a slight weight problem. In fact, 'slight' was the one thing he wasn't. "Why do you eat so much Barney?" Raffles had asked him after the match. He looked up in despair. "It's because I get so stressed." "Why do you get stressed?"

"Because people tell me that I eat too much." It was turning into a lost cause. "You can eat whatever you like if you burn it off with regular healthy exercise." Barney epitomised the forlorn. "Exercise makes me hungry." It was an impasse, but Raffles persisted. "I'll tell you what Barney, report to me just before lunch and dinner every day and I'll tell you something guaranteed to put you off your food." The Barnacle looked genuinely delighted at this new approach. "Thanks Raffles. I'll knock on your door at 8.15."

He had talent though; a talent for soaking up the opposition's attack, draining it of all venom, then accelerating into the weaker bowling with all the latent aggression of a stone wall that's been amiably taking bumps from cars for years, but is now crunching after them up a blind alley and getting its own back for a change.

When the bowling was really difficult to play, Raffles took a single from the first ball of each over and got away from strike. When the easier bowlers came on, he scored in even numbers to keep the strike and then took a single from the final ball to face again at the other end.

'Well you're a good counter, I'll give you that' said The Barnacle, facing, yet again, the harder man.

After twenty minutes of farming the strike in his own favour, Raffles failed to get his required single and Hutchens, the new South African Captain, saw his chance. Van Royden came on. Van Royden the fast. Van Royden the indominatable. Van Royden the thoroughly peeved by Raffles.

'I've been waiting two years for another chance to humiliate you, Raffles.'

'It looks like you spent it eating.'

'Do you like hospital food?'

'Will there be any left?'

I wondered what they usually do about blood on the wicket. Sawdust presumably.

The first ball from the quick scraped the batsman's helmet. The second augured in, beat the defence and thudded into his hip. Bruises are medals. As the crowd winced, the home side's fielders, sensing the rising pressure, ramped it up by discussing Raffles' shortcomings loudly in Afrikaans. Hutchens said something unintelligible and a fielder nodded silently and moved to form a trap just out of Raffles' vision.

Amazingly, A.J. barked a response in the same alien tongue. For ten more seconds the players stared at him, then a surprised fielder shrugged, smiled and moved back to his original position. The ambush was gone.

This was typical Raffles. "It's handy to know the names of the fielding positions and a few crude phrases." Yes, but it sounded... it sounded like he'd been chatting over the garden fence in Afrikaans for most of his life. The truth was almost certainly pitched somewhere in between. Somewhere secret.

The bowler bowled, short this time, and the ball flew past Raffles innocuously. Raffles appeared to be unusually concerned by this delivery and strode down the pitch to the place where the ball bounced, tapping at the earth with his bat.

'We'd better ask for the heavy roller on this in the morning' he related to Batterson.

'Okay. I'll watch out for it' The Barnacle responded.

By now, the bowler clearly believed there was a ridge on the pitch at exactly the point Raffles had tapped with his bat. He must have been thinking that, if he could just hit it again, the ball might deviate and he'd take Raffles' wicket. 'Excellent' he must have thought, 'let's hit it before they get that roller on.'

Raffles took up his stance and prepared to face the next ball. The bowler bowled, the ball touched down at exactly the point on the pitch that Raffles had indicated and, feet in position already, A.J. pulled it for a sublime six straight into the bleachers. The Barmy Army went crazy, Raffles raised his bat and the bowler couldn't believe he'd been so stupid.

Raffles had raised his bat, customary upon reaching fifty, after scoring just fourteen. This triumphal display annoyed Van Royden even further. The next two balls were vertical wides. A.J. ran the second of them and got off strike. The final ball of the over punched into Batterson's stomach and made much the same sound as a wet duck hitting a dry cleaners.

Hutchens, having seen enough waywardness for one day, took Van Royden off.

In case you're wondering, Raffles lost his wicket just after tea by lunging off balance at a loose delivery from a part-time bowler. Westlicott came in, to cheers and boos, but failed to impress, playing inside the line of one and his off-stump shared the ache. England found themselves wiped away within the first day, which didn't look hopeful.

Day two was worse. It's unpatriotic to tell you about that.

On the third day South Africa extended their lead on a flat batting track. England, assuming the worst, appeared to give up trying to get them out and turned to slower bowling and run-saving tactics. The first two sessions were low scoring and thin on wickets. In the final session, they threw the ball to Raffles.

The South African No.4 batsman had known aspirations as a sporting columnist. To this end, as I read later, he'd been taking private tuition in grammar and creative writing at one of the regional colleges.

'This sentence no verb' imparted Raffles, walking briskly past him. Blow me if he didn't concentrate on this new thing and forget the fielding positions! One flap and he was caught behind square, which at least gave him something to explain in the papers.

Raffles' second wicket wasn't credited to Raffles. This happens a lot in cricket and it went like this:

South Africa's premier all-rounder, the same player who'd sledged Barnacle Batterson about being fat, repeatedly lost his wicket cheaply to the great Australian bowler Shane Warne. In fact, many remembered him as 'Warne's puppy.' Since Shane Warne's retirement from International cricket the previous year, this player had grown immeasurably in confidence.

As he settled in, Raffles held an urgent conference with the England Captain, who nodded and they both took up positions as close fielders. The second spinner skipped in and the field focussed. The very first ball spat out of the rough and the batsman played back, tapping down and riding the bounce. The England Captain snapped "Bowled Warnie!" and the suddenly discomfited batsman stepped back onto his own stumps. He went white. Unbelievable! What a dismissal!

The crowd didn't think much of this antic, but it was down in the book. Out 'hit wicket', bowled Leyland for 0. Walking back to the pavilion, he had to pass through the mid-wicket area, where Barney the Barnacle Batterson stood, cheerfully munching a biscuit.

Leaning over the balcony, I could just make out another radio chortling away far below:

'…wasting grass-roots development money on cricket cartoons' it burbled. 'Do you know how much they've spent on the project? £85,000! For cartoons!'

'Four cartoons? Good Lord, were they really that much?'

'Yes Dermot. In the Eighties, they made a whole series of *Night Rider* for that amount of money!'

'To be fair though, David Hasslehoff was very poorly animated.'

'... and the bowler approaches the wicket, the batsman flashes at that one and there's an appeal for caught behind. Is it?'

'Turned down!' the radio confirmed 'like a bedspread.'

Life went on. So did South Africa, finally ending their innings on the morning of day four, more than three hundred runs in the lead. England had a mountain to climb if they hoped to avoid defeat and to their credit, they responded well.

Being under the cosh isn't much fun, but it sometimes brings out the best in a team. By my calculations, England either had to bat one and three quarter days without bothering about the runs or they could bat-out a day and a half to ensure a draw, if (a big if) they could total about four hundred and fifty. Both options seemed unlikely, so I left the ground and spent the most part of the afternoon being a tourist.

When I bundled into a restaurant for dinner, that must have been about eight o'clock, I overheard the score and realised England had done quite well to lose only four wickets. Day five might be tight. I decided not to tell Raffles I hadn't been watching, but was relieved he hadn't done something remarkable. The Proteas needed six wickets and England needed... I calculated runs on my napkin... a miracle.

Later that night, I found I couldn't sleep. I don't think it was worry about England's predicament, so it must have been the heat. Yug, the heat. Yug and biscuit ovens. The temperature must have run so high because I'd switched off the air-conditioning because I couldn't sleep with that endless hum above me. It was the old choice between heaven and hell: In heaven you've got those endless musical instruments to drive you crazy for eternity and hell, of course, has the heat. Given the choice, I think I'd rather be living. It was my fault I couldn't sleep then. Most things turn out to be my fault so I wasn't surprised in the least, threw on a few things and went downstairs to the hotel bar. It was just closing when I arrived, but I managed to talk them into selling me two bottles of Castle beer, with the caps on, for licensing reasons.

Unable to detach the beer lids, I wandered off for a walk along the river, hoping to find a suitably angled stone. The stream was beautiful in the moonlight, a sweeping, twisting, glittering path flanked by strange sounds and darting insects. I hadn't realised the river flowed all the way down to the cricket ground, but I hadn't anything better to do, so I followed it. A mile I walked in the shimmering darkness. A mile of crackling and rustling, alone with my thoughts. Then, unexpectedly, my sweet isolation was broken for there on the far bank I swore I could see a reclining, darkened form amongst the further plimsoll-blackened shadows.

'Is that you Bunny? God, I swear you're part bat.'

'Raffles? Is that you? What are you doing out here?'

'Everyone's got to be somewhere.'

Rather than waste my time in word-play with Raffles, I picked my spot, raised my arms and waded carefully across the slow-flowing river.

'Are there any crocodiles?'

'I have no idea, but it will be interesting finding out.'

I waded faster, but not so fast as to drop my bottles.

Raffles opened them with his teeth – I have no idea where he learnt to do that, on the racetrack, I'd imagine, and he told me tales of many things.

Raffles explained that England must not lose the Third Test as that would give SA a lead in the series. I had worked that out for myself, I told him, but wouldn't it therefore be sensible for him to get a full night's sleep and be fresh to face their bowling the following day?

There was another match, he said, between the wars, when England were pitted against Australia. It was at Melbourne or perhaps Adelaide. I forget the details as a result of the hour. Anyway, I am sure he said it was the only other Test ground in the world located on a floodplain. England, on the final day, were left with a straightforward target to win. So far so good. Unfortunately for the Poms, some of the more inventive Australian supporters spent the moonlit hours damming the Murray River, or perhaps it was the Swan River, but the point was that they flooded the ground.

England spent the following day in turgid conditions, splashing around, trying to bat normally, frequently slipping in the mud and getting slowly picked-off like a coach-load of time travelling day trippers who'd booked the wrong date for an afternoon's historic tour of the Somme. England lost that match, Raffles summed up as if still bitter about a game played eighty years earlier.

'So what?' I asked.

'The conditions are the same today. In fact,' elaborated Raffles, 'the most natural place to dam this river would be at the stepping stones over there.'

'The what? The stepping stones! Why didn't you tell me? You git! Why did you let me wade across?'

O villain, villain, smiling damned villain! I didn't actually say that last bit, but I thought it and my thoughts were exactly the sort of profane and bitter ones that serious playwrights buy you drinks for.

'Calm down Bunny, you're creating a scene'

'A scene? In the middle of nowhere? Damn right I'm creating a scene! An answer if you please'

'It was useful to estimate the depth of the river times the width times the flow. At seventy cubic yards per second, I think as little as ten or fifteen minutes worth of diverted flow would be enough to flood the park.'

'Why didn't you ask me? I might have done it if you'd explained.'

'Free will, of course. I didn't have to. You should re-read your Paradise Lost.'

At least this information was instructive. I've always wondered what the bastard looked like.

I regained my composure. It took a force of will, but I didn't fancy England's chances much if I drowned their seventh batsman. Not that he would drown of course. His sort were immortal. Not immaculate, but certainly immortal.

'Surely no one will remember the flooding incident? It was an age ago!'

'Bunny, cricketers remember *everything*. If it happened a hundred years ago, if it can still help you win, if it can still trick some poor soul out, the bowlers and the captains will file the idea away in the old ammunition store of their minds. Even if you bat just like Don Bradman, you'll find you're facing the traps the bowlers developed in his era to get him out. All around the world, you'd see a lot of in-swing bowling just like Bedser's. You'd see short leg and silly mid-on fielding close, waiting for you to follow that in-swinging ball across you to the leg side and straight into their grateful hands. An old trap, Bunny, but they all know it and remember it, just in case another Bradman comes along.'

'Seriously?'

'Yes. What about the three-card-trick to the tall batsman? Two bouncers up at your throat, then just when your body's getting into the rhythm of moving up and back, there'll be a yorker fired in at your toes, making a dash for the gap you've just made for it. No bowler forgets a good ploy. Believe me, there are people, cricket people, who know this match can be won right here for South Africa, right by those stones. Winning off the pitch is a lot easier than on it, you see? When the bars kick-out, there will be those who think it's a good idea. A clever idea. The Australian fans arriving early for the next series might even *suggest* it to them. They might just be drunk enough to make their way towards this river. If they do, it will be to this bend, Bunny. If they do, I'll latch on to them like a freshwater leach.'

'Have you ever seen a freshwater leech, living in London?'

'No, but I admire their sense of industry.'

'Be serious will you, A.J.? How do you reasonably expect to bat through tomorrow if you're going to stay awake here all night?'

'It's a choice between personal failure and team failure, naturally. I'm not a team player, I'd be the first to admit, but I won't let a bunch of drunks and ten planks of wood pierce my defences either!'

'You're mad' I pointed out, in case he hadn't noticed yet, then stuck out a determined chin and waded back across the river. I got about half way across before I remembered the stepping stones, but by then pride wouldn't allow me to backtrack. So, I rose at the other bank, like Aphrodite of Pallene's bath attendant who happened to go to the same school and shot their rabbit, sloshed up the bank, turned uphill and headed along the river to the call of bed, hoping the African heat would dry my clothes before I reached it.

What a day.

I'd covered perhaps half a mile and was feeling a little better about myself, if not worse about the river, when a pair of local lads passed me awkwardly with a cargo of stakes and planks. I didn't say anything. I didn't even try to stop them, but I do so hate it when Raffles turns out to be right all the time.

You probably need to know this. Why will become clear shortly. Raffles used to practice at school without pads, gloves or a box. "Bruises are medals", he often declared, which is where I picked up the expression. I thought he was mad, I still do, but it wasn't my place to question the captain of cricket.

Years later he confided the real reason. "When I'm settling in at the crease, I don't want them bowling at the stumps. My eyesight isn't perfect and I'd sooner prefer them to bowl at something else. I've got these contact lenses now, which helps, but back then it was downright difficult. I'd go out to bat without gloves and say it was something to do with having a better grip on the handle. The bowlers would see the lack of defence, red rag to a bull, and try to snap my hands. That didn't matter much to me because anything aimed at my hands would be too high to hit the stumps. They just fed my leg-glance, my best shot, until they'd spilled twenty runs or more and I'd settled in for a long innings."

"What about the fine leg fielder?" I'd asked. "If he's in close, I'd glance wide of him for four. If he dropped back, I'll take some pace off the ball and have a series of no-risk singles." "Do they ever hit your hands?" "The glance is my best shot, but sometimes, yes, they have. My card's marked for arthritis twenty years from now, but it's worth it you know. It's worth everything when you're out there."

It's worth everything when you're out there. It sounded, even then, like an epitaph.

If anything, they bowled fast at him in retaliation. He was quick in those days. Yes, it's true, England's premier spinner started off as a fast bowler. I know. I was there. He only had to bowl in a straight line, at ferocious pace, for most schoolboys to step out of the way to him. I do remember that one even personally wet himself as Raffles strode to his bowling mark, before he'd even faced a ball. Yes, the lad was quick. He proved that by breaking stumps every season. He once broke a boy's arm in the nets and the victim apologised to Raffles for playing the wrong shot! Those were the days of tough cricket. Why am I talking about this now?

Let's imagine I had a flashback. It happened as I took my seat, above the snake pit end, on the final morning of the Third Test and watched a familiar figure descend the steps of the old pavilion. A figure without batting gloves. Wearing an old faded England touring cap, a halo of powder blue confidence in place of a helmet. One man in search of a long, long, match-saving innings. One who *really* didn't want them bowling at his stumps. He was going to be hurt, but didn't care, as long as he wasn't out.

This threatened to be an interesting session of play. The other batsman was Westlicott, ahead of Raffles in the batting order this time and known around the counties as a firm punisher of bad bowling. Anticipation ran high for England's new hero, who'd disappointed in the first innings. To an objective observer, Westy already looked shaken. Raffles, by contrast, had salted away a wealth of experience at test level. Westlicott, however, had gone into the match with little more than a bright, new and dangerously hollow Union Jack piggy-bank. The odd thing to me was that the English thought Westy, averaging six at test level, was the last hope to get them out of trouble. A thought influenced by my personal loyalties, I know. The problem was that Raffles could be an idiot too.

'Do you want some chalk?'

'What?' replied Westlicott.

'If you're going to keep hitting it with the end of the bat, we'll get you some snooker chalk.'

Westy looked down, unable to keep eye contact with the staring fielder. Raffles groaned.

They bowled at Raffles' hands for twenty minutes, as he'd predicted, and generously fed his best shot, the leg glance. Raffles, off to a flying start, was taking most of the strike and changing the tide of the game. Hutchens, the wily new South African Captain, altered his tactics to stop the flow.

As they bowled Raffles bouncers he often lowered the bat, allowing them to strike him. I understood that he couldn't be bowled or out lbw or even caught off a bouncer played in this way, but still, it seemed unnecessarily masochistic to me. A painful over ended and Westlicott had the strike.

South Africa's most famous batsman walked over to Westlicott and asked him a question.

'What makes you think you're good enough to play on the same pitch as us?'

Westlicott's confidence looked comprehensively destroyed by that and he went into his shell, unable to score. The wicket keeper then spoke incessantly in Afrikaans to put the batsman off. Westy walked up the wicket.

'I wish I knew what he was talking about, Raffles. It's all traps! They're setting me traps!'

'All the World's a stage, Brian. It's our considered duty to strut and fret a little. After my first tour, I took lessons in the language. Just enough to get me through the sledging. He's reciting takeaway orders, if you must know. Hutchens fancies tikka massala, lamb I think, with a chilli naan and Boorsen at short leg wants a passanda and something I didn't quite catch with definitely no lentils.'

'Really? Cheeky sods. Right. I'm going to tell them to book it for nine o'clock because we're batting through!'

'Don't do that. I'd rather keep it ticking along and see if they're daft enough to discuss tactics.'

The opposition's medium paced bowler launched an absolute quoit, that clattered and jarred uncomfortably past off-stump. The second ball was altogether more fluid, almost sliding up the face of Westy's bat. The third earned him a sketchy single and the batsmen crossed.

'They're bowling door knobs, Raffles. I can't predict the bounce.'

'Yes. Exciting, isn't it? If he can't predict your shots, you're even.'

As Westy's confidence grew against their bowler, the Afrikaners tried the next ploy in their armoury.

'Your wife's Kate, yes? The Buddleshire County Administrator's daughter? We were down there in 2001, remember? I know her. We all know her...'

Westlicott ran down the wicket to the next one, almost missed and managed to run a skiddy edge for two. Raffles moved in to calm him down.

'Don't let him wind you up! Especially that one. I though you knew? He's about as sexually threatening as a panda. Just ask yourself, why's his nickname's 'The Puff Dragon'?'

'Is that really his nickname?'

'Yup, his big friend's that bloke Tandy, in Capetown. You know - always on the television.'

'No! The football player? With the haircut?'

'That's him.'

'Hey, that's really funny. Um, so, why do they call him 'The Puff Dragon'?'

'There's a trick he does in the locker room where he gets down on all fours with a handful of talcum powder and a lighter... On second thoughts, you don't want to know.'

'I don't? Blimey. I thought it was only footballers who got up to that sort of thing. Hilarious! If that wicket keeper joins in again, I'll give him a slap too.'

'That should save him a few quid.'

'That should what?'

'Oh, nothing.' Raffles looked blank.

The bowler couldn't fathom how the batsman had regained his equilibrium so quickly. The 'I know you're girlfriend' line had always been worth a try. His own girlfriend, sorry – his fiancé as she was now, didn't mind him using it. She knew that mind games like that were all part of the job.

From what I could see, the England cricket team's confidence was like... Let me think. Do you remember those old black and white films of bi-planes where a strut would snap and the pilot had to climb out on the wing with a bit of string and tie it back on? Well, Raffles did a very similar psychological repair service for the England cricket team. Only, it wasn't supposed to be like that. It was supposed to be a jet.

His next ball found itself powered away dismissively to the boundary ropes.

'Hey, duckie! I'm seeing it like a football! Give us another' drawled Westy with an air of amused confidence.

What the hell was that all about?

The wicket keeper moved up to receive the ball at the stumps. Westy stared straight into his eyes and slapped the bat deliberately onto his own bum. The keeper worried about that for quite some time. What was he saying?

The SA captain moved to his bowler. 'Give Westy some width. Temp him. If he hits it in the air, we've got four guys to catch it'. The bowler did exactly as instructed, but, as the old hands say, Westlicott was flying. The bowler released and Westy unfurled the same sort of lateral clubbing smash that a yeoman at Agincourt might have used to unhorse a passing Frenchman. The crowd enjoyed half a second of silence, thirty seconds of noise and five minutes of tiresome fussing about, because a cricket ball bent out of shape usually needs replacing.

The nearby radio told me what I could see anyway.

'The bowler's back to his mark, looking a little concerned after that last boundary. Running in now. Bam! Flash, bang, what a picture!'

Two in a row from England, old England. At long last they'd learnt to go down swinging. For surely, go down they must. Westlicott was hitting it in the air – wasn't that a bad thing?

Raffles deferred the strike and, leaning on his bat at the other end, smiled at the anxious faces.

Blat! Another four, cut hard past the fielder at point and into the boards. Westy was dealing in boundaries.

Hutchens conferred with the talkative wicket keeper. His words were Afrikaans, but Raffles heard them. Raffles knew they were about to give him the speech. This was bad. This was very bad and Raffles couldn't solve it until the tea break.

I listened first hand to the feed from the stump microphone. I must say, it was a very well calculated attack. Westlicott was told he wasn't welcome in this country because of all the women and children who died in British concentration camps. He didn't know what they were talking about, but it wasn't long before he retreated into his shell again. At the tea interval, he asked Raffles about this history, only to be rounded on again.

'For heaven's sake! You're in a Test match. Didn't you study the things they could use against you?'

'No, of course I didn't. I thought this was about cricket.' Raffles beamed at him in rapt amazement.

'Seriously? You've got a lot to learn - and I hope you're a fast learner because we've got eleven minutes.'

'Okay. Tell me.'

'It was the Boer War. General Pickering struggled to contain the Boers, who were highly mobile – they raided on horses and then vanished into the wilderness. The Boers were fed and sheltered by ordinary farmers, loyal to their cause.'

'Which was?'

'They wanted to stop Cecil Rhodes nicking their mining rights and, perhaps, to make Africa a little more Dutch. Didn't you take history at school? Never mind that. Ten minutes left, so listen. The only way, according to Pickering, to stop the raids would be to deny the horsemen their food and shelter. He decided to create huge tented encampments, rows and rows of army tents like a jamboree, and relocate all the farmers' families from the Boer farmlands into the encampments. The Boer raiders lost their supplies and shelter, raids declined and captures improved. Pickering was winning.'

'Okay. So it's nothing then.'

'Hardly. The camps were tightly packed. When that happens, the sewage and the fresh water are hard to keep apart. People fell sick with cholera. Cholera, Brian. Lots and lots of civilians.'

'We let them die?'

'No, we absolutely did not allow them to die. Every doctor and nurse available, including every spare medical officer and nurse attached to the army, were tasked to the encampments. They let the fighting soldiers go without medical support so the encampments could have it. Yes, people died anyway. Women and children, yes. Nurses too. It was a monumental disaster, certainly, but it was unplanned, unintended, an accident.

'Okay.'

'They're trying to compare it *in your mind* to the Nazi holocaust, a deliberate planned genocide. This intention is not about justice. It is all about, it's only about, taking your wicket.'

'I see.'

'If they can make you feel guilty, do you see yourself battering extravagant shots? No you jolly well can't because you're a confidence player, Mr Westlicott. Have you seen any tape of your batting? I have. Hours and hours. I need to know how to get you out if our counties meet. Do you think it's just me? Do you think I'm the only one who's noticed that you score very fast when you're in the mood and you trip over your own shoe-laces when you're uncertain?'

Westlicott hadn't thought of that. He made a mental note to secure a tape of Raffles' bowling.

'Honestly Brian. I've seldom seen anything so childish. It's like trying to stop a juggernought one minute and then someone says "boo" and your mind hides itself away in a tiny box. If you let South Africa get a foothold in your mind, it's just a matter of time before they pick you off.'

'It nearly worked.'

'I noticed. Look at it this way: Next time they tell you some unidentified person that the wicket keeper has never met, because they died one hundred and forty years ago, suffered in a medical accident that someone you've never met, because they died one hundred and twenty years ago, didn't foresee, it isn't your problem. Now bundle that incident up into an angry red sphere in your mind, got it? Red ball?'

'Yes, got it.'

'Shrink it to the size of a cricket ball.'

'Okay, check.'

'Pick up your bat and smash it hard into the sun.'

'That's smashed.'

'Gone?'

'Gone.'

'Feeling better?'

'They wanted to make me guilty or just cross?'

'Batting is all about balance. They want to make your mind unbalanced. Which emotion they use is a genuine irrelevance. There are hundreds of little levers. They'll soon learn to pull the one that has an effect on you.'

'They've worked me out?'

'We've all worked you out, Westy. You were picked on your county form, but Test conditions are psychologically different and you're going to have to adapt. I can help you learn, so can Alf and Mickey, but you need to end your relationship with that bowling machine.'

'I should?'

'Yes. That's imperative. Let's start again, shall we? You're still in, aren't you? Feeling balanced now?'

'Yes, but what happens if I'm not balanced?'

'Then you tell me, if I'm still there. If I'm not there, if you sense you're losing balance, try to visualise A.J. Raffles putting his finger on the scales.'

'Alright. Here we go. I promise not to let them get to me again.'

'Good lad. That's the ticket. Keep the good ball out and thrash the bad one.'

'And don't listen to anything they say?'

'Right. Even if they complement you, it's a confidence trick. Dismiss it from your mind.'

'Sure Boss. A.J.?'

'Yes.'

'Thanks.'

'Let's go out there and draw this horrible match, okay?'

'If there's anything I can do for you, Raffles, just say.'

'Well, there is one thing.'

'Yes?'

'If you see them getting any late in-swing, do me a favour - hit the ball in the pool and give it a good soaking.'

'You don't like late in-swing? I'll remember that when our counties play each other, Raffles.'

Raffles laughed and pushed him away 'Now you're learning!'

'Raffles? You don't speak Afrikaans, do you? It was about confidence, wasn't it?'

'Who can say? Try not to learn too fast, Brian. It makes you susceptible to the double bluff.'

'I really thought this was a bat and ball game.'

Raffles laughed, swished his bat and walked out to the middle.

It wasn't long before the assault resumed. Just four wickets to take and Van Royden returned, this time armed with the new ball.

'Did you hear that roar from the crowd, Raffles? Those cheers are for me, not you. They've all come to see *me*.'

'There's no show without Punch.'

'I hope you like hospital food you greasy little English...'

'Do try to be more original. There whole new cuisines to discover and you'll never experience any of them if you only dine at medical facilities.'

I didn't catch the reply, but it looked as though Raffles had done his job and wound him up. He'd stop thinking now and just try to bowl faster and faster. There wouldn't be any more of that nagging line and length he was best known for. No more wickets too, I'd wager. Raffles dug in and trusted his technique.

'He's got a good yorker - a real toe-cruncher.' I let the phrase play around my mind as the patient crowd anticipated a breakthrough. As the sun edged high in the sky, an unconcerned Raffles tugged free some careworn folded thing from the rear of his waist-band and slid on what turned out to be an old Western Province cap. One or two of the Afrikaners registered a murmur.

'Hey! Since when was this Limey git entitled to wear that?'

'Doesn't he know Van Royden's a Western Province man?'

Just to be sure it was noticed, the keeper called out in dialect 'Knock this oke's head off! He's a thief! He's stolen your hat'.

The first ball screamed off the turf and Raffles swayed away fractionally late. The bowler's follow-through took him an unnecessary distance down the track.

'It hurts?' he enquired, with stones instead of eyes.

'Fine thanks' replied Raffles cheerfully. This heroic fool, this nuisance, wore the following ball in his torso. He rose again surprisingly happy.

'Lucky I had sponge pudding at lunch. That missed all my ribs.'

The bowler afforded Raffles a look of hatred and then his eyes registered something wrong about him. The shirt. Raffles was wearing a shirt that buttoned up from the wrong side, like a girl. Van Royden forgot everything but his intention to flatten this man. He turned at his bowling mark and pounded in.

Raffles adjusted his cap so the badge of affiliation shone directly at the incoming bowler. The field sensed blood and crept inward. Raffles took his eyes off Van Royden, imagined a line across the pitch and stared intently at the ground. If it rises from short of that line... For a second, sound faded and the world fell to monochrome, into the sleepy realm of half-remembered things. The ball flickered into being well short of Raffles' line and was sublimely carted into a distant refreshment stand for his second six of the tour.

Jerome De Zemantal, a study in off-the-peg sophistication, who'd spent the afternoon networking, spilled a glass of shockingly red tomato juice straight down his designer cream stretch-fit polycotton trousers. The TV cameras caught it all, an enduring image of the summer.

Was that the end of the incident? No. Raffles continued to tweak the bowler's nerves and Van Royden responded, bowling bouncer after bouncer. Raffles, rather amicably I thought, offered to sell him the cap, if he hadn't got one. The bowler at the other end went un-noticed; the duel was openly between these two. Some balls Raffles avoided. Some he hooked over the heads of the close-field and away for runs. Eventually, an umpire ended the fun and Van Royden was warned for bowling too many bouncers in an over. One more and he'd be taken out of the bowling attack.

Amazing all those who witnessed it, Raffles sprung chivalrously to the bowler's defence, claiming, on his behalf, that he should be allowed to continue. Raffles firmly contested that they were after all only mild long-hops and that nothing that slow should ever be called a bouncer.

The next ball almost decapitated Raffles and Van Royden found himself banned from bowling for the rest of the match. Come to think of it, I don't think he'd bowled a single ball on-wicket in the whole of his spell.

After that, a message came out on the pretext of changing gloves. The Captain had ordered the batsmen to waste time.

'That's typical. He throws away his own wicket and then he tells those who haven't how to do it!'

The umpire he'd been addressing laughed and said it had been the same in his day. Hutchens appeared unimpressed by this lèse-majesté.

Raffles, of course, did it his own way. He got Westlicott so worked up that he hit the spinner onto the roof of the clock-tower. The South Africans switched to a tired pace bowler, who got the same treatment.

'Too short, too slow, get your hair cut!' yelled a happy wag in the crowd.

Raffles rotated the strike neatly and, when the ball went out of play, returned to tell Westlicott what the bowler was trying to do.

Westy hit a six and three fours from his next ten deliveries, which prompted another message to appear with a drink: 'What the hell do you think you're doing? You were told to waste time!' Raffles sent a message back with the empty cups 'Couldn't think of a better way to waste time than making them fetch the ball'.

Westy hit three more boundaries, as if to settle the matter, and England had lost the ball and scored enough to make South Africa bat again. The South African Captain, seeing his chances recede, turned at last to the Vice Captain.

'We have to get Raffles out.'

'Why? He's not scoring.'

'Why do you think Westlicott's still here? It's because Raffles is keeping him alive. Every time someone works Westy over, Raffles swans over and fixes the damage. If there's any chance at all of a run out, tell them to throw at Raffles' end. Full attacking field, okay? Go on, knock his block off, get him retired hurt, anything. I don't care, just get rid of Raffles and we might still win this Test.'

They worked Raffles over, but he soaked up most of it. The runs came every time he beat the in-field, because there wasn't much of an outfield to reckon with. In this way, A.J. reached his fifty and a much deserved one it was too. At the last, when it hardly seemed to matter, his thumb was trapped against the bat handle and probably broken. Raffles would not give them the satisfaction of seeing his pain and so tried to divert their attention from it with a few jokes. I was watching though, as he stood in his batting stance and an occasional drip of bright red blood tapped on his white leather boot.

Two overs to go and the end came early. Hutchens acknowledged that the last four wickets were beyond him and the players shook hands in weary stalemate. Unlikely England had survived to a draw, with Westlicott top scoring and Raffles endings on 61 not out, the highest score I saw him make that season. Westlicott, England's man of the match, left the field to a barrage of photography and Raffles tried to slink away sideways, but didn't manage it. The England captain, a Cambridge psychologist, walked straight past Westlicott and thanked Raffles for saving the game. Raffles gritted his teeth and shook the hand, admitting nothing.

Critics described it as a 'tame draw'. Some even said England's batting in the fourth innings was tedious.

Raffles appeared from the dressing room after a while and made his way to the commentating area for an interview.

'God, man. You're all bust up!' I exclaimed as he passed me.

'Tests don't draw themselves you know. Fair's fair.'

'Was it played fairly?'

'Oh, yes.'

'What about all that chatter?'

'It was a Test Match. That's part of the test.'

Chapter 17

Running the Gauntlet

When I finally rolled out of bed the following morning, I noticed a card had been slipped under my door. It must be Raffles. He's the only person I know who takes 'do not disturb' cards off people's doors because they're convenient to write notes on. It read:

'Gone to a team briefing. 09.30. A bit impromptu – must be a flap'.

I checked the watch. 09.32, I could probably still be in time to eavesdrop for the memoirs.

Eight minutes later, I was dressed, outside the conference room, then loitering about with the same disinterested saunter that I'd often adopted as a teenager whilst trying not to look pathetic and desperate in front of compatible women.

Embarrassingly enough, I'd learnt my sauntering walk from watching Huggy Bear, a 1970s cultural icon. In later years, since the compatible women mostly ignored me, I'd come to believe that this style of walking made me invisible. I walked my walk, the Tour Manager briefed his briefing and the world ignored both of us. The only difference was, like Mr Bear, he was being paid for it.

'These are the facts, people. Last night, the team bowling machine was vandalised. Persons unknown broke into the shed and smashed its internal parts beyond repair. We are now going to have to blow half the marketing budget on another one.'

Some of the players looked pleased. Raffles however shook his head and adopted a mask of exasperation.

'Shocking. Kids I expect. It's the same the world over.'

For a churlish moment, I did wonder if Raffles knew anything about it. I mean to say, where exactly was he yesterday evening?

The tour manager continued.

'Unfortunately, this means that the bowlers are going to have to provide practice manually.'

Most of the audience laughed and then hushed down when they realised he wasn't trying to be funny.

Jerome adored the sound of his own voice. After a few minutes of his pseudo-wisdom, minds drifted.

"Kids – same the world over" Ha! I remembered when Raffles was fifteen.

He'd escape the school curfew by lowering himself down from the dormitory windows on a dressing-gown cord. I know. I had to hold the wretched thing at the top as he descended. The clasp of darkness would take him and off he went until the early hours when he'd pull the cord again, often an improvised bell-rope attached to my foot, and I'd wake up and haul him back in, smelling of beer and tobacco.

'Where have you been this time?' I asked as he changed out of his civilian clothing.

'Flamingos Nightclub.'

'You're joking! How the hell did you manage that?'

'With the birthday cake routine.'

'The what?'

'Simple. You buy a birthday cake earlier in the day from the bakery. You arrive at the nightclub when they're at their busiest and say 'It's my older sister's birthday. Can you deliver this cake to her?' The doormen say 'Sorry sonny, we'll never find her in this crowd with the din and all the lights down', so you say 'It won't take me a second. I'll just drop it off.' When they let you go through, you're not only inside for free, under the age limit, but you've got a whole cake to see you through the evening.'

Raffles, aged fifteen, was either a genius or a lunatic. Probably both.

When the meeting broke up and the players emerged, they mostly broke off into twos and chatted together about how weird everything was getting.

'What would you say that was about, exactly?'

'I'd guess it didn't have much to do with the tour. De Zemantal probably cancelled practice and called us together at short notice just to prove he has the power to do it.'

'There must be more to it than that. If not, what's the point?'

'What indeed? Don't ask me. I'm just a wicket keeper.'

A.J. hadn't bothered to talk to anyone. He'd just cut through the pack and hurried straight downstairs to the reception desk of the hotel. As I edged up behind him, I could hear he was booking a tour.

'So, you can offer me the riding safari or the sharks?'

'Yes Sir. If you haven't been on a safari before, it's really interesting. The horses are very tame and there's a guide vehicle, in case anyone gets sunstroke, packed lunch and there's a thirty percent reduction in the price for children under twelve.'

'Sharks, please. One ticket, oh, hello Bunny. Sharks?'

'Okay.'

'Two for the sharks.'

'One way or return, Sir?

'Hilarious. Do you see that man on the stairs? He's an annoyance. I would like to be on a boat with a significant number of indiscriminately lethal predators between him and me as soon as you can manage. Please?'

'Certainly, Sir' replied the flustered receptionist.

'If he tries to book a tour, don't put him on our boat, okay?' said Raffles, tipping handsomely.

'Are there more boat trips on a Saturday?'

'No. There are just less every other day.'

I decided I didn't like the Captain. There was something altogether fishy about him.

I remember the moment I first saw a great white shark. It's the kind of thing that stays with you. One of those sharp little memories which haunt your comfort-zone or at least change your attitude to surfing.

We'd been pottering along in the boat, a converted fishing vessel which seemed robust enough, and I'd moved well forward of Raffles to get a better view of the Cape fur seal colony that inhabited an island off the bow.

I thought it must be quite a relaxing job, to be a seal. The island teemed with them. They'd haul themselves up the rock, belly-flop about for a bit and then spend an hour or two sunbathing and socialising. It looked like the perfect holiday.

Every few seconds, seals which had been feeding out in the open ocean would make a dash for the rock and flop out of the water with a belly full of fish. Good stuff. Here comes one now, I thought, wishing I'd brought a camera. They were so athletic in the ocean, sliding and zig-zagging through the swell. I wondered vaguely why they did that.

Whack!

Disbelief.

Crash! A huge shark had burst from nowhere and re-entered the sea.

I staggered in shock at the strike I'd just witnessed. Had I just seen what I'd seen? Some of the tourists applauded. Unbelievable. Blood in the water and they wanted more.

So, that was it. That was the point of the tour. At this very spot, the great whites would gather at this time of year and pick-off tired seals from the open sea, making a dash for their tiny island. As it transpired, every ten minutes or so, another seal would be ambushed. They rarely escaped. They knew enough of the species which fed on them, but could they ever understand the species which watched it all for entertainment?

After an hour or so of this butchery, I wanted to leave. The only problem on a boat is that they won't let you. Moving then, to the other side of the vessel, I thought I'd look in another direction for a change. That didn't help. There were seals there too. They seemed to gather and rest alongside our hull for precious seconds of respite before running the gauntlet back to the island.

I watched them with pity, imagining life as a commuter, knowing that one person on the railway platform would be pulled apart in front of me, every single day.

Then I saw a seal, slower than the others. Less athletic and horribly slow in the water, was it injured? Fascinated, horribly fascinated, I steeled myself for the inevitable strike. Swim, you fool, swim! Then, as I watched in useless compassion, something even worse happened.

It waved.

Raffles! God, it was Raffles! He was enjoying it!

Oh no. I was watching Raffles die, wasn't I? This was his suicide, I thought, as he struck out for the island. Swimming now, swimming for his very hide.

Whack!

I froze as another great white hurtled itself into the air and crashed back into the waves.

A seal! It had taken a seal swimming past him. He must have got between the seal and the shark. No, I discounted that. He can't have known either were there. God, what a stupid risk.

They'd all seen him now. Man overboard! The boat turned and motored sedately toward him. It wouldn't get there in time, surely. No, it was okay, he'd reach the island first, if he reached it at all.

Raffles pulled himself out of the water, fully clothed and sat patiently between the bemused Fur seals. When the tour boat pulled level, he rose smartly, picked his way to the furthest edge of the rocks, jumped and clambered up the side of the boat. At least he wouldn't have to swim back. What was he playing at?

'I fell in' explained Raffles.

'You did what?'

'I fell in. It was my own stupid fault, leaning too far over to see the fish under the hull. No one saw me fall and I couldn't climb the side of the boat because it's so slippery, so I made for the island.'

'You nearly got yourself crunched' said the Captain. 'Are you with him? Can you look after him?'

'Yes, absolutely.'

I pushed Raffles to the stern of the boat and asked him what the hell really happened. He wasn't at his most coherent.

'Are you okay? What were you doing, if you don't mind the question? I mean, what the heck?!'

'The World turns with the changing seasons. Winter comes bringing death from the sea.'

'T.S. Elliot on Beckett, wasn't it? Are you trying to martyr yourself, Raffles? Are you still sane?'

'Life is about experiencing things, Bunny. Everything. Anyone who cossets themselves and won't do that might as well be in the land of the dead.'

'Here, drink this. It's from the Captain. I think it's probably brandy.'

'It's 'Mainstay', Bunny. The locals call it 'Mother's Milk'.' Raffles chuckled and cleared his throat of brine. 'He must have been really worried to have given you that.'

'Why did you do it, Raffles? Are you suicidal?'

Would he answer? Tick tock, tick tock…

'When I was fourteen, I made a list. A list of the forty things I wanted to see and do in my life. Within three years, I'd managed thirty-nine. The last was the most difficult of all.'

'What was it?'

He smiled and yet his eyes were sad and far away.

'To bowl a ball at Lords.'

'Well, you certainly did that! To think, I've watched you clear England's finest batsmen from the flattest mid-summer wickets on days that were made for runs.'

'I worked hard and I got there in the end. Nothing meant as much as that first ball though, none of it.'

'Even the Ashes?'

'Even unto the Ashes. For a day or two, after earning my first cap, I thought *nothing* mattered any more. If I were knocked down by a bus, it wouldn't matter. I'd done everything I wanted to do. The rest would be a bonus, or years of treading water.'

'So you achieved your aims and adjusted to life.'

'No, not at all. My palate was jaded. One June afternoon, I sat down on the green grass of Lords, the most perfect lawn in the whole universe of space and time, and I drew up another list.'

I could have shaken him.

'Why can't you just be satisfied? Was this swimming lunacy listed? What number was it?'

'No. It wasn't in my thoughts.'

Raffles smiled again, his eyes full of light.

'I'm on at least list twelve by now. Should I frame them? There aren't so many things left to experience.'

'You are throwing yourself off an edge in the dark. You do know that, don't you? Sooner or later, you're going to get yourself killed.'

Raffles removed his jacket and tried to wring water out of it. He seemed quite calm and detached.

'In the 17th Century, the public went to Shakespeare's plays and watched actors as they revealed the human condition. In the 19th Century, people read novels to understand this same enigma. In the 20th Century, people turned to science for their comprehension. In the 21st, unexplored ground remains.'

'Which justifies what, exactly?'

'Running oneself ever closer to destruction and, in so doing, to confront the question 'What am I?''

I couldn't find words for a minute, so just leant against the rail and watched as he squeezed water out of his socks.

'Raffles, I know that going to a psychiatrist is 'very 1980s', but I could easily fix you up.'

'Bunny…'

'Just say the word.'

'Bunny…'

'It's most discreet.'

'Bunny, do you have any idea what the difference between madness and genius is? Achievement.'

'I think you've forgotten mental coherence. Raffles, you could have such a pleasant life, but you always let this philosophy of yours in through the garden gate and it spends the rest of the afternoon stomping on your petunias.'

'Bunny.'

'Yes.'

'There is no garden. I live in a flat.'

'A flat spin? Are you getting metaphysical again? I'd say it's more of a nosedive.'

'Bunny, just for a day, I saw you ahead of me on the path. I envied you.'

'I don't understand. Thanks for helping and all that, but you're just a little bit mad.'

Raffles made a face and smiled without reason. I presumed that meant he'd decided to drop the topic. Make light of it. Fine, but that's not the same as dismissing it.

Perhaps I'm wrong, since telling you this now probably counts as a separate story. No. I think I will, if only to give you an insight into the indominatable character of the man.

The Captain accepted our explanations and, I think, was pretty relieved to get shot of us. We returned to the hotel that evening in a state of disrepair. Raffles was soaking wet and shaking miserably from the adrenaline. I have no idea why he was so steady at the time, but wobbled hours later. Perhaps it just took that long to sink in? As for myself, worried sick and wondering what to do with him, I needed help.

Raffles didn't want to go to his room, as I'd strongly advised, insisting instead on a large drink at the bar. Feeling suitably shamed to arrive at a smart hotel in such a state, I steered him limply to a corner table, where I prayed we wouldn't be noticed. Of course, we were noticed. Thank providence it was only Dale.

Dale joined the party, or more accurately, since Dale was a 24 hour person and seldom left a party, Dale parked himself uninvited at our table with a fresh bottle of Mainstay.

'Been swimming then?'

Raffles squelched at him.

'You haven't been bothering our sharks?'

'Yes, that's exactly what he's been doing. Raffles fell off the tour boat.'

'Gee it must be shit to be thick!'

'It was an accident.'

'Safe though. A great white wouldn't bite anything that ugly. They're scared of foot and mouth.'

At least we'd made someone happy, or at least contributed one more to his fund of anecdotes. The evening was suddenly going well and Raffles was calming down, controlling the shakes. I wondered a lot about his state of mind though. Could he be cracking up? After this latest scrape, was he mentally strong enough to play more matches? I didn't have to wait long to find out.

The atmosphere shifted again. Improved or worsened, depending on your particular hemispherical perspective. Australians filled the bar. They were here for the international triangular series against South Africa, billed to follow the Proteas' Test series against England. The Aussies would play a few state sides first, then a friendly against a representative English XII. Some of them, the ones needing experience, would also be playing in A.J.'s benefit match. The only problem, as I saw it, was how could they hold Raffles' benefit match without Raffles? The man was a mental wreck.

We dried out, thought our thoughts and drank our Mainstay, until rudely interrupted. To be honest, Dale was always rudely interrupting us, but this was different, this had side.

One of the Australians peered at A.J., trying to confirm his identity.

'Jesus, Raffles. You look like shit.'

He then raised the volume for the benefit of his team mates.

'Hey fellas! Look over here. It's only Dastardly, Mutley and Clunk!'

He stared at us like scum. One of the charming new Australian protégés, I assumed.

'Ignore him' said Dale, but the Aussie persisted.

'You're not drinking at our bar are you?'

'Your bar?' I asked.

'Team Australia mate. We own this town. Hadn't you heard?'

Raffles raised a hand to his mouth and whispered 'Did you know that they actually rehearse this stuff?'

'Seriously?' I was amazed.

'Psychological dominance. Win the match before they play it, that sort of thing.'

'What prats.'

'Yes, but it works. Listen.'

Raffles had made up his mind to talk to the young Australian.

'You haven't been in 'Team Australia' long, have you Jason?'

'Long enough.'

'Just the Sri Lanka series, yes? I couldn't help noticing that Kimbli worked you out.'

'He didn't work me out. He got lucky, that's all.'

'Consistently lucky? Old bowlers like me notice these things. They might even notice *what he was doing.*'

'Get lost.'

'Were there five or six batsmen at the Academy on the day they tried you? They'd probably work themselves to death to get your spot, wouldn't they? They must have followed your career in Sri Lanka with great personal interest.'

'Bugger off, Raffles.'

'Did you work hard? Did you work hard *enough*?'

'What's it to you?'

'So, they've given you another chance? A chance to see if you've learned. A last chance? Against South Africa this time. The only Test nation without an effective spin attack. Ah, but will they still select you against one? You can't just play South Africa, you know. No matter how well you do here, it won't count.'

'Take a hike.'

'What happens when I work you out in the warm-up matches Jason? I wonder what you'll do when I *expose* you like Kimbli did. Will everyone notice, this time? You could try hitting every ball for six. You'd last two minutes. You could always block everything and score off the bowler from the other end. Only... they're looking for match-fixing now and it might look as though you'd taken a bribe.'

No words were forthcoming.

Raffles lowered his voice. 'Does any of that make you feel *confident*?'

Jason was turning pale.

'What will your precious 'Team Australia' think?'

'We've got bowlers in grade cricket better than you' – a flash of defiance.

'A weakness against spin?'

'I haven't got a weakness!'

'In the Australian team? A Test player, shall we say, susceptible to spin? Can't have that. Oh no. Plenty more at the Academy itching to bat. Kids in grade cricket too. How long ago were you in grade cricket? Three years? They're right behind you. Can you feel them breathing down your neck?'

'Get off my case Raffles!'

'What are they doing today do you think? Practicing, learning. Learning to play spin? Such talent. They can't be denied their chance.'

'Shut up, shut up!'

'Don't your family have a taxi company Jason?' The tone relaxed a fraction.

'Yeah, my old man built it up from...'

'Think of it then, a year from now, as you're driving along in your taxi and The Ashes come on the radio...'

'BACK OFF!'

Actually, the young Australian had become so stressed that he'd pronounced 'back' with an F.

At the bar, the Australian captain heard the outburst and looked pained.

'Aww bloody hell! Dunc? Go and rescue the kid. He's getting mauled by Raffles.'

Two of the more experienced campaigners fetched him, with, I couldn't help noticing, a respectful nod in the direction of A.J. The captain wasn't finished.

'Which of you buggers brought us to Raffles' bar? Come on, that's a twenty dollar fine.'

It was the last time I thought of A.J. Raffles as weak.

He still worried me though; for a different reason. I don't know why I regurgitated Blake at that moment, but it was unintentionally audible:

'What the hand, what the eye can frame thy fearful symmetry?'

Dale fell about laughing. At me, I think. I really have to stop doing these things. Get a grip. Gripping now? Good. Keep it up. Regarding Raffles, placed quietly aside with his glass of sugarcane-embalmment, he looked mild and approachable again. Quite the gentleman.

Was it a mistake to fly too close? Was I overdue a singeing as well?

Chapter 18

Strictly Pace

Harold Larwood was the fastest bowler the world has ever seen. We may argue the fact. We may even disagree, but there is nothing whatsoever more we can do about it.

Raffles' words, not mine. I only bring the subject up at this point because few people know that Harold Larwood shaped the development of the young Raffles as a cricketing mind. The story, as I remember it, was this.

A.J. had just been selected from the old school to represent his county in the U-XV colts cricket team slated to play against Middlesex. He was exquisitely fast in those days. Blink and you wouldn't see it.

Bradman vs. Larwood. Raffles reverenced them both. The uncatchable fox pursued by the inescapable hound. The best batsman who ever drew breath, cornered by the fastest bowler the world had ever seen. Same time, same place and on concrete pitch conditions.

In those days, cricket was cricket. None of those helmets, shock-proof bats, soft rubber shoes or indeed (in my lifetime) the latest edition of daft fluorescent pyjamas with names on the back.

Raffles, the sporting talk of the school, held court in the refectory on the subject of fast bowling.

'Jeff Thompson is quick, I grant you, but he wasn't the fastest.'

The singularly pro-Thompson 99mph camp bounced back with a few plausibly un-checkable statistics until one of the right-thinking sort, who couldn't hear Raffles, bounced a bone china mug over their heads. Raffles thanked the Chair and continued pontificating.

'I know they didn't have accurate timing gear for bowlers in those days. What they did have though, was racecourse cameras. They placed these cameras at set distances across a racecourse, with string trip wires set from rail to rail. As the horse tripped the cameras, they got a frame by frame film of a moving horse.'

'So what?' rose a thin voice from the deck.

'So, that's what they did with Larwood.'

'How did the ball hit all the strings then?'

'They adjusted the technique, obviously' explained Raffles.

'They'd have to adjust it quite a lot to make it work' said a doubter.

'Instead of bits of string attached to cameras, they had a camera attached to a clockwork mechanism which exposed a regular reel of sixteen frames per second.'

'A film camera?'

'Yes, if you like.'

'Well why didn't you say so, you utter knob?'

'All they had to do was find the frame where the ball released over the bowling crease and then find the frame where the ball crossed the batting crease twenty two yards away. The number of frames it took, at a sixteenth of a second each, would prove the time it took to complete the distance. So, Larwood the Wrecker bowled and the camera flashed.'

'Where is the film?'

'The only trouble was that the ball didn't show up in the pictures, or it did, but only in one or two of the frames. Oh, and they couldn't be sure which frame he'd released at, but they could work that out by counting backwards, which they did, but the result it produced looked unrealistic.'

'Oh well, that's simple then. Good story, Raffles' called a cynic, probably me.

'Ah, well, there's more. They then brought in a photographic engineer with a camera that took sixteen frames a second, synchronised to a clock which started when you stood on a board at the bowling crease. When they repeated the experiment, the ball only appeared in two frames, but that was enough. In the first appearance, it was just leaving Larwood's hand and in the second it was disappearing out of shot in the seventh frame.'

'You're still a knob, Raffles' came a call, smartly silenced by a sharpened shoe.

'The facts, gentlemen, are evident. In the second experiment, they had the start time and the seventh frame time, plus an accurate seventh frame position, across twenty-two yards of wicket and when you've got distance over time, you've got speed. In other words, how many elapsed sixteenths it took to cover the distance. That's speed, lads. Good old miles per hour. The only problem being, the result was faster.'

'So, what was it?'

'I can tell you they agreed to announce the average of the two experiments: One hundred and twenty five miles an hour.'

The thing I've always enjoyed most about uproar is the sheer spectacle of forty people expressing an opinion and no one whatso- ever listening to any of them. This happens in Parliament all the time, but as school boys, we weren't that juvenile. I remember the phrases 'rubbish', 'bilge' and 'unscientific cabbage rottings' at one point, but then I'm afraid I lost the rest in the clamour. I think the most coherent critique was that Larwood had bowled at around 90 or 95mph in the 1933 Australia series.

'Ah,' Raffles countered, 'that was only because the captain decided to use him as a stock bowler, instead of a strike bowler. He couldn't be expected to bowl that pace through fifteen over spells and yet he was still the fastest in the game! If the captain has used him for three at a time, Larwood would have cranked it up.'

'You're mad, Raffles. That speed isn't possible.'

'So? Even if it isn't, would you accept a 20% reduction to allow for the worst conceivable margin of error? That would still be five mph faster than Thompson.'

The debate rolled on, this time lovingly prosecuted by a certain F.L. Riley-Pitt. 'FLuRP' was a strange one, incorrectly thought of as a sports-field sadist, but more accurately he played his sports strangely unaware of the wake of human wreckage strewn behind him. He was predominantly notable for his high achievement on the rugby pitch.

FLuRP would take a treble dose of painkillers, ironically prescribed by his doctor to alleviate pain from his rugby injuries, and then bulldoze, or 'tank', his way through the opposing team to the try line. Every public school has someone like this. On occasion he'd cross the line with slender opponents still attached, dripping down his shirt like so many remora fish. Riley-Pitt seldom noticed them. He sometimes failed to spot the game was over and found himself with mud across his eyes, a ball in his hand and no one left to run through. This was victory. His debating style was very much the same. Continue all evening if necessary. You've won when you're the only one left in the room.

Riley-Pitt was the son of a private banker. This placed him in a category otherwise only occupied by myself and Raffles: People who's parents paid the full fees. Although there were around two hundred and fifty boarders and fifty day pupils at the old place, most were officers' sons, part funded by the Army, Navy or RAF. The rest were half subsidised by corporations, scholarship and hardship cases or completely paid for as the children of foreign diplomats up in London. Raffles' people paid for him, mine paid for me, from some old legacy and the squeaking dregs of our family coffers. Riley-Pitt floated to the school on the polished backs of newly-minted coin.

FLuRP went for the throat, as usual.

'Is there any documentary evidence for that?'

'No.'

'Then who said it and where?'

'Me. Here.'

'No, honestly Raffles and speaking man to man, you blighted toad, and presuming you don't want to be de-bagged and put up the flag-pole because it's a breezy time of year, where's the evidence? Where is the film kept?'

'I'd say it must be stored in the museum at Lords. With the glass top hat that Lord Harris gave for the first test hat-trick, with Bradman's bat and the famous 'reverse swing' ball from the Pakistan tour. Locked away, probably. You'd have to be an MCC member to view it.'

'Alright Raffles. I propose we should all try to become MCC members. It might take twenty years, but the first one in will find the truth and then I shall want an apology in the Times. There's a waiting list, but I'll get there before you because they wouldn't want an oik like A.J. Raffles snotting up the Long Room. Stands to reason. Then we'll see who's right.'

He never made it to the MCC, but he did join the 'In-and-out' club, so he could always make faces at Raffles from a large bay window across the street from Albany Mews, when the fever took him*. Raffles, I'm sure, went after that film the day he was elected. It didn't take him twenty years either; he took the easy route and played cricket for England (an automatic membership). I'm sure a locked

---

*Nowadays FLuRP can be found prosecuting war-crime defendants in The Hague. His attritional style often wears them down to such an extent that they drop dead before finding justice; an experience already familiar to many of their victims.

drawer wouldn't stop A.J. Raffles, even then. I sometimes wonder what he found. Perhaps I'll ask him to tell you, some day.

A little further into the season, the subject of Larwood took to the field again.

'Larwood's best ball was the off-cutting bouncer.'

'There's no such thing', observed a prefect lurking behind a newspaper broad enough to wrap passing fire-guards. 'You can't off-cut a bouncer'.

'Larwood did it. At Nottinghamshire. Just read Plum Warner and Percy Fender on the subject.'

'Fender was a nut' reasoned the voice of the literati 'an absolute spoon-bender'.

'The fastest fifty of all time' trumped Raffles.

The newspaper sunk down. Oh dear, the situation was shaping into a statistical dogfight.

'Surely, you just bowl an off-cutter at bouncer length?' I mustered helpfully.

'No, it won't go. The angle will smother it.'

The exact words are lost to the history of our culture, but the chorus of 'rubbish', 'bilge' and 'unscientific boiled cabbage-stalk rottings on a plinth' will do for now.

'Why don't you write and ask him then?' sighed the prefect.

Raffles did.

I know. I was sent to fetch the ink.

It took a long time for the answer to roll back. Larwood was in his eighties by then. An old boy in a wheelchair, his sight in tatters. After an afternoon of randomised research, we'd found out he'd emigrated to Australia soon after the war and taken his family with him. His mind though, his mind was as bright and sharp as... let's just say, if you could bottle it, we wouldn't hear the words oxy-acetylene nearly as often.

It wasn't his handwriting, he'd dictated an answer to his son, but the signature was his for sure. Oh yes, we'd compared the collectible cigarette cards for that one.

Yes, he'd written, the off-cutting bouncer was a good surprise delivery. The other surprise was how you bowled it: a) not often, b) not with the angled-seam grip of an off-cutter, but with the horizontal-seam grip of an off-spinner – seam running left to right over the top of the ball, finger joints over the seam. Run in, bowl your bouncer and rip two fingers across that seam from left to right. Bang, into the ground it goes, the batsman sways out of the way and *it follows him*. Too late to change his motion, the batsman might fend the rising ball away with his bat or glove, anything, just fend it off, fend it *in the air*, then c) if it doesn't take the wicket and they look shaken, bowl the same thing again, but put three fingers vertically down the back of the ball and – no matter how fast you try to bowl it – it will come out as a slow ball, the batsman should get out of the way and the ball will casually loop into the stumps.

I remember how Raffles read that bit twice, explained it to me and then wrote the whole thing out again so he'd never, ever, forget it.

Unexpectedly, the next seven-eighths of the letter read like a sermon, aimed at a young lad's mind. The main points, stated and re-stated, were these: Larwood insisted he had never bowled the bouncer to hit people. He'd bowled it to force them to play a bad shot. It was a test of technique, like any other. If batsmen couldn't get out off the bouncer, he wouldn't have bowled it. He also claimed that he hadn't bowled the short delivery very much at all. Was it really an exaggeration?

Accuracy was vital. Practice that, he'd advised. He'd then moved on to something none of us could anticipate. 'Speed alone won't stop runs. Being faster than the next man won't give you more wickets.' What does that, he explained, is bowling to a plan. Seeing the weakness in another's thought or technique and attacking that point. Bowling really fast might get a man out because he's shocked into forgetting technique, reacting instead on instinct. He's out because his training has been abandoned, not because his reactions were slow.

What if, proposed Larwood, you considered reaction times alone. The fast bowler releases a yorker through twenty two yards in the air and the batsman's reaction time may be one third of a second. The spinner however can't easily be played until the ball has bounced, which reveals the direction of spin, so the reaction time against a spinner is not from release to bat, but from bounce to bat. If the spin bowler loops the ball above the eye line of the batsman, he must lose sight of the ground to follow the ball and then re-observe the ground in relation to the ball as it lands. At most, three feet in front of him. One third of a second? What's the difference then, if it's not in the mind? 'Don't just run up and bowl your best ball, young man. Bowl his worst ball. Observe him. Beat his mind.'

Raffles spoke not of pace that term. He spoke of psychiatry. It was late in July, I think, when A.J. received an invitation to join the Hampshire County Colts (under nineteens) for a week's practice. At the age of not quite seventeen, they'd given him a chance, I'd say, based on his extraordinary pace. However, on the day of the match, conditions were so awkward that he didn't bowl a ball of it. He didn't warn his own team in case they vetoed his thinking, opting instead for flight and spin as an expedient variation, *with a field set for pace.* They thought he was nuts, but couldn't argue with his haul of wickets. 'You can bowl what you like', he was told and did so in a much tougher match, a friendly encounter against a full county.

Then Middlesex fell.

Middlesex *noticed.*

●

In case you're wondering, the fastest bowler alive today is a man called 'Hungry', who lives on an island paradise in the West Indies. I won't mention a surname, because you might want to look him up. The reason you've probably never heard of this powerhouse of a bowler is because he is, how should I put it, cursed. Fate has hobbled him and cruelly pruned his wings.

Specifically, Hungry's permanent address is that of a secure psychiatric prison. A permanent address where permanent means *permanent.* The diagnosis? He is a little autistic, okay, and a chronic sociopath, oh dear. So why is he important? Well, Mr Hungry regularly bowls at more than one hundred miles an hour and he thinks about every delivery, analysing *everything.* In fact, he's probably the best analyst in the institution.

Sometimes he takes brown sugar-paper and carefully wraps the stumps that he's broken. It's no one's business to stop him. The shards of stump are signed by captives and jailers alike, all bleached and mellowed in the Caribbean sun. Into the paper they go, crinkled and crunched, stuck and folded. No one's quite sure where they go. 'Maybe he's building a raft to escape on', said one of the more lucid patients.

Dearly I would love to see Hungry play. Just think of it! The natural randomness of the game of cricket would be made complete. In a man. In a moment. In a power and ability unseen before, with no brakes at all on the mind. Bring me chaos on a clean plate.

No, I'm sorry, he can't play for the West Indies. He can't play for his island. The curse is divine, you see? Walk along, have a glass of orange, say hello, move some shoes, break this man's ribs, find a chair to sit in, take out the soap and wash etc, etc. They're all the same value on the scale. He just can't appreciate there's a difference, which is upsetting. In another time or another species, he would be a king.

Where was the sense in the tragic waste of such a gifted monster? An athlete and inspired analyst of cricketing technique, to spend his days locked fast in the sun. Who would be held for pure capability? There were already plenty of Napoleons in this place. What price then, for the sake of the game? There are those who would think it worth a few victims to see him play.

Some evenings, when he was not in trouble, Hungry squatted in his cell and wrote letters to his pen-friend. They wouldn't allow him the dignity of a chair. In a world that wouldn't hear of him, didn't want to gaze upon him, this one knew his name. This one sent him press cuttings, turf clippings from famous test grounds, throughout the great continents, on the *outside*.

In his little garden, Hungry tended his squares of grasses and no one dared to touch them. He wrote again, thinking how easily they might have become each other. He couldn't envy him though; the only one who understood and appreciated his potential. Hungry didn't understand envy and no one spared the time to explain it to him. Was this the only one who thought just like him? The letters were read and censored, of course, before sending. Then they were stamped to announce the point of origin. That ugly prison stamp, always to the bottom left and clear of the address. A mad green smudge and smear, the mark of the curse.

Chapter 19

Raffles' Ashes

5.00am GMT: Lunch-time in Beijing. In a small room at one of the city's teaching hospitals, a child is born who will, thirty-six years from now, invent the system which replaces money. The child's mother worries that she can't afford to keep it.

5.05am: In the last five minutes, 4,409 people across the world have suffered heart failure.

5.10am: Around the World yachtsman, Terry Mitchell, has just fallen overboard. He has three flares.

5.15am: In South Africa, Jason Daskulaki, an Australian batsman, finds it impossible to sleep and so pads away from his hotel to switch the floodlights on in the practice nets. After feeding the bowling machine with forty plastic balls, he swings a bat to wake up his arm. He does not notice the gibbous moon. He blinks three times and freezes like a robber with a club. Balls propel toward him at regular intervals.

Come now, let's listen to his mind.

'Batting now, wake up, fighting, use the feet, that's it, get to the pitch, punching now, turning, head still, play it on the bounce, ride the spin, pushing now, pushing into a gap, play it down, always down, forward then, unexpected, catch it before the turn, focus, watch for the change of pace, middle of the bat now, middle, concentrate, play it late, width there, stamp it, smack, boundary, yes, step to the line, no, watch for drift, don't let him dominate, check the field, now forward to that, watch the hand, spinners, not going to take any of his sh*t, slow ball, erk, a bit uppish, line and length, push forward and smother, wrist spin, stroke it, watch for the stumping, hold the line, balance then, tapping down, that's it, good lad, slapping now, slapping, he's probably got arthritis, short, oh yeah, full swing of the bat, focus, not back and across, turning, too full, punching, I'll show him who's boss, concentrate, loose ball, whop it like a nut...'

Fast forward now,

10.40am GMT: New Zealand, a Brown Island Robin has been killed by a cat, leaving only twenty one of its species in the world. There are plenty of cats.

10.43am: Japan, fishermen have just slaughtered their fiftieth porpoise of the day. It will be packaged and mis-described as whale meat, so a mainland supermarket can sell it for three times the normal food-market price of dolphin.

There are moments in our lives when we remember each detail. Coloured memories, in picture and sound, crystallise and knuckle away like geodes in a wall of wind-blown sand. 10.47am was just such a moment. I remember everything, even the time ticking by on the computer's clock. Raffles had logged onto the Betfine gambling site and was trying to get the best odds available on the match. The great thing about Betfine was that if no one wanted to match the odds you wanted at the moment, you could leave a sort of open-ended offer hanging on the site until someone came along who did.

'The Aussies are universal favourites, Bunny. If the Match-Fixing Syndicate hopes to rake in a fortune, they'll have to bet half a dozen fortunes to get it.'

This wasn't a surprise, to be honest. The Australian team was a battle-hardened unit, capable of re-grouping and fighting for victory from any position. Before their South African Test Series, they didn't want the ignominy of losing a game to a bunch of mis-fits. The 'Rest of the World Team' was a loose assemblage, a mixed bag of age groups and nationalities, often semi-famous names. Some were at the end of their careers and running on empty, two were already retired. The last minute omission of Scottie Small, the New Zealand all-rounder, had been a blow, but the Syndicate had managed to replace him with some teenaged Indian spinner no one had heard of. I had no doubt that Raffles would be doing most of the actual spinning.

I think, to be brutal, that was the point. The Syndicate had created this match. They'd made Raffles captain and they'd hand-picked his foot-soldiers. Their members could accept anyone's bet on Australia and offer dangerously long odds on their own team, simply because both sides would be working for the same result. This was power - they owned the game, bought and paid for, the ultimate fixed match.

I couldn't help thinking Raffles had no chance and neither did those betting on us. What were we doing? Oh well, easy come easy go.

'Do you understand this screen, Bunny? We are seven to one, in a two horse race.'

'Take it then!'

'Patience. Only £28,000 has been matched on Betfine so far. A seventh of that's peanuts to the Syndicate. They will have invested fifty times the amount just to set the game up.'

'So what do we do?'

'Wait. The Syndicate will have to accept bets at much longer odds. They'll only do that at the end, when they panic and go all-in at any price. We will therefore leave our odds hanging, until they take the bait.'

Raffles clicked 'place bet', selected 20-1 and typed in a telephone number. I visibly reeled.

'Is that pounds? How did you get that much money?'

'That's only half our stake. I'll offer the other half at 40-1 and see if they take it.' He caught my expression. 'The money? Oh, that's the rail company's pension fund, nine tenths of a VC, an advance on the diamonds, my flat and the money the Syndicate have transferred to my account to throw this match.'

'You're betting their money against them?'

Raffles smiled a brief and evil smile and I remembered the final seconds of 10.47 forever.

Log off.

Fast forward.

12.41am: Central Africa, a high court judge has ruled a defendant from the political opposition innocent, against instructions he received before the trial from the President's office. Arrangements are now being made. From 7.21pm this evening, the Judge's family will never see him again.

12.45am: South Seas, the Island of Fiji has just experienced its highest tide since the swell of 1754.

12.54am: In Assam province, Northern India, another illiterate child joins the workforce.

12.58am: Terry Mitchell drowns. His wife is boiling potatoes and missing him.

1pm: On an immaculate lawn in South Africa, something important to millions is happening. Observe.

●

The last time Raffles captained a cricket team, he was sixteen years old and I happen to know that because I was the one standing quietly behind him. I can give you longitude and latitude if you like. When conditions were soft or wet and he didn't know whether to bat or bowl first, he'd call "edge" to the spinning coin and leave the decision to the opposing captain. If circumstances revealed they'd got it wrong, he'd subtly hint to the opposition's players that their captain was a little incompetent. Disaffection in the ranks, worms, buds and a few damask cheeks then made the difference between the sides on more than one occasion.

'One day, if there's enough mud' he said 'I might even be right and by Jove they'd remember me for it!' He never got the chance again, with his coins and lunacy, until now.

Alien, Australian fingers spun a golden kruggerand into the air and it came down tails, or strictly speaking, it came down 'antelope'. Raffles hadn't called 'tails' or 'antelope' or even 'heads' for that matter. He'd surprised everyone but me by calling 'edge'.

The Australian Captain looked at him thoughtfully.

'You really do think this is a friendly, don't you?'

'Absolutely' said A.J., adopting a cheerfully idiotic grin.

'We'll have a bat.'

Raffles' tense shuffle changed to an enigmatic smile of satisfaction.

'No, wait up. You wanted me to say that, didn't you?'

He looked at Raffles closely, mistrusting. Neither captain blinked.

'No. We'll give our bowlers a workout. If you're batting at seven, Raffles, you'd better get your pads on.'

In almost every natural habitat of the modern world there are both endemic and exotic species. Endemic species are those which have been localised to the ecosystem for millions of years. They are often perfectly adapted to their niche. Exotic species are those that arrive from a foreign ecosystem and have adaptations that provide an instant advantage over the current inhabitants. They prosper. Throughout the world, exotic species have found themselves in fresh places and plundered them mercilessly. Watching Raffles at the height of his powers reminded me of the exotic and the endemic. They weren't ready for him as his thoughts flicked this way and that, a fluffy cat in the valley of flightless birds.

How should I describe the first innings without cringing into my soup? Actually, getting a bowl of soup in South Africa's a bit of a washout, but you know what I mean. A dismal display, filled with brief cameo performances from The Rest of the World players. They kept doing the same thing: gather a painfully slow ten or twenty runs and then engineer a dramatic way to lose their wickets. It was just as the Pakistani selector had said: Men with reputations for striking the ball hard just weren't hitting. A full toss would always be defended instead of smashed away. In essence, they were all trying to put some runs on the score board, but not too many and not too fast. It looked like they didn't want it to be *their fault*. After the fourth wicket went down, most independent spectators assumed the result. Some assumed the driving position.

The Australian Captain was right. Raffles came in early, but at six, not seven. It's a churlish accusation, as usual, but I think he'd waited until the best bowlers were off, to give himself a better chance of scoring. I remember that he batted uncomfortably, making torrid, but steady, progress. Sometimes he appeared to be over-acting how troubled he was by one or other style of bowling, as if to ensure they continued to bowl it.

At the other end stood a Kenyan batsman called Patrick. In hindsight, I couldn't be sure if he was playing to win or not. He seemed to be doing his best, but the Australian barracking was relentless.

'Come on Patty. Show us one of your famous slog-sweeps. What are you averaging this year Patty? Five? Six? You must know your own average. What is it? Tell you what, we'll let you count your top score. Let's make this fair. How about we give you a ten run head start?'

He firmly blocked the next three deliveries, trying to regain concentration.

'Try not to break any windows Patty'.

That seemed to break the spell. The very next ball, Patrick skipped up the wicket to slog the ball out of the ground, missed and should have been stumped, but the keeper fluffed it. Even so, the Australians seemed mighty pleased with themselves. Ashamed, Patty went back into his shell and blocked the rest of the over. Raffles stepped in.

'Ignore them and hit it into a gap for me, would you? Don't just stand there and block. Last year you got three test fifties, didn't you? Well, this is just a friendly, so relax and knock it into gaps.'

Raffles took a run from the first ball of the next over and Patrick missed the last five deliveries.

'You could put up the pretence of a resistance' said Raffles, between overs. To his credit, that's what he did. He put up the pretence of a resistance and hit the ball into his own stumps ten minutes later. This wasn't going well.

Jason Daskulaki made a point of wandering over.

'Are you enjoying this Raffles? You should be used to collapses. Isn't that what's about to happen to your whole career?'

'You'll be gone long before I am. You'd better get more highlights in your hair. It's the only way anyone's ever going to notice you.'

'Yeah, well, I'm just an uneducated Australian, aren't I? How do you spell 'desperate' then? Huh? Come on Raffles, how do you spell 'shambles'? Tell us captain, what does 'abysmal' mean?'

'I don't know. Your technique against spin?'

'Get lost Raffles. You're all theatre.'

Raffles assumed a rigidly dramatic pose.

'You will rue the day you called me that!'

One of the slips laughed, but a gully and a long-leg didn't think that was funny. The slip dusted himself off and looked embarrassed. Raffles took up his batting stance and poked the ball through a gap.

'Three runs there!' called A.J., back to normal.

Rani, the new batsman, ran two slowly and waited for the ball to go out of play before walking up the middle of the pitch to confer. He regarded A.J. quizzically.

'So, you think I have an engine on my bum?'

Raffles hit the next ball for a single and they exchanged ends. As the first ball to a new batsman, the field closed in.

'One' snapped Rani, piercing the human cordon neatly, and set off.

'Two, two, two!' called Raffles.

'Not a blinking chance of it' cried Rani and stopped after one. Raffles had to swivel back to reach safety.

When the ball went out of play, Rani and Raffles squared up in the middle of the pitch. Raffles opened his mouth to speak, but didn't manage a syllable.

'Do you run after your food in England? We do not do these things. You think I am a mad English hound? You wish to bring me to a grinding halt or what is it? I am a person of inestimable qualities in batting and bowling and rarely to be seen intentionally sprinting against the Olympic Jamaicans, so I can not be expected to run fours and fives for you if I have lost my breath on every occasion. Three is also a quantity to try my patience. If it is to be an all-run four or equal madness, you will perhaps notice a statue of Rani not moving anywhere in a month of Sundays at the other end. Next time I call one run or two, you must dig your ears.'

Raffles returned to his crease, somewhat dazed. Good for Rani. He wouldn't let Raffles stop him doing his job. Raffles saw out the over, but couldn't get the run he needed to change ends. Aware of the weak link, the Australians brought on their last remaining fast bowler. 'Here we go' I mumbled.

Rani smashed the first ball of the over for four, so he wouldn't have to run anywhere. He missed the next three and then wildly connected with the fifth, for another boundary. The crowd cheered, for the first time that day. The first Indian flags peeped around the stands.

By this time, the Australian Captain had guessed Rani wasn't much of a runner, so directed most of his fielders to the boundary and bottled the young player up by only allowing him a single run from what would normally have been his classic boundary shots. After a while, Rani looked hot and tired. When his score rose into the thirties, he missed a nasty late in-swinger which emphatically knocked back his stumps. My heart dropped. It was great while it lasted, but you can't do much if you get one of those.

The eighth batsman was Matthew Hacksley, whom I'm bound to tell you, was a bit of a creep. I spoke to him at the hotel on the second day, but he brushed me off like so much coat-fluff. Raffles said it's because he treats anyone who can't help his career like furniture. Apparently, if they can help his career, he's quite different. Raffles also said he'll travel a long way if there's money in it and that "He tossed the coin once, bent down to pick it up and it hit him on the back of the head", which I suspect isn't true because Billy Connolly said it first.

I never found out what he did to annoy Raffles, but it wasn't the wisest move. The newspapers said Hacksley wasn't of a standard to play for England, so changed his nationality to be Irish (on the basis of some half-imagined grand-parent) and has since carved out a reasonable career bowling for them. In fact, despite not having an Irish bone in his body, I think he got quite lucky in the last World Cup. Even so...

'Two there' called Hacksley, head down and setting off.

As Raffles turned, he could see how far he was short of his ground. In a despairing scramble, he hurled himself at the line, but heard the bails fall before he got there. The decision was referred to the third umpire anyway, which seemed a bit pointless.

Raffles walked up the pitch to enquire of Hacksley whether he intended to deliberately try and run him out off every delivery, or should he expect a back up plan as well? A sea of faces turned their heads to the great television scoreboard, awaiting the decision.

There were still one or two people looking at Raffles though, which he seemed to be very aware of. Bizarrely, Raffles chose that moment to yell "Telegraph" at the stands (an ancient phrase calling for the score to be updated) and, as every remaining eye gazed in the score-board's direction, Raffles stamped his spikes firmly into the other batsman's foot.

'Awwww!' complained Hacksley, crumpling.

Raffles explained to the umpire all about cramp and then turned to Hacksley again.

'It hurts?'

'Yes.'

'Upsy daisy.'

'Good try, but that won't save you. I'll have to go off.'

'No, you'll stay and have a runner.'

'Only I've lost some blood, you see. That'll make me dizzy in a bit. I'll probably miss the next straight one.'

'Then I'll make sure they don't bowl you any.'

'One of your tricks? Caught then. I could be out any moment. You'd best let me go back.'

'No, no' said Raffles heartily 'I can't leave you brooding in the pavilion, clasping your hands and wondering forever what might have been. You'll stick around and have your runner.'

'Oh, good' said the skewered bat, with a helping of irony.

Then the decision came. Not out! Fantastic! It was not out. Why wasn't that out then? It certainly looked out to me. Heads turned to the big screen overlooking the score board. Oh, I see. The wicket keeper had displaced the bails with his gloves before the ball arrived. Phew, what a let off!

Raffles, in his role as captain, spoke to the Umpires and set off on a long trot to the edge of the pitch. Having discussed the matter with the opposing captain, he signalled to me in the crowd. I couldn't imagine what for. As I didn't understand, I made him walk across the outfield.

'What?' I said. 'Do you want a bottle of water or something?' I just hoped he didn't want me to change the bet. Where would I get an internet connection around here?

'Quickly, get these whites on. You're coming on as a runner.'

'You can't be serious! Why me?'

'You're twelfth man.'

'What do you mean I'm twelfth man?'

'One of the professionals dropped out at the last minute, so I put your name on the team sheet.'

'You thought it was funny?'

'To award you your first international cap? Yes, I suppose so.'

'Can't you change it?'

'Nope. I need my twelfth man, right now, so none of these other duplicitous slugs can run me out!'

'Rani did okay for you, didn't he?'

'Yes, but he's not much of a runner and I absolutely can't trust the others. I can trust you, so you're on.'

'Best of luck is all I can say to that! What will you do? The match-fixer's got this in the bag!'

'I agree. Our little friend has probably advised his clients to bet their whole stack. Just think, both teams! Forty or fifty to one though. It's a once in a lifetime opportunity. No, there's nothing for it. We've got to play it out and try to beat both sides which is, frankly, all I've ever done anyway.'

'Fat chance, A.J. The bloody cheats have won already!'

'I think we can beat the massed ranks of organised crime without swearing, can't we Bunny?'

'Oh, yes. Sorry. Well, what else can you possibly do?'

Raffles' blue-grey eyes, once relaxed and distant, clutched and set like steel a-quenching. He paused and turned to face the pitch, a little like Henry V might have done in his most noble moment (in-between bouts of dysentery) on St Crispin's Day of 1415. The breeze ruffled the trees behind us and in a nerveless voice, the resolution came:

'How can they prize this hollow cup? I can give them something different, something fresh. I can give them fear of a summer's day.'

What was that all about? Did he mean gamesmanship? I couldn't tell and, to be honest, couldn't spare time to think as I pulled on whites and gloves and all manner of things I had barely thought to see again. "One more such victory and we are lost" as King whatnot paraphrased to thingee after the battle of whatever it was. Look it up if you don't believe me. I could see, with bribes and things, their behaviour would lose in the long run, but one less victory right now would admirably suit us. I just hoped I wouldn't be the one who ran him out.

Picture me now, padded up and scampering onto the pitch. Back up and rise. No, it's not a knighthood, think of it as a camera instruction. Zoom back, that's right, you're getting the hang of it, then slip your attention in through the open window of the Press Box.

'The runner's on.'

'Who is that?'

'Good Lord. It's O'Manders of *The Evening Bacon*.'

'Well he's certainly got a scoop this time. Lucky blighter.'

'What exactly is *The Evening Bacon*?'

'It'll be one of those internet cricket journals, I would have thought.'

'Who'd you say that was?'

'What?'

'Blowers says who is it?'

'O'Manders. Voice of cricket on the internet.'

'He certainly seems to know Raffles.'

'Young bloods like that are the future. Good luck to him, I say.'

As I walked onto the pitch, 'self-conscious' my motto, Raffles distributed reassuring advice:

'Don't be run out, Bunny, whatever you do. Clear calls of 'yes', 'no' or 'wait'. If they try to throw down the stumps, get yourself between the wickets and the fielder.'

'What would you do if a batsman does that?'

'I usually accidentally throw it very hard into his spine. Don't worry; it hurts a lot less when you know you're not out - and you usually get an apology.'

'Super.'

'That leaves an obvious problem. What can we do if the other batsman actively tries to get caught? There are two options to obviate this problem. Option one is to monopolise the strike in such a way that the other batsman never gets to face a ball. Option two is to direct the bowler's thinking in such a way that he only bowls deliveries the batsman can not possibly be caught off.'

'Eh? That one went past me a bit fast, sorry.'

He explained it again.

'Option two sounds complicated.'

'Yes. I'd be surprised if it's ever been done.'

At first, Raffles solved this dilemma the hard way, by 'farming the strike' and, as he explained to me breathlessly, only taking single runs from the last ball of the over. In the first five deliveries, on no account should the batsmen be allowed to cross, scoring twos or fours only, thus denying the other player the chance to face any bowling whatsoever.

In the end, as you can imagine, this wasn't possible. Raffles deftly tickled the ball into a gap which suddenly wasn't there. A brilliant piece of fielding at backward point killed the run from the final delivery and one of the best fielders in the game returned the ball as if he'd done nothing out of the ordinary. A stop was as good as a wicket by then, since A.J. would not now be facing the next over. Raffles glanced at Hacksley and walked up the pitch as if tapping down a divot with his bat.

'Yond Cassius has a lean and hungry look.'

'Yes, I'd gathered that. I'm not totally thick.'

'If I ask how many balls are left in the over, it means we will run a single as soon as the bowler has bowled, then we take a bye as the ball flies through to the wicket keeper, okay?'

'Okay. Um, Raffles? How do you know it won't be aimed at the wicket?'

'I don't.'

This sounded horribly risky. Was there a better option? I thought earnestly about obstructing the fielders, but you can be given out for obstructing the field, can't you? That wasn't quite on. What could I do? The Australian Captain trotted over for a conference with his bowler.

'This one's all over the place, Clive. If you can push him back in the crease with the first two, that'll unsettle him. Something he can't keep down. Ok? Rough him up a bit and then knock his toes off.'

Damn. Hacksley was judging the distance to the Point fielder. Was he trying to get caught? What could I do? The bowler brushed past me on the way to his mark. I spoke to him. I actually spoke to him.

'Where did you get that shirt?'

'What's that? Oh, the shirt! I got it at Feldsteads in Melbourne. It used to be called *Harrods*, but the lawyers made them change the name. It's a hard-wearing linen, you see. Really good and strong, but the air circulates. Have you ever been to Melbourne?'

'No, but I'd love to go one day.'

'Ah, mate. Look us up. I'll order a shirt for you.'

'Thanks. That's very kind. If there's anything I can do for you, just ask.'

'You can start by telling me how to get this bloke out' he kidded.

'Sure' I replied 'I played against him in Galway. He's a real sucker for the cut shot. Swing it out past his right shoulder and he'll hit a catch to Deep Square every time. Never fails.'

'Jees, thanks mate' he said and instantly forgot everything his captain had told him. For the first three deliveries, the bowler aimed wide and high of the wicket and Hacksley did exactly what I'd said. He wasn't caught though because the Australian Captain, expecting different bowling, hadn't placed any fielders square of the wicket. In fact, Hacksley accidentally scored two boundaries and the bowler had a row with his own captain. This couldn't last.

'Umpire' called Raffles, 'How many balls are left in the over?'

'Three to go, Mr Raffles' confirmed the Umpire.

As the bowler stormed past me in a breeze, I ran. I didn't stop running until I was twenty yards past Hacksley. Raffles was grinning all over his face, but the other batsman looked mortified at losing the chance to get out. I'm told that's the point the radio latched onto my performance.

'What a run! He's saved the injured player. Brilliant work from O'Manders, bringing home the bacon.'

Raffles, in a policy of ignoring easy singles in the first five and taking insane ones in the sixth, worked his way up to a respectable 44 runs, then Umpire 'Chalky' White gave him out in a dreadful leg before wicket decision when he'd clearly edged the ball. The tailenders threw their wickets, as predicted, and I saw for sure something I knew on paper already. The 'Rest of the World' team had been undeniably 'fixed'.

All out for 146, a dismal score and one I considered all but impossible to defend against the Australians.

The players went to lunch. I followed them, but sat apart at a corner table by the door. I tried to take my mind off the game. In truth, to pass the time, I tried to think-up some new collective nouns. A lapping of jellyfish. A raid of pine martens. A shower of managers. No, it was no good. I couldn't think of any good ones. A boast of property agents? No. A waste of slimmers? A dunk of lifeguards? The closest I came after that was 'a jobbie of railway carriage lavatories', which wasn't very pleasant at all. I gave up and wondered what Raffles was doing. He looked deep in thought. Probably not about collective nouns, knowing Raffles. It would be about something dark and saturnine, wouldn't it? Like how to frame someone as a cannibal so they wouldn't be allowed to bat in the second innings at Dunedin. In what furnace was thy brain, old boy? He surely wasn't still thinking about winning?

After the shockingly dire first innings, I re-took my seat in the stands for the second. They'd patched-up Hacksley and, based on his assurances and barely credible claims to the laying-on-of-feet, the Umpires reluctantly allowed him to re-take the field.

Bowling now. Raffles should be at home with that, except, it wouldn't be him, would it? No one had opened a fist class match with spin since the days of Ritchie Benaud. No, I was right, Raffles opened with his medium pacers. What were they doing? Un-troubling the batsmen? It looked to me like a row of identical deliveries, bowled straight through a sausage machine.

They got slaughtered, of course. At least, they did toward the end of the spell. Early on, the Australians just seemed keen to play risk-free strokes and settle in for a long innings. Raffles watched, quite helpless, as his opening bowler gave away extras, one going straight between the wicket keeper's legs for an unruly four. A strange bowler. He launched a mixed bag, but the man simply wasn't hunting for wickets in the way he should be. Actually, what a ghastly little pug. I wondered what his county must have thought of him.

I wouldn't say it if he were in the room, but I'd guess that Raffles panicked. It's the most likely reason why he'd put himself on to bowl at the other end so early in the proceedings. That's it, I thought, he'll use up his overs when the ball's too hard to spin and then the surviving Aussies will attack the bowling which comes after. By this throw of the dice, A.J.'s spell might have to take ten wickets. No, don't get your hopes up. That's a fantasy if ever I've heard one.

Raffles wasn't a defender who took defeat lying down. He'd lie down and watch you charge into the palace and think you'd won, then he'd nip out the side door, slip the bolts and burn down the whole building with you in it. With this strategy clearly in mind, he bowled a couple of slow, looping, off-breaks which only served to draw the batsman forward. 'At least this slow rubbish isn't going for runs' said a nearby spectator. 'Yet' said another. Any moment now, I felt, he'd loop one in and they'd pounce onto it and hoist him for six into the car park. The third ball, when it came, was a surprise, for a spinner. It was none other than the fast ball I hadn't seen for fifteen years, an unforgiving javelin-style bouncer directed at the throat. The batsman, who'd guessed wrong and leaned on the front foot early, got into a dreadful muddle, lowered his head to duck underneath and was struck a mallet blow to the helmet. I'd say he crumpled and fell like an over-stuffed bag of laundry. Others would disagree. The radio said a bag of spuds, but I've never seen one of those fall over.

Raffles, bless him, was the first to run up to the felled player, looking righteously shocked at his handiwork. The victim managed a pained grin, acknowledged and waved away Raffles' profuse and sincere apologies. There were nods and pats on the back as he accepted the spinner's explanation that his grip on the ball had slipped. Raffles walked back to his bowling mark looking remorseful, to say the least of it.

The dazed batsman tested his feet, adjusted his pads, aligned his helmet and settled into an accustomed stance awaiting the next delivery. Which was another lethal bouncer aimed at the neck. I must say, it was the last thing I expected, anyone expected, including the batsman, whose gawky top edge pistoned the ball limply skywards. The wicket keeper was already standing beneath it and in not so much as a crowd's gasp Raffles popped up next to the gloveman, his own hands at the ready in case 'it bounced out'. It didn't of course. I had to concede, the keeper did have some pride. 'He's the best keeper in the World!' yelped someone in the row behind. 'He'll drop the next one', I told them, and so he did. An edge, a palpable edge, but a clever drop as the wicket keeper went the wrong way as if to field an inside edge instead of an outer.

'Why do you use that enormous bat?' asked Raffles, out of the blue. 'Are you compensating for something?'

The last ball of the over had the new batsman plumb leg-before-wicket. Raffles appealed for the inevitable, but had it rejected by

Umpire 'Chalky' White, much to the crowd's dissatisfaction. A replay on the big screen supported Raffles' side of events, to the accompaniment of boos and whistles.

The surviving Aussie opener looked fairly relaxed, highly experienced and was probably seeing this as just another practice session before the tricky one day series against South Africa. Leaning on his bat, he decided to take an interest, if only to take the pressure off his batting partner. He turned to Raffles, shook him firmly by the hand and said 'Mate, I still think you're a great bowler' then paused for a heartbeat 'I don't care what the other fellers say.' Raffles smiled appreciatively at that little gem and filed it away for future campaigns.

Longstock, the other bowler, charged down the run-in and his ball was met with a significant prod. Beating a fielder who hadn't reacted, the batsman called 'He's dreaming' and took two runs where there should've only been one. The next delivery went for four, when there should have been two. This was getting beyond a joke.

Raffles spoke to Longstock. I'd assume that was an instruction to bowl fuller. If the bowler bowls the ball on one side at just one length, the batsman can only reasonably hit the thing in predictable places. Even if the bowler were trying not to take a wicket, the captain could set a field to control the scoring. Raffles then secretly instructed two fielders to move back to the Long-On and Long-Off positions. They did, but instead of doing it quietly, they peddled backwards as fast and eye-catchingly as they could, just to make sure the batsman could see them. Very helpful.

Raffles knew the batsman had seen. Oh well, there was still pride.

'This is a trap', he explained in resignation to the Australians, pointing to the pair of fielders. The batsmen nodded wearily.

Longstock pelted in and bowled full, his usual rubbish, only to see it smacked straight back over his head and down to the Long-On fielder, who dropped it. Oh, no, he hadn't! He tried to drop it, but the ball got stuck in the folds of his jumper and when he picked it out... that was a catch!

'I tried to hit it over your trap' explained the Australian opener as he walked away. Two down.

In the next over, Raffles was then called 'no ball' for overstepping the front line of the popping crease, which he hadn't. 'What is wrong with this umpire?' I asked aloud to the world in general. The world in general told me to 'Shhhh!' because they were trying to hear a radio three rows in front. How quickly my achievements had been forgotten.

Despite the inadequate total and a forlorn hope of defending it, Raffles did not react. The umpire then called "no ball" again. Raffles asked what he did wrong this time.

'You were outside the side-line at the back of the popping crease'.

'Oh, I see. My foot was right here? In your blind-spot, you mean?'

If so, this judgement was technically correct. What was down-right magical was the way the umpire could observe the placement of boots that were landing behind him. What should have been the second to last ball of the over was thinly sliced to the wicket keeper and caught on reflex. 'No ball' was the unbelievable call that smothered our cheers.

'You've got two fielders standing behind square on the leg side.'

Raffles looked across and saw it to be true. So, another one of them had betrayed him. A fielder this time, a little creep earning his pieces of silver. The ball was re-bowled, tapped into the gap for two and the tortuous over ended. No, I must have miscounted, what with all those re-bowled deliveries.

When I was young, we were told the umpires should be regarded as God's personal representatives on Earth. "If you ever think something is different to the way the umpire has seen it, lad, you need your eyes tested". As I was taught it, if you are quite sure about your contention, then it became a matter of theoretical physics: there are two realities and you are living in the wrong one.

I could see what they meant though. Accepting the umpire's decision at the higher levels of the sport conditioned the lower levels of the game to always accept an umpire's authority. Without having cameras everywhere, an impossibility in the leagues of village cricket, one simply has to leave decision making to the umpire or the game would become intolerable to play. The principle of the umpire's decision made playing the game possible. We all understood that. One must be philosophical, so I calmed myself down and accepted the decisions.

Raffles was then called by Umpire White for 'throwing' and I'm afraid I lost my temper. Raffles took himself out of the attack and brought in a swing bowler who totally failed to swing the ball.

'Hold it across the seam' instructed Raffles.

'Why?'

'You're not getting any swing, are you? At least that way I might get some unpredictable bounce.'

The bowler couldn't argue with that, but looked a little put out.

Bang, bang, bang. It was horrible. The straight-line bowling the man served up was a gift to the batsmen. One into the advertising hoardings, one into the crowd, the shots were spectacular, but each one of them stabbed into my soul as only an Australian performance can.

Raffles turned to Maubrey, the famously reliable New Zealander, who let him down too. He asked to come out of the attack after two overs, complaining something about "an off day".

Three overs later, and Chalky tried again.

'No ball.'

'Might I ask why, this time?'

'The bowler didn't specify his action.'

This was absurd, so Raffles did the absurd in turn. He brought himself back on. At least, I'm not sure it worked like that. I think A.J. wouldn't have done it if it hadn't been suggested. What happened was this:

At the end of that over, the field re-arranged itself for the bowler at the other end. Head down, Raffles trudged past the second umpire, a hugely respected West Indian commanding over a decade of experience in the Tests. He, at least, would not remain silent.

'There's Voodoo in the air today, Mr Raffles.'

'That there is, Mr Mallow, that there is.'

'Voodoo don't work so good on me, Mr Raffles.'

'I know that, Mr Mallow.'

'So you bowl true and you'll have straight answers from me.'

'Thank you, Mr Mallow. That's all I ever ask.'

'No, you ask more that that, most times. You've got a voodoo of your own, Mr A.J. Raffles.'

Raffles regarded him closely, but didn't speak.

'You'll be changing ends too, I reckon.'

'Yes, I think I might have a little bowl from your end.'

From the distant stands, I was as surprised as anyone to see a fresh spring in A.J.'s step.

Raffles had changed his tactics, tossing the ball above the batsman's eye-level. The slow bowling looked easy to play when viewed from a seat in the stands, but losing sight of the pitch meant the batsman had to play his shots after the ball bounced and couldn't easily capitalise. Then I watched as a familiar play unfolded, preceded by a footwork-driven four, popped over the in-field. Not a percentage shot, as A.J. would have said. One that would have cost a wicket once if attempted twice and so... Raffles used the batsman's confidence against him.

'Excellent. A superb shot' applauded Raffles, openly showing his appreciation.

'Thanks.'

'Honestly, that was straight out of the MCC coaching manual. Look on the big screen; it's worth watching that shot again. Oh, no. It's a shame.'

'What's a shame?'

'The camera missed it. He must have dropped his sandwich.'

The spectator with the Radio turned it up to find out what all this was about, but only heard the commentators rattling on like geriatrics about the spirit of the game.

'Raffles being the last great sportsman, of course.'

'Absolutely Peter.'

'Look at him congratulating Russell Franks. That's the mark of a great player. I don't think I've seen a cricketer applauding the opposition since, oh when was it Derek? Somerset at Lords in the final of 2002?'

'Who was that then?'

'Raffles again, probably.'

'What a generous man. A fine example to young people today, coming up through the game...'

Franks mimed the stroke he'd used, swishing his bat through the air in practice, just in case anybody else had missed it. Raffles walked back to his mark, trundled in and repeated the ball, the batsman committed himself forward, repeated the shot and, stunned to see it turn the opposite way, hit a return catch straight back to Raffles. Out! No question this time, out and walking.

Three down. Not enough. Not nearly enough. Ah! The next batsman in, I think you'd recognise. It was Jason, the brash young player Raffles psyched-out in the bar. Poor lad. He must have run this match through his head all night. All credit to his work ethic though. The radio had something relevant:

'The ground staff told me this morning he'd been up and batting in the nets since 5am for this match.'

'I did see him practicing in the nets earlier this morning, Derek.'

'He was there again through lunch. What's it now? About 4.30 and I must say he's looking extremely tired. Too tired to face Raffles, surely?'

'That's right. Well, he'd better concentrate now. The bowler's circling, ah! No, he's just beaten the bat. I thought that was a thin edge, but he's still there.'

A few balls later, A.J. went round the wicket and drifted the ball into the footholds. The batsman, too slow and scared to use his pad, meekly tapped it in the air for a consecutive caught-and-bowled! I leapt out of my chair.

Jason Daskulaki walked off the pitch and returned to his own seat in the pavilion balcony and finally realised that he'd been tricked into another of Raffles' whopping great elephant traps. I felt sorry for him. I don't know why. The Australians never felt sorry for us.

Four down and only five overs of the Captain's allocation remaining.

Another Australian arrived and immediately started scoring. The tactic Raffles used was to ask the batsmen to hit the ball to just one fielder. Not exactly ask, no. He packed the on-side with fielders he believed had little intention of holding their catches and then encouraged the batsmen to hit against the spin to the near vacant off-side, where Patrick was the only man within the close circle. If any of his players were honest, Raffles reasoned that it would be the ones who weren't expected to have the talent to turn the match. The obvious choice was Patrick, so he would have to be the one to do it.

'Patty, in a few seconds' time, you'll have more cricket balls whizzing past your ears than you'll know what to do with. They won't be able to place them accurately, but they think there's a good chance you won't hold onto any of them. Patty? Send one of these arrogant beach-boys home for me, would you?'

Raffles walked toward the keeper, passed him without a word and collected the spare helmet. Walking back, he laid it down to one side of Patty and continued to his own position in the field.

'You can't do that! It'll be five runs!' cried Maubrey.

'Yes he can', confirmed my, by now, all-time favourite umpire. 'There's nothing against it in the laws.'

The next three major shots flew past Patrick's snapping hands and off into the outfield.

Raffles changed tack, talking again to a batsman.

'I thought you were a footballer.'

'I was. Victoria Under-XXIs. You can't do both though, can you?'

'C.B. Fry?'

'Ah, mate, that was the old days. You can't manage it now. Sport's gone too professional.'

It was unusual to be so friendly at the end of the over, when Raffles would be bowling to this player next. I didn't hear all of it, but he told me later it went like this:

'Still. It must have been good to have the option.'

'Yeah. Reckon so. Still, I made my choice and I'm okay with it.'

'I bet you'd like to be kicking the ball now, kicking the ball now...'

What was this? Hypnotic suggestion? Raffles crossed the wicket and bowled his first effort in as few seconds as he could manage. The delivery was one of the Maurice Tate variety, with horrible forward spin. The batsman tapped it down ahead of him and attempted to run a single as A.J. dived to collect the wobbling ball. The Aussie lashed out a leg as he ran and swept the ball from Raffles' path. The batsmen crossed and the wise old West Indian umpire nodded to the world in general.

'Out, for hampering the field.'

At first, the crowd couldn't work out what had happened. They could see the fuss though. It's not often you see an Australian throwing his prawns out of the barbie.

Five down and the batsman scored in twos for the rest of the over.

Out! Then six, off the medium pacer this time, as the new batsman sliced his first ball straight to Patty. Hooray for Kenya! It's not often you ever hear that, so I thought I'd be the first to say it. Well done, that man. Chalky must have forgotten to no-ball it.

Raffles again, from the other end. A big leg break. Heads up! The deck was suddenly turning.

Another big leggie. That one fizzed and spat.

The next is... bowled! Out! It's the three card trick and the googly's done him!

'Well that is an important piece knocked off the board' chattered the radio.

Raffles finished his ten over spell, with the opposition a wonderful seven wickets down. It was a good try, but we both knew one player would never be enough. We'd failed and the cheats and the money-men had won. I located the ring pull and opened my one remaining beer. It might even be my last one. I remember thinking 'they could try to kill me tonight. If they've even noticed me', so I felt doubly determined to enjoy it. The tin can had warmed unpleasantly in the sunshine. *Typical*. I sipped and slipped into a bitter mood.

The young Indian spinner Rani Papta Patel, probably an afterthought in team selection, then clean bowled an Aussie with a loopy googly that gated the batsman's defences wonderfully. The clatter of those stumps, that shattered disarray, carried further than it should. Perhaps, I thought, because not every fielder was cheering. Raffles, standing square of the stumps, couldn't see the movement. He thought the Australian had played and missed at a straight one. What a stroke of grace that would have been, but no, I saw the replays. It twisted like a mongoose. This bowler was *trying*.

Eight down and still all of forty to win. That should be done and dusted by the normal standards, but not when the bowling side aims to give the runs away. There was an interruption as next to the last batsman strode to the crease. A middle aged hooligan, soberly dressed, ran wildly onto the playing area. He seemed very familiar to me, that sad pitch-invader. Ranting for support despite his utter solitude, careered toward a group of fielders and desperately pleaded.

'Do something! Aaaannnnyyything!'

The players looked alarmed and backed away.

'I bloody own you!' he ranted after them.

As the crowd waited politely, security guards rugby-tackled the lunatic to the ground and those nearest tried to make out his increasingly desperate cries as he was manhandled away.

Raffles sensed a change in the tide and moved himself to the mid-wicket boundary.

The Aussie number nine kept piercing the mid-off boundary, diametrically opposite Raffles, where there was nothing at all he could do. The score ticked along.

Bowling at the other end, Rani kept generating catches, but four different players managed to drop them. Spectators became uneasy and started to ask what was going on. The radio didn't have an answer. In fact, the commentators fought each other to get off-air and away before the impending riot.

Sensing they wouldn't be dropped forever off Rani, the batsmen simply blocked out each delivery of his spell and took their runs from the other bowler. They were scoring, yes, but running out of time.

Needing twenty or so to win, the bowler from the other end tried to hand them the match from his six balls alone. Easy balls, full tosses, long-hops, even an old fashioned lob. The batsmen misinterpreted this bounty and thought he was trying to buy the last wicket, to have them caught on the boundary. Finkel, the Australian opening batsman, had been around far too long to fall for that sort of thing, so tapped each ball down for an easy two runs and kept the weaker player off-strike until the sixth delivery. To keep facing the bowling, to protect the last batsman, Finkel would be required to hit a one or a three from the final ball of the over and change ends.

The bowler obliged the Australian cause with another half-volley and Finkel prodded it safely, all the way along the floor and out to Raffles at the mid-wicket boundary. The batsmen ran the three runs they needed and took a rest. Even the ball seemed to run out of steam as it trickled towards the fielder. All eyes were on Raffles, who then... deliberately folded his arms.

The radio loved it.

'That's right Clive, he did nothing at all to prevent the ball rolling past him for four! That's the most apathetic piece of fielding I've seen in all my days of cricket.'

'Actually Charles, I think he's been extremely clever. They've now got the Australian number ten batsman facing the new over and, judging by his average, he isn't sure which way up to hold the bat.'

'That's a good point Clive. Lateral thought. Yes, I hadn't appreciated it like that. How very clever.'

The over was over and my favourite Bengal tiger returned at the other end. With a master class of turn and flight, the young Indian spinner's first three balls did everything right but take a wicket. The fourth defected off the Australian tail-ender's pad and, blessing his luck, he ran through to safety.

A coiled spring replaced a wet one as the more experienced player focussed on the fifth delivery. Despite a good effort, sliding across the face of his bat, Finkel tapped the ball off the batting square for a single, which he then decided not to run. Full protection then, for the weaker batsman.

'He won't take the risk and let the tail-ender face a single ball if he doesn't have to!' burbled the radio.

How many runs to win? Six? Seven? I tried to make out numbers on the scoreboard as the theme tune of the match repeated itself: The batsman would require a one or three to retain the strike at the other end.

Fielders moved in to stop the single, although I had little confidence in them doing so. Rani had seen his Captain's ploy and delivered a palatable half-track delivery, which the batsman again pushed out toward Raffles on the boundary. Raffles deliberately folded his arms and I winced painfully at perhaps his greatest gamble yet. They didn't run this time. If Raffles was going to let it go, they'd need three to win and they'd have half a dozen overs to get them. Did it matter if the tail-ender faced that dreadful bowler at the other end?

Like a panther. That's how the radio described it. As the ball rolled past the disinterested Raffles, he kicked it neatly into his hand and fired it back in like a meteorite. Australian faces fell. They'd hit it an awful long way for no runs at all! Oh, and look who's on strike for the next over! Was this the birth of a new ploy?

The Australian batsmen conferred in the middle of the pitch. Finkel took the initiative.

'Don't think about it, okay?'

'Look, the crazy old coot's coming in now.'

'He's going to field close and try to put you off, so you're going to ignore him, alright?'

'Sure.'

'No, really ignore him. Don't underestimate a thing he says or does. You must give them no chances in this over. Don't leave your crease. Don't think about running. Leave anything wide of the wicket. Don't get greedy and think you can score. Block, just block. I need you to keep six balls out and then I'll score the last seven runs off the spinner. Got it?'

'Got it. Don't listen to Raffles. Defend six. No worries.'

'Right.'

The bowler tried everything to present the last batsman with easy runs. Again and again he pitched too short or two full with tempting 'buffet balls'*, all of which sailed through to the keeper unmolested. Seeing the opportunity slip, the bowler handed out a wide and a full tossed no-ball to keep the scoring rate up. That made two more un-run runs to Australia, which I think made it single figures to win. The number ten had almost passed the post and the odds moved in his favour. Seeing this, the bowler bowled a straight, medium-paced delivery, which the batsman slapped back, deflecting off the bowler's legs. He made no attempt to get his hands to it, hoping the deflection would skid away for runs. It didn't. The wicket arrested its flight. Out! That counted as a run-out! The bowler didn't seem up to celebrating.

Raffles checked the score and had no choice but to cast his dice through the hands of the spinner. He still wasn't sure about Rani, but I was. 'That's it' I said aloud 'Give him the ball and pray.' Was it the final over? No. Pity. It would have been good if it was the final over, but nine runs to win and an acknowledged batsman on strike put the equation well into Australia's favour.

'This looks like the last chance, Rani. What are you going to bowl?'

'Do you think I would tell you how to do your job in such a circumstance?'

'No, of course not Rani. As your Captain, all I meant…'

'You just be quiet and stand there. It is my over, is it not?'

'Yes, but…'

'Well then. Zip it. To the midwicket with you and remember to hold your catches with two hands.'

'Yes Rani. I'll try to do that.'

'Are you still here or what is it?'

An admonished Raffles 'zipped it' as instructed and returned to his mark.

Rani huffed and puffed and turned on his toes and readied himself for bowling.

Raffles bit his lower lip and looked as nervous as ever I'd ever seen him.

It didn't take long. The first ball was hittable. Bang, it was hit. Rani stuck out a leg like the Australian had done and deflected it. Two runs. The second spun forward as it touched the ground and the batsman miss-timed his shot. He pulled the bat down late, but the ball couldn't quite grub underneath. Forward spin! Better than Raffles and amazing to me as I think the great Maurice Tate couldn't have bowled it better. The third ball was defended, from respect to the second. The

---

* *'Help yourself' deliveries.*

fourth was launched at, with a mighty arc of the bat, but biting the earth and turning late, it ended as a failed connection. A close fielder picked the ball up and threw it at the stumps, which it passed at velocity and ran away to the boundary as four overthrows.

I closed my eyes and couldn't watch any longer.

'Technically, everything was wrong with that' said the radio 'Three to win.'

There it was then, the equation I mean. The Syndicate's fortune and perhaps their very existence against our own stake – itself more money than I'd ever seen or had a right to part with. Had we got the forty to one on Betfine? The odds wouldn't matter if Finkel hit a four, so I tried not to count our imminent losses.

The fifth ball spun the other way and the batsman slogged it down in front of Raffles. They didn't risk the run.

I remember thinking that last delivery must be a magic bullet, nothing less to contain Australia's finest.

Rani pounced into the popping crease like a cat, bending his supple spine and whipping an arm vertically to clip across his ear. I also remembered Raffles' lecture – that if his arm clipped the ear, it had to be a googly, jumping right, or otherwise the straight one because anything else bowled from that position would effectively be impossible.

Looping from the batsman's eye-line and dipping late, Australia's last hope and best bat was early on it. Not early enough to adjust the shot though, as it broke against all reason to leg. In a wild attempt to restore the laws of physics and nudge the impossible thing away from his stumps, the batsman flung his bat, a white flash of willow as it caught the sun, and snubbed the ball with a leading edge, tapping a dolly catch straight back to the bowler. Rani put it in his pocket.

OUT.

I've never heard anything so silent.

Raffles exploded.

I've never heard anything so loud.

The crowd exploded too and made quite an unnecessary mess for someone else to clear up. I tried not to worry about that and laughed instead, until the tears reddened my eyes.

Nowadays, the stewards don't let you onto the field after a match, but I went anyway as a pitch-invasion of eight hundred people is a pretty hard thing to stop, unless you knew something Canute didn't. As I caught up to Raffles, I dismissed the pitch-invasion fine out of hand. I would pay a fair price for this moment. Raffles turned aside, seeking out the teenaged spinner amongst the melee.

'You didn't take the money, did you Rani?'

'I wouldn't do it to you Mr Raffles.' Their eyes locked. 'When I was a boy, I watched you on television in my Uncle's shop. My father spoke of you. I wanted to bowl just like you, so I practiced.'

'Thank you Rani. That means a lot to me.'

'I practiced bowling with the ball *and* with the mind. Is that not your way?'

'Yes. Yes Rani, that is my way. I think the game will study you though, from now on.'

'I have a lot to learn, Mr Raffles.'

'You are too modest, too humble. I rarely see such talent. Could I ask you a question?'

'Certainly, Raffles.'

'That ball that broke the wrong way. The vertical leg break. Where did you learn to bowl it?'

'I learned it from my father. He speaks of you sometimes. He calls you 'The one who should have been born Indian' and I would like to say that he even took your wicket once.'

'Canterbury, 1989?'

'You do remember! Excellent.'

'I remember the mess it made of my mind.'

'"Bowl the ball sparingly" he said, "Do not waste it on idiots. Save it until all the gods are watching".'

'Please convey my regards. Tell him, I think you should tell him…'

Raffles smiled a deep and grateful smile as weights finally fell from his shoulders.

'Tell him all the gods were watching. Yes, Rani. Tell him that.'

They were both smiling now and warmly they shook hands, but Rani hadn't quite finished.

'That trick with the cap in the Test Match was truly splendid.'

'I got it on Ebay, just to break that one player.'

'Very good, Mr Raffles, very good. I too shall be a collector of caps.'

They said their farewells and the sun sank to the sea. I drank that cooked tin of beer anyway, in the late afternoon and the heat. To me, it tasted like hot champagne, which was... different.

I remembered my Lucan: Ab Hyrcanis Indoque a litore siluis. From Hrcanian woods and the Indian shore, marvels may find us.

Chapter 20

Raffles Leaves the Country

That evening, we checked out of our hotel. At least, when I say 'checked out', I should qualify it by saying nothing's as easy as it sounds. A.J. did the paperwork and gathered our passports and I went upstairs with the swipe-cards to clear the rooms.

Mine didn't take long as I never have much to carry. I took a final look round, closed the door and headed along the corridor to Raffles' room. 3212, 3213, 3214... Ah! Here it was, but strangely enough, there too was the pleasant girl from Reception loitering about outside it.

'I was just wondering if Mr Raffles was looking for any more tours.'

'No, I don't think so. He's downstairs checking out, you see?'

'Is he? Shit!' She ran for the lift.

Having made it past the resident strange person, I accessed the room and located the bags. His were a lot larger than mine, but I suppose he had to carry his ego around in them. As I scanned the room for anything else I'd missed, something unusual caught my attention. The jug of fresh orange juice beside the bed seemed to have a layer of sedimentary snow at the bottom of it. Two-tone orange juice, how flash. What was that then? Blood orange over normal orange? Only, it wasn't quite right, was it? They should at least have the same density. I made a closer inspection. A few seconds later I found the phone and dialled Reception.

'Can you put me through to Dale McKenna's room? No, I know this room is supposed to be checked-out, but I need to speak to Mr McKenna. It's quite urgent actually. Please?'

Various clicking noises and I'd caught him.

'What now?'

'Dale! It's Bunny. How much authority have you got? What? No. I mean, what would you do if someone tried to murder Raffles?'

'That's easy. I'd hold their hat for them while they do it. The man's a menace.'

'Room 3216. The swipe card's under the pot-plant. Someone's poisoned his orange juice.'

'It's probably from Natal. They make crap orange juice.'

'Dale! The damn stuff's precipitating!'

'That sounds bad. I'd better look it up.'

'You do that, Dale. Then get the police. They're trying to kill Raffles.'

'So am I. I had a bet on the Aussies.'

'Just do it, will you? Tell them to bring a forensic chemist and check *fast* for cypermethrin. It evaporates.'

'Gees, you do talk a load of...'

'Just do it! Now please. Cypermethrin.'

I hung up, surprised at the sound of my own voice, turned and walked past a mirror. I then looked into that a couple of times, surprised at my own expression. I closed the door and hoped to high heaven that Dale would be loud and persuasive enough. Actually, who was I kidding?

The bags and I descended smoothly in the lift and I dropped and burst forth across the ground floor in my finest impression of a water-bomb. Ah, right, there he was. I swerved around the random wandering receptionist, rounded-up Raffles and marched him away from the Foyer and off to the car-park entrance.

Unfortunately for us, Jerome the Tour Manager stood up from a chair. Damn! He'd spotted Raffles jumping ship and must have thought it was his job to stop him leaving in a huff, which it wasn't.

'Hey, hey, hey. Let's take this runaway truck off the highway for a moment. You've heard the squad for the Fourth Test, am I right? Okay, so we won't let you knock over another coconut if you won't wait in line. Get with the programme! You know the whole structure feeds up to the Urn. You're just looking at a line item!'

'Have any of you people ever heard of free will?' replied Raffles.

'Yeah. It's a concern. I've commissioned a report from Nick Broker about this. He believes cricketers should be predictable, like production in a business. He thinks it can be solved with tighter contracts.'

'Rubbish. Let me through.'

'Come on, Raffles. We're all fans. He described your bowling as 'prime chutney.'

'He did what?'

'Look, man. The Ashes is a whole base jump and you're just one string on the England parachute. I've heard your thoughts about selec-

275

tion before and they're *good thoughts*, believe me, I know you mean well, but let's park that conversation for a while and talk turkey.'

Jerome made a sort of two-handed parking mime which resembled a fish being slipped through a letterbox and then followed it up with a talking turkey mime, which is quite difficult actually and probably takes hours of practice in front of a full length mirror with a real talking turkey.

'If we want to win, first of all we've got to head up the business team. Slice and dice. Spin out the paper trail, see what we've got and replace key systems. Then we have to have a good analyst.'

'What about good players?'

'We can build good players.'

'No. At best you can train athletes to conform to the disciplines of cricket, but the best cricketers of the last three hundred years have all been naturals. They just appear one day from out of the sticks. An Australian sheep station gave us Bradman. Genuine isolation. He didn't have another cricketer to play against! He just learned the game from the radio and used to hit golf balls against water butts with a stick!'

'That's a one-off.'

'In a nation of millions you're going to have a dozen naturals, one-offs. Some will never know the game. Of the rest, almost all of them will find being noticed too difficult or the other job offers too tempting, particularly when there's rent to pay, and they'll leave cricket for silly work in offices or banks. Acorns on tarmac. In England, one or two in a generation will break through. Then people like you will say they're not worth the risk because they don't have the standard bowling action or they take too many risks with the bat. It seems to me that you're here to keep them out or at least leave them jobbing along in the counties until they're too old. This year there's a bumper crop and instead of giving them a chance, you want to control long-term failure by filling the team with consistently, predictably, athletically average performers. If I named the ten best cricketers of all time, you'd have blocked them all at youth level, wouldn't you?'

'Freakshow stuff. You can only manage consistency, in any real business sense. Consistency must be demonstrated over time.'

'So you pick people long after you've seen the best of them? Then you'll be beaten by freak natural brilliance. Predictably and often. When you find it in the opposition, you won't be able to contain it. What about Anwar? Think of it. A teenager gets tired of herding goats up a mountain in Pakistan, arrives at a cricket club in the foothills, picks up a bat... and *they can't get him out*. He made the Pakistan team at the age of sixteen and scored a hundred opening the batting against England! You can't build that. You can't build a bowler like Murali. You can't build a keeper like Knott. You can teach a bowler the laws, but you can't build cunning.'

'Look bowler man, I'm not sure that particular mythological monkey ever hatched.'

'It's people like you who kept out Steele and Fairbrother. Short-sighted selection policies like yours kept Fraser on the sidelines for years! Do not repeat those mistakes.'

'A.J., my man, listen to me. There are three gates to the England playing field and I've got the keys to all of them. For us, that's the 'fit point'. We can live with flexibility. It's built into the curve.'

'What are you talking about?'

'Look, you want to be there when we populate that dressing room. You can forget those five kids you've put forward for the New Zealand tour. So what if their heads are screwed on the right way, they don't have a track record. There are fifteen players who should be in that team, but we've only got eleven places. I don't know how we're going to square that circle, but we have flagged up there's a circle to square. We need systematic support flow and there's a push from the counties to look at our consistency in the success criteria.'

'Are you aware that people don't understand what you're saying most of the time?'

Jerome pretended not to hear that. He hardly ever took account of what other people were saying.

'We've got to be on the same page here. Test cricket has to be a poster-child for the real money spinners like Twenty Twenty matches. Twenty overs a side, forty quid a customer, TV rights, pop music, cheerful costumes, drinks and food concessions, buckets of cash and a bunch of happy county grounds! It's a pound a punter for every six balls! Now that's what I call commercial achievement. In any real sense, Test cricket has to be hyped as an advertising campaign for the real product. Otherwise, we'll never get this gravy train Stateside.'

I don't think I've ever seen Raffles so offended. I wondered whether I might be about to witness a murder. I got ready to help.

'We've got to be future proof! Raffles, Raffles, admitting to your weakness is a *strength*. Man, you've got to knock all those old ideas of yours into the long grass. This is the age of aluminium woods! You gotta realise it's no good being the brightest candle money can buy if it's an electric world!'

'Really? I'm told even the brightest bulbs house a vacuum.'

Raffles had heard enough of this. We were going.

'You're witty. Good. I like that. Help me Raffles. Let's wash England through and blow out the chaff! It's all to do with that old chestnut 'team'. 'Team' depends on the collective view. The collective new, *the collective now!* I mean, are we looking out of the same window? Our team vision.' Jerome was at it again, as he mimed the action of opening curtains. 'I see trees, poplars, all lined up and marching to victory! What do you see?'

'A twat. Good day' and with that, Raffles left the country.

Jerome yelled after the dangerously volcanic figure of Raffles 'Listen to me! You can't win cricket matches on your own you know!' screaming now 'WE WON'T LET YOU.'

'You've certainly done your best.'

Oh dear. Raffles, old England, scourge of the counties, will you be redeemed by love or war? For, I'm fairly certain cricket is making you worse.

Chapter 21

Raffles Takes a House

Raffles took a taxi "to the airport" in full view of everyone. I presumed this to be a deception. No, I'm not being clever all of a sudden. It just gave me a clue when he shoved a 'do not disturb' card with a list of instructions into my hands on the way out. I read instruction number one and let him go without explanation.

1. Don't read this now you fool! Make yourself scarce.
   Okay, fine. I could just about manage that. Always with the orders.
2. Can you collect my kit-bag from the porters? I've told them to expect you.
3. Don't go near my room. It's cleared, but it might be watched.
   I know. I cleared it. How far in advance had he written this?
4. I've taken the number of the public telephone by the soft drinks kiosk. I'll call you there in two hours.
5. Pack your bags. Eat something, but remember – stay in very public places. No wandering off.
6. Sea-green incorruptible? Find an internet connection and move all the money in the Betfine.com account to the bank account number below. The user name is 'Bunny',
   That's hardly secure, I thought.
   '… in Latin'
   Oh.
   Was that 'lapin'? No, that was French. Never mind – it would come to me.
   'and the password is Paradichlorobenzine.'
   Actually, that bit's quite secure.
7. Ask the receptionist if you can use their shredder.

   - Must dash.

Constant as the northern star, or perhaps lacking the imagination to try anything original, I spent the time fulfilling each of these points in turn. The hardest of them being number five, to stay in public places. I mean, how does one go to the lavatory in full view of as many people as possible? Surely, this was a matter easier said than done. Should I wait until a coach party comes in or run the risk of being arrested? I did ask to use the shredder, but I must admit that I tore out and kept the bit that about paradichlor-whotsit because I felt I needed a crib. This turned out to be the chemical they put around cased moth and butterfly collections to keep the moisture out. It isn't in the usual dictionaries or the usual shops.

As I found out later, Raffles had behaved very strangely at the airport. It seems he'd queued up in the departure area and run his eyes along the bags of passengers waiting in line to go to Rio de Janeiro. The parent of one cricket-mad child had said something like 'Just go up and ask him. It'll be okay.'

Raffles was then asked to sign an autograph, so he took the pen and paper they supplied and did so. 'I think we can do better than that' he'd added and fished out his rumpled England cap for the lad and signed that for him too. Then, it seems, he pocketed their pen and walked away. Raffles returned to a suitcase bearing one of those double-sided tags with to/from on it and wrote down the South African 'from' address.

At the appointed time, Raffles rang me from a taxi driver's mobile phone and explained the situation:

'Bunny? Is that you? I've taken a house' and 'We'll stay there until the hounds lose the scent.'

'That's a good idea. Can you trust the letting agent not to say?'

'They don't work weekends. This is between myself and the owners. Did you move the money?'

'Yes. No problems. I've deleted the account too so they can't reverse it.'

'Well done. I'll be outside soon after eight I'd say. Twenty minutes then. Look for a cab with an advert for *Petracodo Motor Oil* on it.'

'Will do. Bye.' I hung up. At least he was still in one piece.

When the taxi rolled to a stop, I took the long route around the back of the hotel and approached it. No one appeared to be in the back, but I could soon see Raffles, below the line of the window, apparently tying his shoe laces. I loaded up the bags and got in next to the driver.

'Go, go, go' said Raffles. We did.

At the next traffic lights, I arched around to speak to him. I was alarmed to see his bruised cheek and a cut beneath one eye.

'God! What happened?'

'I stole a child's pen.' He dismissed the damage with a wave 'The father.'

Ah, ok. Even so, the nervous energy he was broadcasting at this moment made me see threats everywhere. I kept glancing behind and in the mirrors to see if we were to be forced into an exciting car chase. Just as I thought it to be inevitable, Raffles stopped the taxi and got out. Oh. What an anti-climax.

'Have you got everything?'

'Yes' I replied 'Three bags and a coat.'

'Do we really need the coat?' asked Raffles, striding past me and towards an old car at the traffic lights.

'It was my Father's and I've always been rather attached to it.'

'Dump it' he replied and knocked on the car's half-open window.

'Yes? What's your problem?'

'I have no idea how much this pile of African money is worth. I have no idea how much your car is worth, but I'd hazard a guess that half of this would buy me five of them. Would you sell?'

'Sure mon. Jeesh! Are you guys being chased by the mob?'

'We are the mob' said Raffles, getting in.

We drove for some time. To be honest, it's pretty hard to accurately quantify time when the adrenaline's pumping, but I suppose it would have been for well over an hour.

Raffles found a map in the glove compartment, which helped. I had a lot to think about, so couldn't tell you an awful lot about the journey. He seemed to know where we were going and, as the street lights took over, I was glad no one would be relying on my navigation. Okay, so I'm not bad a map-reading from the back of a Land Rover on Salisbury Plain, but in an urban environment, with street signs everywhere, I was hopeless.

We arrived at what I could only assume to be the right address and parked in the driveway. It was the only house in the street without illumination, which didn't help. The signs looked pretty bleak and, when Raffles tried the lock, he found his key didn't fit it. Hell, I thought, what are we supposed to do now?

I remember thinking it was unusual for a door key. It was more the sort of thing you'd use to open a locker. They must have given him the wrong one, which was just typical. I'm not sure what it was typical of, but it was certainly *typical*. There was nothing for it, Raffles asserted, we'd have to break in.

I helped him with a leg up to reach the window, clicky clack click and then... Uncle Bob. He was quite efficient at breaking in, which also surprised me.

So, it was the R&B show again. We scouted the place, turned on a few lights and settled in. I chucked my bags into the best bedroom, leaving the one with the shower to Raffles. He took a plink or two at the piano and then foraged around the kitchen for something to eat.

'This house has everything!'

'Apart from the key, you mean.'

He'd discovered a larder packed with smoked meats, plenty of tins and a rack of interesting varietal wines. Raffles reassured me that the owner wouldn't mind if we replaced whatever we used or paid the equivalent value before leaving. Fine. Shower, shave, shausages and sleep. I was most looking forward to a wash and sleep. Trawling around the back roads of South Africa in a car without any hint of air-conditioning can fairly take it out of you.

At about eleven o'clock, the doorbell rang and my heart stopped working. I looked at Raffles and between us we elevated a wild selection of eyebrows. Raffles got up from his chair and calmly opened the front door to find out whatever whoever it was could possibly want.

There were five people at the door. I'd say they were all in the same mid twenties age group and they also showed signs of a wearisome journey. I wasn't sure if it was safe to breathe yet, which compounded the tension.

'Hi! This is Kieran's parents' house isn't it?'

'That's right' replied Raffles with a winning smile.

'Oh. It's just he said that his parents would be away, so we should pitch up and he'd be along tomorrow.'

'Did he mention this to them?'

'Um, I reckon not. It's a sort of student party, you see. I don't think they're meant to know.'

'Ah.'

'I suppose that kills the fun this weekend then.'

'It's okay. You're secret's safe with us. We're supposed to be house-sitting while they're in Brazil. Burglars and so forth; you can't be too careful.'

'Um, is it okay if we stay tonight? We haven't got money for a hotel.'

'No problem at all' Raffles granted magnanimously, 'Any friend of Kieran's... I'll help you with those bags.'

'Thanks! I'm Kimberley, this is Pippa, that's Knotty, this one's Faye and that's Jacques.'

'Hi, I'm Jacques' said Jacques unnecessarily.

So now we were seven. A.J. had a hell of a lot to learn about 'low profile'.

It wasn't long before I'd adapted to the names and faces. Knotty was almost certainly male and had a matted bleachy mop of simulated rotting hair, Kimberley or Kim was cheerful enough and reminded me of an oyster-catcher pecking for whatever it is oyster-catchers peck for; presumably not oysters nowadays as times are hard. The others were dissimilar enough not to be confused: Pippa – hard on the eyes, Faye – easy on the eyes and Jacques seemed a heavily-built lad with a graveyard demeanour. Probably a scrum-half, I speculated.

When describing South Africa, I wouldn't want to paint you a picture of a land dripping with honeys, because it isn't. However, I have to admit that Faye was okay, in a demure girl-next-door kind of way. She'd probably go on to marry some boorish farmer who'd treat her abominably, but there wasn't much I could do about that.

Form the outset, they all got on well with Raffles and then Pippa asked what he thought of Kieran. A.J. fielded this diplomatically, explaining that he was more of a friend of the parents. This surprised me, as he'd never mentioned them before. I guessed they must be friends from a previous tour, like Dale, so I accepted all this without asking. It transpired that Kieran was a postgraduate student and doubled as some sort of musician in a band at their university. For this reason, he planned to travel down tomorrow as there wouldn't be enough time after the performance tonight.

Raffles latched onto this. 'I suppose we'd better hand the place over to him tomorrow morning then. We'd feel like the most unwelcome of intruders if there was a member of the family here after all.'

You know those preacher chappies who have to go along and confess their doubts? Well, I knew how they felt. I began to have my doubts, heaps of them, about the exact nature of Raffles' rental agreement.

Away from the pack, I took my chance. 'A.J.?' I asked quietly. 'You don't know this Kieran or his parents, do you?'

'No Bunny. I don't. Does it really matter?'

I choked, lost for words, but if I hadn't been, the words would be these: And thus I clothe my naked villainy. Shakespeare's, not mine, but he had Raffles to a tee.

I've never understood how Raffles remains so aloof and confident at times like this. I was so nervous that my stomach acid was tying me in nasty little vinegary knots. I sometimes wonder whether Torquemada's assistant felt the same. I mean, how exactly does one explain it to the families?'

My mind raced. How were we supposed to get out of this? I was all for leaving now and shooting off into the darkness like one of those dogs with a fire-cracker tied to its tail in an RSPCA video. When I got the chance, I pushed Raffles back into the kitchen and asked him to tell me precisely what he'd done.

'I took a house. I told you that before we came.'

'I thought that meant renting a house, not *taking* one!'

'Be realistic for one moment, will you? If we'd been on a hotel register somewhere, the Syndicate would have found us by now. That would be a bad thing Bunny, a bad thing. Understand? A 'no toes to count your blessings on' bad thing. We're here and we're safe. Our guests are an unfortunate complication, but nothing that can't be overcome. Leaving now would appear a rather guilty action, don't you think?'

'Our guests? Raffles, you're deplorable.'

'Yes, but I have added a certain mystique to your life. Has it ever been dull? No? I hope you'll come to think of that as my gift.'

I thought about this for a bit and decided I still didn't like it.

'Raffles, you know that verse in *Kings* where Pharaoh captured Gezer, burned the Canaanites with fire and gave a city full of cooked dead people away as a dowry to his daughter?'

'Yes?'

'Well this is just like that. Thanks for nothing.'

'You're welcome.'

We both looked at each other, but no one backed down. Raffles broke the silence.

'Did he really do that?'

'Yes.'

'I'd like to have met him.'

We went back to the main room.

The evening progressed carelessly and we worked our way through the wine supplies. I couldn't relax, but, being the only one, I tried hard to disguise it.

'Are you all South African?'

'Yes' said Faye, 'but the only one who's really, really, South African, you know, three generations back, is Jacques. The rest of us have all got bits from other places. I always think you need to be slightly foreign to be interesting. Meeting you two is great because it isn't like talking to Jacques about the same boring things all the time.'

Jacques looked fed up at this and returned to an open bottle. It was the same bottle Knotty had been reaching for, but he didn't seem to mind.

'You're not musicians then?' I asked.

'No. Just mates. The band members are all playing now.'

Stupid of me. I must be tired.

'The problem with student bands is, just when they've got used to each other, one of them gets their qualifications and they're off. Kieran's lost most of his original band that way.'

That was Pippa. In the land of the word-slurrers, the girl who can just about make herself understood when placing an order for a cheese and tomato sandwich, easy on the onion, is queen.

Raffles said he quite understood. For years he'd played Jazz Piano and he'd never yet managed to find a comfortably settled jazz band. The other members were always ending up in hospital or falling out. Of course, they had the same complaints about him being unavailable through the summer. I clutched the arm of my seat. He surely wasn't stupid enough to tell them what he did? Who he was? Then we'd be for the high-jump and no mistake.

I needn't have worried. Lucky for us, they seemed more interested in hearing him play the piano. Raffles protested briefly, claiming to be terribly rusty, but I don't think he put up any serious opposition. Kimberley said she hated the occasions when someone was really good at something and wasn't interested in doing it. That was enough for Raffles. He played and was superb. I wasn't aware he'd practiced or even mentioned this hidden talent in decades and, if he did, I can't have been listening. Yes, I'll say it for the record. He was damn good. It may have been my personal illusion, but yes, like all the best pianists and pickpockets, he seemed to have a few more fingers at his disposal than I.

Raffles leaned back from the piano to ask me something. I listened dutifully.

'Bunny? There's champagne in the fridge. Be a good lad would you and fetch a few glasses?'

This was typical. 'Draw me a bath, would you Bunny?' 'If you wouldn't mind pouring a dozen glasses of champagne.' He had absolutely no idea what it was like to be a slave.

'Are you musical too?' Kimberley asked as I set off for the wine.

'Oh no, not really' I confessed freely.

'He's being modest, of course' whispered Raffles. 'Bunny has sung with the Rolling Stones and Madonna.'

'Really? Wow!' she said, her eyes shining in delight.

'I'm afraid my friend is exaggerating. There were thousands of people in that audience and I wasn't the only one singing along.'

Kimberley made a face at Raffles, who struck a humorous chord as I slipped out to the fridge for champagne.

An hour drifted pleasantly by on piano tunes and stolen wine. The evening had been a long one, but it looked as though Raffles and I could rest easy. We were above suspicion now. Knotty and Faye had pushed off upstairs to explore the various bedrooms. Pippa and Kimberley were stifling their yawns and Jacques had drunk himself into a morbid silence. Conversation petered out and thoughts turned to the sleeping arrangements.

A pair of bare feet clipped lightly down the carpeted stairs. By the time the knees came into view, I realised it was Faye. I had a sudden vision of what Mr Knotty's feet might look like and yielded an involuntary shudder.

'Sorry everyone, but we've got a little problem. There aren't enough rooms for everyone, so some of us are going to have to share.'

Faye's eyes scanned the room and settled on me.

'Well, you got here first Bunny. Who would you like to share with?'

'That's okay' I volunteered without hesitation 'I'll spend the night on the sofa down here. It's comfortable enough, when you get used to it.'

'That just leaves one more' said Faye, adjusting her skirt and turning to Raffles. With a bright smile and wide eyes she asked A.J. 'Would you like to share with me?'

I spent a wakeful night on that sofa, as I had openly volunteered to do. This uncomfortable item of furniture, smelling of badly-cured leather, dog hairs and state drinks, being some eight inches shorter than myself and giving me terrible back pain in the morning, wasn't the leading objection. My main complaint was being kept awake until half past two in the morning by the ecstatic giggles and mechanical creaking from upstairs. I had half a mind to tell Raffles that he might... come to think of it, what could I tell him?

After a while, I tried to take my mind off the situation by composing an epitaph for my tombstone. I decided upon this, which will have to suffice until I come up with something better:

'The trouble with being a gentleman is that one day you might wake up and realise you're the only one.'

Chapter 22

Big Game with the Lion Hunters

'D'you know Raffles, I've been thinking of taking up ricket again.'

'Good for you. I'll spare you a bat.'

'Thanks.'

'I've got a Newbery somewhere. Low moisture content with a bowed low centre and a thick edge. I don't think it's really me. I'd much rather be intelligent than demonstrative.'

Although I'd normally redirect a statement like that to those eminent code-breakers at the *Plain English Campaign*, I had to let it go because a free bat is, essentially, a free bat, even if it's deeply bowed wet and the edge thick with jibbies.

'Just club level. Nothing grand.'

'In the South West?'

'Yes. Perhaps Taunton.'

'No.'

'Not Taunton?'

'I'll put you in touch with Alan Jackson down at Yeovil. You can learn a lot there.'

'Will you introduce me?'

'Pass over one of those postcards would you? Thanks.'

He took a pen, glanced at the picture, wrote something neatly on the reverse and slid it back to me across the baking roof of the car. The card wasn't bad, as cards go: a sunset view with lions at the waterhole. Oh, look - the back ridge of a crocodile paddling into shot. I turned it over and read:

'A.J., fresh meat for the grinder, A.J.'

Sometimes, I find, it's not easy to tell if he's being serious.

What's that? Our location? I should probably bring you up to date. We'd sneaked out of the house at 7am and set off along the coastal road to the East. As a trained map reader on a long, straight and uncongested road, I shouldn't be lost. Just to make absolutely sure I wasn't, we stopped in a lay-by to stretch our legs. Don't look at me like that. The sun was in my eyes. No, really it was.

'Okay, I've got it' I said, following the line of the road with my finger. 'That's the place you asked for and this is more or less where we are now. I'd say two hours at most.'

'Good. Pop back in then.'

I don't know if you've ever driven along the coast road east toward the wine regions, but it's a trip to scrabble the mind of any naturalist, geologist, poet or painter. Actually, I suppose hefty proportion of poets and painters have their minds pretty scrabbled already, but, in the words of the Tour Manager, that's a goose I am unqualified to pluck.

As the ever-rising sun reduced its dazzle, I had my chance to gape at the monumental visions before me. The sea a deeper blue, the land a rushing Kew of botany, an overload of fantasy terrain. I took in as much of it as I could and I shuddered. When I recovered my composure, I shuddered again, just to get it over with. Why was this continent not leading the world? It must be, I supposed, the curse of human nature.

After fifty or sixty miles, I reluctantly turned the car inland and the scenery changed again. Endless vineyards stretched across the slopes around us. Accurately tended and yet without so much as a human head in sight. Did they work at night, I wondered?

'How I would love to have been a winemaker' I said to Raffles.

'Viniculture or viticulture?'

'Eh?'

'Growing or squeezing?'

'Both, I suppose. Either. Just think of it! The chance to nurture and ferment your own vintage!'

'Even if you were skilled, they wouldn't issue you with a work permit if a South African citizen could do the job. Even if you got a work permit, the transnational retailers would squeeze your profit margin to nothing and negotiate to maximise their own profits. If you had a bad year, that would be the whole thing over and gone. Suicide. Would you bet your life, every year, on a good crop? Just think of it.'

'You're quite a negative person, aren't you?'

We drove on.

'Raffles?'

'Yes.'

'Look at that sign up ahead.'

'It's a private business. If you're hoping for a picturesque outdoor restaurant, we've come too far.'

'No-no. That's not what I mean.'

'Explain?'

That was typical Raffles. Brevity ahead of manners one minute and then, at another pass, making a huge effort to put some stranger at their ease even when he'd never see them again. A contrary fellow.

'It's just that I've seen their logo before. It's a tour company or something. *Malibu Tours?*'

Raffles leant forward across the dashboard and peered through the window. Satisfied, he relaxed back.

'*High Calibre Tours?*'

'Yes! How did you know that?'

He gestured loosely at a placard on the opposite side of the road to the direction I'd been staring. It read 'High Calibre Tours – this way to the premier reserve' and an arrow.

'Lucky you weren't in the Observer Corps.'

'Thank you for that.'

'You were saying? What is this place?'

'They breed lions. This is a lion farm.'

'To supplement the wild population? I'd heard that numbers were tumbling. Apparently survival is all down to the size of the gene pool.'

'No, for execution.'

'What?' said Raffles, genuinely shocked.

'They have a website. They offer a service. For a set amount of money, people can send their children to South Africa, where they can shoot through the bars of a cage and kill a captive-bred lion. Accommodation, a certificate and photographs are included in the price. Absolute safety guaranteed.'

'You're joking? Although I suppose you can't be.'

'The lions are bred for shooting, reared, transferred to small cages in which they have trouble turning around and are then shot at point-blank range by child-tourists poking rifles through the bars.'

'You've just said that.'

'Probably because I feel so strongly about it.'

'Turn in.'

'Myself? What for?'

'Turn into this driveway.'

'Oh. Why?'

'I want to see it.'

'Only if you promise me you won't buy shares.'

We drove through the improvised gateway (arched wooden carvings of elephant tusks) and made our way up to the accommodation complex, tastefully appointed the 'Undiscovered Africa Game Lodge'. Yes, this was certainly a part of Africa that the world should hear about. Under a shady tree, a shady character sat.

Aware of our approach, the figure got to its feet, crushed a cigarette underfoot and stepped into the light. It was a man, incongruously attired like an early colonial hunter, with a cartridge belt slung bandana-style across his belly. I applied a selection of brakes, until one of them eventually worked, then flicked open the door. As I tried to deliver my speech about being lost, A.J. spoke straight over the top of me.

'Roger, am I right? – No, you can't be Roger, that's *Waterhole Tours* isn't it? You're *High Calibre*, of course you are. Sorry – we've got such a tight itinerary and I've lost my sheet of contact names. It really is too far to go back for it. Sorry – I should have said. This is Russell and my name is Mungo, from *Adventure of a Lifetime (Paris-Kettering-Munich and imminently Munchen-Gladback)* and you're expecting us. Am I right?'

'No, I can't say we are. You're who?'

'What? I can't believe those incompetent twits at the office would do this to me again! Russell, when we get back, remind me how angry I am.'

'OK boss.'

Raffles went back into the fray.

'Right, now let's get off on the right foot, shall we? Your name is?'

'Neilson, Paddy Neilson.'

'Which means you do what?'

'I'm the Head Ranger.'

'How do you arrange heads exactly? Just my joke. Excellent. Always start with the man the whole thing's built around, I say.'

'Thanks. You didn't tell me what you're here for. If I can help...'

'You could whistle-up a drink. It's like a desert out here.'

'It is a desert out here.'

'Is it? Well, like I said.'

Mr Neilson stuck his head around a doorway and called, presumably for drinks, in a wonderfully pronounced tongue. The very idea of learning such a language killed my dream of vineyards in the sun.

291

Raffles continued and I listened carefully as it was the first and only briefing I'd get on our cover story.

'As you should already know from the letter…' Raffles scanned the ranger's face for signs of recognition.

'You didn't get the letter, did you?' and turning to me 'Give the office a rocket, would you?'

'Yes Boss.'

'Damn right 'Yes Boss'. Make a note. Right, where was I? Oh yes. *Adventure of a Lifetime*, actually we can't use the acronym AOL because the software people had it first – although that didn't stop Apple Computers and Apple Records, did it? Ha! I think they ruled it was a tangible difference, so maybe we can use AoL one day and see if we get away with it? Worth a go. Make a note Russell.'

'Sir.'

'What was I saying? Oh yes. *Adventure of a Lifetime*, is the number one fastest expanding tour operator in our field - through the UK, Netherlands, Benelux and German markets. Really, number one. We've got ABTA, IATA and fully comp. and never forget our sunglasses! Do you know why we're the number one? It's because we offer something different. Who wants to go on some sad little package holiday to the Costas and sit round the pool with a bunch of slobs if you can pay a whole lot more to us and have the Adventure of a Lifetime! Am I right? Of course I'm right! Make a note Russell.'

'So you're checking us out?'

'We're checking all our potential subcontractors out. Commercial credit checks too, I'm afraid. We always do that before offering a fixed contract. Did I say? We're into the African market! At least, since Thursday, because that's when we signed the first two deals. Hang-gliding across waterfalls in Tanzania, swimming with great whites and now, stand aside Tarzan - BANG! - bag yourself The King of the Jungle!'

'I wouldn't advise swimming with great whites. That's too dangerous.'

'I know' said Raffles with a secret smile, 'but precautions have been thought of.'

'What are those?'

'The customers pay in advance and we never give 'em our real names!'

'Great, mate. That's really funny. Do you mind if I use that in my welcome talk?'

'Go ahead. Please, can you show us the format?'

'No problem. Follow me.'

We tracked behind Paddy as he proudly introduced us to all aspects of the business. The Undiscovered Africa Game Lodge looked comfortable, all squared off into neat little rooms.

'It's open plan, but each entrance twists, you see, so the other guests can't see in. We figure that if the clients can pay 1 8 , 0 0 0 , although the tour operator skims 30%, they're rich enough not to spoil it by poaching each other's wallets.'

'If they do?' I asked.

'Insurance. We've got insurance for everything here. It's the fathers I worry about. Some of them think they're Ernest Hemmingway and stick their hands in the cages to impress their sons. One oke couldn't pull his hand back quick enough because his bloody diamond Rolex stuck out like a block! He nearly messed himself. The drugs were the only thing that saved him.'

'Drugs?'

'Yah, I'll come to that.'

We passed a series of hundred year old portraits full of big game, dead big game and colonials in jalopies. Breaking out into the sunshine again, I felt the temperature leap in an instant. Paddy resumed his tour.

'Over here, we have the mature lion compound.'

'Right by the housing?'

'Yah. It makes a good first impression and the guests love to hear the growling in the night.'

'How old's mature?' asked Raffles.

'Two years. Three if we separate the males and let them grow a mane.'

'Your turnover must be quite good then.'

'We go through about fifteen a month. It could be more if we had the lions. We try to captive-breed wherever possible, but when demand's high we can do a sneaky refill from the wild. It's not permitted, but if I show you fifty lions, I bet you can't tell me which one shouldn't be in there.'

We walked past some of the cages which, I think, I'd already seen on my screen at Heathrow. Paddy toned it down a bit here as if knowing it was wrong but just another part of the job.

'Why do you shoot them so close?'

293

'They can't shoot it from further away because the shot might hit one of the bars. Anyway, you can't trust the tourists to hit it otherwise. They get so excited, anything could happen.'

'The lions look very quiet'.

'Yah, we hand-rear them, so they're used to people. They still get sedatives on pay-day though. We can't have any accidents.'

'What rifles do you use? The barrel seems unusually long' I asked conversationally.

'This is a .308 and we've got FLNs or a 7.62 that takes NATO rounds. Most of them have a barrel extension.'

'To stop muzzle-flash?'

'No. We *like* muzzle-flash. That's why we load extra powder into the shell cases, so plenty of it burns outside the barrel. The kids love a real blast. It's what they see on the movies. It's the same with the extension. On the trophy photos it looks like they've made a tricky shot at long range, when you and I know they can't bloody miss. The 'touch and feel' is a big part of the experience. If we clean it up or reduce it to pressing a button, who'd pay? We even let them sleep with their rifle in the room, for confidence.'

'Do they ever chicken out?'

'Yah. Some of them puke. Today's group look tough enough. The father runs an outfit that makes loans to farmers who can't borrow at normal rates from anywhere else. Somewhere in the Mid-West. He's hard enough to take their farms out from under them when they can't pay the interest. It only takes one bad harvest at that. The kid's a brat. He says he's been shooting his pets since he's been big enough to hold a weapon.'

'Charming. Profitable though.'

'Yah. Today's their acclimatisation day. The kid's allowed to drink tonight. He's well under the age for that back home. He's supposed to leave here a man, you see. All part of the experience.'

'Of course.'

We stopped outside the cage of a slumbering cat. Its breath stank to high-heaven.

'Then he gets to shoot Pluto here in the morning.'

'If you don't mind my asking, how did you end up in this job? I mean, it's a bit unusual' I asked.

'Ah, that's a long story. Are you sure you want to hear it?'

'Yes, I think so. I like to know who I'm dealing with' said Raffles, suddenly the businessman.

'I used to be a National Parks warden. One day I took a party of German tourists out to meet the lions in the bush. I found a pride and led the tourists as close as I could to the group, from down-wind. I was ahead of them all, with my revolver, when I heard this 'humph' sound and a lioness I hadn't seen charged out of some bushes to the side of me. It was all over me, teeth and claws, mauling.'

The Ranger lifted his safari shirt and showed us a lattice of claw marks across the middle of his body.

'The tourists drove off as quick as they could and left me, the creeps. I can't forget the stinking breath in my face as the lion tried for my throat – it made this fella's breath smell like flowers' he said, indicating Pluto. The lion looked back at him expectantly. He probably thought it meant dinner.

'How did you survive?'

'I got hold of the pistol and shot it. I was badly cut though. Only just got back. You wouldn't believe what the bloody tourists did. They only complained their tour guide was defective. They asked the company for a refund!'

'We shouldn't book any German clients then?'

'Book who you like. I don't care. I'm not crazy about tourists or lions or stories from stupid old buggers who say they've met Hemmingway. I'm just doing the best job I can and I'm trying not to think about it.'

'Thanks for your time' and that was it. We departed.

11pm. Hungry now, we tried to sleep on the seats of the car.

12pm. Sounds in the bush, we extended our vigil.

1am. Distant lights at the ranch went down. One minute they were there, the next minute their bulbs flicked to orange spots on blackened squares and faded, memories of the eye. I thought of galleries in London who'd gladly buy that effect and sell it to some 'must have' advertising loudmouth from Notting Hill.

1.30am Raffles and I got out of our seats, shook off weary torpor and crept with minimum noise back to the compound.

Whatever your view of Raffles, you can't say he wasn't brave. My job was to keep watch and watch is indeed what I did. I'm not sure if this was because I wasn't trusted enough or whether it might be because Raffles reserved each individual thrill and risk for his own delectation. I watched.

I watched as Raffles entered the Ranger's office, by the simple device of hooking his fingers over the upper frame of an open sash window, pulling himself off the ground and swinging his body, feet first, beneath the raised window pane. In the heat it seemed that few windows were kept closed for long.

I watched as he exited carefully through the door, his actions cloaked in silence. Raffles reminded me of one of those grass-snakes you see about the place - sliding and sneaking soundlessly through the rough. Except, to match Raffles, the grass-snakes would have to do it all on tip-belly.

I stared harder into the gloom. I could just make out, in his hand, the compound's keys and a small plastic suitcase, which presumably contained animal tranquilisers of some description.

I watched as he crept skilfully into the Undiscovered Africa Game Lodge and I had to hold my breath for minutes until he stepped out again with his prize, a bundled weapon.

I worried he could have got it wrong and it might be murder. He'd assured me of the plan. It would be impossible to use the dart gun, because of the noise. No, it would have to be a jab job. Sedating the father in his sleep would be easy and I shouldn't think the dose might kill him as Raffles would estimate it by weight and reduce accordingly. Yes, fine, but what did Raffles know about guessing people's weight in the dark? What could he possibly know about tranquilisers? I had a horrible thought he might have used them on the opposition in cricket matches, but even Raffles wouldn't stoop to that.

Actually, come to think of it, I know he had a club-cricket theory about orange juice. Am I going off-piste here? I am? Oh, okay, I'll be brief. When drinks came out on a boiling hot day, he'd advise the tea ladies that his own side should have well diluted orange juice to quench their thirst, but the opposition side should be given sparingly diluted orange juice so they'd return to the field with an even greater thirst. It's not the same as tranquilising people, but club cricketers have to work with what little they've got.

I watched as he picked his way towards me, passing from shadow to shadow through the scrub.

'Bunny! I've got an idea. Help me carry the brat over to one of the lion cages and when he wakes up, he'll get a splendid fright!'

'You're mad. You've got the gun you came for, so let's go.'

'Bunny, please?'

'This really is the last time. Alright then, but on your head be it.'

When I entered the lodge, I could see the fearful truth. Both guests were drugged and snoring quietly.

'Raffles, if these ones are tranquilised and the Warden's asleep in the other hut, why are we still creeping around?'

'Three more guests. In the room at the end. They must have shootings arranged for two days in a row.'

'Let's get out.'

'Yes, but with this little jerk.'

'Why?'

'He wanted sport. It's only sport if the quarry gets their chance.'

'If you say so.'

We grabbed one end each of the slumbering teenager and hauled him, blanket and all, out into the night and down to the cages.

'Blast!' said Raffles.

'What now?'

'None of them are empty.'

'Great. Let's go then.'

'Not yet. I have a solution! We'll simply let one out.'

'I've had enough of this, Raffles. You're crazy. I'm going back to the car.'

I snatched the rifle, still in its bundle of bedclothes and walked off down the track. Just to be sure, I paused and squinted into the shadows to check that he was okay. Yes, I could see, the madman had released a lion - the one with the halitosis. Yes, he'd locked the superfluous youth into the vacant cage and disguised his sleeping form under a tarpaulin.

Then there was then a bit of a dangerous moment when Pluto didn't want to go away, so Raffles shook some keys at him. I believe he even said "Woof!" and "Bad Boy!" which I thought a little impractical. As he returned the keys, stretching for a nail through the open window, I waited by the roadside for his return.

We ran through darkness and down to the car, trying not to trip and with Raffles failing to suppress his laughter.

'Mission accomplished?'

'That was the most entertaining... I mean to say, that was the most...'

'Raffles, I think we've done something awful! It's that lion. I think we've left the door to the lodge open!'

Raffles descended into such an uncontrollable heap of mirth that I had to wait a nervous five minutes for him to recover before we could start the car and escape.

We escaped. As a matter of fact, so did most of the tourists.

Chapter 23

Play, Play Up and Play the Game

'You know those shining beacons of hope that the politicians bang on about?'

'Yes... what?'

'Beacons of hope.'

'Oh. Those. Probably.'

'Well, I haven't seen many about the place lately.'

We drove on in silence. A parade of thoughts and accusations bashed a sullen path through our heads. Raffles stopped the car around and behind a convenient mound of reddened sandstone and we popped the doors.

'Be a good lad and pass the bag up from the back seat?'

'Okay, will do' I said and reached where indicated. We continued on foot across bumpy land and in the general direction of a brittle upward slope. I didn't bother asking what we were doing there.

'Raffles, what do you want with this wretched gun? It looks antique. It looks exaggerated. I mean, look at the barrel-extension. That's the barrel of an inadequate man.'

'Will it work?'

'Well, yes, of course.'

'We'll need it.'

'Will we? There's just one, I see. What am I meant to use? The mesmeric power of persuasion? Look, A.J., the police aren't after us. If they are, it's only because someone's reported a gun missing. Can't we take a roundabout route and try the airport? There's sure to be a flight with unsold seats. We could go to Istanbul, Rio, Budapest, New York America, San Paolo, Kuala Lumpur, anywhere!'

'True enough, Bunny. The money's in an online account, so we can move it anywhere.'

'Now you're talking! Anywhere's got to be better than this face-of-the-moon boulder repository.'

'Bunny, we can't turn back on the road we've just used. We are being followed, mile by mile they close upon us. Very soon we will be hunted down.'

'I've heard about this before. The paranoia of highly strung athletes. What you need is a dose of reality. I could kick you in the ear if you like? It won't take a moment. Just lie down and make yourself comfortable.'

'Bunny, they will be here soon. They will be armed and they won't be friendly.'

'Why do you think that?'

'I left them a note.'

'You did *what*?'

'A note. I said we'd be here tomorrow. If they're ex-army, they'll want to be here the day before. They'll want to circle-in and be sure it's not a trap.'

I knew this stuff already, which didn't stop me being livid with him. It was standard operating theory for making a rendezvous without being ambushed. Had he been reading books? Had he been reading *my* books?

'Listen Mush, back up and let's re-cap. You have to stop me if I get this wrong. You left a note saying we'll be here tomorrow, please come and kill us? Is that right?'

'Yes.'

'Oh, fine. No reason. That's absolutely… WHY?'

I booted a nearby rock and hurt toes quite badly.

'Was that necessary?'

'Yes' I whimpered.

'As a professional sportsman, my job involves standing still in the middle of a wide piece of open land wearing highly visible clothing. Not only that, but the newspapers actually *publish* where I will be standing up to a year in advance. The only way to finish this is to bring it to a head and get the damn thing over with.'

'Either way?'

'Either way.'

'Bonnie and Clyde died, didn't they?'

'Yes, but I have a secret weapon.'

'You have? What's that then?'

'You.'

'I don't follow.'

300

'Good. I don't want you to follow. I want you to lead. This is your area of expertise, Bunny. We're going to move up to the summit of that escarpment, find some cover and you're going to take the gun and use it to shoot them. Numbers should be irrelevant.'

'What?' I said again. It was rapidly becoming my word of the day.

'Gun. Point. Shooty shooty.'

'Eh?'

'I've brought you a long way for this. Don't go soggy on me now.'

I stared at the madman and tried to assess what he was asking.

'We are being chased by civilians. You want me to shoot civilians in a time of peace?'

'It's no worse than shooting civilians in a time of war.'

Good point, but I still couldn't take this in. Raffles took hold of my shoulder and gripped hard.

'Bunny Manders, you are a soldier. You are also, if I can bolt this through your wooden skull, one of the best long distance rifle shots in the world.'

'Oh, I wouldn't say that.'

'After your triumph at Braemar, Her Majesty the Queen Mother herself described you as "Scotland's most outstanding shot".'

'That was a misquote by the paper.'

'Oh, come now Bunny.'

'No, really. That's not what she said.'

'Don't be so modest.'

'Raffles! I'd just run over a corgi.'

We walked on.

'Bunny, I can't do this job. You can. We are moving to the high ground and you are taking this gun. There is no alternative. When they try to kill us, that's KILL us, Bunny, you are going to have to shoot at them. It's no longer a game. You have been trained for this moment, not for those stupid barracks, pointless tent encampments in Wales and spending the rest of the time soaking up cocktails in be-nighted London nightclubs. Eating your breakfast off the back of a Landrover is not what it's about! Being a trained soldier makes you more disciplined, more inhuman and better adapted to horror than the men on the other side. Otherwise, if you can't do that, they won't give up. They are going to shoot us, Bunny, unless I can persuade you to shoot them. Simple enough?'

Simple as death. About as encouraging too.

I couldn't believe I was agreeing to this. I felt pretty sure they couldn't kill him. At least, there's probably some special technique involving garlic and silver bullets, but it would take ages to contact Peter Cushing and get the research details.

'You're talking about murder. Mine in fact. This isn't good.'

'You were born for this!'

'No. I was born to be a gardener.'

'You're an officer!'

'Okay, a head gardener.'

'Bunny, just think of it this way. We've got a few hours to live. We're dead people. I'm giving you something interesting to do whilst we wait. See how many of them you can shoot before they reach us. If you can hit all of them, you can go home. Step up, every ball's a coconut.'

'No need to be facetious. You knew it would come to this, didn't you? You knew you needed me.'

No answer. We foot-slogged upwards. Is there anything worse than dying? Yes. Falling out with people and then dying. Oh, sod it. It sounded like an interesting challenge.

'Alright, I'll do it.'

'That's the spirit.'

We yomped upwards.

'Why did you join the army, Bunny?'

'Several reasons. Family expectations I suppose. Phrases like 'cowards die many times before their deaths' rattling around in my hind-brain. Being used to institutions too, but looking for one with a little less claustrophobia.'

'Less than...?'

'Have you met my family?'

'Ah.'

'My application was good. It even had reference letters from two Dukes and a General. Everyone really wanted me to get in, so I was carried along on the momentum. Of course, when you're young and don't know what you want to do, it's a time when you're more susceptible to suggestion.'

'So you signed on the dotted line.'

'It wasn't that easy. They don't just dish out commissions, you know. Especially a Guards regiment in a year when they're cutting back from two battalions down to one. Lots of spare officers in a year like that.'

'I can imagine.'

'Still, there's a few year's pause while they stuff you through military college, so they booked me in anyway. I was called for an interview, which went alright. The Brigadier was the son of our family doctor so I knew him already, in passing. My godfather was a Brigadier in the Greenjackets of course, and General Anderson built my toboggan, which might help get you through the door, but it doesn't matter who you know after that. It's up to your performance at the interview. My inquisitor was a Royal equerry. I didn't ask for whom because I thought they might think my motives for applying were pretentious. 'Why are you applying for this particular regiment? What's your connection with Scotland?' That sort of thing.

They send you for a medical, which you'd presume is a formality. Mine was on the same day as the Trooping of the Colour. I remember there were hundreds of brightly decorated soldiers in the parade square warming up their musical instruments and levelling their hats. It seemed to me like one of those Victorian affairs where bands play and the regiment marches on board a steamer for the colonies.'

'So, you passed the medical?'

'I failed the medical, actually. "Short sighted, low blood pressure, return your ticket and get out of line. Next!"'

'Low blood pressure? What's that got to do with it?'

'If an officer responsible for perhaps thirty men gets wounded, it's not going to help anyone's survival if they fall about fainting all the time and can't stay conscious long enough to make rational decisions.'

'Ah, alright, I see.'

'Anyway, my family were not at all impressed. My father's last word to me in this world was "weakness". They made me have laser surgery to the eyes.'

'Charming people.'

'Quite. I wrote to the regiment again and made my case. The eyes were fixed. The low blood pressure helped me shoot.'

'Ah, that's the reason.'

'I enclosed my last card from the mile-plus range at Banchory and asked whether they happened to know any rifleman in the British Army or indeed any army who could match that? To be honest, I think they took another look at me because they couldn't believe my cheek.'

'So you made it. I'd have hardly believed you had it in you. Well done. Well well.'

'My hardest achievement and now I've messed that up too.'

'Yes, you have, but you will always know you can achieve much, much more, if pushed.'

'Perhaps. I don't want to be pushed though. I want to go home.'

'At heart, Bunny, you're probably cut out to be a gardener. I'm sorry I got you into this stressful mess.'

'Didn't I get you into it?'

'We're probably square.'

He was most likely right. The great difference between us was that, clearly, he was thriving on it.

'It's time I told you Bunny, you're not an addict.'

'I'm not?'

'No. You don't think about it fifty times a day.'

Something whistled straight past me, quite close. My mind registered the whistle before my ears tuned into the preceding crack. Sod everything, someone was firing at us. We ran, tumbling upwards like spiders, into the line and cover of a weathered groove, forever up and away from our new and unseen tormentor. Crack, closer now, the shot absorbed by intervening rock. Why were they shooting at me, not him? Oh yes, I was carrying the gun-case. Clever. They must have military training.

They always teach the snipers to shoot the officer's uniform first, then anyone with a transmitter, then anyone with binoculars and then the machine gunners and specialist soldiers. Looking harmless was usually quite safe. In fact, Raffles was lucky he hadn't thought to take the rifle himself. We pinged between a cobbled outcrop like chamois avoiding a shearing appointment and reached the cover of a natural cave.

Crack, top of the cave, not even close and yet another wasted shell. As a lad in the Scottish Highlands, I'd be issued with a single bullet for my hunting trip. I'd walk nine miles or so to take my shot and if I missed, I can tell you, it was a very long walk back.

Crack - beshiiing. Impacts at the top of the cave confirmed they were therefore much lower on the slope. Did they think they could get us with ricochets?

I looked into his eyes. He wasn't scared. He was excited.

'You want to be chased. You actually need them to try and kill you. You'd be upset if they turned back, wouldn't you?'

He set off again, crab-like across the crumbling floor and deep into shadow.

'What is it with you, Raffles? Are you mad? Why the hell am I with you Raffles?'

He didn't look back as the reply came.

'Because you're like me.'

'No, I am absolutely not.'

'You're fascinated. You want to find out what happens next... just as much as I do.'

'You're insane!'

'Who's the fool?'

'Why am I here, Raffles?'

'It's your show now, Bunny Manders. I remember the day you earned your name. The school rabbit. No one thought you could make that shot, across two cricket pitches and up between the old school buildings. It's your time again, Bunny. Another shot. Prove it to me, best out of three.'

'Raffles, we're not at school! This is about people's lives!'

'Bunny, you agreed! Let me tell you something.'

'You'd better be quick!'

'Every molecule in your body is replaced within a twelve year cycle.'

'This had better not be about Ninjas again.'

'Bunny, listen. There is *not a single molecule* of your body which was with me at school.'

'Oh. So you're saying you have no allegiance to me whatsoever?'

'Why are you always telling me what I'm saying? What I'm saying Bunny, what I'm trying to get you to appreciate, is that the thing you think of as YOU really is NOT the physical matter you are made from.'

'Alright. So why am I getting a philosophy lecture at a time like this?'

'It is because, although I'd prefer to pick you up and shake you, you have to stop carrying around all this mental baggage!'

Crack. Puug.

Some rock or something, maybe lead, had dealt the side of Raffles' head a heavy slap. He was groggy, correction, unconscious. Why did he always have to have the last word?

Okay, blood, that's not good. I checked for swelling on the outside. I just hoped there wasn't swelling on the inside. Relieving compression on the brain was more or less impossible under these circumstances. Back at college, officially, I was the worst in my class at field-bandaging. I didn't even have a bandage this time, only a torn scrap of white shirt. Never mind, a knot or two to finish. I couldn't ask for help now.

I thought about negotiating. I waved the rest of the white shirt.

Crack.

Perhaps not then. I suppose I'd better shoot at them after all, I thought, unwrapping the bag. Oh great. The modern sight was floating around separately to the aged rifle, presumably removed by Raffles to make it fit into the holder, which was logical, but unhelpful. Never mind. I would be surprised if anybody had ever set it in, the scope that is. Ah, okay, I'd found an Alan-key. Part A to lock A, Part B to the sight rail, a few twists with the fiddly little stick. Now I just had to fish out a coin to adjust the scope with. No coins? No. Would Raffles have one? Was it worth standing up?

Crack. Ziiiing. No rush.

This was like flatpack furniture, wasn't it? Okay, coin, coin, no, but my watch buckle would do. Sod it, the manufacturer had put a strong plastic wrapper over the wheel cap on the sight-guard and no one had ever bothered to cut it off. Fantastic. Better use teeth. Okay, spitting plastic, but done.

Click-click.

Elbows forward, up to the cave mouth and...

Boom.

I hadn't fired at them. I'd fired instead at a wide, flat rock face about 700 yards away. It was well over their position, but enough to tell me the trajectory on this un-ranged rifle. Up 'till now all its targets had probably been four yards away, so I would have come as a breath of fresh air, or cordite depending upon your personal engineering status. The puff of dust told me where the shot had pitched and I tracked and adjusted the scope accordingly.

Metres, just my luck. Tricky little foreign measurements. I stopped swearing in my head, lucky you didn't hear any of that, drew a deep breath and carried on. I think in yards of course, so had to calm down and do some arithmetic. I glanced back at Raffles and didn't quite have my great epiphany, but started to connect a few of my recent insights into his behaviour.

'Okay Raffles. This is what you saved me for. I'll show you how it's done.'

Shot two...

Boom.

Okay, better, but with room for improvement. The watch buckle went back into the adjustment wheel on the side of the scope, click-click-click a quarter of a degree per ratchet. Ready, shot three and... I saw the hat. Okay, I'll let the rock off this time, lucky rock, and shoot the cheeky muppet slinking around behind that ridge whom, I bet, has no idea I can see him. Probably forgot he's wearing a whoppingly obvious hat. Too stupid to live and...

Boom.

Shards of rock scattered, but the hat just sat there. Okay. Elevation. Two points up and I've got it set in record time. Well, not exactly *the* record. There was a bloke called Dawes in the East Lothians who... sorry, never mind about that. Fingers like elastic bands though – incredible. He could gut, joint and salt a rabbit in thirty seconds when it takes me most of a minute to peel a potato.

Click-click... no, don't fire. Calm down and make sure of it. Relax, far away now, soft and quiet.

Crack.

Ignore that. None of this is actually happening. Calm, drifting away, see the tunnel, fall into the tunnel, slow breathing, slow the heart, focus down, down again, look through the hat, feel the cloth, feel the mind and...

Boom. Gotcha!, I think.

The hat flopped a foot or two into the air and span away amongst the rocks.

I necked around to check on Raffles. He was drifting in and out of consciousness.

'How are we doing?'

'Fine. Pipe-down and go back to sleep.'

'Where are we? Do we have any tea?'

I wasn't sure whether I should divert my attention and talk to him.

'Yes, but there's no milk.'

He looked pained.

'It's a living nightmare.'

Raffles crawled along the holed and rutted floor, slowly clambering towards me like a drunk making an unsteady course along the taxi handles of a late-night rank in Leicester Square. As one of his hands slipped down a hole in the floor, Raffles stuttered something incoherent about an atrocious track at Sabina Park. Uncharitably, I thought to myself, 'These cracks would swallow your lousy cricket ball nine times out of ten you complete fool. So what of it? Stop, please stop *distracting me!*' In his condition, I couldn't blame him for getting things out of proportion. Just, just... not now Cato. Of course, he wouldn't shut up.

'For each action, there is an equal and opposite reaction. Take tea in the bath. Take a bath in the tea.'

It's been about a month since I first brought my plight before Raffles. In that time, I've travelled widely in his company and I think I can finally say that I have come to see what he truly represents. I'm not a very good instantaneous judge of character, but I like to think I get there in the end. For instance, I took the poet Lucan for my dissertation. It was only after two years of intensive and adoring study that I realised just how truly awful he really was.

'Shut up Raffles.'

'Remember Bunny, you pay for your trip on the way out.'

'Enough! Quiet now!'

I switched back to the matter in hand and scanned the field of play for movement. I couldn't believe it. The hat was back! A little further away this time, but still propped up, bold as you like, amongst the rocks. What was this? A coconut shy? Okay, so this wasn't what I'd call shooting at long range, but it was long enough at short notice.

Crack.

It was also very difficult to note where the shots were coming from, because of the distorted echo in the cave. My other difficulty was being too excited to go into my usual shooting trance, my trademark.

Crack.

Something had cut my ear. Oh well, can't be helped. All in a day's work for O'Manders of *The Evening Bacon*.

Hang on! Hang on a mo! There was the movement. Right down by the road three quarters of a mile or so away. Ha! The sniping gentleman. 'He thinks he's out of range' I told myself. I settled down and tried once more to fall into my trance. Slow now, daydream, a mile away, a mile of cotton. A minute or two of silence reigned. The odds were swinging around to me. Less than a run a ball required, as Raffles put it. I had the high ground, I had the equipment and the training. I was genuinely good at this. Slow now, sleepy, focus and...

Boom.

Something fell off the distant figure's shoulders. It wasn't a hat on this occasion. I couldn't believe I'd just done that. To this thing of darkness, I acknowledge mine. Mother would be appalled.

Raffles, apparently unaware of our predicament, began soliloquising:

'The primeval folk of the British Isles believed that simple streams mark a division between the worlds. Living, running water made a gateway between our world and a beautiful, timelessly ethereal plane. The line between these places has never belonged to us; as in cricket, the line is not your friend. None of us are pure enough, wise enough or one of the fey, to stand at once between the water margins, the boundaries of the two realms. The willow tree alone grows there.'

'You're waffling, Raffles.'

'Yes.'

'Shut up then.'

Crack, went the wall.

'What is the…?'

'Shhh! Stay still and stay down!'

The field bandage slipped and draped itself over his shoulder like white opera gloves. He circled awkwardly, propped his back to the rock wall and began edging upwards.

'Whenever a fellow says life is bad, I just tell him the facts. It could be worse, you could be eating a lemon. Go and find anyone who's eaten a lemon and they'll tell you that your troubles are nothing.'

'Get down!'

Raffles didn't comprehend, still trying to stand, clawing upright inch by inch.

'Get down! You'll be shot.'

Crack.

The ceiling rained aggregates into my hair. Another one. Still coming. Persistent, aren't they? The Syndicate really got their money's worth from this crew.

'Idiot' I cursed, realising I'd have to stand and go after him. Upright now, tall and concussed - an easy target.

'Raffles?'

I stood up, lined up and kicked him very hard between the legs. He stayed down that time.

Now, where was I?

Retaking position, I found my heart was beating out of my chest. No chance of the Zen approach now then. How could I regulate my breathing enough to shoot straight? I realised I could always try the method A.J. came up with at school. Nothing to lose now. For the life of me, I couldn't think of any songs. Honestly, my mind went creakingly blank.

Crack! Pssssssssttt, the hiss of death passed over me and fled into the shadows.

The hat was back. Unbelievable. The man in the iron hat. Okay, think of a poem or something.

Click-click. I shuffled forwards.

"The sands of the desert were sodden red, red with the blood of a square that broke"

Boom. Click-click. Goodbye hat.

"The Gattling's jammed and the colonel dead, the ranks half blind with the light and smoke"

Boom. Ah, movement. I see you.

"And the voice..." click-click "of a schoolboy rallied the men"

Are you going to jump the rock or not? Do mind the gap. The management takes no responsibility...

"Play, play-up and play the game."

Boom.

Crack. Crack. Crack.

Where did those come from?

"There's a breathless hush"

Crack!

Closer now. I'd better budge back a little. I've probably got this poem back to front, haven't I?

"An hour to play and the match to win"

Click-click.

"And it's not for a season's glory or a ribboned coat"

Boom. Stitch that! Goodnight Padstow.

"But the Captain's hand on your back when he spoke. Play, play up and play the game."

So much for Newbolt.

Click-click.

Jump between them then. Go on; tell yourself I can't be that good. Three two one move...

Boom.

Instant abstract expressionism.

Actually, he had sprayed rather wildly across the rocks. What was this thing firing? Wadcutters?

At least it gave a whole new meaning to the phrase 'he's just popped across the path'. No, don't move! Ooh, that's got to hurt. I am so, so sorry about that. Please don't stand up again.

The hat was back. This was becoming weird and suspicious, like a pineapple. What's going on here? I had a feeling it wasn't dark enough. Hang on. Is this cave open at the back? Who ever heard of a cave that's open at the back?

One of those sinking sensations you sometimes hear have been hanging about and clinging to people seized its moment and clung onto me. It slowly occurred that, potentially, I might have been outwitted. It wasn't the first time. I'd best check they hadn't any slippery friends creeping up from the other direction. That would explain the whole hat-decoy thing at least, wouldn't it? Of course, I still had the distinct advantage of defended ground. Surely I was technically better at this than them? I stood up, then, something surreal.

'Poc poc apoco-poc' said the rocks behind me. Had someone thrown a doorknob?

'I've never seen a real grenade before' said Raffles matter-of-factly. 'Aren't they pretty?'

Now I knew how Bradman felt.

My attention latched onto the intrusive ball in a frenzy of alarm. Perhaps it was a fit of anguish. Either way, he was right. A small and delightfully formed fragmentation grenade bounced and puckered, with a hollow and echoing playfulness, into the cave with us. I realised I'd been out-thought. Okay, so Raffles might have a point about Padstow. The hat was just a hat. On a rock. A hat on a rock. They'd drawn my attention and circled around the back instead. How Napoleonic. The strategy I mean, not the hat.

'Now that's cheating'

Raffles nodded. 'Think like a mushroom.'

I sighed in resignation. It assuredly wasn't cricket. Without thinking much about my actions or mushrooms, I turned the rifle in my hands and, swinging the wooden stock like a batsman, tried to punch the little device back out of the cave and off in the general direction of our tormentors.

'Booung... a-poco-poc.'

I wondered for a fleeting second whether that might be a purely functional word for something light-hearted and domestic in an early Meso-American language. Perhaps a word that no one's heard these last three hundred seasons. Maybe Toltec. Maybe 'corn pot'.

I'm sorry, but that went down as my last recollection before memory failed.

In fact, I think I might be out.

Chapter 24

A Green and Pleasant Land

They say that when a sun dies, it expands, it fills your vision. You feel the heat and marvel at the sharpness of the light as it cuts through every last hiding place. It blinds you and then it dies. It just dies. And takes you with it.

I fell to earth, I know not where. Only, no, this wasn't. This was something different. I woke up in daylight, strangely rested and the tears were wiped from my eyes. There was no pain here and death had no meaning. Nothing I had considered important in my life before had the least relevance in this place.

It was truth. Nothing mattered, nothing, for the former things had passed away.

I could feel the sunshine warm and soothing against my back. Broad and ancient trees anchored the fields about me. I could sense something very familiar, something from my childhood. Ah, yes, that was it! The smell of freshly mown grass.

If they had called me back, I wouldn't go. I liked it here.

Who were 'they' anyway? I couldn't remember.

I saw figures in that meadow, standing peacefully on a perfect lawn. Their white clothes made them look like angels. Perhaps they were? I felt as if I might be welcome amongst them.

Was that really a collie dog watching me?

Et in Elysium ego.

Post Script

In 2007, the remarkable Nobel-nominated Italian philosopher Nico Odoni advanced the following theory:

Everything natural is pure and beautiful. Everything man-made (even when constructed on, in or from nature) is ugly. Even art, for example, appeals to us because it tries to seamlessly mimic the natural rather than the constructed.

Therefore, he reasoned, if we could run an algorithm or, in terms of a thought-experiment, construct a type of telescope through which we could pick out ugliness, it would be a simple matter to point it at the stars and identify any and all extraterrestrial civilisations.

When asked what would happen if he pointed his theoretical 'Belissiometer' device at our own Earth, Odoni concluded the following: We would be able to visually classify everything that has had its origin in the activity of Mankind. Conversely, we would clearly see everything in the natural realm which has evolved through survival and natural selection. The only exception might be the game of cricket. Seemingly man-made yet also a clear echo of the life experience itself, it may be the only, otherwise inexplicable, statistically indicative evidence we have for the existence of a Creator.

However, if recent articles in the Italian press are found to be accurate, Nico may have already punctured his own reputation. The popular newspaper *Milanese Reporto* allegedly discovered Professor Odoni openly claiming that he had constructed such a device and the only reason he was to be found in a disreputable city nightclub, in what appeared to be a clumsy attempt to seduce impressionable young ladies, was merely 'for calibration purposes'.

●

Telegraph Office, London.

FAO: Night Editor.

I've gathered as many quotes as I can find. Will you let me know if these are useable?

PRESS REPORT————————— PRESS REPORT—————————
PRESS REPORT————————— PRESS REPORT—————————
PRESS REPORT————————— QUOTES ONLY—————————
TREAT AS UNCONFIRMED————————— LATEST:

"The importance of these men's achievements can not be over-stated" said Mr Simon Trent, Media Spokesman for the English County Committees.

"The Anti-Corruption Team has earned the first major feather in its cap. They will root out the bad apples in cricket and if that some-times means burning down someone's diseased orchard, then so be it." – Dr Zamadee, President of the Association of International Harmony through Sport.

"Our investigator, Mr McKenna, has delivered the most spec-tacular of successes. After forming an association with the heroic investigative journalist Mr O'Manders, they have swiftly crushed the largest and most troublesome organisation that has ever spread corruption within a game." BREAK "The selfless nature in which the exemplary English cricketer A.J. Raffles risked his own life by agreeing to infiltrate the gang should earn him the heartfelt gratitude of players and spectators around the world." – Official Statement by the World Cricket Development Anti-Corruption Team.

"Mr O'Manders always preferred to stay with us and we're proud to have supported him and the wonderful sport of cricket. His favourite drink, the *Garden of Proteas*, is served exclusively at our hotel. It's based on the national flag of South Africa." – Heidi Rodriguez, hotel spokesperson.

"As the Press have already suggested, I can confirm that Mr Raffles, under instruction from a representative from the Anti-Corruption Unit, accepted the match-fixing syndicate's terms and in so doing cleared the way for heavy betting on the outcome of a one-day cricket match in which he was a Captain. By turning the match and producing a result opposite to the outcome previously agreed, members of the corrupt syndicate were undoubtedly left to pay a heavy price, if not bankrupted. This is why they attempted to murder him, firstly with chemical poisoning at his hotel and, when that failed, by kidnapping. The use of the toxic compound cypermethrin has led to the recent investigation by the Jamaican authorities to be re-examined. The South African Police will also, thoroughly I might add, review the death of Hansie Wepper in light of recent events. – Police spokesman."

"The evidence indicates that Mr O'Manders attempted to protect Raffles by taking him into hiding at an address in the neighbouring province. After being discovered by agents of the Syndicate, both were kidnapped and taken to a remote location, we believe for execution. Strong disagreement broke out amongst gang members, perhaps over the possibility of a ransom payment. We can confirm that weapons and explosives were found at the scene. The explosive device intended to murder the hostages seems to have triggered in a natural depression by the mouth of the cave, masking the lateral angle of the blast at floor level. This explains the primary injuries across the head and upper bodies on most of the victims. Believing that both captives were no longer alive, the remaining gang members withdrew. – Chief Investigative Officer, SAF."

"Police are still looking for a red pick-up truck which might have signs of blood on the doors, windows or seats. Garages throughout the southern Cape are being visited as we speak and will be left with a full description." – Spokesman for the Pretoria Divisional Serious Crimes Unit.

"Why are they calling him O'Manders all the time? It's an assumed name! He booked into the hotel as Mr Manders. He called himself something entirely different when infiltrating a corrupt pensions company in his last job before leaving England. He introduced himself in a London nightclub as Mr Kenneth Compote, for heaven's sake! I don't think we will ever know what his real name was. This man is like The Jackal. He's the eternal spirit of journalism, absolutely our Journalist of the Year." – Editorial, the London Press Review.

"I can confirm that Mr Raffles is on the road to recovery, but will not be well enough to answer your questions for a few more days. He has suffered concussion, some fracturing and associated soft-tissue injuries to the head. We have removed a small amount of shrapnel from his body, as located in an MRI scan we conducted yesterday. Mr O'Manders remains in a critical condition having suffered blast injuries to the abdomen and some bleeding within the brain." BREAK "He is resting, but unaware, in a condition similar to induced coma. For the time being, we are using a life-support system to ensure Mr O'Manders' survival and give the body time to repair itself. I'm afraid we have no way of telling if his mental functions have been permanently damaged. If any of his relatives or colleagues know who he is, The Director of Hospitals has asked me to encourage them to come forward." – Dr Tasiekenyeri, Senior Surgeon, Makamba District Hospital.

"I have spoken to representatives of Her Majesty's Government this morning. I fully support their recommendation that it would be appropriate for The Queen to consider civilian bravery awards for Mr A.J. Raffles and Mr... Mr Pomander. Oh, for heaven's sake! Can we please confirm these people's names? Could someone at least tell me what the A.J. stands for?" – The President of The Republic of South Africa.